Goldenrod

Also by Ann McMan

Dust
Hoosier Daddy
Festival Nurse
Backcast

The Jericho Series
Jericho
Aftermath
Goldenrod

Story Collections
Sidecar
Three (plus one)

Goldenrod
—— a Jericho novel ——

Ann McMan

Bywater BOOKS

Ann Arbor

Bywater Books

Print ISBN: 978-1-61294-083-0

Bywater Books First Edition: July 2017

Printed in the United States of America on acid-free paper.

Quote on page 77: Burnford, Sheila. *The Incredible Journey*. New York: Bantam Doubleday Dell Books for Young Readers, 1960/1988.

E-Book ISBN: 978-1-61294-084-7

Cover designer: Ann McMan, TreeHouse Studio

Bywater Books
PO Box 3671
Ann Arbor MI 48106-3671
www.bywaterbooks.com

This novel is a work of fiction.

For Susan Jane Barraclough,
who made me promise to keep telling my stories

"Suffer little children,
and forbid them not, to come unto me:
for of such is the kingdom of heaven."

—Matthew 19:14

Prologue

She didn't fear the water because it was deep.

In fact, it wasn't deep. Not right here. She knew that much from experience.

If she took her time and chose a route that involved jumping from rock to rock, she could pretty much make it all the way to the other side without getting too wet. That was the most important part—not getting wet. And this part of the river had a lot of bigger, flatter stones that spread out just above the surface of the water. They looked more gray than brown in the late afternoon sun. That meant they weren't wet and they'd be warmer on the bottoms of her bare feet. Her shoes and a book were cinched up tight inside a plastic grocery bag. She was careful to hold it high above the water while she crossed.

This was one of her favorite spots—this bend that wasn't visible from the house or the narrow stretch of road on the opposite side that followed the river most of the way into town. That made it the safest place for her to cross without being seen.

She didn't want to be seen.

The last time he had caught her trying to make it to the other side, he was so angry that he stormed right out into the water wearing his dress clothes to grab hold of her and drag her back to land. She remembered watching the sunlight flash in the spray that roared up from his surging feet. He was moving toward her like an angry wave, and when he reached her he delivered his first crude lesson about how dangerous the river was.

He held her face below the surface of the water for only a few seconds, but it was long enough for her to realize that if she kept her eyes open she could make out the smooth contour of the amber- and green-colored riverbed. It was strewn with ancient tree limbs and long, smooth stones that had been pushed deep into the soft ground by winter ice floes. It looked calm and simple. What a contrast it was to the world she inhabited above the surface, where heat and human passion took what should have been order and created chaos.

She was lucky that time. The water was cold—colder than usual for this early in the season. It didn't make him less angry, but it made him more eager to get out of the slow-moving current that soaked his shoes and flattened his best pants against his spindly legs. Still, his rage was strong enough to carry them back to shore where he threw her against a pile of rocks and towered over her, shouting out a promise to leave her on the bottom of the river if she ever dared to defy him like this again.

Then his rage took an uglier, more predictable turn.

It took him days to calm down after that episode. She'd had to steer clear of him after work until he changed out of his suit and left for the evening. He was gone a lot more these days. So if she timed it just right, she could get back well before dark and be locked inside her room when he stumbled back in for what was left of the night.

That was her hope today.

She looked at the angle of the sun and tightened her hold on the bag. If she hurried, she'd have plenty of time. She hopped across to the next flat rock. Water swirled around it like it was caught up in some kind of crazy dance. The way it rolled and gurgled beneath her feet was almost funny.

She didn't fear the water because it was deep.

She didn't fear the water at all.

It was land that terrified her.

Chapter 1

The hardest part of this job was all the waiting around.

Well. Maybe that was the *second* hardest part. Learning how to drive this damn truck was no cakewalk either—especially for her. *Navigationally challenged.* That's what her father called her. But that didn't seem fair—or accurate. She didn't have trouble *finding* things—she just had some problems parking once she got there. Sometimes, though, she got lucky and that task wasn't as difficult as it was most days.

Like today. This stop on the route was one of the simpler ones because it was in a fairly desolate location where there wasn't a lot of traffic. It was really just a crossroads. A spot in the middle of Jefferson County where the two-lane blacktop that ran alongside the river veered off and intersected a wide gravel lane that led to a bunch of farms. All she had to do here was get the truck pulled over to the edge of the gravel without slipping into the runoff ditch.

That had already happened. Twice.

But now she knew better and she had some good visual markers to help her know how close she could get without going too far. She had figured out that if she lined the left wall of Joe Baxter's corncrib up with the right front bumper of the truck, she'd be positioned in a way that she could make a clean U-turn when it was time to leave. Not having to back up was a good thing. In her life, that bit of wisdom always held true, even when it had nothing to do with driving this bookmobile.

It seemed incredible to her that so many of the things that helped her in this job were also true in the rest of her life. It had taken her a while to figure that one out. Charlie said that was because she tended not to look at "the big picture," but instead stayed focused on all the things in her path that might trip her up.

Roma Jean found it hard to disagree with that assessment. She'd always been pretty famous for falling over things. Especially when those "things" were great big distractions that loomed up out of no place and obscured her ability to see anything else. It wasn't fair that real life didn't offer up its own brand of visual markers that worked like Joe Baxter's corncrib. More than once she wished for any kind of reference point that would keep her from sliding into *other* kinds of ditches. But if those markers existed, she sure didn't see them. Not often, anyway. Consequently, she found herself spending a lot of time hauling herself out of the ditches that ran along both sides of the middle ground that defined her life.

The good news was that she tended to emerge from these forays less banged-up than the bookmobile. It helped that nobody else could really tell when she went off the rails. That's what her uncle Cletus called it when somebody acted crazy. "Off the rails." Of course, he was usually talking about Gramma Azalea, and in her case, that was a pretty accurate description.

It was slow here today. She'd already been parked in this spot for nearly fifteen minutes and nobody had shown up yet. That made her worry a little bit. Henry Lawrence was nearly always here waiting on her when she pulled up. He'd been living with his father in a small apartment over Junior's Garage since last summer, when his dad got out of the army. James Lawrence had lost a leg when the transport vehicle he was driving hit a roadside bomb in Afghanistan. Now he divided his time between working on engine repairs at Junior's and delivering mobile homes for Cougar's Flag Cars. When the mobile home business was good and James was away on overnight trips, Henry would move back into his room at the farm with Dr. Stevenson and Miss Murphy.

It wasn't hot outside today, so she didn't have the air conditioning going. She jumped at any excuse not to run the van's noisy generator, even if that meant not being able to have the inside lights on. The gas-powered generator shook, rattled and thundered like a jet airplane engine, and it made the books on the shelves vibrate. Miss Murphy had sent the truck out to Junior's twice to have it checked out, but both times Junior said there was nothing wrong with it except that it was old. Miss Murphy wasn't surprised by that. She'd bought the thing secondhand from some small library system in central North Carolina and everything on it was pretty beat-up. They'd had plans to fix it up, but Miss Murphy wanted to get it into service as quickly as possible. That meant they'd be having it worked on it during the days it wasn't parked along some county road. At least Bert Townsend's boy, Buddy, came by the library and kept it all washed and shining. Still, she wished they had time to paint over the ginormous red, yellow and orange sunburst logo that proclaimed "GET CHECKED OUT!" in two-foot-high, psychedelic letters. That part was *really* embarrassing—especially when Roma Jean was first learning how to drive it and kept crashing into mailboxes, trash cans and the drive-through awning at Aunt Bea's.

The first time she pulled the big van into the lot at Freemantle's Market (and nearly took out a row of gas pumps), her father came outside, took a gander at it, shook his head, and told her the dang thing looked like a mobile dating service.

They'd only been running it on the weekends but now that summer was here, Roma Jean would be operating it full-time. That meant a lot more stops in remote locations like this one. Miss Murphy was excited about extending library services to people who lived out in what she called the "backcountry" areas of the county. "We have an obligation to reach out to people who don't have the ability to travel to the branch in Jericho," she told the county supervisors. Of course, they all agreed with her, but they were unwilling to commit any more money to the library. So Miss Murphy made them a deal they couldn't refuse: Put up the money to pay the salary for a summer intern, and she'd buy the damn bookmobile herself.

So here Roma Jean was, late on a Friday afternoon, making her last stop of the day. She heard the telltale creaking of the metal steps that announced the arrival of a patron.

Finally.

She got up from the driver's seat and ducked back into the darker recesses of the bookmobile.

A young girl was standing there, blinking her eyes to adjust to the low light. She smiled when she recognized Roma Jean.

"Hey, Miss Freemantle." The girl held up a plastic Food City bag. "I finished that book you gave me last week."

Roma Jean reached out to take it from her. "Hey, Dorothy. Did you like it?"

Dorothy nodded. "A lot. Are there more books like this one?"

Roma Jean pulled the copy of *To Kill a Mockingbird* out of the bag. "I bet we can find something else you'll like just as much."

"I might need two books this time. I won't be able to come back next week."

"Oh, really?" Roma Jean checked Dorothy's book back in and returned it to a shelf. "Is there a school holiday or something?"

"No." Dorothy shook her head but didn't offer any other details.

Roma Jean was tempted to follow up with more questions, but something about the girl's expression made her think twice about that—not something she usually did. But they had read *Pride and Prejudice* in her freshman English class, and she was trying hard to be more like its heroine, Elizabeth Bennet. "Keep your breath to cool your porridge," Miss Bennet told the arrogant Mr. Darcy. Then she went on to play the piano and sing.

Roma Jean couldn't play the piano worth anything. And her singing voice made her father's beagles howl.

"Do you play the piano?" she asked Dorothy.

The girl blinked at her.

"I'm sorry. I guess that was kinda random. I just read a book called *Pride and Prejudice* in school, and all the ladies in it play the piano."

"It's okay," Dorothy said. "We don't have a piano."

"We do. But it's ancient and half the ivory is gone from the keys. I used to get splinters when I had to take lessons."

"Why'd they make you take lessons?"

Roma Jean shrugged. "Beats me. Mama said it was supposed to teach me *deportment*."

Dorothy looked confused. "What's that?"

"It has something to do with being a lady."

"How does playing a beat-up piano make you more of a lady?"

"If I knew the answer to that, my life would be a whole lot simpler."

Dorothy seemed to accept that explanation at face value. "I don't know very many ladies, so I don't know how they're different from the rest of us."

Roma Jean thought about Dr. Stevenson and Miss Murphy. Nobody would argue that *they* weren't ladies. Even though they didn't have an ordinary relationship—at least not by Jericho standards. "I think they handle stuff better."

"What kind of stuff?"

"I don't know. *Stuff.* Like how to react when things don't go your way. Or what to do when you're really frustrated and nobody else understands it." She thought some more about Elizabeth Bennet and her run-ins with the awful Lady Catherine de Bourgh. "Or how to defend yourself when somebody really mean accuses you of things you didn't do."

Dorothy rolled her eyes. "That last part would be good to know even if you weren't trying to be a lady."

Roma Jean thought that was an odd comment. "Is somebody being mean to you, Dorothy?"

Dorothy never got a chance to answer because they were interrupted by the sound of feet pounding on the gravel outside. Little Henry Lawrence skidded to a halt just outside the door of the van. He was out of breath and his arms were full of oversized flat books. Half of his shirttail had come untucked and his bangs were hanging down in his eyes. He shook his head and tried to blow the hair back away from his face. He was only moderately successful. He smiled when he saw them both inside.

"Hey, Miss Freemantle. Hey, Dorothy. Am I too late?"

"Nope." Roma Jean walked over to meet him. "Come on inside. You've still got plenty of time to pick out something new."

"Okay." He climbed up the metal steps. "Do you have more of those Harry books?"

Roma Jean took the stack of Gene Zion classics from him. "I don't think so, Henry. You pretty much read them all."

His face fell. "I like that dog."

Roma Jean reached across the narrow aisle and pulled a book off a lower shelf. "I think you might like this one a lot, too. It has two dogs in it—and one of them is a yellow retriever."

His eyes grew wide. "Like Pete?"

Roma Jean smiled at him. Pete was Dr. Stevenson's dog. "Like Pete with short hair. Only not as old." She handed him the copy of *The Incredible Journey*.

He opened it and quickly scanned the pages. "It has a lot of words."

"It does. You'll have to ask someone to read it with you."

He sighed and handed the book back to her.

Dorothy reached out for it. "How about I check it out and help you read it, Henry?"

He looked at her with excitement. "Really?"

Dorothy nodded. "But you keep it at your house and bring it with you on bookmobile days." She looked at Roma Jean. "Can we keep it an extra-long time?"

"You sure can." Roma Jean smiled at her. "Now let's find a new book for you."

"Two books, if that's okay," Dorothy reminded her.

"Wanna try this one?" Roma Jean handed her a copy of *Cold Sassy Tree*. The Olive Ann Burns book was one of her favorites. She didn't worry that the book was too advanced. She knew that Dorothy was already reading things that were far beyond her seventh-grade level. "It has a small-town setting, too."

Henry pulled a dog-eared paperback off a shelf. "This one

must be good, too." He handed it to Dorothy. "There are *nine* copies of it. I counted them."

Dorothy showed the book to Roma Jean.

Fifty Shades of Grey.

"Um." Roma Jean held out her hand. "Probably not this one."

"Why not?" Henry looked confused. "What's it about?"

"It's about . . ." Roma Jean deliberated. "Games. Grown-ups who play games."

"I like games." Henry looked at Dorothy. "Don't you like games?"

Dorothy was too busy watching Roma Jean to reply.

"There are a lot of copies," Henry continued. "We can both get one."

Roma Jean knew she was blushing.

Dorothy seemed to take pity on her. "I don't think this one is right for us, Henry."

"How come?"

"I think maybe it's too . . . *advanced.*"

Henry squinted behind his bangs. "What does that mean?"

They all jumped when they heard a throat being cleared.

Dorothy and Henry turned in unison toward the open door. A tall, blonde woman wearing sunglasses and a brown uniform stood just outside. She had an odd smile on her face.

"Charlie!" Henry raced toward her.

Charlie Davis scooped Henry up and gave him a warm hug. "How're you doing, short stack?"

"Good!" Henry hugged her back. "Roma Jean is giving us some books to read, Charlie."

"So I see." Charlie pushed her sunglasses up on her head and took note of the book Roma Jean was holding. "Interesting choice. Care to elaborate?"

"Oh." Roma Jean waved the book around in an ill-fated attempt at finding a place to stash it. She finally gave up and dropped the hand holding it to her side. "I wasn't . . . they weren't . . . we didn't . . ."

"It's about *games*," Henry clarified. "But Dorothy says they're too 'vanced for us."

Charlie set Henry back on his feet. "I think Dorothy is right, pal. But I have to wonder," she smiled sweetly at Roma Jean, whose face was now beet red. "Does our librarian here think these games are too 'vanced for me, too?"

Charlie smiled at her with that smug expression that always caused Roma Jean's heart to do somersaults.

Roma Jean closed her eyes.

It was always the same. Two seconds after Charlie showed up, her composure would evaporate and she'd veer right off the rails into the nearest ditch.

Do not pass go. Do not collect $200 dollars.

She dared to look over at Charlie, who was still smiling at her with those incredible blue eyes.

Maybe the view from inside this ditch isn't so bad after all.

"I don't get it."

"What do you mean you don't get it? It's pretty straight-forward."

"Maybe to you." Maddie handed the flat purple and white bit of plastic back to Lizzy. "What am I supposed to be getting here?"

Lizzy held up the device. "See the little plus symbol in the window?"

"Of course." Maddie leaned back in her chair.

"Well, what do you think it means?"

"Is this a hypothetical question?"

Lizzy tipped her head back and glared at the ceiling of Maddie's office.

"Look." Maddie tented her fingers. "Why don't you just cut to the chase and tell me what we're discussing here?"

Lizzy sighed. "It's a home pregnancy test."

"I gathered as much."

Lizzy raised an eyebrow.

"That big 'EPT' emblem stamped beside the Walgreen's logo was a dead giveaway."

Lizzy dropped into the chair opposite Maddie's desk.

Maddie watched her for a moment. "Care to tell me why we're having this conversation?"

"Isn't it obvious?"

"Not to me."

Lizzy looked amazed. "You know what, Dr. Stevenson? There are a lot of people who would pay big money to see the list of things that *are* obvious to you."

"Now you sound like Syd."

Lizzy agreed. "A woman after my own heart."

"Yours and many others."

"I won't disagree with that."

"So." Maddie took off her reading glasses and tossed them atop a stack of file folders on her desk. "Wanna clue me in on why we're discussing a low-tech, OTC device?"

"Sometimes they get the job done more quickly. Especially when you're already sure of the outcome."

"Which in this case means?"

Lizzy stared back at her without speaking. Her expression was unreadable.

Maddie decided to pick up the clue phone. "This is yours, isn't it?"

Lizzy nodded. "I'm pregnant."

Maddie didn't say anything, mostly because she wasn't sure what to say. The only sound in the room came from the measured ticks of an ancient wall clock that had been a fixture in her father's office for decades.

After a few labored seconds, Lizzy glared at the clock.

"I've always hated that thing."

Maddie followed her gaze. "Why?"

Lizzy shrugged. "It's a crude reminder of how much of my life I've wasted."

"Maybe this is an opportunity to change that."

"Are you kidding?"

"Um. That depends on whether you view my anecdotal comment as a profound insight or a sophomoric insult."

Lizzy gave her a halfhearted smile. "This is a colossal mess."

"It doesn't have to be."

"Meaning?"

"Meaning you have options. As many or as few as you choose."

Lizzy didn't reply.

"Does Tom know?" Maddie asked.

Lizzy shook her head.

"Are you going to tell him?"

"Before I answer that, should I be offended by your automatic assumption that Tom is the father?"

Maddie smiled. "It did occur to me to wonder about Sonny Nicks. You two looked awfully chummy last week at the fire department barbecue."

"It's true." Lizzy sighed. "Old Sonny has unsung talents."

"I thought you made an adorable couple when you were arm wrestling over that last biscuit."

"I nearly had him until I got distracted by his tattoo. The man has some seriously good ink. In the end, I let him win."

"Is that the secret to a successful relationship?"

"Only the ones with men."

Maddie didn't reply. The second hand on the wall clock continued to mark time with its sequence of loud clicks.

Lizzy watched it in silence for a moment before shifting her gaze back to Maddie.

"I think I'm hosed."

"You don't have to be."

Lizzy threw up her hands in frustration. "How could I be stupid enough to let something like this happen? I'm a damn *nurse*."

"Meaning you should've known better?"

"Meaning I should have my credentials revoked for being such a careless idiot."

"It doesn't work that way."

"Oh, really? What do you think Dr. Greene will say when he finds out the resident Clara Barton in his precious little philanthropic project is knocked up?"

Maddie sighed. "Believe me when I tell you that the last person you need to worry about is Dr. Greene. Besides, he and Muriel are now spending most of their time flitting about on what can conservatively be called *esoteric* cruises."

"Someday you'll have to explain that to me."

"We'll both be happier if I don't."

"Whatever."

"Do you want to have a proper examination?"

Lizzy nodded. "But not when Peggy's here."

Maddie didn't disagree. If her loquacious nurse found out, the news would travel faster than a norovirus on a school bus. "We can wait until she leaves for the day."

"Thanks." Lizzy got to her feet.

"One thing before you go?" Maddie asked.

"What?"

"Tom. Are you going to tell him?"

"I honestly don't know." Lizzy shrugged. "Not right away."

"Okay."

"Do me a favor?"

"Sure."

"Don't say anything to Syd about this? Not until I know what I'm going to do."

Maddie thought about that. Tom was Syd's brother. Even though he drove his sister nuts, Maddie knew Syd would be beside herself with excitement at the prospect of having a niece or nephew to spoil. Especially since Henry had left them to live with his father. It would be next to impossible for her to keep this quiet for very long. She was lousy at keeping secrets from Syd, who could always see through any attempt at subterfuge like it was a worn-out negligee.

"I'll try." She leaned forward. "But promise me you won't take too long."

"Too long at what?" Peggy Hawkes filled up the doorway to Maddie's office. "Are you going to lunch early?" she asked Lizzy. "If you are, can I get you to stop by Aunt Bea's and pick me up one of those pointy breasts and a biscuit?"

Lizzy took it all in stride. "Something to drink?"

15

"A large Cheerwine."

"How about you?"

Maddie started to reply but Peggy cut her off. "She's having lunch with the mayor."

Lizzy raised an eyebrow. "Do tell? You and Jericho's own Pat McCrory?"

"He's not that bad."

"Said the last canary in a room full of alley cats."

"Shhhhh," Peggy wagged a finger at them. "He's out there in the waitin' room."

"I think I'll take this opportunity to duck out the back door." Lizzy waved at them. "See you a bit later."

Peggy watched her go. "Is it just me or is that girl gettin' wider in the slats?"

Maddie cleared her throat. "Did you say Mr. Watson was in the waiting room?"

Peggy nodded.

"Please tell him I'll be there in just a minute."

"Okay, doc." Peggy bustled off.

Maddie sat and stared morosely at her father's clock.

Syd is gonna kill me . . .

"Tell me again why you thought this was a good idea?"

Celine was running her hand over a bank of tin ceiling tiles that now covered most of a wall in her new kitchen.

Bert and Sonny exchanged glances.

"Well," Sonny began. "There was these big cracks in the plaster back 'ere."

"Big cracks," Bert added.

"And me 'n Bert thought that these here ol' tiles from the hardware store—the one that got all tore up in the tornado last year—would fit in real good with all them fancy steel appliances you got ordered for in here."

Bert agreed. "There wasn't no way we could fix that wall up, Miz Heller. It was too far gone."

16

"Yes, ma'am. We'd a had to bust it all out and put up sheetrock." Sonny took off his paint-spattered ball cap and scratched his head. "We know'd you wouldn't want that. Not with how hard you been workin' to keep this all authentic."

Celine tapped her fingers against her leg as she regarded the wall. It had been a shock when she first saw it. But now? Now it looked almost . . . right. A quirky but nearly sublime departure. Again. She shook her head.

"I don't know how you two keep coming up with these inventive solutions."

Sonny demurred. "It was really Harold's idea. He reads all them home design magazines."

Sonny's son, Harold, ran the local beauty shop, Hairport '75.

Bert agreed. "Last time I got my hair cut, I was talkin' about how bad these walls was in here and how all them big rains last year just did for this plaster. Harold showed me some pictures of some movie star's house in California where they done this same thing. Course, they had to order them tin tiles from some joker who was tearin' down farmhouses up in Saskatchewan. But me and Sonny remembered that all that stuff from the hardware store got hauled out to that back lot behind Junior's and was free for the takin'."

Sonny took up the narrative. "We thought it'd be somethin' we could do while we was waitin' on that permit for the electrical to come through."

"We knew if you didn't like it, we could just take it down." Bert tapped the cracked plaster that was visible above a row of the tiles with the blunt edge of his tinners hammer. "It ain't like we'd done nothin' to make this worse or anything."

Celine had to agree. Her decision to buy and restore this old shell of an abandoned bungalow that had sagged proudly for generations on a grassy hillside near Bridle Creek had been spontaneous. Its river views were spectacular. And its relative isolation was perfect for her, even though she argued—convincingly—that it was barely two minutes off a main road and only five miles from town.

17

Her daughter thought she'd lost her mind—in spite of being thrilled with her decision to retire from her teaching career in the medical school at UCLA and return to the tiny mountain community. But that initial reaction from Maddie was nothing new. When it came to taking chances, Maddie was about as reckless as a box turtle. Thank god that reluctance to veer off the beaten path didn't extend to her personal life. It was fortunate that Maddie took after her late father in more ways than one.

Celine looked around the old kitchen. This room had been an afterthought—added on years after the original structure had been built. That wasn't uncommon. Many of these old houses built in the mid- or late-nineteenth century relied on summer kitchens—outdoor sheds where the cooking took place.

She had plans for this room. Bert and Sonny were going to extend the side wall and add a big, open seating area surrounded by glass doors that would lead to a garden. Space. Color. Light and air. All the things she'd given up during her years in California. Now she could have them in abundance. Now she could lead an intentional existence that wasn't an afterthought. Breathing new life into the dark recesses of this ancient and neglected house was more than an exercise in aesthetics—it was an effort to reclaim her soul.

Yes. The tiles were right. Exactly right.

She smiled at Bert and Sonny.

"Carry on."

"I'm hoping you can talk some sense into your friend."

Maddie lowered her cup of coffee. "Excuse me?"

Gerald Watson dabbed at his upper lip with a paper napkin—about the fifth one he'd made use of since their plates of food arrived. A tidy stack of the discarded squares rose beside his plate. He was plainly fastidious about keeping his moustache clean. That being the case, a barbecue sandwich loaded with runny coleslaw was probably not the wisest lunch option. But in Maddie's experience, people rarely made what she'd call "operational" choices that dovetailed in rational ways with their personal proclivities.

"It's not safe for him and his partner to be holding those weddings out there at that farm." Watson added another paper square to the heap. "There's a lot of talk about it in town. It's bad for business and this is an area that thrives on tourist traffic."

Maddie didn't want to have this conversation. The mayor's inflection on *partner* and *those* was impossible to mistake.

"Mr. Watson, I hope you'll understand that having this conversation with me will be of little value to get you closer to whatever outcome you have in mind."

"I disagree. He listens to you."

Maddie felt her ire rising. "Even if that were true, this is not an area where I have any right or inclination to interfere. David and Michael are experienced businessmen who are capable of making their own decisions."

He shook his head. "Friday is the first of June, Dr. Stevenson."

Maddie waited for him to add clarification to his statement, but none seemed forthcoming.

"I fail to see your point, Mr. Watson."

He gave up on holding his sandwich and picked up a knife and fork. "I suppose that's not very surprising given your own circumstances."

"Pardon me?"

"Even you must realize that June is a popular month for weddings, and that this is an industry that drives commerce for many of our local businesses."

Maddie chose to ignore his implied criticism of her personal life. "If that's true, then it would seem that David and Michael are helping the local economy, not creating a hindrance."

"No, ma'am."

Watson wagged an index finger in front of her like a metronome on tilt. The simple gesture was oddly arrhythmic. Maddie was half tempted to spear his finger with her salad fork. It was difficult not to follow the halting gestures with her eyes. If they had been seated in her examination room instead of on mismatched straight chairs at the Midway Café, Maddie would have been tempted to give the mayor a neurological exam.

He continued to drive home his point. "Good and God-fearing small business owners in this town do not want to be forced to participate in rituals that condone immoral acts."

Maddie had had enough of this conversation.

"What good and God-fearing business owners might you be referencing, Mr. Watson? The florist? The hairdresser? The caterer?" She paused for effect. "The local physician?"

Watson's face turned red. A throbbing vein in his forehead telegraphed that it wasn't from embarrassment. "I had hoped that you, as a person of sense and education, would see reason and use your influence to help your friends avoid the unhappy consequences of their reckless decisions. I see now that I was mistaken."

Maddie leaned forward. "On that point, we certainly agree, Mr. Mayor."

He abruptly pushed back his chair and got to his feet. "I bid you good day, Dr. Stevenson."

Maddie noticed two things about his indignant departure from the restaurant. Even in his haste to be away from her, he took time to extract a half-dozen more paper napkins from the metal dispenser on their table.

He also failed to pick up the check.

Maddie stared at the grease-stained slip of paper that sat beside the mayor's plate.

Jerk.

"We shouldn't be doing this here."

Charlie was kissing along the side of Roma Jean's neck, inching closer to her collarbone. Roma Jean knew it was getting out of hand. *Again.* It was always this way when they ended up alone together. The last time it happened, Charlie had stopped in to see her when she had the bookmobile parked near the low-water crossing on Greenhouse Road. There were several houses strewn

20

along that stretch of gravel road that was really like two ruts bisecting a rolling expanse of pasture. It was dotted with little copses of trees shading cattle weary of grazing in the hot afternoon sun. That day, the only thing that had stopped the couple's inevitable progress toward what the locals surely would consider unnatural acts was a wayward heifer that decided to seek relief in the convenient square of shade thrown across its path by Roma Jean's truck. Of course, the heifer butted its expansive hindquarters into the side of the bookmobile—twice—before it settled to the ground with an accompanying grunt. Roma Jean and Charlie had bolted apart like escaped felons caught in the sweep of a searchlight.

It took Charlie forty-five minutes to convince the heifer to get up and mosey along.

It took Roma Jean forty-five seconds to resolve to be more careful in the future.

Today, though, the location was less trafficked—by patrons or cattle. After Henry and Dorothy departed with their books, Roma Jean and Charlie sat close together inside the dimly lighted mobile library and talked in fits and starts about safe topics.

"Safe" topics were defined as any subjects related to Roma Jean's classes at Radford, Charlie's work for the sheriff's department, or innocent gossip about any of the county's more eccentric residents. Fortunately for them, that last item provided an unending number of discussion topics.

Today it was Roma Jean's ninety-year-old grandmother, Azalea.

"Zeke Dawkins told me that he saw your Gramma and Uncle Cletus at Waffle House yesterday. He said they were in deep conversation with a couple of slick-looking Yankees in suits."

Roma Jean rolled her eyes. "I know."

"Well, what was that about? Zeke said your Gramma won't even stay in the same room with a Yankee, much less sit down and eat waffles with a pair of them."

"It's embarrassing."

"What is?"

Roma Jean shrugged.

"Come on," Charlie nudged her—which Roma Jean knew was really just an excuse to scoot a bit closer. "What were they doing?"

"They were going over her contract with Rockstar. Gramma is going to be a beta tester for *Grand Theft Auto VI.*"

"For real?" Charlie was incredulous. "I thought those rumors about a version VI were bogus?"

"Gramma says they just wanna keep it on the DL. They're gonna roll it out, all right. And she's persuaded they're gonna set it in someplace offbeat—like Troutdale."

Charlie's eyes grew wide.

"No kidding. I mean, after knocking off Junior's garage and escaping in a beat-up Oldsmobile, what other heists could they plan? Stealing retread tires off the rooftops of all the trailers out there? She's crazy."

"I just can't believe this. They really hired her?"

Roma Jean sighed and nodded. "She's gotten pretty famous in the gaming world. Her Snapchat posts have gone viral and most of them are about her *GTA V* record-setting totals for The Big Score."

"Azalea's on Snapchat?"

"Yeah. Her handle is *@AzaLeavesNoPrisoners.*"

"Is this a joke?"

"Nope. Uncle Cletus had to have ApCo do a heavy-up on the power to their apartment because Gramma kept blowing all the circuits, and Aunt Evelyn said all the pennies she kept sticking inside the fuse box were gonna burn the place down."

"Roma Jean—"

"Uncle Cletus tried putting a lock on the fuse box but Gramma just blasted it off with her .410. That was a real mess because when the lock blew apart it took out about four dozen jars of tomatoes Aunt Evelyn and Nadine put up last summer for the café."

"Sweetie—"

"Aunt Evelyn said when she got home the apartment looked like a scene from some old movie called *Helter Skelter.* She was pretty mad. But Gramma was oblivious. She just sat there in the living room on Cletus's recliner, staring at the TV screen with the game controller on her lap, capping hookers."

Charlie ran a hand over her face.

"Uncle Cletus says the only good thing about Gramma's obsession is that she hardly has to take any arthritis medicine any more. I guess manipulating all the controls on that game console night and day has really reduced the swelling in her hands."

"Baby, you need to stop."

Roma Jean gave Charlie a sheepish look. "I was blathering again, wasn't I?"

Charlie smiled at her. "I wouldn't say that."

Roma Jean dropped her eyes. "What would you say, then?"

She knew she was being a flirt, but right then she didn't really care.

Charlie inched closer to her. They were sitting next to each other on the step that led up to the driver's compartment on the truck.

"I'd say it's been too long since we had a chance to do this."

Charlie leaned over and kissed her. It was a gentle touch, more like a brief brushing of her lips across Roma Jean's. It wasn't a tease. It was more like an invitation. Charlie was always like that. Slow. Considerate. Not too pushy. Not really pushy at all, when Roma Jean compared her to the other people she'd shared simple intimacies with. Of course, the others had all been guys and each of them had attacked her mouth like starving men who were persuaded that she was concealing the last morsel of food on the planet.

It was pretty gross.

But Roma Jean allowed it because she thought that's what she was supposed to do. Playing tonsil hockey with a succession of boys who had roaming hands and bad complexions was something she never got used to. That used to worry her. A lot. But all of that changed when she met Charlie. Now she found herself fantasizing all the time about being alone with Charlie. She thought about all the things she'd like to do and imagined herself behaving boldly— like Elizabeth Bennet, who went into any kind of situation with composure.

Charlie smelled good. Like cinnamon and strawberries.

She wondered if Mr. Darcy smelled this good. And whether that made it as hard for Elizabeth to stay focused as the sweet mixture of air shifting around inside the truck was making it for her right now.

"Are you okay?" Charlie's soft voice was close. So close Roma Jean could feel the warm puffs of air that carried each word to her.

Was she okay?

She shifted closer to Charlie. There wasn't much light inside the truck. But not even the little bit that managed to filter its way in from the driver compartment separated their bodies now. Charlie's figure was framed against a backdrop of shopworn classics—books that had been held a thousand times by as many pairs of hands. *Treasure Island. Robinson Crusoe. The Mill on the Floss. My Antonia. Pride and Prejudice* was there, too. If she closed her eyes, she could almost imagine Elizabeth Bennet smiling down at her.

The truth was that she was more than okay. She was something miles ahead of okay. Finally. Wonderfully. *Entirely.*

She raised her hands to Charlie's face.

"*Yes.*"

Syd gave up waiting on Maddie to make it home in time for dinner. She fixed herself a large summer salad and sat on the wide front porch, enjoying the last hour of daylight. Pete dozed on the big glider but kept one wakeful eye fixed on the driveway for any sign of Maddie's Jeep.

The salad was wonderful. It was a tumbled conglomeration of lettuces pulled from their small garden and fresh, tender peas clipped from the lattice of lines that Henry had helped her string before the last frost in April. The mound of cherries and strawberries were treats that she picked up at a roadside stand on her way home from the library. All of it was topped with a simple vinaigrette and a few tangy bleu cheese crumbles—an indulgence she could enjoy because she was eating alone. Maddie hated bleu cheese.

Celine wasn't home yet, either. Maddie's mother had been staying with them while renovation work proceeded on the dilapidated house she'd bought out near Bridle Creek, but that wouldn't last much longer. Celine was already talking about scheduling a time to have the PODS containing her furnishings delivered. And lately she'd been making day trips to larger urban centers like Roanoke or Winston-Salem to shop for fixtures or more retrograde bits of hardware than those readily available at the big box stores that defined shopping alternatives in the smattering of larger towns closer to Jericho.

It was a quiet evening. A couple of deer felt confident enough to risk venturing out from behind a stand of trees to drink from the pond while it was still daylight. Pete seemed not to care, although Syd saw him raise his head and at least think about chasing after them.

Henry's pet Hereford, Before, was equally unfazed by the intruders. She stood placidly beside the rail fence that ran along the lane, chomping at random clumps of taller grass that sprouted up on the pasture side of the barrier. Keeping a seven-hundred-pound heifer as a "pet" was ridiculous. But Henry had grown uncommonly attached to the calf that formerly had been part of Joe Baxter's herd. The calf, known originally as B4, had consistently sought out breaches in the fencing that divided their two properties, appearing to prefer the less congested dining options presented by their pastures. Henry's penchant for collecting buckets full of fat garlic bulbs and liberally doling them out as treats hadn't done much to dissuade the calf from contriving ways to visit. Last year, when Henry left them to live with his father, Syd decided to make Before a permanent part of their family. That way when Henry returned for occasional overnights or weekend visits, he could be surrounded by his menagerie of animals. It was growing to be an impressive list. Before. Pete. The odd assortment of fat fish in their pond. And Rosebud—a black and white stray cat with tuxedo markings who'd taken up residence behind a bin of castoff vacuum cleaner parts in Maddie's workshop.

Of course, Rosebud hated Maddie. She had a fondness for sleeping on the hood of the Jeep and peeing on its tires. She also enjoyed evacuating beneath the workbench.

Syd smiled. The animus was mutual.

In typical fashion, Maddie tried chasing the cat away, but it was useless. She would grumble in the evenings when she got home from work and fresh examples of Rosebud's handiwork were evident.

"Why is that damn tuxedo cat still hanging around?"

Syd would shrug and say nothing. She knew it wasn't wise to let Maddie know she was sneaking food to the stray.

They indulged in this game of thrust and parry for a few weeks. Then one night, Maddie seemed to turn a corner. She stormed into the house from the barn and dropped onto a stool in their kitchen.

"That tuxedo cat is a total pain in my ass."

Syd nodded from the island where she was washing vegetables. "I know, honey."

Maddie glowered and drummed her fingers on the tabletop.

Syd took pity on her. "What do you want to do?"

Maddie thought about it. "Buy some cat food, I guess."

They named the intruder-cum-antagonist "Rosebud" because Maddie insisted that the cat would likely hold the key to some great, as-yet unsolved mystery in her life.

Syd did not disagree. Mysteries they had in abundance. It was answers that were in short supply. Especially lately.

She looked at her watch. *Nine-thirty.* Maddie said she'd be home by eight.

Her mug of tea was cold. She thought about taking it inside and sticking it into the microwave to heat it up, but why bother?

She stood up and collected her dishes. "C'mon, Pete. Bedtime."

They were halfway to the door when Pete stopped, turned around, then bolted for the steps that led to the yard. His figure was a yellow flash in the fading light as he bounded toward the Jeep that was slowly making its way up their lane.

Maddie was home.

Syd deposited her dishes and followed Pete at a more sedate pace. Maddie waved when she saw her coming.

Syd followed her into the barn. Maddie parked the Jeep and grabbed her bag off the passenger seat. Before she turned to greet Syd, she stopped to scrub Pete's head and steal a quick peek at the ground beneath her workbench.

"Any presents?" Syd asked.

Maddie shook her head and smiled. "Not tonight."

They hugged.

"You're late."

"I know," Maddie said. "I'm sorry. I was on my way out and I made the mistake of answering the phone. There's a new pharmacist at the Rite Aid in Wytheville. He somehow managed to screw up about twenty prescriptions. It was simpler just to write new ones than to try and figure them out over the phone."

"Did you get any dinner?"

"No. And I'm starving." Maddie linked arms with her and they started walking toward the house. Pete ran on ahead of them. "I didn't think you'd still be up."

"I nearly wasn't. I was just on my way up to bed."

Maddie gestured toward the empty parking space behind the house. "Where is mom?"

"I'm not sure. Roanoke, maybe?"

"She didn't call?"

"No."

"That's strange. This is the third night this week she's been out late."

Syd thought about giving her a pass on the comment, but changed her mind. "It must be a family value."

Maddie stopped walking. "Are we going to have an argument?"
"About?"

"Oh, I don't know. Lemme see. Climate change?"

"Sarcasm won't get you off the hook."

"That's precisely my point. Why am I *on* the hook?"

Syd plucked at a faded yellow bloom on the rosebush that was slowly overtaking the steps that led to the porch. She really needed to prune this thing. It was gangly and unkempt. But now was not the right time. She'd missed her window. The early spring weather had come and gone without warning, and now it was too late in the season. The thing was already putting on new growth. She dropped the withered petals and looked up at Maddie.

"You're not caught on any hook you couldn't dislodge with just a bit of effort."

"Am I supposed to know what that means?"

"Are you saying you really don't know?"

Maddie didn't reply. In the half light, Syd could see that her face was tinged with worry. And maybe defeat. But still, her blue eyes glowed like night fire.

Syd relented. "Let's go inside. I'll make you something to eat."

"You're not mad at me?"

Maddie's tone seemed so contrite that even if she had been mad, Syd would've found it impossible to stay that way. She leaned in and slid her arms around Maddie's waist.

"No. I'm not mad."

"Thank god." Maddie hugged her closer and kissed the top of her head.

"I miss you," Syd murmured into her chest.

"I'm right here."

"Not always. Not lately."

"I know I've been working too much. I'm sorry."

"Maddie?" Syd raised her head. "Don't kid a kidder. It's not work. It's Henry. And you're not alone in how you feel. I miss him, too. But not coming home to avoid the fact he isn't here won't make it any easier—for either of us."

"Is that what you think I've been doing?"

"In a word? Yes."

Maddie gave her a shy smile. "Are you watching Dr. Oz again?"

Syd pinched her on the butt. "Nice try."

"Getting fresh with me won't advance your cause."

"Cause? What makes you think I have a cause?"

"Well. The fact that your hands are now performing deviant acts might be a clue."

Syd kissed her. "Nobody ever said you weren't good at rendering a diagnosis, Dr. Stevenson."

"Trust me." Maddie kissed her back. "I'm a whole lot better at cures."

"Are you? I don't remember."

"Maybe I can jog your memory." Maddie dropped her bag and got serious about reminding her.

Syd was losing focus. Why were they standing here in the yard when they had a big house full of obliging beds?

A big *empty* house . . .

Syd drew back. They both were breathing heavily. "Do you still want something to eat?"

Maddie gave her a roguish smile.

Syd rolled her eyes. "Pervert."

She grabbed hold of Maddie's hand and led her into the house.

Chapter 2

"Would you mind repeating that?"

David made a dramatic eye-roll. He was having a hard time concealing his excitement. As soon as he had got the notification, he called Celine and asked her to meet him at the café for an early lunch so he could give her the good news in person. But she wasn't getting it.

He snapped his fingers in front of her face.

"Earth to Celine? I said *The Tales of Rolf and Tobi* just won a ManMeat Award."

Celine seemed unimpressed. "Is that a good thing?"

"Good thing? *No.* It's not a 'good' thing. It's a *great* thing."

"Well then, I'm very happy for you, David."

David dropped back against his chair. "Why do you sound like I just told you that the dryer finally coughed up my missing sock? ManMeat Awards are a *big* deal in the independent publishing world. They're voted on by the readers."

"The readers? The readers of what, exactly?"

"Duh. The readers of top gay fiction books published within the last year. And, lucky for us, that includes self-published books, too."

"I'm sorry. I don't mean to rain on your parade."

"Hey?" David interrupted her. "It's not just *my* parade—you were the editor on this gem. Half the credit is yours, Dr. Heller."

Celine's jaw dropped. "You didn't use my real name on this, did you?"

"Of *course* not. I used your nom de plume, 'Stanford Hopkins.' Your reputation is safe."

"Thank god."

"But, listen. You must know that recognition like this is *huge*. We have to get busy right away."

"Busy?" Celine looked wary. "Busy doing what?"

"Duh. Writing volume two, of course. We've got to strike while the iron is H. A. W. T."

"Wait a minute." Celine held up her hand. "I am not reprising my role in this debatable enterprise."

David's face fell. "You have to. I can't translate those stories without your help."

"David . . ."

"You said it was *fun*."

"David . . ."

"You said the work was *instructive*."

"David . . ."

"You said it opened a door to a world you knew *nothing* about."

"David . . ."

"You said it would annoy the *piss* out of Maddie."

Celine opened her mouth to speak, but seemed to think better of it.

"Gotcha." David flashed her a brilliant smile.

"Much to my chagrin, I have to admit that last inducement does have merit."

David nodded energetically. "I've always thought so."

"I have to say." Celine shook her head. "You certainly never can predict how things will turn out."

David plucked a fat biscuit out of the basket on their table. "Tell me about it."

"If you'd asked me a year ago if I would be living back in Virginia, renovating a condemned house and moonlighting as a translator of German porn, I'd have said you were nuts."

"*Ex-cuse* me?" David cleared his throat. "Porn?"

"Sorry," Celine amended her statement. "Erotic fiction."

"Thank you."

"Still. It's quite a transformation."

"It is for sure," David agreed. "And you didn't even mention your new inamorato."

"My *what?*"

Before David could answer, Nadine Odell arrived at their table carrying two plates loaded with food.

"I guess I don't have to ask which one of you ordered the fried catfish." She plopped the large serving of fish topped with French fries down in front of David. "You need any kind of sauce with that, young man?"

David smiled up at her. "That depends."

"Depends? Depends on what?" Nadine placed a large arugula salad in front of Celine.

David snagged a French fry and bit it in half. "On who fried the fish. Was it you or Michael?"

Nadine propped her hands on her hips. "What if I said I made it?"

"Then it won't need a thing." He beamed at her. "It'll be perfect."

Nadine rolled her eyes. "I don't know why that man puts up with you."

"Same reason you do." David winked at her. "My infectious charm."

Nadine clucked her tongue. "I don't doubt for a second that 'infectious' describes a lot of things about you, boy—but 'charm' ain't likely to be one of 'em." She looked down at Celine. "Am I right?"

Celine didn't reply. She was still gaping at David.

Nadine looked back and forth between them.

"Now what on earth is the matter with you?" She pointed an index finger at David. "Is he telling you stories about what the two of them get up to when the lights go down?"

"Of course not," David replied. "She's just in shock because I mentioned her new beau."

That comment was enough to help Celine find her voice. "David . . ."

33

"Boy, you got some kind of nose for news." Nadine pursed her lips in obvious disapproval. "No wonder that partner of yours says he could use you to find truffles."

David smiled sweetly at her. "He told you about that game?"

Nadine popped him on the side of his head. "Don't you blaspheme in here, boy." She looked at Celine, whose face was a study in mortification. "Listen. Even the biggest idiot can get things right once in a while. So, if he's talkin' about you and that good-lookin' hunk of Sheriff, I say *ride* that pony, sister. Life is short."

The swinging door that led to the café kitchen banged open. Nadine's husband, Raymond, filled the opening. He was holding a mop and a large plumber's wrench and he did not look happy.

Nadine sighed. "Exhibit A in the circus parade. Let me go deal with my own bunch of flyin' monkeys." She patted Celine on the shoulder. "You got a shot at lettin' us all live the dream, sister. Don't mess it up by worrying about what people think."

She strode off toward the kitchen, angrily snapping a hand towel at her perpetually distressed mate.

"What she said," David added. Then he proceeded to swap their lunch plates. "You gonna let me have some of your French fries this time?"

Celine continued to stare across the table at him. Then she gave him a slow smile.

"Yippee ki yay."

"Gimme one of your smokes."

Jocelyn Painter was going over the budget with their new dispatcher, Natalie Chriscoe.

The business at Cougar's Flag Cars had grown so much, she and Deb Carlson had been adding staff. First came Natalie, who'd been the bookkeeper at the Bixby Bowladrome before it got demolished in the tornado the year before. A few weeks ago, they had hired her sister-in-law, Rita, who formerly ran the shoe concession. Hiring Rita was a no-brainer because she'd spent most of the last year working as a substitute bus driver for the consolidated school district. That meant she already had her multi-axle license. Rita now handled a lot of the overnight runs, delivering manufactured homes to retail lots in Kentucky and West Virginia.

Natalie pushed her open pack of Camels across the desk. "I thought you quit?"

"I tried them e-cigarettes, but one of 'em kicked back on me and the flare-up about burned off my adenoids."

"You still got your adenoids?" Natalie blew out a long plume of smoke. "I had mine took out back in October when I had that hysterectomy. I know'd it was just a matter of time before they went bad on me, so Mack and I thought we should take advantage and get a twofer on the deductible."

This kind of shrewd thinking was precisely why Jocelyn and Deb wanted Natalie on their team.

"You got a good head for business, girl."

Natalie shrugged. "With this Obamacare, you gotta figure out new ways to game the system."

"Ain't that the truth? We're gonna go broke if we don't take on more business to cover insurance costs for our full-timers. And the more drivers we hire, the more we gotta shell out in premiums."

"At least you got them government coverages. The rest of us ain't so lucky."

It was true. Jocelyn held on to her day job delivering mail just so she could keep her USPS benefits. But that kept Cougar's short-staffed during the day until she finished her route. Right now, there was more work than Deb and Rita could handle. They *had* to hire more drivers. But traipsing down that path was what her daddy always called a *sticky wicket*, because right now the manufactured home business was booming—but nobody could predict what might happen if the area got hit by another recession.

"Well, I been thinkin' about some ideas that might just work out." Natalie pulled her cheaters down from the top of her head and opened a loose-leaf notebook.

"Don't keep me in suspense." Jocelyn fired up a smoke. "Tell me what you got in mind."

"For starters, I think there's a bunch of opportunities out there in some of what they call 'underserved markets.' Things like this." She passed over a folded piece of paper.

Jocelyn took the flyer and opened it up. After she'd scanned its contents, she regarded Natalie. "What the hell are Poppin Johnnies?"

"Them ole timey, two-cycle tractors John Deere used to make." Natalie waved a hand. Her fluorescent nail polish all but left skid marks on the air between them. "But that ain't the part that piqued my curiosity. It was *this*." She pointed at the lower half of the flyer. "That's what I been fixatin' on."

"*Wheatland Swap Meet and Show?*" Jocelyn quoted. "I don't get it."

"It's a ginormous convention they have every year out in Wichita. Big-time collectors travel there from all over the country just to stand out in the middle of some dried-up field showing off their antique machines and drinking up tons of cheap beer. That got me to thinkin'. All of them wanna-be farmers have to move them tractors out there *some* way—and not everybody has the time to take a week off to drive across country to get there. That's where we come in—or could come in."

"You mean we'd use our trucks to haul these Poppin Johnnie things?"

"*Of course not.*" Natalie ground out her cigarette. "Forget about them damn tractors. I'm talkin' about usin' our trucks to haul *anything*. Across town or across country. Anyplace. *Everyplace.* Get it? I'm talkin' about gettin' out of the flag car business and embracing the brave new world of *lo-gistics*."

"Logistics?"

"It means *relocation*. Moving. Moving anything that needs moved. That right there is the pot o' gold at the end of the truckin' rainbow."

Jocelyn finished her smoke and thought about it.

"Well I'll be damned." She looked at Natalie with wonder. "It just might work."

"Count on it. This plan is the key to your success. And it's poised to roll right up the byways of America on *our* trucks—the trucks that have this day been reborn as Cougar's Quality Logistics."

Cougar's Quality Logistics.

Jocelyn tried the words over and over in her head. They had an almost reverential ring to them. Yes. It could work. She didn't even worry about telling Deb. She knew in her heart this was right. It was the way forward.

"I'll be damned," she said again.

Natalie was nodding and smiling at her. "And I got us a lead on our very first long-distance haul."

"What is it?"

"Bert Townsend told me that Doc Stevenson's mama was looking for somebody to fetch her piano and move it here from California." She tapped another cigarette out of her pack and winked at Jocelyn. "I think she's playin' our tune."

A piano? Jocelyn didn't know much about music, but she was pretty sure they could handle it—with the right crew on board.

But who could they send? A job like this would require their crew to be gone for eight to ten days, minimum. They didn't have any employees who could take on that kind of commitment. Most of them had to work two jobs just to make ends meet.

"James Lawrence."

Jocelyn looked at Natalie. "Say what?"

"James Lawrence," Natalie repeated. "I already asked him. He said he'd do it. He said he moved bigger stuff 'n that in the army."

"Well, shit fire." Jocelyn shook her head.

Things were lookin' up.

Henry was distressed. "Why didn't he take the animals?"

Dorothy lowered the book. They were sitting together in the shade created by a cluster of Heirloom pear trees that proudly staked their claim to a section of sloping bank above a switchback along the New River. Today was their bookmobile day, and Dorothy was making good on her promise to read *The Incredible Journey* to Henry during their times together after school.

"He couldn't take them along, Henry," Dorothy explained. "He was on his way to a fishing cabin that was very far away."

"Why couldn't they go, too? Why couldn't they stay with their family?"

Dorothy was beginning to think this book wasn't the best choice. She wondered why Miss Freemantle had suggested it to Henry. For one thing, he was too young to read it by himself. For another, it was a pretty sad story. At least it was so far.

"The family was in England, across the ocean," she explained. "This man was taking care of the animals for them—until they got back."

Henry nodded. "Like Maddie and Syd took care of me when Daddy was in Afistan."

"Yes. Just like that."

Henry stared down at the pages full of words. "I think Maddie and Syd would take me if they went fishing. Pete, too."

"What about Before? They couldn't take your cow along."

Henry thought about that. "I guess not."

"And they couldn't take Before to a kennel, either. They'd have to have somebody come in to feed her."

Henry looked up at Dorothy. "She eats grass."

Dorothy sighed. "How about we stop reading this for today?"

"Does that mean we have to go home now?"

"Not if you don't want to." Dorothy looked at the angle of the sun. "I can stay a little bit longer."

"Okay. Daddy has to work late."

"How late?"

Henry shrugged.

"Are you gonna be home by yourself tonight?"

"No. Buddy is going to come over and stay with me 'til daddy gets there. We watch TV. He changes channels all the time."

"It's nice he can come over."

"He washes cars for Mr. Junior. I like him. He can read my library books backwards."

Dorothy was surprised by that. She'd met Buddy a few times when her father hired him to clean the gutters or repaint the porch posts on the weather side of their house. He'd ride up on his little red scooter, wearing his bright orange vest and a silver helmet with a jaw strap. Then he'd go right to work. He was always nervous and shy whenever she tried to talk with him, so she learned early on not to bother him when he was out there working. He'd leave without saying goodbye as soon as he finished his chores. People in town all said he was slow, but harmless. She knew that last part was true. She never felt afraid of him. But it seemed strange to her that he'd be able to understand a book, much less read it backwards.

"Does he read to you?"

Henry nodded. "Can you read me some more?"

Dorothy was still working her way through *Cold Sassy Tree*. The only other book she had with her was *Lord of the Flies*. They were reading that one in English class. She didn't think either of those would work for Henry.

"I don't have any other good stories from a book today. But maybe I can tell you a different one?"

"Is it about dogs?"

"No. But it has a horse in it. A *magic* horse."

Henry's eyes grew wide. "What kind of horse is that?"

"One that knows how to fly."

"Is that one of Miss Freemantle's books? Can I get it?"

Dorothy shook her head. "No. This one was in a big book of stories that belonged to my mama. I found it in a box in our attic."

"Does it have pictures of the horse?"

"A couple. It has more words than pictures."

"I don't like those books as much." Henry picked up his copy of *The Incredible Journey*. "I can't read this many words."

"You will someday. You just have to keep trying."

"Is that what you did?"

"Yeah. I didn't have anybody to help me, either. So, I just kept practicing. When I got to really hard words, I'd write them down and ask about them."

Henry sighed. "When daddy is home, we watch TV."

"You could ask your teacher?"

"He doesn't like me."

Dorothy knew Henry's teacher. She'd had him as a substitute teacher, too. She wondered why so many people who hated kids taught school. It didn't make sense. But then, not much about the things adults did made sense.

"Maybe you could write things down and ask me? Or ask Miss Murphy or Dr. Stevenson?"

Henry nodded. "Okay." He looked up at her. "Syd always helps me with my homework when I go back there to stay."

"See? That sounds really nice."

"I like that part better than piano lessons."

"They make you take piano lessons?" She thought about Miss Freemantle and the book she described about how all ladies played the piano.

Henry nodded. "Gramma C. does. She's going to have a big piano in her new house. She said that maybe I can come stay there sometimes, too."

"You're lucky to have so many nice people who want to take care of you when your daddy is gone."

"I know. Who takes care of you when your daddy goes away?"

Dorothy looked out across the river. She could see swarms of gnats buzzing around close to the water. They moved around in crazy patterns and looked golden in the afternoon light. That meant the fish would be swimming close to the surface, trying to catch an early dinner. She loved to watch them flash and pivot in the slow-moving water. It was like they had all the time in the world.

But she didn't. And she knew she was skating dangerously close to the time she needed to be home.

"My daddy doesn't go away."

"I bet you like that," Henry said.

Dorothy decided to change the subject. "How about I tell you the magic horse story? Then I have to head home."

"Okay." Henry put down his book and laid back against the soft grass. "I'm ready."

Dorothy closed her eyes as she began the story.

"A long, long time ago, before the world we know now was

created, the heavens were controlled by a big family of gods and goddesses. They all had scary, special powers and lived on top of a mountain called Olympus. They were a very warlike family and fought many battles against other gods and monsters. One of the major gods on Olympus ruled over the oceans. His name was Poseidon, and he was made from big, angry waves. The flying horse called Pegasus was his son. His job was to soar across the heavens and carry thunderbolts for the head god, Zeus. They said that wherever the feet of Pegasus touched the earth, a spring of water would appear. One day, after Pegasus helped the gods win a big battle against a fire-breathing monster, Zeus rewarded him by turning him into a constellation of stars that could be seen forever."

Henry sat up. "He's in the stars?"

"That's what the story says."

"Can I see him tonight?"

"Not tonight," Dorothy corrected. "But in the fall, when it starts to get cold and the night sky is very bright. You can see him then."

"Have you seen him?"

"Lots of times." Dorothy nodded. "I look for him from my upstairs window. He's always there, too. High in the northern sky above the trees, running free through the night with his wings spread wide."

Henry gazed up at the snatches of blue sky that were visible between the maze of leaves and branches above their heads. "I can't see anything from my window. There's a building right in front of it and a bright light that stays on all night. Daddy says that's so people won't try to steal the cars."

"Maybe you could look for him when you're out at Dr. Stevenson's farm?"

"Do you think I will see him there?"

Dorothy smiled down at him. "I bet you will."

Henry seemed satisfied with that answer. He dropped back against the grass. "When will the fall be here?"

"Not for a while. The summer is just getting started."

Henry sighed. "Good things always take too long."

Dorothy understood his implied corollary. There was no waiting period for bad things.

It was past time for her to go, but she decided to risk it and stay just a bit longer. She lay back on the grass beside him and pointed up at the tree canopy above their heads.

"Let's look for pictures in the branches."

"You need to calm down."

"Calm down? *How?*" David was striding back and forth across Maddie's office like a caged beast. "That man doesn't have the good sense God gave a gnat."

"David? If you don't sit down, I'm going to tie you into a chair and give you an injection of Thorazine."

That stopped him dead in his tracks. "Really? Can I get a dose to go, too? Because when Michael hears about this I'm going to have to scrape his ample ass off the ceiling fan."

Maddie pointed at a chair. David finally complied and dropped into it with a grunt.

"Now," Maddie continued. "I'd love to offer sage advice, but you haven't stopped fuming long enough to tell me what's going on."

"It's that rat bastard mayor."

"Gerald Watson?"

"Duh? You know any other rat bastard mayors here in Shangri-La?"

Maddie raised an eyebrow.

"Okay, okay." David waved a hand in frustration. "Byron Martin showed up at the inn this afternoon and served me with papers outlining all of the new outdoor event ordinances just passed by the county supervisors. Effective immediately."

"Byron served you?"

David nodded. "I don't blame him for being the bearer of bad news. He was apologetic about the errand. It's that homophobic, chinless kumquat who's the problem. That man ain't happy unless he's pissing in somebody else's Froot Loops."

"I didn't know the supervisors met. It's not even close to the first of the month."

"Oh, hell yes. It was one of those dead-of-night, 'emergency' sessions. You know. Like the ones they use to pass all the gay smackdowns in North Carolina?" He reached out and grabbed a tin of cinnamon Altoids off her desk. "Mind if I have a few of these? There was a ton of onion on my salad at lunch."

"Help yourself. What are these new ordinances?"

"Are you kidding me? They're a collection of ridiculous restrictions that have only one purpose: to systematically shut down the outdoor wedding industry in this county."

David shook out a large handful of the cinnamon candies and popped them into his mouth. "I wish you'd get the peppermint ones. I don't like these as much."

"All evidence to the contrary."

David munched away while Maddie took a moment to process his information. She was truly stunned by how swiftly Watson had made good on his threat. Getting the rest of the board of supervisors to go along with him would have been easy. Most of them were octogenarians who'd held their seats on the board for decades. They were not known for their progressive stances on anything.

"What are the new restrictions?" she asked.

"Oh, let's see." David ticked them off on his fingers. "They now require wedding or event planners to apply for the permits at least *sixty* days before the event, and to provide advance notice to neighbors within five miles of the property. *Five miles.* I suppose in our case, that's so noise from the celebrations don't disrupt the solitude of any geriatric stray goats grazing out there in all those abandoned fields that are contiguous to our property. The measure also requires us to notify the County Sheriff's Office and local fire department fifteen days before the event so they may be on alert for potential public safety issues. I mean, you never know when some of those crockpot Vienna sausages might combust and take out half the county, right?"

"I agree with you that these are unnecessary hoops to jump through. But they sound more annoying than onerous."

David shook his head. "*Au contraire, mon petit chou.* I saved the best for last. Every private venue is limited to a maximum of four events per year. Oh, and finally, only properties of *ten* acres or more are approved to apply for the permits."

"Let me guess. You and Michael own fewer than ten acres?"

"Bingo, Cinderella. We own precisely 8.765 acres. And this, our unenlightened public servant knows all too well."

David shook the remainder of the Altoids into his palm and promptly tossed them into his mouth.

"You gaa ayy mo a deese?"

"No. And don't talk with your mouth full."

He gave her the finger.

She sighed. "So. What are you going to do?"

David slumped down in his chair. The posture of defeat made him appear smaller—the way he used to look when they were kids and he'd follow her home after school to avoid his father, who worked third shift at the glass plant.

"I honestly have no idea. This will ruin us financially. We're still trying to recover from all the rebuilding after the tornado. We already have twelve weddings booked. If we have to cancel? Well. Michael might end up having to sling hash with Nadine full time."

"What about the inn?"

David made a slashing gesture beneath his chin.

"How many of the weddings are for gay couples?"

David seemed surprised by her question. "About nine. Why?"

"Just searching for a motive."

"Well, news flash from planet *obvious*. What do you *think* his motivation was? That man has been systematically working to undermine every gay-owned business in town ever since he crawled out from beneath his rock and acceded to the mantle of power."

Maddie did not disagree with him—mostly because she suspected he was right. After all, it was no accident that most of the businesses in Jericho that would be adversely affected by this new ordinance were not only tied to the wedding industry—florist, hair salon, caterer—but all of them were owned and operated by gay men, too. That had become true last year when Gladys Pitzer sold the florist shop to Harold Nicks' partner, Ryan.

"How much time do you have before you're required to send cancellation notices for the parties you have booked?"

"About two weeks. I honestly see no way around this one. At best, we'll have to pull the plug on eight of them—and that's only if we can figure out a way to get an exception for the acreage requirement."

Maddie chewed the inside of her cheek. "I think I have an idea about that last part."

David looked hopeful. "What is it?"

"Be patient, white rabbit." Maddie reached for her phone.

"More Altoids would help," he muttered. "You know I have to eat when I'm stressed."

Maddie opened a desk drawer, pulled out a candy bar, and tossed it to him. He snagged it in flight.

"A Zagnut bar? Seriously?" He sniffed it. "Has this been in there since your dad ran this joint?"

"Take it or leave it." She punched some numbers into the phone. "Beggars can't be choosers."

David unwrapped the candy bar and took a cautious bite. "This thing is disgusting. Maybe I should have you update my tetanus vaccination?"

"Where you're concerned, a case of lockjaw might be considered a charitable act." Maddie smiled sweetly at him. "However, if you want the vaccine, I'll be happy to oblige." She raised the receiver to her ear. "Just take off your pants."

"On the other hand," he took another bite. "This is hitting the spot."

Maddie waved a hand to shush him. "Hi, mom? Quick question. When you bought the Bridle Creek property, wasn't there an option to add some extra acreage?"

David perked up.

"Uh huh. Yeah. That's what I thought." She gave David a thumbs-up. "I think we may just have figured out a use for it. Thanks, mom. See you later." She hung up.

David was incredulous. "You're kidding me, right? Celine owns some of that land that backs up to our property?"

"She does right now, but that's about to change."

"What do you mean?"

Maddie glanced at her father's ancient wall clock. "I mean that dinner tomorrow night is at six-thirty. Henry's coming so we're having tacos." She smiled at him. "Bring your checkbook."

"I apologize for that, James." Celine lowered her cell phone. "It was my daughter."

"That's okay, ma'am." He seemed embarrassed. "I appreciate all they do to help out with Henry."

"It's a labor of love for them, as you know." Celine noticed how James kept shifting his weight from one leg to the other. "Why don't we go sit down where it's cooler?"

She pointed to a battered picnic table that Bert and Sonny had hauled in from someplace. They'd set it up beneath an old hickory tree. They'd also added an ancient hibachi grill. Bert and Sonny liked hot dogs. They bought them by the gross from Freemantle's Market.

James followed her to the table and sat down sideways on one of its benches so he could stretch out his leg.

"Is your prosthesis bothering you today?"

He shrugged. "It comes and goes. Most of the time, it's fine. But some days, it's like I just got it."

Celine nodded. "Do you worry at all about the effects of driving so many hours?" James was there to talk with Celine about hiring Cougar's to move her Steinway back to Virginia from California. Her other belongings had already been packed up and loaded into modular PODS that would be delivered once the renovations on the house were completed. Only the piano remained behind in her Brentwood house.

"No ma'am." James regarded her with his clear blue eyes. "On long hauls, I can rest it when the other driver spells me. It won't be a problem for me at all."

"I'd love to hire your company, James. But I'm sure you understand that moving a grand piano is a very specialized kind of process."

"Yes, ma'am, I do. But Natalie's been in touch with a place in Los Angeles that can take it apart and have it all wrapped up and tied down right. All we'd be doing is picking it up and driving it back here."

"Did she give you the name of the firm in LA?"

"Yes, ma'am." James fished a card out of his shirt pocket. "Santana Piano Movers and Storage," he read. "They have good references and can have it all crated for us. Natalie said to tell you they're bonded and insured." He handed her the card. "Natalie said you could give them a call if it would set your mind at ease."

"It sounds like Natalie pretty much thought of everything."

He nodded. "They want to move their business more into this kind of work. I volunteered to do this trip. Another new hire of theirs, Rita Chriscoe, will go with me. We'll share the driving. We should only be gone six to seven days."

"This won't interfere too much with your work for Junior?" Celine knew the answer was none of her business, but she couldn't resist asking.

"No, ma'am. Truth be told, there isn't really enough work at Junior's right now to keep us both busy. I was going to have to look for something else to fill the gaps. Driving for Cougar's will do that, but it has a downside, too."

"Henry?" she asked.

"Yes, ma'am."

Celine had a hard time reading his expression. It was guarded, but there was something about his countenance that hinted at weariness, too.

"It's hard to be a single parent," she offered.

"You did it."

The energy behind his quick response surprised Celine. It rang out more like an accusation than an observation.

"I did, yes. But only part of the time. Maddie spent the summers in Virginia with her father."

James seemed embarrassed by his retort. "I'm sorry, ma'am. I don't mean to be rude."

"James? Please call me Celine. I think we know each other well enough by now and 'ma'am' makes me feel like I'm a hundred years old."

That got a small smile out of him. He was a good-looking man but that detail was easy to overlook because the set to his features was usually so dour. When he smiled, the years and the worry seemed to drop away. He looked younger. He looked hopeful. *He looked like Henry.*

"I try to be a good dad to him, but I don't get it right most of the time."

Celine was surprised by his comment. She wondered if James could read her mind. "Why do you say that?"

He shrugged. "I'm not very good helping with his schoolwork. And I think maybe he's alone too much."

"You mean because of the extra work you've taken on?"

"That and . . . other things."

As tempted as she was to follow up and ask him to elaborate on what "other things" meant, she knew she had to tread carefully.

"Are you still getting good support from the VA?"

"Sometimes. I can't get up to Roanoke much these days."

"Maybe there are some local groups that could be helpful?"

"What kind of groups?"

"That would depend on what you think you need."

He didn't reply.

"I'd be happy to assist you with this, James," she said gently. "Or with anything else that helps you and Henry."

"You and your daughter already do too much for us. I wouldn't feel right asking for anything else."

"We think of you and Henry as family. Don't ever worry about asking us for help."

"They already said they'd keep him if I did the California trip."

Celine smiled. "Did Natalie take care of that, too?"

That got a laugh out of him. "No, ma'am—*Celine*. I asked Syd when I called about dropping Henry off at the library tomorrow."

"That's right. We're all having dinner together tomorrow night. Why don't you join us?"

"I'd like to, but I can't. I have to do a run over to Bristol for Cougar's. Syd and Maddie are keeping Henry overnight."

"Well then, we'll be sure to save you some tacos."

James got to his feet. "Thanks for talking with me today."

"Of course." Celine stood up, too, and extended her hand. "I appreciate you coming all the way out here."

He gave her hand a modest squeeze. "It's okay." He looked over the setting and the scattered piles of construction debris. It was clear that Bert and Sonny were making good progress on all the tear-outs. "I kind of wanted to see what all was happening out here."

"It's a work in progress. But you are welcome to stop by any time."

"Thanks."

He was halfway to his car when Celine called out to him. He stopped and turned to face her.

"Tell Natalie that I'd be honored to have you fetch my piano," she said.

"Really?"

She nodded. "This place will be far enough along for me to move in by the end of next week. The sooner I have my piano, the sooner I can begin inflicting regular lessons on your son in earnest."

He laughed. "I won't tell him that."

"Good. We need to keep some things just between us."

He took a second to think about that before waving goodbye. "I'll have Natalie call you about the move."

"You do that."

Celine stood beside the freshly underpinned front porch of her new home and watched as James's white Ranger pickup made slow, deliberate progress back along the rutted lane that led to the county road. Luckily for her, Bert and Sonny had plans for how to remedy that, too.

She still had the small white card in her hand.

Santana Piano Movers, someone had written with a soft-lead pencil. The script was a florid combination of loops and squiggles. She felt certain the handwriting did not belong to James. There was a phone number, too, but part of it was too badly smudged to be readable.

Celine smiled and tossed the card onto a nearby pile of debris.

"If they're good enough for Carlos, they're good enough for me."

Henry was outside, busily making his rounds and reconnecting with the menagerie of animals at the farm. He'd already finished his homework, and Syd told him he could play outside until dinnertime. When David arrived, Henry quickly conscripted him and took off for the pond with a large can of fish food.

Maddie remained behind so she could help in the kitchen with dinner preparations. Right now, Syd was chopping vegetables and Maddie was grating cheese. In fact, Maddie was doing more complaining than grating—which was typical for taco night.

"I fail to understand why we keep buying these mammoth blocks of cheddar."

"You mean why do *I* keep buying them?" Syd didn't bother looking up from her task.

"Yes. *You.*" Maddie stepped back from the island and waved the ancient cheese grater in the air with disgust. "This damn thing is a relic. And it's dangerous."

"It was your father's."

"I *know* it was my father's. It still has his blood stains on it."

"Maddie . . ."

"I just don't get it." She resumed grating. "I mean—they make those wonderful zipper bags packed with shredded cheese. The dairy aisles are *full* of them. You want some shredded cheese? *Presto!* You just open the bag. No fuss. No muss. And no skin grafts when you're through."

"Oh, good lord." Syd turned around to investigate. "How much have you done so far?"

Maddie tipped her bowl so Syd could assess her handiwork. It contained what generously could be called a trace element of grated cheese.

"Seriously?" Syd returned to her task. "Keep grating."

"*Oh, come on.* How much more do you want?"

"More than that," Syd said over her shoulder. She resumed her energetic chopping.

Maddie muttered an epithet and proceeded to grate. "Where's mom?"

"She's outside with Henry and David. They went down to the pond to feed the fish."

"I wonder if they'd like some of this cheese?"

"Don't even think about it, sawbones."

Maddie took a break from her grating and picked up her wine glass. They'd opened a bottle of Invetro because the full-bodied super Tuscan was big enough to stand up to tonight's menu. Maddie sniffed it and let its dazzling aroma fill up her senses. She took a conservative sip and savored it while she listened to the staccato sound of Syd's knife contacting the chopping block.

"What are you doing over there? It sounds incredibly tedious."

"I'm making salsa."

"*Making* salsa? What's wrong with the kind that comes in the jar?"

"Maddie?" Syd turned around again. "Keep it up and you'll be eating Marshmallow Fluff for dinner."

Maddie brightened up at once. "Do we have some of that?"

"I'm going to kill you."

"You'll have to get in line."

Syd rolled her eyes and walked to the stove to stir the ground meat and seasonings. "I'll claim prior privilege."

"That might work."

"Not that any special inducements are required, but who else wants to kill you?"

"Today, or in general?"

Syd laughed. "Let's start with in general and go from there."

"Oh." Maddie picked up the brick of cheese and gave it a couple of halfhearted grates. "I think I let Lizzy down."

"About?"

Maddie shrugged.

"Yes, I can see why she'd be disappointed by that." Syd tapped her spoon against the side of the skillet before returning it to its rest.

A wonderful medley of intoxicating smells wafted across the room. Maddie's nostrils flared. "Did you put too much cumin in that again?"

"No," Syd replied. "Do you wanna give me a bit more to go on about this thing with Lizzy?"

"I can't, really."

"Patient confidentiality?"

"Sort of."

"Are you two in disagreement about a diagnosis or course of treatment?"

Maddie was surprised by Syd's acuity. But she shouldn't have been. Syd always managed to cut straight to the chase. "Yes," she replied. "That's it exactly."

"Is it a situation where you might have to overrule her?"

Maddie shook her head. "No. In this case, she knows the patient much better than I do."

Syd wiped her hands on a towel and picked up her own glass of wine. "This is all pretty ironic. I have a similar kind of dilemma right now with Tom."

Maddie slipped with the grater and caught the end of her knuckle on one of its metal protrusions.

"Damn it!"

"What happened?"

"I scraped my knuckle on this implement of torture." Maddie sucked at her finger.

"Is it bleeding?" Syd asked.

Maddie inspected her wound. "A little bit."

Syd took another sip of her wine. "Don't get blood on the cheese."

Maddie glowered at her. "Thanks for your concern."

Syd blew her a kiss.

The door to the porch opened and Celine came in carrying a bunch of fresh cilantro. She took note of the standoff between the two chefs as she made her way to the prep sink to wash the herbs.

"What's going on?"

"Your daughter just lost her cage fight with the cheese grater," Syd explained.

"Grater? What grater?" Celine asked.

Maddie held it up.

"Oh, good lord. I thought your father threw that thing away forty years ago." Celine shook excess water off the herbs. "Why don't you just use the food processor?"

"Food processor?" Maddie glared at Syd.

"Yeah." Syd poured Celine a glass of wine. "You aren't checked out on that yet, honey. It has too many moving parts."

Maddie rolled her eyes at Syd and regarded her mother.

"So, Mom? It's actually nice to see you in the *daylight*."

"Isn't it?" Celine replied. "I found the prospect of spending an evening with Henry held greater appeal for me than shopping for kitchen fixtures."

"Right," Maddie agreed. "Because those all-night plumbing supply stores tend to be a drag after a while."

Celine picked up her wine glass and smiled sweetly at her daughter. "Nice try."

"Oh, come on, Mom. Don't you think it's time you told us what you've been doing every night?"

"Let me see." Celine took a moment to consider her answer. "No."

Syd laughed.

"But, you will be happy to know that David and I reached amicable terms on the exchange of assets."

"You sold him the land?" Syd asked.

Celine nodded. "Two acres. Just enough for them to make their land requirement to hold the weddings." She smiled. "I drove a hard bargain. Ten dollars and a pledge that Michael will supply me with all the shrimp and grits I can eat. Of course, we'll have to have the land surveyed, but that's a technicality."

Maddie raised an eyebrow. "Not if Gerald Watson has anything to say about it."

Celine agreed. "I fail to understand what motivates that man to be such an unrepentant pain in the ass."

"That one isn't hard to figure out." Syd gave the meat mixture another stir.

"What do you mean?" Celine asked her.

"You know I hate to gossip . . ."

Maddie interrupted her. "But in this case, you'll make an exception?"

Syd nodded energetically. "The backstory is that Watson's late wife was very unhappy in her marriage . . . not hard to imagine. In the years before her death, she became involved with someone else and was planning to leave him."

"There was another man?" Maddie asked. "Hard to blame her for that," she added.

"Oh, no." Syd held up an index finger. "Not another man. According to Harold Nicks, the object of Eva's affection was one Rita Chriscoe."

"Another *woman?*" Maddie shook her head. "Well *that* explains a lot about the mayor's proclivities."

"Did you say Rita Chriscoe?" Celine asked. "The woman who drives for Cougar's?"

Syd nodded. "Yep."

"Well, that's ironic. She's the woman who's going to help James move my piano."

"Apparently, she used to work at the bowling alley. I gather that's how she met Eva. She and Harold's mom were in the same league with Deb and Jocelyn." Syd shook her head. "Harold said Watson threw a rod when he found out about Eva and Rita. He said it was an epic scandal."

Maddie laughed. "Are there any *other* kinds of scandals in this town?" She regarded her mother. "Word to the wise, here."

Celine rolled her eyes. "I'm going to do us both a favor and ignore that."

Maddie threw up her hands. "Don't say I didn't try to warn you."

"Well right now, I wish you'd go outside and warn David and Henry that we're about five minutes away from dinner." Syd collected their wineglasses and carried them to the kitchen table.

"I'll do it." Celine refilled her own glass and left the kitchen.

"You know I'm right," Maddie called after her.

Celine waved a hand over her head before disappearing down the hallway that led to the front door.

Maddie joined Syd at the table. "Okay, *that's* a first."

"What's a first?" Syd looked up at Maddie, who was staring at her with an open mouth.

"I think Mom just gave me the finger."

"Really?" Syd chuckled. "That's only about forty years over-due."

"Forty?"

"Don't pout, dear." Syd reached across the table and patted Maddie's hand. "You've always been an overachiever. Embrace it. Honor it. Make it work for you."

"Are you reading those Melody Beattie books again?"

"I don't need self-righteous dirges about positive thinking to know what's best for you."

"Well, *there's* a true statement." Maddie was staring down the hallway with a glum expression.

"Honey?" Syd asked.

"What?"

"I wasn't kidding about turning this into something useful."

"Okay." Maddie sighed. "How do I do that?"

"Well for starters," Syd smiled sweetly at her, "go grate more cheese."

Twenty-two and seven. Twenty-two and seven. Twenty-two and seven.

There were twenty-two boards in seven piles. Twenty-two and seven were right. The load of cut boards made exactly seven piles of twenty-two.

Buddy stacked the boards in tidy rows along the back wall on the shady side of the porch. Papa told him to pile the boards beside the kitchen door, but he knew this was better. It was going to rain. It always rained on the first of June. Sometimes it rained after lunch, but it always rained before three o'clock.

Twenty-two and seven. There were two thousand, two hundred and twenty years between Abraham and Jesus. *The time of the patriarchs.* Sixty-six books in the Bible. Three times twenty-two. God created twenty-two things in the first seven days.

Twenty-two letters in the Hebrew alphabet. He knew them all. He could say them backwards seven times. He would say them for Henry when they watched TV. Henry liked letters.

Twenty-two and seven.

Pi. They all called it "pi." But pi was more numbers. More than they could count. Pi was right. Pi was twelve point one trillion digits. It would wait there until they found more room. But it would always be made from twenty-two and seven.

Papa came around the corner of the house. "Buddy, why you puttin' that lumber there?"

"It's going to rain."

Papa looked at the sky. "It's not gonna rain."

"June 1st. It always rains on June 1st."

Papa went back to work.

Hammers and saws. *Papa said we'd go home after the Quiet Lady came.*

The Quiet Lady came every day.

Twenty-two and seven.

BERTRAND LEAR TOWNSEND JR.

Twenty-two letters. Born on seven fifteen. Seven plus fifteen equals twenty-two. One nine eight four. One plus nine plus eight plus four equals twenty-two.

The Quiet Lady liked music. It played from the radio in her car. Yesterday he counted it. One hundred fifty-seven beats. Half of three-one-four. Half of pi. The car stopped before it could play all of pi. Half of pi was not finished.

The Quiet Lady needed to finish pi.

Twenty-two and seven.

The boards were all stacked now.

It was time to wait. He knew how to wait. He could count how to wait.

Soon the Quiet Lady would come. She would finish pi. It would rain and they would all go home.

Chapter 3

Henry knew he'd missed the school bus again.

On days when his daddy had to work late, Buddy would meet him at the bus stop in Troutdale and stay with him at the apartment. But on days like today, when he had to stay late after school, Buddy would ride over on his scooter and pick him up. Henry never figured out how Buddy always knew when to do this. He just did. So, it didn't surprise him when he walked outside after detention and saw Buddy waiting for him near the beetleweed plants along the far edge of the parking lot.

It looked like Buddy was fussing with the white flowers that covered the plants—plucking off dead or wilted leaves. The last time he had picked Henry up, he said they were blooming too early. Henry knew Buddy thought that was a bad thing, because Buddy was always bothered when things happened before they were supposed to.

Buddy didn't like change.

Henry was happy that Buddy would be taking him home today. His teacher had made him stay after school because he didn't bring a lunch. That happened sometimes when his daddy got home really late and didn't wake up in time to pack anything for him to take. Henry didn't understand why his teacher got mad about that. He figured it might be because he didn't always have his homework done, either.

Detention was hard because he missed the bus—but it was mostly hard because other kids made fun of him for always being stuck behind with Gabriel Sanchez—who got detention a lot, too. Or they'd tease him about being "dumb" like Buddy. That made Henry mad.

Gabriel was one of his best friends. And Buddy wasn't dumb.

Gabriel got in trouble for not speaking English very well. But Henry never had trouble understanding him. He was going to ask Dorothy if she would help Gabriel with his reading, too. He knew she would if they could figure out a time to work on it. Dorothy always had to be careful about not staying out too late after school. But once school was over for the summer, she would be taking care of him during the daytime. He hoped maybe he could get Mrs. Sanchez to bring Gabriel over so they could go to the bookmobile together. He knew Miss Freemantle would have ideas about good books for them to use to practice learning bigger words.

"Get away from those flowers, you idiot!"

His teacher was yelling at Buddy. Henry hadn't even seen him come outside—but he was standing in the parking lot beside his shiny, big car.

"Move that scooter off the grass, too. What's the matter with you?"

Buddy held up the wilted blooms he'd collected. "Too early," he said. "They finished too soon."

"What is that supposed to mean?" His teacher yanked his car door open and tossed his briefcase on the front seat. "Those plants are school property. You have no right to deface them."

Buddy didn't say anything. He just stood there holding the pile of dead blooms and leaves in his hands.

Henry ran as fast as he could to get to the other side of the parking lot. He didn't want Buddy to get yelled at any more. "He . . . he won't hurt the . . . plants." He was out of breath from running. "I promise. He's . . . really good with things that . . . grow."

His teacher slammed the car door closed. "Are you talking to me, young man?"

"Yes, sir." Henry was still out of breath. "I'm sorry, sir."

"Unless you want to earn another day of detention, I suggest you remember the correct way to address me."

Henry nodded. "I will, sir."

The big man pointed a finger at Buddy. "Now tell your mentally challenged friend to get his vehicle off the grass and to stop tampering with private property."

Henry wasn't exactly sure what "mentally challenged" meant, but he knew it wasn't good. He also knew it wasn't *right*. Buddy cared a lot about things that weren't right, and he always worked hard to make them right when they weren't. But Henry didn't want Buddy to try to fix what was wrong with what his teacher thought. That was because the round end of his teacher's nose turned red when he got mad—and right now it was starting to look like an unwrapped Fireball.

"Yes, sir," he said. "Come on, Buddy. Let's go home." Henry hurried over to where Buddy stood. He unfastened the straps on his backpack and held open the empty book compartment. "We can put the dead stuff in here and we'll throw it away when we get to Junior's."

"It grew too fast, Bluebird," Buddy said. "Now it's over."

"What's he babbling about?" His teacher was tapping his hand against the side of his leg.

"He calls me Bluebird. It's just a nickname," Henry explained.

"Tell him to move that thing, *now*."

"Yes, sir." Henry closed up his backpack. "We're leaving."

Buddy helped Henry put on his homemade helmet. They climbed onto the scooter and Buddy started it and carefully backed it out.

Henry couldn't see him, but he knew that his teacher was still watching as they left the parking lot and turned onto Main Street to head for home.

"I'm not ready to have this conversation."

Byron's face was a study in confusion. "What conversation?"

"The one you keep hinting at every time we're alone together."

He laughed at her. "Celine? I don't believe I *hint* at anything when we're alone together."

She had to smile at that. "You know what I mean." She was annoyed with herself that it was a struggle to remain on task.

"Is that why my chair is way over here?"

Celine had carefully positioned their chairs so Byron's faced the prospect of the rolling field that led to the river. She'd set hers at a respectful distance from his, with her back toward the house. They'd taken to coming out here on the nights they could meet, just so they could have a private place to talk and enjoy the unseasonably warm evenings. Soon Celine would be living here and they'd always have a private place—and a new set of problems.

Something flashed above the tall grass behind Byron's chair. *A firefly?*

Impossible. It was too early.

She saw it again—unmistakable this time. More evidence that summer was coming early to the mountains this year. Another irony. This chapter of her life was shaping up to be a poor remake of *The Roman Spring of Mrs. Stone.*

"I thought you should have the better view tonight," she told Byron. She knew it sounded weak, even as she said it. But she had to retake control of this situation. The fact that she even thought of it as a "situation" was problematic. She wasn't used to having *situations.* She'd engineered her life to avoid them.

"I'm not looking at the view," he said. "I'm looking at you."

"Then maybe I should move my chair?"

"It won't make any difference. I'll still be looking at you."

"Byron."

"Celine."

This was getting them nowhere. And it wasn't helping that the setting sun was bathing everything around them in golden light. It made the setting seem surreal—like a movie set. *A movie.* That's exactly what this was like. One of those horrid Hollywood tropes about women with faded charms and grasping, pathetic needs. She could be the next Maggie Smith—or Shelley Winters. *No.*

Her situation was more epic in its total flight from reason. Set hers to music and she could be starring in a Strauss opera. She was the Marschallin of Jericho—a half-crazy, deluded spinster preying on the attentions of a younger man. It was pathetic.

The evening sun was illuminating red highlights in Byron's hair. He looked bronzed and handsome.

"This can't happen." She said the words aloud—more to remind herself than to caution him. "You have to know that."

He leaned forward. "What can't happen?"

"This." She waved a hand back and forth between them. "Us."

"That's the first thing you've said tonight that I agree with."

Finally, they were getting someplace. "So you agree?" she asked.

"I agree with you that there is an 'us.' I think the rest is a bunch of hooey."

"Hooey?"

He nodded. "I think hooey pretty much covers it."

"*Hooey* is an unscientific categorization without meaning. It ignores the facts."

"Really?" He looked over the hard-packed ground that would become her patio. Wire-caged towers of slate stood in a semi-circle around their chairs like druid monuments. "I see about as much hooey piling up out here as slabs of rock."

"This can't happen," she repeated.

"Correct me if I'm wrong, but I think it's *already* happened. And it's terrific." He smiled at her. "Isn't it?"

She closed her eyes and nodded.

"So what's the problem?"

"Byron. I'm twenty years older than you."

"Twelve," he corrected.

"Don't prevaricate."

He rolled his eyes. "Celine? Have you ever noticed how you lapse into professor-speak whenever you get uncomfortable?"

"Professor-speak?"

"Yeah. That's what I call it."

"I do not do that."

"Yes, you do. Your syllables increase with your level of agitation."

Celine drummed her fingers on the arm of her chair until she saw Byron drop his gaze to her hand. She abruptly stopped drumming and folded her hands on her lap.

He laughed. "Busted."

"Something you'd be familiar with, of course."

He raised an eyebrow. "I won't deny that getting to arrest a woman of your caliber stands out as one of the high points of my career in law enforcement."

"Women like me?"

"Yeah." He nodded. "Classy types. Most of the women I've busted in my time have either been too drunk to stand up or too busy trying to cut their boyfriends' throats with broken beer bottles."

"I suppose I should be gratified for providing you with such a high-toned diversion."

"I won't deny that I'm happy to be diverted by you."

She stared at him. "This is precisely what concerns me."

"What is?"

"This. That it's a 'diversion.' Something you'll regret—something we'll both live to regret."

He sighed. "I don't think so."

"How can you be so sure?"

"How can I be sure we *won't* regret it? How can you be sure we *will?*" He leaned forward. "Celine, I'm not naïve enough to suggest there won't be hurdles to jump over—although I think most of them are the ones you keep throwing up in front of us. But I'm old enough to know that everything about this feels different. You feel different. I'm different with you. And it's a difference I like. I'm not afraid of it, and I don't think you should be afraid of it, either."

"What if it doesn't last?"

As soon as she said the words, she felt ridiculous. Exposed. She lowered her gaze because she was afraid to look at him—afraid to see her own fear reflected in his hazel eyes. She knew she was behaving like the scared adolescent she once had been—

the shy, awkward girl who always refused to look at herself when she passed through the hall of mirrors that led to her mother's dressing room. It was there, in the darkest recesses of their Manhattan apartment, that the ghosts and golems waited for her. "Dybbuks," her British tanteh called them. "They haunt the dark places, ziskeit. They will trick you and lure you into things. Do not look at them for they want to steal your soul."

Was her attraction to Byron a trick? A ruse? Did Byron want to steal her soul?

Or was she willingly offering it up to him?

"Are you a thief?" she asked. The words sounded thin and hollow—as if they had traveled for decades along the frayed cord that stretched from her childhood to this very moment. "I'm sorry," she added quickly, before he had a chance to respond.

He blinked. "Am I a what?"

She shook her head. "Never mind."

"Am I a thief?" he repeated. "Is that what you asked?"

"Byron. Please. I'm just rambling."

"No," he protested. "This is important. I can tell that it matters."

"It doesn't matter. I was just thinking out loud."

"About whether I'm a thief? A thief of what?"

She didn't reply.

"Your virtue?"

She had to laugh at that. "Hardly."

"Your reputation?"

"Byron . . ."

He scooted his chair closer. "Tell me."

She gave up trying to conceal her escalating consternation. "I don't trust myself—not where you're concerned. And that scares me. It isn't who I am. It's not how I live my life."

He shrugged. "What we believe about how we live our lives can change. If it doesn't, we won't be living them for long."

"Do you really believe that?"

"Celine, every day I deal with the messes created when people think their choices are only about as wide as the scrap of dirt they call a lawn. So, yeah. I do believe it."

"I'm foundering." She shook her head. "I don't know which end is up."

He held out his hand. "How about you just hang on until you find some equilibrium?" When she didn't reply, he gave her a shy smile. "I promise I won't let you fall—not unless you ask me to."

It was completely dark now, but she didn't need light to see him. She knew his features by heart. Perfectly. She saw them all the time. Waking. Sleeping. Dreaming. His image was always before her.

Another firefly lit up the space between them. It danced crazily on the warm night air, flashing its tiny beacon off and on. It was like a channel marker, warning her that one side of this emotional journey offered safe passage through open water—but the other was shallow, less certain and lined with jagged rock.

But which side was which? From this vantage point, it was impossible to tell.

The firefly's movements on the night air were ungraceful, halting and arrhythmic—just like the erratic beating of her heart. She had no idea what to do. She closed her eyes and fought to steady her breathing. *Do not look at them for they want to steal your soul.*

It was ridiculous. She was a woman of sense and education. *A scientist.* What was there for her to fear?

Nothing.

She opened her eyes and dared to look at him.

Everything . . .

It no longer mattered.

She took hold of his hand.

"I'm going to do it."

Michael didn't look up from the pie crust he was rolling out. "You're going to do what?"

"Hello?" David snapped his fingers. "Haven't you been listening to me for the past fifteen minutes?"

"Of course I have. To which of the nine topics are you referring?"

David rolled his eyes. "Could you please give me your full attention?"

"Not right this second." Michael wound the pie crust around his rolling pin and positioned it over a banged-up metal pan. "I'm at a critical stage here."

"You're *always* at a critical stage." David dropped onto a stool. "I mean, global warming is critical. Azalea Freemantle in grillz is critical. Nuclear proliferation is critical. Pie crust? Pie crust is *not* critical."

Michael looked up at him. "Azalea Freemantle wears grillz?"

"Duh." David waved an index finger in front of his own teeth. "Big, shiny *silver* ones. Impossible to miss—I mean, impossible to miss for anyone who isn't obsessed with pie crust."

"Where the hell did she get grillz? Most people around here can't even manage to find dentures that aren't five sizes too big."

"Buddy."

Michael blinked. "Buddy?"

"Yeah. *Buddy*. You know, Bert's son." David shook his head. "That man is a genius with car tape."

"Car tape? What the hell is car tape?"

"Do you *live* in this county? After pork rinds and Cheerwine, car tape is the top-selling product at Freemantle's Market. Two-thirds of the truck windows out in Troutdale are held together with that stuff. Junior says it sticks better than shit to a blanket."

"Buddy made grillz out of car tape?"

David nodded. "Of course. He used it to fix the bell on Nicky's clarinet, too, after Roma Jean backed over her case with that damn bookmobile. Strange. It changed the written pitch on that thing to a flawless C. I think Buddy did that on purpose. He has an incredible ear."

Michael didn't comment.

"You know . . . it just occurred to me that nobody knows Junior's last name. They say his people are from up around Stuart, but Junior's been out in Troutdale running that body shop since Methuselah jacked up his daddy's Oldsmobile. And in all the years I've known him, I've never heard him called anything but 'Junior.' Have you?"

Michael stared at him without speaking.

David shrugged. "Oh, well. Maybe he's just 'Junior.' You know? Like *Cher*."

"David?"

"What?"

"You're giving me a migraine."

"So what else is new?" David rolled his eyes. "If you think this is bad, just wait until the campaign starts."

"Campaign?" Michael squinted at him. "What campaign?"

"Have you not heard a word I've said?"

"Even though I tried to ignore you, a few words still managed to sneak through my wall of indifference."

"That's going to have to change. Once this campaign heats up, you'll have to be out there doing some of the heavy lifting."

Michael sighed. "I reiterate: what campaign?"

"Mine."

"Yours?"

David nodded.

"What the hell are you campaigning for? And don't tell me it's that harebrained 'Full Monte Carlo' calendar idea again."

"It's not the calendar."

Michael narrowed his eyes. "Is it those edible, sriracha-flavored assless chaps?"

David shook his head.

"Well, at least there *is* a god."

"Hey, bucko. I didn't see you expressing umbrage the last time *I* wore a pair to bed."

"True. But in fairness, I was coming off a cleanse."

"That's one word for it," David snorted. "I had to boil those sheets in lye."

"So, are you gonna tell me what you're talking about?"

"Our dip wad mayor."

"Gerald Watson?"

David nodded.

"What about him?"

"Oh, good god." David threw back his head. "You couldn't connect a row of dots with grappling hooks and six hundred feet of chain."

Michael's eyes grew wide. "You aren't resurrecting that BDSM version of Twister, are you?"

"*No.*" David blew out a slow breath. "Let me simplify this for you. I have decided to run for mayor. Against Gerald Watson."

Michael's jaw dropped.

"Did you hear me?" Michael remained silent. David snapped his fingers in front of his face. "Hello? Earth to Galloping Gourmet? Anybody home in there?"

"You can't do that."

"It lives!" David raised his hands toward heaven.

"David? I'm not kidding. You *cannot* do that."

"Why not?"

"Well, for one thing—you just won an award for translating gay German porn."

"It's not *porn*—it's erotica."

"A difference without distinction here in the red states."

"Au contraire," David wagged a finger. "Virginia voted for Hillary."

"Not *this* part of Virginia."

"Well . . ."

"David, please? Watson is already waging a campaign to have us all run out of town on a rail. Why add fuel to his fire?"

"*Why?* Precisely because he *is* waging a campaign against us. The best way to call him out is to *be* out. And loud. And proud."

"It's crazy."

"It's not crazy—it's genius."

Michael raised a hand to his forehead. "Now I really am getting a migraine."

"You just need a little time to adjust to the idea." David reached out and patted his arm.

"More time is *not* what I need. Having Maddie renew my Xanax prescription—*that's* what I need."

"You mull it over, baby cakes. I gotta scoot." David drew a heart in the dust of flour that covered the countertop. "I'm meeting Mama at ten. She's helping me write a campaign jingle." He pointed down at Michael's pie crust. "The edges on that are drying out. You might should mist it." He hopped off his stool and headed for the door. "TTFN."

Mist?

Michael dropped his gaze.

No amount of mist was gonna salvage this one.

He watched David leave before lifting the pie tin and dumping the dough into the trash.

"C'mon. Talk to her for me."

Syd was lining the shelves of a book truck with returned titles. She'd already organized them in tidy rows by call numbers. Not many people knew that this simple, rote task was something she looked forward to every morning. After she unlocked the small storefront library, turned on the overhead lights and started a pot of coffee, she'd grab a hefty canvas bag and trudge outside to retrieve the tumbled contents of the book return box. Back inside, while she waited for the coffee to finish brewing, she'd unpack the books, check them in, and prepare them for reshelving.

Creating order from chaos. It was delicious. *Addictive.* Returning things to an order that made sense had always been one of her guilty pleasures.

Intervening in her brother's relationships, however, was not something she enjoyed.

Ever.

She looked up at him over the tower of books.

"Tom? I'm not doing your dirty work for you."

"Dirty work?" Tom seemed offended. "I'm not asking you to do any dirty work. I just want you to talk with her and find out what's going on."

"Why don't *you* ask her?"

"I have asked her."

"And?"

He shrugged. "She says nothing is going on."

Syd sighed. "Here's a radical idea: How about you believe her?"

Tom ran a hand through his wavy blonde hair. He needed a haircut. He always needed a haircut.

"You know Lizzy, Syd. The quieter she is, the more it means that something's not right."

"Ask. Her."

"Why are you being so difficult about this?" He pulled a book off the truck and examined its cover.

"Do you mind?" Syd snatched the book away from him and returned it to its slot.

"Hey? Maybe I want to read that."

"Why? Did your subscription to *Mechanix Illustrated* finally run out?"

"Very funny." Tom plopped down on a stool. His expression was so morose that Syd relented.

"I'm sorry, Tom."

He looked at her with surprise. "It's okay. I know I act like an asshole most of the time."

"It goes with the job description."

"What job description?"

"Little brother."

He smiled. It made him look just like their father—cute and engaging enough to be forgiven for his bouts of annoying behavior. How many times had she seen their mother roll her eyes and cluck her tongue at the two of them? *Peas in a pod,* she'd call them. *The rotten kind that break your teeth.*

"So." Syd pulled a stool over and sat down, too. "What's going on?"

"I don't know." Tom waved a hand in apparent frustration. "It's like you all speak some kind of different language. I feel like I'm always on the outside trying to operate with only half the alphabet."

"By 'all,' do you mean women?"

71

He nodded.

"Tom. We don't speak a different language. You just need to listen with better ears."

"Am I supposed to know what that means?"

Syd sighed. "Probably not."

"Great. What else you got?"

"For starters, what makes you think there's something wrong?"

"I don't know." He threw up his hands. "Lately she just seems so—distant. Like she's a zillion miles away. And . . . well . . ." He shrugged. "She's been distant in other ways, too."

"What other ways?"

"You know." He made an oblique gesture. "*Other* ways."

Syd narrowed her eyes. "You mean sexually distant?"

He nodded. "And believe me, that's not an area where we *ever* had problems."

"Yeah." Syd held up a hand. "TMI, bro."

"Hey, don't act all shocked. I mean, it's not like the whole county doesn't know that you and Maddie hit it like rabbits."

"Excuse me?"

"Don't tell me you're going to deny it?"

Syd was flustered. "Why on earth would I deny . . . We don't . . . It's not . . ." Her words trailed off.

Tom laughed at her.

"What-*ever*. You're such a jerk." She yanked the book he'd been looking at earlier from its spot on the cart. "Here. Maybe you *should* read this."

Tom took it from her.

"*I Used to Miss Him, But My Aim Is Improving*." He looked at her. "Is this a joke?"

"Of course not. It's the ultimate breakup survival guide. We have six copies, and that's just in this branch."

Tom read over the book's description. "'Make an ex-boyfriend voodoo doll. Lose the guy, keep the jewelry. Stalk responsibly to keep him on his toes.'" He handed the book back to her. "Yeah. I don't think so."

"Hits a bit too close to home for you?"

"Not exactly. The idea is not to break up at all."

"Is that what this is about?" Syd reshelved the book. "Do you think she wants to break up?"

He shrugged.

"Tom? Are you serious about Lizzy?"

"Define 'serious.'"

She sighed. "*Serious*. Noun. Not joking or trifling. Being in earnest."

He nodded. "I think so."

"You *think* so?"

"Yeah."

"Maybe when you *know* so, she'll be a bit more receptive to your queries."

"Meaning?"

"Meaning you need to make up *your* mind before you start worrying about *hers*."

"It's not that simple."

"Really?" Syd dropped her voice an octave. "Enlighten me."

"I have one more year of vet school. I don't know where I'm going after that—or even what I'll be doing."

"Hopefully, you'll be fixing broken animals."

"Maybe. Maybe not. I could go into product development. Either way, I'm not likely to be around here."

"Have you told Lizzy that?"

"She knows my plans for the future are open-ended right now."

"Gee, Tom. What thinking woman wouldn't jump at the chance to hitch her wagon to that?" Syd shook her head. "And you wonder why she's being distant?"

"Hey. That's not fair. I never promised her anything permanent."

"Then why are you having so much trouble with her returning the favor?"

"So you think she's shutting me out because she knows I might be leaving soon?"

"No. I think she's shutting you out—if, indeed, she *is* shutting you out—because you're a spineless asshole."

He blinked at her.

"Your words, not mine."

"I never said I was 'spineless.' You added that part."

Syd smiled at him. "I did, didn't I? See what happens when you pay attention? You ought to try it, Tom."

He ran a hand through his hair again. "How about we reboot this conversation? What you're saying is that you won't talk to her for me?"

"Bingo. See? Sometimes half an alphabet is all it takes to get the job done."

"Fine." He stood up. "I'll ask Maddie."

"Whoa." Syd held up a hand. "Hold your horses, Hoss. That's not a good idea."

"Why not? They're close. They work together. She sees more of Lizzy than I do."

"Yeah. Therein lies the problem. They *work* together. Maddie is Lizzy's boss, Tom."

"You're saying she won't intervene in something personal?"

"Let me put it this way. Have you ever seen one of those land speed tests they do at the Bonneville Salt Flats?"

"Sure."

"That's nothing compared to how fast she'll lay a patch to get away from a conversation like this."

"Even when it relates to someone she cares about?"

"Especially then."

"Then I don't know what the hell else to do." He turned away from her and walked toward the door. "She won't talk to me about it—whatever 'it' is."

The way his shoulders slumped made him look so genuinely miserable that Syd took pity on him. *Today if ye will hear his voice, harden not your hearts.* She sighed. Why did those damn aphorisms continue to roll and clatter around inside her head like loose marbles? It made no sense. They were raised Catholic. They didn't even *read* the Bible.

She blamed library school. She hadn't been born a human Rolodex; it was an acquired characteristic. One she wished she could jettison. Especially right now.

A high-pitched sequence of beeps sounded.

The philosophers were all wrong. Authentic being *did* exist—and it was dispensed to wayfaring pilgrims in ten-ounce cups.

The library's ancient coffeemaker had been leaking for months. Even Maddie couldn't fix it. Syd had finally given up and stashed it in a closet until she could take it to the dump. She'd been resigned to hauling a thermos around until she had time to buy a new unit at the Walmart in Wytheville. But one day after Buddy had been there cleaning the library, the thing reappeared. Its cracked reservoir was wrapped with shiny metal tape. Now it hummed and brewed and dispensed liquid wisdom like a minor prophet.

It appeared that sometimes broken things *could* be mended—not just set aside or replaced.

Her brother was nearly to the door.

"Tom?"

He stopped and turned around. Syd thought his eyes looked wet.

She knew she'd live to regret it, but she stepped into the void anyway.

"Go and get us each a cup of coffee, and we'll figure something out."

Buddy was reading Henry's copy of *The Incredible Journey*. Backwards.

Henry didn't mind. It was different from listening to Dorothy read. She was always very careful and took time to make sure he understood each word. But Buddy never slowed down—not even at the ends of sentences. His words all ran together and sounded the same, too. It was a lot like listening to water drip from the kitchen faucet.

He'd do that at night when he couldn't sleep.

Listening to Buddy read didn't ruin the story for him at all. It was more like having two books inside the same cover. Besides, he liked that Buddy's story started from a happy place. It was hard when you had to wait for things to get better.

He knew a lot about that part.

His daddy was working late tonight. Buddy would stay with him until he got home. Sometimes that was before bedtime, but mostly not. Henry would lie down on the couch when he got sleepy, but Buddy would stay awake. He'd sit in the big blue chair beside Henry and watch TV with the sound off. He'd stare at the screen and change channels until it was time for the weather—which happened a lot.

"Weather on the eights," he'd say.

Then he'd click the remote again until the next eight rolled around.

Daddy would leave food for Henry to eat, but it was always cold stuff. He wasn't allowed to use the stove. But tonight Buddy brought hot food from town. Chicken and mashed potatoes. Green beans. Two brownies. They were all tied up in a bag with a note from Syd. "Dinner for two handsome men."

It was Tuesday. On Tuesdays and Thursdays, Buddy cleaned the library.

Syd knew that Henry's daddy was going on a trip tomorrow. That meant he'd be staying at the farm for a while. He'd sleep in the big front bedroom with all of Maddie's airplane pictures—and Pete would lie across his feet.

He missed Pete. And Before. He got to see them every week on taco night. The black and white tuxedo cat was coming in the house now. Henry wanted her to sleep on his bed, too. But she wouldn't.

Rosebud always slept on Maddie's desk in the downstairs office. At first, Maddie chased her. But then she put an old fuzzy blanket in a box and left it on the floor in there.

It didn't work.

Daddy was going to California to get Gramma C.'s piano. He didn't understand why Gramma C. wanted another piano when she already had one at Maddie's house. But Dorothy said Gramma C. was a lady, and that all ladies had pianos.

Buddy was still reading. It looked like he had only about half the pages left to go. He was in the middle of a row of words when he stopped and clicked the remote to turn the TV volume on.

Henry didn't worry about Buddy stopping. He always remembered his place.

Another eight had come around. It was time for the weather. Henry wondered how Buddy always knew what time it was. He didn't wear a watch and they didn't have a clock out here. But he was always right. Buddy was always right about everything.

They watched the screen as big blobs of green and yellow jerked their way across the map. Sometimes, a bright wedge of red mixed in, too. The colors inched closer to them every eight minutes.

"Too soon, Bluebird," Buddy said. "Low pressure. Too much warm air."

"What does low pressure mean?" Henry asked him.

Buddy clicked the volume off and picked up the book.

"Low pressure. Too much warm air. Unstable."

The stream of words started again.

Henry could hear rumbling that sounded like the noise the dumpsters at school made when the big county trucks emptied them and dropped them back to the pavement.

Something started tapping on the windows that overlooked the road.

Buddy kept reading:

> him brought had that river the towards night the in wraith a like stealing go him watched she tears of blur a through . . .

The tapping noise got louder, but Buddy's voice stayed the same. Henry had to strain to hear him over the tapping and rumbling:

> shadows the among lost was form running swiftly low the soon . . .

The lights in the apartment flickered. Off. On. Off. On. Before the next weather eight could come around, they went off and stayed off.

Buddy kept reading.

Bright flashes turned the windows white and filled the room with big, dark shadows. Everything looked different—like it had all been painted blue.

"Too soon," Buddy said. "Unstable."

More thunder rolled. The white flashes came faster.

"Do we need to go in the closet?" Henry asked.

Buddy's shape was part of the blue of the chair now, but Henry could tell he was shaking his head.

"Will you stay with me until Daddy comes home?"

Buddy held the book up higher and kept reading.

Henry listened to the unbroken stream of words that floated above the sound of the rain and thunder. He grew sleepy imagining what meaning they had. A story was a story, no matter where it started—and sometimes, waiting for the beginning to happen was better than knowing the end.

For the second time that week, Maddie managed to make it home in time for dinner. After the meal, they carried their glasses of wine out to the porch and watched the sun set over the pond.

Pete was busy working the perimeter. His slow-moving figure cast a long shadow along the edge of the water before disappearing into a thicket of fuzzy, white-topped cattails. The tall stalks swayed on the night air. Their fat winter seed pods had already been mostly dispersed by warm winds that continued to push through from the south. Syd couldn't recall the last time spring had come and gone so soon.

Rosebud had followed them to the porch. The cat jumped up onto Maddie's lap and got summarily removed so many times that Syd started counting the exchanges. It was like watching a carefully choreographed pas de deux—with six feet instead of four.

Maddie returned the cat to the porch floor for the fifth time.

"She's not going to give up, you know." Syd pointed out the obvious. "Why don't you just let her stay?"

"And ruin my slacks?"

"I don't think she'll ruin your slacks."

"Have you seen her talons? They're like mini can openers."

"Maddie . . ."

Rosebud jumped up again. Maddie put her back down.

"Honey," Syd tried another approach. "Even if she does snag your pants, it's not like you don't have nine other pairs exactly like these."

"That's beside the point." Maddie shook her head. "I refuse to condone aberrant behavior."

"She's a cat."

"So?"

"Cats don't have aberrant behavior."

"This one does."

Thunder rumbled in the distance. A storm was brewing. It was still miles away, but apparently the threat was portentous enough to distract Rosebud from her errand. She bolted from the porch like her tail was on fire and made a beeline for the barn.

Maddie watched her go. "That cat is a spaz."

"This weather is unnerving. It's too warm, too soon."

"I know." Maddie re-crossed her long legs. "Everyone in town is on edge about it. It's too reminiscent of the pattern that led to the tornadoes."

"How can people continue to insist there's no climate change?"

"They're idiots."

Syd looked at her in surprise.

"Well?" Maddie shrugged. "Am I wrong?"

"No. But that doesn't sound like something you'd say."

"I'm just tired."

"You're working too much."

Maddie sighed. "I won't argue with that."

Syd didn't want to waste the opening. "So? Why not change it?"

"I can't. Not right now."

"Maybe you could pay Lizzy for some overtime? Have her help take up some of the slack?"

Maddie took a moment to respond.

"She's . . . not able to take on extra hours right now."

"Why not?"

"She just can't. She has other priorities."

"Other priorities?" Syd was confused. "What other priorities?"

"Look," Maddie drained her glass. "I'm not at liberty to discuss this, okay?" She stood up. "Want some more wine?"

"Oh, no you don't." Syd held out an arm to block her passage to the door. "Put your tastefully clad butt back in the chair. We aren't through with this conversation."

Maddie sat back down.

"Look, Syd. There isn't anything else to discuss. Not about this."

"I don't see why not. Lizzy isn't your patient."

Maddie didn't reply.

Syd smelled a rat. "Are you saying that Lizzy *is* your patient?"

"I haven't said any such thing."

"Then why are you being so cagey?"

"Honey . . ."

"Something is going on. Tom came to see me today. He's all het up about his relationship with Lizzy. He says she's become distant and withdrawn."

Maddie shrugged.

"He asked me to talk with her and find out what the problem is."

Maddie looked alarmed. "Syd . . ."

"I told him no."

Maddie's features relaxed.

"Before I agreed to do it."

Maddie closed her eyes.

"He's my brother," Syd protested. "What was I supposed to do? He's miserable."

"Stay. Out. Of. It."

"So there *is* an *it*." Syd narrowed her eyes. "I knew it."

"Oh, good god." Maddie raised a hand to her forehead.

"Come on. Tell me."

"No."

"So you admit you *do* know what the problem is?"

"I admit nothing of the kind."

"Then why won't you talk about it?"

"Because it's none of my business. Or yours, I might add."

"He's my brother."

"Yes," Maddie nodded. "And your *brother* should be the one to talk with Lizzy."

"He *has* talked with Lizzy. She won't tell him anything."

"I reiterate. Stay out of it."

"Come on. Those two have been inseparable ever since they met. And I know it's not her job—you said she was going to renew her contract to stay on another year."

Maddie drummed her fingers against her empty wineglass.

"What else could it be?" Syd asked. "Is she sick? Is that it? Is that why you can't talk about it?"

"Syd . . ."

"Well? Is she?"

"No." Maddie waved a hand in frustration. "She's not sick."

"Well, if she's not sick, then she must be . . ." Syd's eyes grew wide.

"Don't." Maddie leaned toward her. "Don't say it. Don't ask me. *Please.* Just. Don't."

Syd dropped back against her chair.

It started to rain. A soft pattering on the metal roof became louder. More insistent. Something bounced off an eaves spout and landed by her feet.

Hail?

More thunder rolled around them, but this time it was preceded by bright flashes of light. She could see Pete loping across the lawn toward the shelter of the porch.

Maddie said something but Syd couldn't make it out. Her voice sounded like it was coming from miles away.

"What?" Syd asked her. "What did you say?"

"I said we should go inside." Maddie was back on her feet again. "It's probably not safe to be out here right now."

The flashes of light were coming faster now. The thunder was having a hard time keeping up.

Her mind raced along with the storm.

Was Maddie right? Were they in an unsafe place?

The yard was filling up with tiny pellets of ice.

"Syd?" Maddie touched her on the shoulder. "Are you coming?"

"In a minute." Syd gazed up at her. "I just need another minute."

"Okay." Maddie seemed to hesitate. Syd thought she might say something else, but she didn't.

After a moment, Maddie withdrew her hand and retreated into the house.

Chapter 4

Buddy was raking out the cramped crawl space beneath the porch that ran along the west side of the house. All manner of winds and weather systems were pretty much constant from this direction and that meant dried leaves from all four corners of the county managed to make their way here and pile up beneath the sagging floorboards. The big rains that had rolled through the county several nights in a row had made the surrounding area safe enough for Dorothy's father to decree that today would be a good time to burn the big piles of debris that ringed the property like burial mounds.

An old, rusted burn can stood in a clearing just out of sight, beside a path that led down to the river. Buddy had been working there most of the morning, shifting tall piles of compacted sticks and leaves closer to the can so her father could soak them with oil and set them ablaze.

He didn't trust Buddy with matches.

It was easy to forget Buddy was there. He worked quietly and never said much. Still, having him nearby always gave Dorothy a feeling of calm. Especially on days like today, when her father was at home.

It was Saturday, and they were doing chores around the house. That meant her father would stride around like a bantam rooster and bark orders at them. He wouldn't bother to change out of his house shoes and he seldom left the porch. But he always had strong opinions about the work that needed to be done, and he gave them a running commentary about how badly they were doing it. Sometimes he'd threaten to come do it himself. But that rarely happened. And it never happened on days like today, when he started the morning with a drink in his hand.

Dorothy did her best to stay out of his way. She set to work behind the house, determined to move several partly decomposed piles of leaves that had sat neglected for many seasons because they were out of sight. The leaves were dense and heavy. Any grass that once thrived on the ground beneath the piles had long since given way to thick, black dirt that she knew was rich enough to use in what remained of her mama's vegetable garden.

She scooped up the matted debris with a pitted shovel and piled it into an ancient wheelbarrow before pushing it down the hill to the burn can. It was hard work, but the air today was warm and fresh. The sun was already inching above the treetops. Good weather like this meant her father would soon lose interest in chores. Before long, he'd be dressed and on his way into town. With luck, she wouldn't see him again until after supper.

Each time she rolled one of her heavy loads past Buddy, he'd stop raking and stand at rigid attention until she disappeared below the rise. The third time she approached him, she told him not to stop. Not to wait. She didn't want her father to notice that he stopped working—even for a few minutes.

"Don't stop raking, Buddy," she whispered, as she pushed the creaking wheelbarrow past him.

"Watch for Goldenrod," he'd mutter. "Goldenrod is here too early. Warm weather. Too soon."

Buddy always called her "Goldenrod." At first, she didn't understand it. But eventually she decided the odd nickname was because of her hair color—gold like her mama's had been. Buddy tended to do that—to identify people by some odd quirk or characteristic. It was like solving a puzzle to understand his meaning. Most people didn't bother to try. But nobody was better at it than Henry, who always seemed to know what Buddy was talking about.

"Hush, Buddy. Keep working." She'd keep her voice low and hurry past him, hoping her father wouldn't notice their exchange.

He didn't like it when Buddy spoke to her.

Her father never paid Buddy much for the work he did for them, but he wouldn't hesitate to pay him nothing if he thought Buddy was slacking off. Most of the time, though, he acted like Buddy wasn't even there—except when he found a reason to shout insults or criticize the way he was doing something.

"Fucking retard doesn't know his ass from a hole in the ground . . ."

Once she was safely back behind the house, Dorothy noticed a rhythm to Buddy's raking. She began to follow along with him. Twenty-two quick scrapes of the rake. Pause. Seven more. Then twenty-two again. It was a good pattern. It split their work into smaller parts. It was a lot like the story in the Bible that described how God divided land from water and day from night. It made sense because little things were easier to manage. People could live through anything if they knew for sure it had an end.

Dorothy filled her wheelbarrow again and started her slow trek toward the burn can. This time, she gave Buddy a wide berth, hoping he wouldn't stop when she passed. It didn't work. As soon as she got behind him he stopped raking and stood at attention.

"Buddy, no," she hissed. "Don't stop."

It was too late. This time, her father noticed.

"What the hell are you doing?" he bellowed. "I don't pay you to stand there like an idiot. Get back to work."

Buddy didn't move.

"Buddy, please," Dorothy pleaded. "Don't make him mad."

Her slow progress toward the clearing came to a halt when the front tire of her wheelbarrow hit an exposed tree root, causing the whole load to lurch to one side. She did her best to hold it upright, but she wasn't strong enough. The rusted metal tire bracket gave way and the front end of the wheelbarrow collapsed. Leaves and broken sticks spilled out across the area Buddy had already cleared.

"God damn it!" Her father threw his plastic tumbler at them. It landed near Buddy's feet. "You worthless pieces of shit are no better than a couple of Mexicans."

Buddy stood rooted to his spot like a beanpole. He was staring straight ahead, but Dorothy knew he wasn't looking at her father. He wasn't looking at anything.

"Are you ignoring me, boy?" Her father stepped closer to the edge of the porch.

Dorothy intervened. "I'll clean it up, Papa."

"You'll clean it up?" He scoffed and shifted his gaze to her. His eyes were like dark smudges on his face. "Just like you clean up every other mess you make?"

He came down off the porch and shoved Buddy hard enough to knock him down.

Dorothy resisted the impulse to run. She didn't want to leave Buddy alone with him.

Little things were easier to manage.

She saw her father's expression.

Today wasn't going to be a little thing.

He approached the broken wheelbarrow and kicked at it with disgust. Then he slapped her so hard it made her ears ring. "Who's going to pay to fix that?" He grabbed her by the arms and shook her. "You? That worthless moron?"

Dorothy closed her eyes. She didn't want to be there. She didn't want to be anywhere. But she needed to stop him. She needed to protect Buddy.

I won't fight you . . .

He shook her again. "Do you have something to say, girl?"

She opened her eyes. "I said I won't fight you."

Something flickered across his face. It was there and gone so quickly it would've been easy to miss. But she saw it. She always saw it.

His hands tightened on her upper arms. He hauled her forward. "Why do you make me do this?"

Bourbon and Old Spice. The smell burned her nostrils and made her stomach churn.

"Why do you make me do this?" He repeated. He shook her like he was trying to force out an answer.

She didn't have one. Not now. Not any time he asked this question. And he always asked.

He shoved her backward. Her leg smashed into the side of the upended wheelbarrow. It was sharp. She could feel something wet on her leg.

"Get in the house. *Now.*"

She stumbled to her feet and turned around.

Buddy? Where was Buddy?

He was gone.

Dorothy half-walked and half-ran across the uneven ground, nearly tripping over Buddy's rake. Her father was fast on her heels. She was midway up the porch steps when she smelled it.

Smoke . . .

Her father smelled it, too. He stopped and jerked around.

Large columns of thick black smoke rose like a curtain ahead of the tree line.

"*Son of a bitch! That fucking moron will burn the place down!*" He took off running toward the clearing. "*Call the goddamn fire department!*"

She knew he'd kill Buddy if he caught him.

But he wouldn't catch him.

Dorothy looked out toward the lane in time to see a flash of bright orange before Buddy's scooter disappeared around a bend.

"There's a good place right up here. We can tank up and get something to eat at Denny's."

Rita pointed at the exit sign. They'd been cruising along I-64 in Indiana for some time. James never realized how big it was—wide and dull. "Gateway to the rectangular states," Rita had declared when they crossed over the Ohio River in Louisville.

James nodded and started gearing down. They weren't driving one of the big rigs. They didn't need all that cargo space for this trip—even though Natalie had floated the idea of having them drop off a few loads of pipe stems and mirrors on their way across country. Jocelyn had nixed that idea. "I don't want to slow them down. This is Cougar's first cross-country haul, and I want to bring it in under the wire."

James didn't bother telling Jocelyn that "under the wire" meant barely on time. The army had taught him to just roll with whatever his commanding officers said. Things worked better that way.

He did agree with her, however, that getting back quickly was a good idea, although he had a hard time imagining Dr. Heller getting too bent out of shape if her piano showed up a day late. She didn't seem like that kind of person. The other thing he was sure about was that his son, Henry, wouldn't complain about the chance to skip a few more lessons.

Everything was all set with Santana's. The LA-based piano mover had the six-foot Steinway broken down, strapped tight and crated. It was being stored in a climate-controlled warehouse until they got there. All they had to do was load it up and make a giant U-turn.

So far, they were making good time.

"What's this town?" he asked Rita, as he slowed down at the end of the exit ramp.

"Haubstadt. Not much here but a couple hotels and one of them roadside graveyards for aborted babies."

James looked at her.

"They ain't real babies," Rita explained. "Just crosses set up in somebody's side yard."

"Why do they do that?"

"Don't ask me. It's Indiana. Folks here have time to do stuff like that." She shrugged her narrow shoulders. "Seems like they'd do better to take in all the kids that ain't dead—but they pretty much don't give a rip about 'em once they're born."

James didn't comment.

"Pull into this truck stop and park. We'll get some dinner first before we fill up and get back on the road."

"Where're you thinking about spending the night?"

"Columbia, Missouri. That's about four hours from here."

They were taking a more northern route because Rita said she didn't like driving across Oklahoma.

"That whole 'panhandle' gives me the willies." She opened a new pack of Dentyne and popped a stick into her mouth. She was trying to quit smoking. "You have to ask why they didn't lop off that little hunk and make it part of Texas. Mark my words—nothin' good is going on in Oklahoma."

James didn't have any opinion about Oklahoma, but he'd spent time at Fort Hood in Texas, and he had no fond memories of the place. It was where he met Henry's mother. Sheila worked at a local dry cleaner's and she was what his own mother called a "camp follower." James found out the hard way what that phrase meant. They got married when Sheila told him she was pregnant, but he knew it wouldn't last. She wasn't cut out for military life—or for motherhood. She wasn't cut out for much of anything that didn't involve hard drinking, self-injected drugs and other men. She disappeared a week before his Permanent Change of Station to Fort Irwin in California. He had no idea what happened to her until he got a call shortly before his deployment to Afghanistan. She'd been found dead in her apartment in a small town in Ohio.

He parked the truck and they hopped out for the short walk to Denny's. Rita noticed his gait.

"That leg giving you a fit?"

He nodded. "I probably need to take this thing off for a while."

"Well, hell. Why didn't you say so earlier? I could a done some of the driving before now."

"It's okay." He held the restaurant door open for her. "I was gonna ask if you wanted to do the next leg."

"Ha!" Rita slapped him on the arm. "*Next leg*. Good one."

James smiled. He was normally pretty sensitive when people asked him anything about his prosthesis. But something about Rita made him feel at ease. He liked doing trips with her. She was laid-back and a straight shooter. She didn't mince words. You never had to wonder what she was thinking or where you stood

89

with her. After so much time having people tiptoe around him, he found that refreshing. Rita made him feel . . . normal. Like he wasn't missing any parts that mattered.

They seated themselves in a booth near the front window.

Rita liked to keep an eye on her rig.

James studied her while she looked over the shiny menu. She was probably in her mid-fifties. A little on the hefty side, but still nice-looking. Her hair was bright red—a color not found much in nature. But she had pretty green eyes that suggested it might once have been natural. She always seemed to be smiling. He knew she was Natalie's sister-in-law, and she was single, but he didn't know much else about her.

He decided it was time to change that.

"What's your story, Rita?"

She looked at him over the top of her menu. He couldn't make out her expression because it was hidden behind bright pictures of pancakes and chicken-fried steak.

"I'm sorry." James apologized for his impulse. "It's none of my business."

"Hell." Rita lowered her menu. "Lord knows I don't have no secrets." She waved the waitress over. "Let's get some food and I'll give you the 4-1-1 on Rita Chriscoe."

They both ordered big skillet dinners—steak, eggs, potatoes and cheese. Rita asked for a side of ranch dressing for dipping.

"Damn. I'd kill for a smoke." Rita drummed her fingers on the table. Her nails were short but neatly trimmed. She didn't wear any polish—unlike Natalie, whose nails probably glowed in the dark.

"Do you wanna go outside? I'll call you when the food gets here."

Rita shook her head. "Nope. I gone this far without givin' in. I reckon I can make it through another day."

"I know that feeling."

She nodded. "I just bet you do, young man."

They sat in silence for a minute.

James knew it was his turn to say something. "I think I get it wrong most of the time."

"What?" Rita asked.

He gave her a small smile. "You aren't going to make this easy for me, are you?"

"Why should I? Nobody ever made nothin' easy for me."

He was quiet again.

"Look it." Rita picked up her glass of iced tea. "You ain't the only person to feel like life dealt you a handful of shitty cards. We're all stumblin' around half-blind, tryin' to get it right."

"You feel that way, too?"

"Hell to the yes, I feel that way. You think driving these beat-up rigs is a dream come true for me? You think I like living alone in that fleabag apartment over my brother's garage?"

James was embarrassed. "I guess not."

"You *know* not. I had dreams once, too. And plans. And none of them involved ending up a near-broke spinster with a broken heart and no prospects for nothin' better."

James didn't know what to say.

Fortunately for him, Rita was on a roll.

"You think you're a failure as a parent? Everybody in hell and half of Georgia thinks I'm a failure 'cause I never got to *be* a parent." She shook her head. "We don't always get to pick our poison, boy. Sometimes it gets doled out whether we ask for it or not."

"You wanted to have kids?"

"Not really. I came close once, but it wasn't meant to be. And that ain't what I'm talkin' about, anyway."

"What *are* you talking about?"

"I'm fixin' to tell you." She drained her tea. "I have what our God-fearing friends and neighbors in Jericho like to refer to as a 'checkered past.' Know what that means?"

"In general or in particular?" he asked.

She laughed. "In *this* particular, it means I don't play for your team."

"My team?" He was confused. "What team?"

"You don't get out much, do you boy?" Rita rolled her eyes. "It means I ain't straight. Or wasn't. I don't know what the hell I am these days."

"Oh." James wasn't sure how to reply. "I didn't know that."

"Well, I don't know how in the hell you missed it. It's all but posted up on that bulletin board in the canteen next to them lost-time posters."

"I don't talk much with people at work."

"You don't talk much with nobody about nothin', do you?"

"Not really."

"You might should try it."

"Why?"

"Well, for one thing, you'd know that you ain't alone in feelin' like a failure. For another, you'd know you can relax on these long hauls 'cause I ain't fixin' to get into your drawers."

He blushed.

"Am I right?"

"I never thought that about you, Rita."

"Not even once?"

"Well." He smiled at her. "Maybe once . . ."

Rita sat back and seemed about to share something more when the server arrived with the food, ending their conversation. James was too shy to try to restart it, and Rita seemed fine to let it drop and concentrate on eating.

Forty-five minutes later, they were back on I-64, heading west into the setting sun.

"I need to show you something."

Syd held a folded piece of paper out to Maddie.

"What is it?"

"It's a note Henry brought home from school. I just found it in his lunchbox."

Maddie took the paper and unfolded it. "He didn't give it to you?"

Syd shook her head and sat down at the kitchen table and watched her read the note. She watched Maddie's eyes widen.

"Suspended?"

Syd nodded.

"He's *suspended?* For what?"

"Insubordination." Syd pointed at a line of type at the bottom of the paper. "Apparently, he was rude to his teacher."

"*Henry?*"

Syd nodded again.

Maddie refolded the sheet of paper. "That's impossible."

"I thought so, too."

"Did you ask him about it?"

"No. I thought it was better for us to talk with him together. Besides, he hid this from us."

"Well, he must've known we'd figure it out when he didn't go to school today."

"You'd think. When I went upstairs to wake him, he said he didn't feel good."

"I don't doubt it." Maddie sighed and looked at her watch. "What do we do? Call James?"

"I thought about that, too. But James won't be back for three more days." Syd picked up the paper. "I think we have to handle this."

"Oh, man . . ."

Syd patted her on the shoulder. "Don't worry, sawbones. I've got your back."

"*My* back? What about *your* back?"

"Sorry. You're the Ward Cleaver in this domestic drama."

Maddie rolled her eyes. "I don't see why."

Syd smiled at her. "You're taller."

"Oh, give me a break."

"You look better in cardigans."

"Nice try." Maddie pushed back her chair and stood up. "What else you got?"

Syd glanced at her feet. "You wear wingtips."

"These are *not* wingtips. They're Josef Seibel lace-ups."

"You say tomato . . ."

"All right, all right." Maddie feigned umbrage and stared up at the ceiling. "Boy. I never saw this one coming."

Syd stood up, too. "Me, either."

"Okay. Let's get it done before I lose my nerve."

They were halfway across the kitchen when Henry appeared at the bottom of the back stairs. He was still wearing his Scooby-Doo pajamas and his hair was tousled from sleep. He seemed surprised to see them standing there together. It didn't take him long to notice the sheet of paper in Maddie's hand.

"So, Sport?" Maddie began. "Is there something you need to tell us?"

Henry started to cry.

Syd fought an impulse to rush over and pick him up.

"Come on, Sport. Don't cry." Maddie reached out a hand to him. "Let's sit down and talk about this, okay? You know you can always tell us anything. Right?"

Henry nodded.

"We aren't mad at you," Syd added. "We just need to know what happened at school."

Henry sniffed and followed them to the table. Syd pulled out a chair for him and they all sat down. Maddie unfolded the paper and placed it in front of him.

"Syd found this note from the principal in your lunchbox. Did you forget to give it to us?"

Henry shook his head no.

Maddie sighed and looked at Syd for support. After a moment's consideration, Syd got an idea.

"Henry?" she asked. "Did the principal tell you to give this to your daddy?"

He nodded.

Okay. Now they were getting someplace.

"Sweetie?" Syd continued. "Since your daddy is on a trip, Maddie and I are filling in for him—kind of like substitute parents."

At her mention of the word "substitute," Henry's eyes filled with tears again.

"He doesn't like me," he stammered. "He picks on me."

"Who?" Maddie asked. "Who doesn't like you, Sport?"

"My substitute teacher. He says bad things about me and Buddy. He makes me stay in during recess."

Syd quickly laid a restraining hand on Maddie's arm. It was clear to her that Maddie was trying to remain calm. It was equally clear that the elementary school would be her first stop on her way into town.

"What's his name, Sport?"

Henry looked up at her with owlish eyes. "Hose Beast."

Maddie's jaw dropped. "*What* did you say?"

"Hose Beast," he repeated. "Mister Hose Beast."

"Honey," Syd took over the inquisition. "What's his *real* name?"

Henry seemed confused. "Mister Hose Beast *is* his real name. That's what everybody calls him."

Syd dropped back against her chair. *So much for that whole "suspended" mystery . . .*

Maddie ran a hand over her face.

"Sport?" She tried again. "What is your teacher's *proper* name?"

Henry had to think about that one. He looked back and forth between them.

"Darren?"

"Dar . . ." Maddie looked at Syd.

Syd dropped her eyes to keep from laughing. But when she did, she noticed something in the fine print at the bottom of the suspension notice. She picked it up and held it out to Maddie.

"Read the last line at the bottom. Aloud." She pointed at the entry.

"'Supervising teacher: Darren Hozbiest,'" Maddie read. "Hozbiest?"

"You can't make these things up," Syd replied.

"I told you that was his name," Henry insisted. "He doesn't like me. He's mean to Buddy."

"Okay, Sport." Maddie put the paper back down. "Let's start from the beginning. Why do you think Mr. . . . Mr. *Hozbiest* . . . doesn't like you?"

"He makes me stay after school."

"Why does he do that?"

Henry shrugged his narrow shoulders. "Sometimes I don't bring a lunch so he has to stay in the classroom with me."

It was Maddie's turn to lay a restraining hand on Syd.

"Why don't you have a lunch every day, Sport?"

"Daddy forgets sometimes."

"And Mr. Hozbiest makes you sit in the classroom while the other kids are eating?"

Henry nodded. "He makes me stay after school, too. He's mean to Buddy."

"Does he make you stay after school because you don't always have a lunch?" Syd asked.

"No." Henry lowered his eyes. "Sometimes I don't have my homework done."

Syd began drumming her fingers in agitation.

"Henry?" Maddie asked. "How does Mr. Hozbiest know Buddy? Buddy doesn't go to your school."

"I miss the bus when I have to stay late," he explained. "Sometimes Buddy gives me a ride home on his scooter."

"And Mr. Hozbiest doesn't like that?" Maddie wasn't sure she liked that idea, either. Not because she didn't trust Buddy—but because it didn't seem safe for the two of them to be riding so far on county roads.

Henry shook his head. "He calls Buddy bad names."

"Okay." Maddie sat back. "I'm going to stop by the school today and talk with your teacher. Everything will be just fine. We don't want you to worry, okay?"

Henry nodded.

Syd pushed Henry's dark hair back from his forehead. "After breakfast, you can go with me to the library today. Would you like that?"

Henry nodded with enthusiasm. "Can Héctor and Gabriel come, too? I won't get to see them after school is over for the summer. And Dorothy?"

"I'll call Mrs. Sanchez and see if Héctor and Gabriel can come after school. I'm not sure about Dorothy."

"Miss Freemantle sees her all the time. Maybe I can ride on the bookmobile with her?"

"Maybe. We can ask her. But first you have to finish your

homework." She bent down and touched her nose to his. "*All* of it. Even the math."

"Okaaayyy."

Syd stood up. "How about some breakfast?"

"Hear, hear." Maddie pushed back her chair. "Who wants pancakes? Raise your hand."

Henry's arm shot into the air.

Syd glared at Maddie.

"What?" Maddie feigned innocence. "We're *celebrating*. You don't eat yogurt and twigs when you're celebrating . . . do you, Sport?"

"No!" Henry slid off his chair and raced to the fridge. "I want berries in mine. And chocolate chips."

"You know," Syd drawled. "I'm tempted to kill you—but if I wait long enough, I won't have to. Your diet will do it for me."

Maddie beamed at her. "I'll get the griddle."

Roma Jean had nearly finished restocking the bookmobile for the day's route. This often was the hardest part of the job. She had to anticipate what the regulars at each of her stops liked to read, and do her best to rotate her inventory to be sure she had things on hand that would appeal to a very diverse group of interests.

Sometimes, that was more complicated than it seemed.

Nelda Ray Black, for instance, liked any book about Jesus. But the straight-laced old woman flew into a rage after Roma Jean suggested she read *Another Roadside Attraction* by Tom Robbins. In retrospect, that had been a bad choice—but how could people expect Roma Jean to have read every book in the library? It wasn't fair.

When she told Charlie about it, Charlie just threw back her head and laughed. She said Mrs. Black didn't have the sense of humor God gave a schnauzer.

Roma Jean didn't know much about schnauzers, but she guessed this observation meant they didn't find many things funny.

Today's route was less volatile. She had four stops. Most of them were in the western part of the county: Volney, Grant and Troutdale. But her first stop was at the county prison unit. That one usually gave her a case of what her Gramma Azalea called "the yips." It wasn't that it was dangerous or anything. It was a minimum-security detention center—even though some of the inmates were in for super-bad stuff. Charlie said that any men staying out at this facility were considered safe and hadn't exhibited any disruptive behavior for more than twenty-four months.

Roma Jean wasn't sure she shared Charlie's view of what constituted "disruptive" behavior. One of the men asked her to locate back issues of *Inside Detective* magazine. When she asked him why, he puffed out his chest and said, "There's an article about me in there." And a couple of times now, men who'd been released had stopped by the library to "visit" with her or invite her out for "coffee."

Miss Murphy put a pretty quick stop to that. Roma Jean was glad. She didn't do too well managing unwanted attention—especially these days. Miss Murphy told Roma Jean she needed to be more careful. The way she said it made Roma Jean wonder if they were still talking about ex-convicts. She wanted to follow up with her and find out if Miss Murphy was really making a reference to Charlie, who still managed to meet up with her a couple times a week at some of her more remote stops. They weren't doing anything all that inappropriate. Well. Not yet, anyway. But Roma Jean knew things between them were starting to get out of hand.

She had tried to talk with Charlie about that yesterday, when she was parked out at Creola near Baywood. It had been a slow day and not many people had ventured out for books. Still, she was scrupulous about staying at each stop for the full hour. You never knew when somebody might show up.

Like Charlie.

It was only her lunch break, but Charlie stopped by to spend what was left of it with Roma Jean. Charlie said it had taken her nearly thirty minutes to make the drive to Creola because she'd been at the opposite end of the county, delivering a message for Byron.

"He had me talk with the owner of the Christmas tree farm up on Whitetop," Charlie explained.

"Why?" Roma Jean asked. "What did he do wrong?"

"Nothing yet." Charlie shrugged. "But the mayor told Byron he hasn't filed I-9 forms for all of his workers."

"What are those?"

"They're tax forms that verify eligibility to work. You only have three days to do that after you hire somebody."

"I don't get it. Why would the mayor care about who grew his Christmas tree? He bought one last year from Daddy's lot—and those all came from Whitetop."

"It's not hard to figure out. Most of the workers up there are from Mexico."

Roma Jean thought about the implications of that. "You mean like Carlos Sanchez?"

Charlie nodded.

"But Carlos and his family have lived here forever."

"That won't matter if they don't have papers to prove their right to work."

"Does that mean they'll be arrested? Or deported?"

"I hope not. That's why Byron had me go up there—to tell the farm owner that our mayor is planning on deputizing local law enforcement to act as immigration agents."

"He can't do that, can he?"

"Yes, ma'am, he can." Charlie nodded. "Under Section 287(g) of the Immigration and Nationality Act."

"So, we have to warn Carlos and Isobel."

Charlie didn't say anything.

"Charlie?" Roma Jean laid a hand on Charlie's arm. "We have to warn them."

Charlie sighed. "Roma Jean. You know I can't do that."

"Why not?"

Charlie pointed to her badge. "I'm a deputy sheriff, Roma

Jean. If I warned them, I'd be breaking the law. And we don't even know what their status is. They could have green cards."

"What if they don't?"

Charlie shrugged.

"I don't get it. Wasn't Sheriff Martin breaking the law when he sent you up there to warn the tree farmers?"

Charlie shook her head. "I didn't go to *warn* them. I went to advise them to get their paperwork in order—which is good legal advice on any average day."

"This is all so confusing."

"I agree."

Roma Jean got an idea. "So, you can't warn them, and Sheriff Martin can't warn them because you'd both be breaking laws. Right?"

Charlie nodded.

"But nothing says that *I* can't warn them. Right?"

"Roma Jean . . ."

Charlie tried her best to talk Roma Jean out of getting involved, but it was too late. Her mind was already made up. She vowed to talk with Mrs. Sanchez on her next trip to Volney. But she knew Charlie would never stop trying to dissuade her, so she decided to distract her. It wasn't hard. All she had to do was scoot a bit closer and ask how much more time they had before Charlie had to head back to town. She pointed out that they never knew when a patron might show up, so they had to make the best of the time they had.

It was a new experience for Roma Jean to realize that she held some power in a relationship. That had never happened before. At least, if it ever had been true, she'd never been aware of it—much less clued in about how to leverage it to her advantage.

Right then, that leveraging worked out just fine. The problem was it hadn't taken long for Roma Jean to forget all about trying to distract Charlie. The process of doing so quickly overwhelmed her ability to think coherently about anything.

She knew they were probably skating precariously close to

what her Aunt Evelyn called "heavy petting"—although she wasn't one hundred percent sure what all was comprehended in the phrase.

"Don't you be all hell-bent on exercising them feminine wiles, young lady," Aunt Evelyn had said, wagging a finger at Roma Jean. She'd caught up with her in the parking lot on Sunday after church. "You keep gallivanting around with that flame-red hair and that bosom of yours and you're gonna end up in a steaming pot of hot mess."

It wouldn't do Roma Jean any good to point out to Aunt Evelyn that she couldn't do much about her hair color or her bosom. They both pretty much got to be what they were all on their own without any special effort or enhancement.

Aunt Evelyn always seemed to be the one in the family tasked with having the "serious" talks. Roma Jean was pretty sure her mama had engineered this one. Ever since she started driving the bookmobile, her mama had been acting antsy—like she thought Roma Jean was up to something unsavory. But she'd never be the one to ask her about it. They didn't have that kind of relationship. So instead, she sent Aunt Evelyn barreling in like a tank to clear a path for the infantry.

"I'm not exercising *anything*," Roma Jean whined. "And I can't help walking around with this bosom." She gestured at Aunt Evelyn's chest. "It runs in both sides of the family."

Aunt Evelyn's big brown eyes grew larger. "Are you giving me sass?"

"No, ma'am." Roma Jean sagged against her car door. She was still driving her uncle's ancient Caprice. It would be another six months before she had enough money saved to buy something used from Junior's.

"Well you just mark my words." Aunt Evelyn drove her point home. "No good can come from carrying on with the wrong kind of people."

Roma Jean thought for a moment about the assortment of options available in Jericho.

It was a pretty short list.

"So," she asked her aunt. "Who would the *right* kind of people be?"

Aunt Evelyn lifted her chin. "You know what I'm talking about, missy."

"No, ma'am. I don't. Not if 'carrying on' with the right people means I have to pick out somebody like one of the Lear twins."

"Oh, those two are just idiots," Aunt Evelyn scoffed. "And you know full well that ain't what I'm talking about."

"But, I don't, Aunt Evelyn. I swear I don't."

"Let me make this simpler for you. You know it wasn't easy for your Uncle Cletus to bring me back here to live after we got married."

Roma Jean nodded. She'd heard all the stories about what a scandal it was when her uncle married a black woman and brought her to live with him in Troutdale.

"Well, believe me," Aunt Evelyn continued, "my people didn't much care for it, either. Hell, the only person around here who gave us the time of day back then was your Gramma Azalea—and that was only because she'd rather die than live with a Yankee like your mama. Everybody else acted like we'd committed a crime against nature. And it ain't much different today, mark my words."

Roma Jean opened her mouth to say it wasn't like that with Charlie, but the words dried up before she could get them out. Besides, saying anything about her feelings for Charlie would just open up a can of worms she wasn't ready to deal with yet.

Sometimes it seemed like she was racking up so many unopened cans of worms, she ought to give up on library school and open a bait shop.

Aunt Evelyn was still staring at her. "You've got a good head on your shoulders, girl. We all expect you to use it."

"Just like you did?"

"I can't say as marrying your Uncle Cletus was the smartest thing I ever did. But even though he drives me crazy, he's a good man and I could a done a lot worse." She looked at her watch. "I gotta go. Nadine's gonna string me up by the short hairs if I don't show up and get them biscuits started."

"I just want to be happy." Roma Jean muttered. She knew it sounded pathetic, but she couldn't think of a better way to express what she was feeling.

"Honey?" Aunt Evelyn's voice dropped down from what her daddy called its normal resting place in nosebleed country. "We all want to be happy. But sometimes, we need to accept that being smart is a better choice."

Was being smart a better choice?

Had Miss Murphy been smart when she divorced her cheating husband and moved in with Dr. Stevenson? Not everybody in the county had good things to say about that. Yet the two of them sure seemed to be happy.

It was true that the world was changing and people had more freedom these days. But it wasn't the freedom to choose who you were—she was beginning to understand that you pretty much got dealt that hand of cards at birth. It was more like you had the freedom to decide if you were gonna do what Aunt Evelyn suggested—pick being "smart" over being happy.

All these ruminations would just have to wait a bit longer.

Besides, maybe she'd live long enough to get lucky.

Maybe one day, people wouldn't have to choose.

Maddie was working late.

Her last appointment had been at four-thirty, and she was in her office, trying to get caught up on paperwork—the bane of her existence. She had no trouble understanding why so many residents gave up on their dreams of opening their own practices. Had she not inherited this one from her father, she seriously doubted that she'd have had the temerity to persist. She spent as much time pushing paper as she did seeing patients. And her practice was too small to add the requisite staff to manage it. So, for now, she was the one tasked with the Herculean feat.

At least tonight when she rolled in late, she wouldn't face the wrath of Syd. There was a library board meeting this evening and they'd agreed ahead of time to grab dinner together in town before heading back to the farm. Henry was at home watching a movie and eating a "TV dinner" with his beloved Gramma C. Maddie's mother had discovered some retro, divided-compartment dinnerware while scouring around in an antique store looking for vintage drawer pulls. The plates were ceramic reproductions of the ubiquitous aluminum meal trays that took the nation by storm back in the mid-1950s. It was amazing what Celine could coerce Henry to eat if the moveable feast was served up on an iconic monument to television.

In retrospect, it was hard to blame Henry for being an unwitting victim of the ruse. Even she had to admit that four tiny flowerets of broccoli did look less daunting when they were encased in their own small compartment.

But tonight, she was holding out for Waffle House. A big plate of smothered, covered and chunked hash browns sounded like ambrosia to her.

Fat chance on that one . . . no pun intended.

Syd was still enjoying her tenure as cruise director on Maddie's dietary hell tour of the Pritikin Islands.

She'd been entering patient data into their records system for about an hour when she heard the voices. The sound surprised her because she assumed that everyone else had left shortly after the clinic closed at five. One of the voices belonged to Lizzy. She couldn't make out the other until the voices grew louder. Then she recognized it.

Lizzy was having an argument. With Syd's brother.

Maddie sat back and closed her eyes.

They could only be arguing about one thing. Which must mean that Lizzy had decided to tell Tom about her pregnancy.

At least, she hoped that's what it meant.

Maddie could hear them clearly now. They'd left Lizzy's office and were headed toward the back door of the clinic.

"I can't *believe* you'd keep something like this from me."

Tom's voice. Maddie wondered if she could climb out a window?

"I told you. I wasn't ready to talk about it yet."

Lizzy's voice. She sounded exasperated—and angry.

"Well, when the hell did you *think* you would be ready? After the baby got here?"

Bad approach, man. Conciliation would get you a lot further.

"You know, Tom. It's really none of your business."

"None of my business? How dare you. It's totally my business."

Maddie didn't have to see Lizzy's face to imagine her next response.

"Tom? It's not your business. It's not your body. It's *my* body—and it's my decision."

"You can't just shut me out of this."

Oh, yes she can . . .

"Oh, yes I can. You've made your position on the future perfectly clear."

"What's that supposed to mean?"

"It means that you've gone out of your way to demonstrate that you have no interest in making any kind of long-term commitment to me. So why should I expect you to make any commitment to a child?"

Here it comes.

"Look. I'm Catholic, okay? These choices aren't so easy for me."

Oh, man. I should just give you a shovel so you can dig yourself in deeper . . .

"I cannot even believe you'd say something that selfish and insensitive to me."

"Insensitive? What was insensitive about me being honest and sharing my beliefs with you?"

You might have to pull up a chair for this one.

"Do you want a list? If so, you'll have to sit down because it'll take a while."

Maddie stared at the back of her door with an open mouth. Why did people say she sucked at serious conversations? So far, her handicapping of this one was right on the money.

But Lizzy wasn't through yet.

"You know, Tom? You might want to pay attention to the fact that you haven't mentioned your feelings for me *one time* in this entire conversation. Nor have you bothered to ask me what *my* feelings are, or even how I'm doing—not just with the news but with the physical aspects of being . . . pregnant. And in case you're interested, I'm not doing great. So, unless you want to wear what I had for lunch, I suggest you get the hell out of here. This conversation is over."

Maddie heard the clinic door being unlocked.

"Are you kicking me out?" Tom sounded incredulous.

Sounds like a big 10-4 to me.

"Bingo."

"Fine." Tom sounded angry now. "You know how to reach me if you change your mind."

Don't hold your breath.

"I wouldn't hold my breath on that one. Goodbye, Tom."

The door slammed shut. She could hear Lizzy's footsteps retreat along the hallway that led to the clinic.

Maddie deliberated. Should she open the door and let Lizzy know she was there? Or should she follow her instinct and hide beneath her desk until she was sure Lizzy was gone, too?

It was a toss-up.

She didn't get much time to weigh her options. The footsteps stopped outside her door.

"Maddie?" Lizzy knocked gently on her door. "Are you still in there?"

Maddie cast a futile glance toward heaven.

"Maddie?" Lizzy knocked again. "Can I come in?"

"Yeah." Maddie stood up and walked toward the door. "Of course. Come on in."

She didn't know what to expect when she opened the door and saw Lizzy. Tears, maybe? A face flushed with anger and disappointment? But Lizzy appeared to be neither of those things. If anything, she looked . . . relieved.

"I assume you overheard all of that?" Lizzy dropped into a chair.

"I did. I'm sorry."

"Don't be." Lizzy waved a tired hand. "He's an asshat."

"He's . . ." Maddie wasn't sure she'd heard Lizzy correctly. "I'm sorry. What did you say?"

"I said he's an asshat. First quality. A selfish and self-absorbed little shit." She ran a hand across her forehead. "Do you have anything to drink in this place?"

"Um. If you mean alcoholic, no. Besides, that isn't advisable for someone in your . . . um. Well. I wouldn't recommend it for you right now."

Lizzy stared at her for a moment. Then she gave a short, bitter-sounding laugh.

"I guess you're right, doctor. No booze until I make a decision."

"Better safe than sorry. There's too much going on with your system right now."

"Yeah. Not only my system. My mind's pretty much on sensory overload these days, too."

"I'm sorry about that. I know it can't be easy to be facing this alone."

"Well." Lizzy sounded resigned. And tired. "Tom is actually making this easier, not harder."

"How so?" Maddie perched on the edge of her desk.

Lizzy squinted at her. "You did say you heard our conversation, right?"

Maddie nodded. "Mostly."

"I reiterate. Tom is making this decision easier."

Maddie felt an impulse to agree with Lizzy. But she couldn't. She knew Tom, and she knew how much Tom genuinely cared about Lizzy. He was guilty of being immature, clueless and probably scared—but not much more. She was sure about that.

"Look," she said. "You know I'm usually the last person on the planet to butt into the middle of anyone else's life, right?"

"But in this case, you'll make an exception?" Lizzy asked.

"Sort of. I know Tom Murphy. And I wholly agree with you that he's got some growing up to do. It's true that he reacted like a selfish frat boy and you're right to hold him accountable for that. But I'd be remiss not to remind you that he's a decent guy with a big heart. His feelings are probably just hurt that you waited so long to tell him."

"Tell him?" Lizzy gave Maddie a surprised look. "I didn't tell him."

"You didn't?" Maddie was confused. "Who did?"

"Syd."

"*Syd?*"

"I thought you knew that."

Maddie was speechless. She slowly shook her head.

"Oh, man. You *didn't* know that? I just assumed . . ."

"I didn't . . ." Maddie struggled to make sense of Lizzy's revelation. "I didn't tell her. She was fretting about how upset Tom was about your relationship. He went to see her at the library and tried to enlist her to talk with you—to find out what the problem was. She asked me for insight. I didn't tell her anything. But she just kept pressing and asking me if I had any idea what was going on with you." Maddie shook her head. "She figured it out on her own. *Of course.*" She gave Lizzy an apologetic look. "I've always been lousy at hiding things from her. I am truly sorry."

"It's okay. Really." Lizzy held up a hand to stop Maddie's mea culpa. "Once I had time to get over my initial anger, I was actually relieved to find out he knew. It was past time for me to stop licking my wounds and behaving like a complete chickenshit." She touched Maddie on the knee. "Don't grow a tumor over this, okay? I'm not mad."

"You sure?"

Lizzy nodded and got to her feet. "And I promise to consider what you said about Tom. But it won't be tonight. All I want right now is to crawl in bed with a box of saltines."

Maddie smiled at her. "You'll call if you need anything?"

"Girl Scout's honor." Lizzy rolled her eyes. "Well *that* oath kinda falls flat given my circumstances."

"At least your sense of humor hasn't deserted you."

"True. And don't let yours desert you either."

"Mine?"

"Yeah. *Yours.* Take it easy on Syd. She was trying to do the right thing."

Maddie sighed. "I'll try."

The phone on Maddie's desk rang. Maddie glanced at the caller I.D.

"It's Syd."

"Go ahead and take it." Lizzy waved at her. "I'm outta here. And remember what I said, okay?"

"I'll do my best."

Maddie watched her go.

The phone kept ringing. She stared at it.

Lizzy said she wasn't angry about Syd's interference.

The phone rang again.

She said she'd already dealt with it.

Another ring.

I guess it's my turn, now.

Maddie was already seated in her regular booth at Waffle House and was halfway through her first mug of coffee when she saw Syd's battered Volvo rattle its way into a parking space.

The coffee was hitting the spot. Her young server, Coralee Minor, had started brewing a fresh pot of decaf as soon as she saw Maddie's Jeep pull into the lot. They had an understanding. Coralee made sure the coffee was always hot and plentiful—and she never divulged to Syd that Maddie contrived to sneak into the short order joint at least once a week for lunch.

Maddie watched Syd walk toward the entrance to the restaurant. It was a new experience to see her and feel a sharp pang of trepidation poke at her insides. Reactions like that evaporated years ago when they finally wised up and quit denying their attraction for each other. But this?

This was something different.

She was angry at Syd for betraying a confidence. That had never happened before. And it was bigger than Maddie's personal sense of betrayal. In this case, it was a HIPAA violation, too. One that, under other circumstances, could get her sued for malpractice. Of course, that wouldn't happen with Lizzy, but it didn't diminish the seriousness of Syd's inappropriate decision to tell her brother about Lizzy's pregnancy. Nor did it excuse Maddie for her personal breach of ethics when she confirmed

Syd's suspicion about what lay behind the estrangement between Tom and Lizzy.

It was a mess all the way around. They both were culpable. And even though Lizzy had made it clear that she was no longer upset about the interference, it was still a problem—one they needed to address. Now.

Syd waved at Coralee on her way to Maddie's booth.

"Hey, Miss Murphy." Coralee held up the coffee pot. "Want some decaf?"

"I'd love some. Thanks, Coralee."

She deposited her bag on the padded seat before sliding in to sit opposite Maddie.

"Hi there."

"Hi."

Syd noticed her unsettled demeanor right away. "What's wrong?" She squinted her eyes. "Why do you look like something Rosebud dragged into the barn?"

Maddie saw no reason to forestall the discussion.

"Tom came by the clinic this evening."

Syd dropped back against the booth. "Oh, no."

"Oh, yes. I take it you spoke with him about Lizzy's predicament?"

Syd closed her eyes and nodded.

Coralee appeared with the pot of coffee. She filled Syd's mug and topped Maddie's off.

"Do you folks need a minute before you order?"

"That'd be great, Coralee," Maddie replied. "Thanks."

Coralee smiled and walked on. Syd watched her until she was out of earshot.

"Are you angry?"

Maddie nodded.

"I'm sorry. Truly sorry."

"I hope you are." Maddie tore open two packets of sugar and prepared to add it to her coffee.

Syd reflexively reached out to stop her, but seemed to think better of it. She withdrew her hand.

"Maddie? I *am* sorry. It was wrong of me to break your confidence."

"It wasn't just my confidence you breached, Syd. Lizzy trusted me with that information—not just as a friend, but as a healthcare professional. When you figured it out and I didn't deny it, I broke the law."

"Oh, god. I never even thought about that." She hesitated. "Is Lizzy angry?"

"At me or at you?"

"Yes."

As frustrated as she was, Maddie still had to fight an impulse to smile. "She was, but she isn't, now. She said you actually did her a favor by telling him."

"I kind of doubt that."

"Why *did* you do it, Syd? I've thought about this six ways from Sunday and I still can't figure it out. It's not like you."

Syd was absently shifting her coffee mug back and forth between her hands.

"It's hard to explain. Tom is my little brother. And even though he makes me crazy, I still feel responsible for him. I love him, and I don't want to see him get hurt. Lizzy is the best thing that's ever happened to him. I didn't want him to mess it up." She sighed. "I knew as soon as I told him that it was a big mistake. I never should have done it. I owe Lizzy a huge apology." She reached across the table to touch Maddie's hand. "I owe you one, too."

"You didn't think it was a mistake until you told him?"

"Of course not. I knew it was wrong and that I had no right to share the information. I just . . ." She slowly shook her head. "I just made a bad decision. And even though it might seem disingenuous now, I was going to tell you about it tonight."

Maddie didn't reply.

Syd squeezed the top of her hand. "Do you believe me?"

Maddie nodded. "But I'm still disappointed, Syd."

"I know you are. I'm disappointed in myself."

"We're both lucky that Lizzy isn't more bent out of shape about it."

"Did you see Tom?"

"No. But I did overhear their conversation—unintentionally."

Syd looked perplexed.

"They were arguing in the corridor outside my office," Maddie clarified.

"Arguing?"

"Yeah. Loudly."

"Oh, no."

"I didn't want to overhear it, believe me. But it was unavoidable. Lizzy appeared to know I was still there, too. But it didn't stop her from unloading on Tom."

"That can't be a good sign."

"Trust me. He deserved it. He was acting like an ass."

Syd laughed. "That's not hard to imagine. Most of the time, he *is* an ass."

"Well, he didn't do himself any favors in this conversation, believe me."

They were both quiet for a moment.

"Does Lizzy know what she's going to do?"

Maddie shook her head.

"Tom's going to blow it. He's *already* blowing it. He doesn't understand that good relationships don't grow on trees. Windows of opportunity like the one he has now with Lizzy open once in a lifetime. And that's if you're lucky."

"You don't think he knows that?"

Syd shrugged. "He may know it. But he doesn't realize that those windows can close just as quickly."

"He's not unique in that."

"No." She squeezed Maddie's hand. "But thank god I realized it when you came around."

Maddie smiled at her. "Are you trying to butter me up?"

"That depends. Is it working?"

Before Maddie could reply, Coralee arrived to see if they were ready to order.

"You bet we are." Syd handed her the menus. "I'll have a bowl of chili with a house salad. Italian dressing on the side. She'll have the chili, too, but over hash browns. Smothered, covered and chunked."

"Got it." Coralee sailed off toward the kitchen.

Maddie stared at Syd with what she was sure was a stupid expression.

"What?" Syd asked.

"That whole buttering up thing you're doing?"

"Yes?" Syd smiled at her. "What about it?"

Maddie picked up her coffee mug.

"It's working."

Chapter 5

Syd was halfway through her first cup of coffee when she heard the street door to the branch open.

Five past nine was early for the first patron of the day, but she was relieved to have the distraction. She'd been checking in returns and setting aside books with waiting lists. The blue request slips were clipped to the backs of the circulation cards and she had quite a stack of them piling up. It was a terribly low-tech operation, but a surprising number of her patrons in the small mountain community continued to have no access to email. She'd be on the phone for the better part of the morning, calling folks to let them know it was finally their turn to dive into the latest release by Nora Roberts.

If only it were that simple.

She'd fall on bended knee and thank an obliging creator whenever an answering machine picked up. But that wasn't the norm. The average phone call lasted anywhere from fifteen to thirty minutes. After all the "Hey, howdy" and "We hadn't seen you at church lately" comments, the conversations would naturally drift into prolix ruminations about recent or upcoming hip replacements, apocalyptic weather events or whoever was occupying the top spot in the cheating spouse category.

That last one was pretty hotly contested right now.

It had been a hard winter.

Syd shifted the tower of romance novels to the side of her desk and left her office to go and greet her patron.

It was Byron Martin.

"This is certainly a surprise. Are you here to arrest me," she smiled at him, "again?"

"No, ma'am. Not unless you're the one who spray-painted obscenities all over the mayor's Buick."

Syd's eyes grew wide. "Really? Someone did that?"

Byron nodded.

Syd lowered her voice, even though no one else was in the building with them. "What'd they write?"

"You don't want to know."

"Oh, but I do."

"Let's see." Byron ran through the list. "Fearmonger. Chinless bigot. Hate is not a family value. And—my personal favorite—Read *These* Lips—accompanied by an anatomically correct illustration of female . . . parts."

"Oh, my god. That's quite a display."

"Isn't it?"

"He must have a big ride."

"It's a LaCrosse," Byron explained. "Roomy inside and outside. Those Buicks are good cars."

"Well, it couldn't have happened to a more deserving object."

"True. But it's still a crime."

"Any suspects?"

"A few." He laughed. "Actually a 'slew' would be more accurate."

"Is that why you're here this morning? Or did you want to use the full force of your office to butt in line ahead of the two dozen women waiting to read *Island of Glass, Book Three in the Guardian Trilogy*?"

"Um. No."

"No, you're not here about the vandalism or no, you're not interested in the book?"

"No on both counts."

"Too bad about the book. I hear it's a real page-turner."

"I'll wait for the movie."

Syd smiled. "Well, it's always lovely to see you, whatever your motivation is."

"I'm not sure you'll feel that way after our conversation."

"Oh, come on, Byron. I was having *such* a good morning." She sighed. "Are we gonna need coffee for this?"

"It wouldn't hurt."

"Come on back to my office then, and ruin my day in style."

He followed her into the small room behind the circulation desk and dropped into an ancient Bank of England chair while she fixed him a cup of coffee. Syd thought he looked tired. Probably his errand.

Or it could be all those late nights with Celine.

She handed him a bright yellow "Hello Kitty" mug. He frowned at it.

"Is this the only one you have?"

"Of course not." Syd sat down behind her desk in the room's only other chair. "I'm trying to lighten the mood."

"I'm afraid that will take more than festive drinkware."

"Byron? You're killing me here. What is it?"

"It's about Roma Jean. And Charlie."

Syd closed her eyes. "Oh, no."

He nodded. "Apparently, some God-fearing citizen complained to the mayor's office about the two of them meeting up on some of her bookmobile routes."

"Are you kidding me?"

"No ma'am."

"Who was it?"

"I'm not at liberty to say. But I have been directed by our mayor to insist that you impose disciplinary measures on your young employee." He took a sip of his coffee. "For the good of the Commonwealth, of course."

"This is absurd."

"I agree. But the mayor shares the concerned citizen's worry about exposing children to unnatural behavior."

"*Unnatural?*"

"His words, not mine."

"Oh, I *so* do not believe this. Doesn't that man have better things to do?"

117

"Apparently not."

Syd fumed. "Have you spoken with Charlie?"

He nodded.

"What was her response?"

He laughed. "You mean after she turned about thirty-four shades of red? She was mortified."

"Do you think they've done anything wrong?"

"I think that depends on your definition of 'wrong.' Charlie made it clear that she wasn't avoiding her work, and that she only met up with Roma Jean on her lunch breaks. Knowing the two of them, it's pretty hard to imagine they'd ever do anything inappropriate in front of kids."

"I agree."

"Still," he stretched out his long legs, "it does give the appearance of sneaking around."

"I know. I've already tried to caution Roma Jean. I guess I wasn't specific enough in the way I went about it."

"You need to know that Watson intends to approach the library board if the meet-ups continue. Hell. Knowing him, he may do it anyway."

"If he thinks the board controls our funding for the bookmobile, he's got another think coming. I pay for that service myself—out of pocket."

"But doesn't the board pay for Roma Jean?"

Syd sagged against her chair. "Shit."

"I'm going to ask you something that's really none of my business—and I understand if you don't want to answer, okay?"

"Okay."

"Do you think it's possible that the mayor—or anyone else in this town—might believe that you . . . influenced Roma Jean in this relationship?"

Syd was tempted to throw her coffee at him, but she managed to remain calm—at least overtly.

"I cannot believe you would ask me that."

"Wait a minute." He held up a hand. "Before you go off the

rails at me, you need to know that this is likely what he's going to allege—if this escalates."

"Why the hell would he do that?"

"Because he's a homophobic asshole—with the moral compass of a rock. And, Syd? As stupid and offensive as his views are, he is not alone in possessing them. Life in this county isn't always a stroll through Candyland."

"Ain't that the truth. Especially lately. It's like a national damn epidemic."

Byron sighed. "I predict it will get worse before it gets better."

"Jericho, or the rest of the country?"

"Yes."

Syd laughed. "Okay. You can tell our kumquat of a chief executive that I'll deal with my wayward employee."

"I've already told Charlie to stow it during work hours." He shook his head. "It's hard for them, though. It's not like they have many other opportunities to see each other."

"And they won't. Not until Roma Jean figures it out and talks with her family."

"Charlie's a good kid. She won't push her into anything she isn't ready for."

"Byron? Some time, you'll have to fill me in on your relationship with Charlie."

"Oh, it's not that complicated. Charlie went through a pretty rough patch with her own coming out process. Her father damn near beat her to death when he found out about it. After that, she spent the rest of her teen years in and out of foster care."

"My god."

"I gave her a job when she turned eighteen. You pretty much know the rest." He smiled. "She's a good officer. One of the best I've ever had." He finished his coffee and set the cup down on Syd's desk. "You don't have to worry about her. She has a good head on her shoulders." He got to his feet. "I need to let you get back to work." He gestured toward the tower of books on her desk. "Eight copies of the same thing?"

"I told you. Romance is in the air." She stood up and smiled at him. "But I don't have to tell you that, do I?"

He gave her an exaggerated eye-roll. "Nice try."

"Oh, come on, Byron. The two of you aren't exactly being discreet."

"Do we *need* to be discreet?"

"Not as far as I'm concerned. I think it's wonderful."

Syd could tell he was trying hard not to smile. It made him look shy and adorable—wholly at odds with his imposing frame, uniform and gun.

"I think it's pretty wonderful, too," he said. "What about Maddie?"

"What about her?"

"What does she think?"

"You mean about the relationship her mother is *not* having with you?"

"Yeah." He nodded. "That would be the one."

"She thinks her mother is nuts."

"Really?" Byron looked surprised.

"Not *that* kind of nuts," Syd clarified. "She thinks her mother needs—in her own, high-toned words—to get her head out of her ass and quit worrying about what other people think."

"I knew I liked her."

Syd nodded. "She's pretty much a keeper."

Byron quietly regarded her for a moment. "I think you both are."

"Thanks. Maybe share that with our august mayor?"

"You think it would help?"

"No. But it couldn't hurt."

He laughed. "Maybe I *should* take one of these books."

"If you're looking for a user's guide, Celine doesn't have one."

"No?"

Syd shook her head. "Trust me. They threw away the molds after they made those two."

"Lucky us."

"Yeah." She smiled at him. "Lucky us."

◊ ◊ ◊

James and Rita delivered Celine's piano exactly eight days after they left to fetch it.

Their arrival dovetailed nicely with her decision to move into the house, even though Bert and Sonny still had a fair amount of work left to complete. The interior was all but finished, and needed only a bit of touch-up painting here and there. They were almost entirely focused on exterior work now, and that part would proceed more slowly. She was confident that any dust or mess could be confined to outdoors, although Bert stipulated they would want to close off her studio and cover the piano when they started cutting flagstones for the patio area.

Celine was fortunate that David's mother, Phoebe, knew a piano tuner who'd worked for years out of a Steinway showroom in Richmond before retiring to Abingdon. When she called to schedule an appointment, she explained that her Model A salon piano had just made the long, cross-country trek, and asked how long she needed to let it acclimate to its new surroundings before having it tuned.

"Well, that depends," he said.

"Depends on what?" she asked.

"On how you had it moved."

It became clear to her that Marty Fassbinder would take his time getting to the point.

"By truck," she clarified.

"What kind of truck?"

Celine thought about replying that it was a big white truck with red stripes, but she resisted temptation.

"A commercial step van," she explained. "The piano was professionally packed and stored in a climate-controlled facility prior to making the trip."

"Was the truck climate-controlled, too?"

"I don't think so."

"Then storing it in a climate-controlled facility was kind of a waste of money, wasn't it?"

"Probably. But it was only in storage for a week."

"Well. You could a done a lot worse. Some folks wouldn't think twice about moving one strapped to the bed of a '57 Chevy pickup with no shocks."

"That wasn't the case here."

"Where is it now?" he asked.

"Here. In my studio."

"Summer's coming on early. You got AC in there?"

"Yes."

"Is it on?"

She bit back an expletive. "Yes. I keep it set at sixty-eight degrees and have a humidity regulator."

"You got any plants?"

"Not yet. I just moved in a few days ago."

"Well then, I'd say you can have it tuned whenever you want to."

"Really?" Celine knew she'd probably be sorry, but she decided to ask a follow-up question anyway. "Why did you want to know if I had any plants in the studio?"

"They attract moisture. Especially if you overwater them like my wife always does."

"I think I can promise to keep Mrs. Fassbinder away from my houseplants."

That got a laugh out of him. "Don't be too sure. That woman is wily."

"So, how soon can you come out here?"

It turned out that Marty had an appointment in Wytheville the following day, so he showed up at Celine's just before noon. He was fast and efficient and he expressed surprise that the big Steinway was still relatively in tune.

"It's not on concert pitch, but considering all the potholes it survived getting here, I'd say it's in good shape." He gently tapped his tuning wrench on the side of the cast-iron frame. "Nice job, girlie."

When he'd finished, and was packing up his tools, he dropped one of his tuning tips and had to crawl beneath the piano to retrieve it. While on the floor, he appeared to notice something on the underside of the frame. He fumbled around inside the pocket of his jacket and fished out a penlight to take a closer look.

"Well, I'll be."

"What is it?" Celine was afraid that he'd discovered a crack or some other imperfection.

"Did you know your piano was autographed?"

"Autographed?"

"Yep. Right here. In ink. 'Raymond Parada. 28 January 1986.' There's something else, too." He peered closer. 'Challenger exploded today.'" He sat back. "If that don't beat all." He looked up at her. "You wanna come take a look?"

"You bet I do."

Celine got to her knees and crawled beneath the massive instrument. Marty handed her the penlight and pointed at the spot where he'd discovered the handwritten message.

She ran her fingers over the tidy script. "Who was he?"

"Unless I mistake, Raymond Parada was one of the best tone regulators at Steinway. He'd be the man who gave this hunk of metal and wood its voice." He shook his head. "Though I didn't know he ever worked on the salon series. He was better known for the concert grands."

"Raymond Parada." Celine repeated the name. She laid the flat of her hand against the underside of the frame that held the soundboard. "So, he taught you how to sing?"

"Oh, no, ma'am," Marty corrected. "He gave it a voice. *You* make it sing."

Celine and Marty sat together beneath the big piano like children hiding in a homemade fort. It was a curiously intimate experience, vaguely like sharing secrets with a stranger.

"Did you buy it new?" Marty asked.

"No," she shook her head. "I bought it from a member of the music faculty at UCLA. But she got it new in New York, when she was at Juilliard."

"That makes sense. She probably bought it right out of the showroom in Queens."

"My parents were both musicians." It was a random comment, apropos of nothing. She was embarrassed by her candor. "I'm sorry. I don't mean to babble."

"Talking about music isn't babbling. Talking about politics or the weather, or who's gonna win the World Series—that's babbling."

"I suppose."

"So, you're a musician, too? Like your parents?"

"Me?" Celine shook her head. "No. It's just a hobby."

Marty laughed. "Pretty expensive hobby."

She shrugged.

"And you paid a private contractor to haul this thing all the way across the country?"

"I tend not to go out much."

"Tell you what? How about you take this thing for a spin and see how it sounds?"

Celine was surprised. "Don't you want to test it out?"

"I already did my part. Besides, I don't play the piano."

"You don't?"

"Nope. Never learned." He held up his hands. "I have a great ear but I was born with eighteen thumbs."

"But you tune pianos for a living?"

"No. Not for a living. I do it because I love music. As a hobby. Kind of like you."

She found it hard to argue with that. "Fair enough."

They retreated from their cave beneath the piano and got to their feet. Celine took her seat at the keyboard.

"What should I play?" she asked him.

He sat down on an ottoman near the window. "Surprise me."

She decided on a Schubert *Impromptu* because its main theme allowed her to get a feel for the keys, the sound, the pedals, and the instrument's full dynamic range—especially in the middle section, where the notes fell faster and tested the action. It didn't take her long to forget that Marty was in the room. The lush sound filled the space and wrapped around her like a silk cocoon. As she played, she could hear echoes of her mother's voice, reminding her to note the accidentals in the second part of the Trio.

Playing her piano was like resetting her internal gyroscope. It anchored her. Righted her center. Reminded her that a tumultuous world was always navigable as long as she maintained a stable reference point. It didn't really matter where the journey took her as long as she remained balanced and had both eyes fixed on the horizon ahead.

The piano was performing brilliantly—just as it was built to do. Sitting at the keyboard and running through the *Impromptu* was more than a good way to test the tone and agility of the instrument, it was a way for her to reconnect with her simplest and most authentic self.

She could imagine Raymond Parada smiling.

She didn't finish the piece. She didn't need to. She knew the piano was perfect. She lowered her hands to her lap and closed her eyes so she could focus on the faint reverberations of the final notes. They seemed to hover in the air a bit longer than normal— as if they were taking their time getting acquainted with the contours of the new space.

"Well?" she heard Marty ask. "What do you think?"

Celine smiled. "I think it's more important to ask what *you* think."

She turned around to face him and was surprised to see they were no longer alone in the room. Buddy was standing just behind Marty in the doorway that led to the patio. He was still wearing his helmet and his blaze orange vest, so she knew that he'd probably just arrived. That meant Bert and Sonny would be along shortly, too.

"Oh, Buddy," she said. "Come in. Meet Marty Fassbinder. He tuned the piano for us."

Celine got to her feet and addressed Marty. "Marty, this is Buddy Townsend. Buddy is helping with the renovation work on the house. He loves music, too."

"I kinda thought so." Marty extended his hand. "Nice to meet you, Buddy."

Buddy glanced at Marty's hand but didn't shake it. He nodded his head and stared at the floor.

Marty didn't seem offended. He casually folded his arms. "What'd you think of the performance, Buddy?"

"Not finished."

Marty looked confused.

Buddy was staring at the tops of his shoes.

"He means I didn't play the whole piece," Celine clarified. She stepped closer to Buddy. "That's right, Buddy. I didn't need to finish it. It was only a test to see how the piano sounded after being moved here from California."

Buddy looked at her with his clear eyes. "Half is not finished."

She smiled at him. "How about you and I meet here a bit later, and I'll finish it for you then?"

Buddy didn't reply. Celine patted him on the arm before turning back to Marty.

"Let me walk you out?"

Marty nodded. "You make her keep that promise, Buddy. I want to hear the rest of the music, too."

This time, Buddy did look at Marty. "Half is not finished," he repeated.

"No, sir. It is not. But one thing we know for sure is that when Ms. Heller here does finish it, it will be perfect." He winked at Celine. "Raymond Parada took care of that."

They left the house through the patio door and walked across Celine's unfinished garden to reach Marty's car. Buddy's scooter was neatly pulled in beside it.

"Autistic, right?" Marty asked. "He a savant?"

Celine began to make an automatic reply, but thought better of it.

"You know, Marty, I'm not sure what Buddy is. I only wish science had a way to clone his goodness, bottle it, and freely dispense it to the rest of the world's population—starting with me."

"I think I know what you mean." He opened his car door. "You'll let me know when that magic carpet of yours needs another tune-up?"

"I promise. Thank you, Marty."

She watched and waited while he backed out and began his long trek down the lane that led to the county road.

The morning mist had all burned off and the sun was now holding court in a deep blue sky. It was shaping up to be a warm and beautiful day—another one for the record books. The redbud trees ringing her pasture were all shimmering with branches full of bright pink blooms. The tall grass between them was full of white and yellow oxeye daisies. *A nuisance plant*, as Bert explained. They'd have to be rid of them if she wanted to use her pasture for anything useful.

Yes. Bert and Sonny were sure to make good progress on the patio and garden today.

And Byron was coming for dinner tonight—the first meal she'd be able to cook for him in her new kitchen.

Remember the accidentals, ziskeit . . .

She did remember them. To forget them wreaked havoc on pacing and tempo. Destroyed the power and nuance of the transition from minor to major. To remember them meant preserving the delicate balance and counterbalance of the minuet. Because in the end, a dance—like life—was always about balance. Always about careful give and take. Always about grace, syncopation and a hint of mystery.

Yes, she whispered to the spirit of her long-departed mother. *I remember the accidentals.*

As she drew closer to the house, she heard the music. The notes floated toward her on warm currents of air, blending so seamlessly with the color and scent of early summer that she could barely distinguish them from the pastiche of nature spread out around her.

But as the music went on, she did distinguish it. It was the Schubert. All of it. Accidentals. Harmonic ambiguity. Cascading semiquavers. Played just as she had played it for Marty.

No . . . not *just* as she had played it. *Precisely* as she had played it.

She stood outside the house in stunned silence until the music stopped—exactly where she had stopped.

Buddy.

She entered her studio through the patio door and found him sitting quietly on the bench in front of the Steinway, still wearing his helmet and his bright orange vest. His hands were resting on his knees.

"Buddy?" She took a step toward him.

"It isn't finished," he said.

"It isn't . . ." Celine didn't really know what else to say, so she didn't say anything. Instead, she crossed the room and took a seat beside him on the padded bench.

They didn't speak.

A pair of tree swallows landed on a branch outside the window and started trilling. They seemed anxious for her to get on with it.

They were right. Buddy was right. *It needed to be finished.*

She raised her hands to the keys and played the rest of the *Impromptu* for him, picking up from the spot where they'd each stopped.

When the piece was finished, Buddy didn't say anything.

He got up from the bench and left the studio as quietly as he'd arrived.

"Are you sure I can't help you out?" Maddie picked up a shiny whisk and tested its heft.

Michael took the whisk away from her and returned it to its place in a queue of devices.

"Don't. Touch. Anything."

"Oh, come on, Michael. I'm a *doctor*. You don't think I can handle a few of these crude implements?"

"Crude?" Michael glared at her over the rims of his glasses. "Did you say *crude*?" He picked up the whisk. "I'll have you know that *this*," he waved it aloft, "*this* is not an 'implement.' This is a Kuhn Rikon French wire whisk. And it's far beyond your level of expertise."

"Oh, really? Next time you need your gallbladder removed, be sure to call on someone with a higher level of expertise, okay? Maybe they can just *whisk* it out." She smiled at her own joke. "No pun intended."

"Oh, don't get your panties in a wad."

"I just don't understand why you can't get over that damn mixer incident. It was years ago."

Michael sighed. "Years ago, and it seems like yesterday." He gazed up at the faded, framed photograph of an industrial-sized stand mixer that adorned the shelf above his work area. "I miss you, Gloria."

Maddie picked up her wineglass and took a healthy sip. "You're a head case."

"Hey, I take my work very seriously—just as you do yours."

"Yeah? Well I don't name my *tools*." She held up a palm before he could correct her. "My partners in the craft."

"That's more like it."

"What's so special about this Wrath of Khan thingamajig, anyway?"

Michael rolled his eyes. "Kuhn Rikon."

"Whatever."

"It's the only whisk that won't break the mayonnaise."

"Break the . . ." Maddie changed her mind. "I don't even want to know what that means."

"Probably wise. You've already proved that you can't be trusted with the information."

"What are you making, anyway?"

"Amuse-bouche. These are white cheddar and thyme gougères with black lava smoked sea salt." He sighed. "But Nadine will insist on calling them 'finger food.'"

Maddie laughed. "What's the occasion?"

"They're celebrating. Apparently, Azalea signed some big contract with a video game company and she's giving Evelyn and Nadine enough money to pay off the note on the café."

"No kidding? That's great."

"Yeah, except we have to plan *two* separate meals because they're hosting two parties—on the same day."

"Why?"

"You know Azalea. She won't eat with Yankees."

"Oh, good god." Maddie refilled their wineglasses. "Didn't her War of Northern Aggression end about a hundred and fifty years ago?"

"Not in her mind. That's why I need the mayonnaise whisk. I have to make a vat of broccoli slaw for the second party. You and Syd will be invited, by the way."

"Great. Dare I ask to which party?"

"Don't get your hopes up, Cinderella. You won't be getting the fried chicken."

Maddie's face fell. "Why not?"

"Duh. Syd is from *Baltimore*. Ring any bells?"

"Maryland is below the Mason-Dixon Line."

"Not good enough. Azalea's Mason-Dixon line is more of a moving target. To her, Maryland was nothing but a 'buffer zone.' She's very specific about these nuances of geography." Michael added a mound of freshly shredded cheese to his dough mixture. "Astrid isn't allowed to attend the later event, either. David will be apoplectic."

"Astrid?"

Michael nodded.

"Well that's hardly surprising. She *is* a dog."

"That isn't why. David got her from a breeder in Rehoboth Beach."

"Astrid is from Delaware?"

"Of course." Michael shrugged. "All the best Papillons are."

Maddie thought about it. "I guess that makes an odd kind of sense."

"Tanning. Drag shows. Parading your candy-ass dogs. It's a beach town trifecta."

"Well, however the dueling parties unfold, it looks like your experiment with Nadine has worked out beautifully. You two seem to have settled into a perfect arrangement sharing kitchens."

Michael did not disagree. "That woman is a master chef— although she'll forever reject the distinction."

"How's business been since you two combined forces?"

"Great. Nadine has been a godsend helping with all the wedding catering. We'd never manage without her."

Maddie watched him fill a pastry bag with the seasoned dough and began covering prepared cookie sheets with dollops of the mixture.

"So, I guess that means adding the extra land you bought from Mom succeeded in getting the mayor off your backs?"

He paused mid-dollop. "Not exactly."

Maddie didn't like the sound of that. "What do you mean?"

"Now it seems we have to apply for special permits to serve food to groups larger than twenty-five."

"Does that man lie awake at night inventing new ways to be a cretin?"

"If so, he must never sleep."

"I just don't get it." Maddie shook her head. "What does he gain by working so hard to antagonize everyone in the county?"

"For starters, it's not everyone. There are plenty of people who appear to be just fine with the mayor's methods. I mean, there hasn't exactly been a groundswell of angry mobs picketing his office on Main Street."

"I suppose he's riding the so-called 'populist' wave that seems to be driving political discourse these days."

"That's one way to put it. I'd be inclined to take a less charitable view."

Maddie helped Michael carry four large pans of the upscale "finger food" to a massive wall oven. He slid them all inside and set the timer.

"Those'll take about fifteen minutes to bake. Let's have a seat and I'll tell you why I asked you to come over here tonight."

They walked back to Michael's prep area and perched on a pair of mismatched stools.

"I was wondering if you planned to keep me in suspense. Syd was pretty intrigued when I couldn't tell her why you summoned me."

"What's she doing tonight?"

"She and Roma Jean took the bookmobile to a state library

symposium in Roanoke. They'll be home late tonight." She looked around the kitchen. "By the way, where is David?"

"That's part of what I wanted to talk with you about. He's out canvassing."

"Canvassing? Canvassing for what?"

Michael sighed. "He didn't call you, did he?"

"Call me?" Maddie was immediately suspicious. "What about?"

"Brace yourself." Michael refilled her wineglass. "He's decided to run for mayor. As a write-in candidate."

"*What?*" Maddie was flabbergasted. "That's completely insane."

"Trust me." Michael held up a hand to halt her tirade. "I already went the distance with him on this one. There's no stopping him."

"Come on, Michael. This is *David* we're talking about. Until last year, he thought the electoral college was an online university. How the hell can he run for *mayor?*"

"You're preaching to the choir. I told him it was a harebrained idea. He's persuaded that the only way to get Watson to back away from his crusade to drive the queers out of Jericho is to beat him at his own game."

"He's really serious about this?"

"Deadly."

Maddie ran a hand over her face.

"I saved the best for last."

Maddie dropped her hand. "Do I wanna hear this?"

"Probably not. But I'm going to tell you, anyway. He's going to challenge Watson to a public debate—at the river, during the town Fourth of July celebration."

"Oh, good god. What the hell is he thinking? Watson will eat him for lunch."

"I think that's part of his strategy. The more Watson comes after him—or any of us—because of our sexual orientation, the more David can publicly call him out. Right now, any protests are about as effective as pissing into a stiff wind." He held up an index finger. "But as *candidate* Jenkins, he has a bully pulpit."

"I'm . . . speechless."

"Well, don't be because he needs you to help him."

"Help him?" Maddie narrowed her eyes. "Help him how?"

"He wants you to write his speech."

"What?" Maddie bolted up from her stool. "Why the hell would I write his speech?"

"He says you wrote all of his papers in high school."

"That was different."

Michael raised an eyebrow.

"It *was*," Maddie insisted. "Writing a five-page report on the life cycle of a planarian is hardly the same as taking on a seasoned politician."

"Maddie? Have you ever actually *looked* at Gerald Watson?"

Maddie took a moment to consider his question. There was some truth to the comparison. Like David's planarian, Watson had two heads . . .

"I see your point."

"Besides," he continued. "It's one speech. We both know he doesn't have a snowball's chance in hell of winning."

"True."

"So, what could be the harm in helping him?"

"You mean apart from the ridicule and endless self-loathing I'd endure if it ever came out?"

"Precisely."

Maddie sighed and dropped back onto her stool. "Let me think about it."

The wall phone behind them rang.

"That's probably David." Michael got up to answer it. "Hello? Oh, hey, Nadine. What's up?"

Maddie could hear Nadine's voice on the line. She sounded rushed and agitated, although Maddie couldn't make out what she was saying.

"What?" Michael asked. "*What?*" he repeated. "When? Just now?" Michael began striding back and forth. "He did *what?* How many people were there?" He threw his head back and closed his eyes. "That rat bastard," he muttered. "I hope he broke his damn jaw." He took a slow, deep breath. "Yeah," he said. "I can handle everything until you get back. Just tell Nicky to keep topping off the iced teas. Uh huh. Right. You just stay calm. We don't want you *both* in the slammer." He glanced at the wall clock. "Listen, I've got four pans of gougères in the oven. I need about five more minutes, then I'll be on my way." He started to hang up the phone, but Nadine said something else. Michael listened, then rolled his eyes. "*White* cheddar, like we discussed." He nodded. "*Yes.* I used the *smoked* sea salt." He nodded again. "Yeah. I'll be at the café in fifteen minutes." He hung up the phone and turned to face Maddie.

"That was Nadine."

"I gathered as much. What's going on?"

"She was calling from the jail. Raymond's been arrested."

"*What?* Why?"

"She didn't give me all the details but, apparently, he got into a shouting match with the mayor about some shrubs and ended up slugging him. Watson charged him with assault."

"Shrubs?" Maddie was incredulous. "When did this happen?"

"About an hour ago—at the café. Watson was there giving Raymond all kinds of face about some landscaping faux pas, and it snowballed. She said the restaurant was full, too . . . some church bus from Patrick County." He shook his head. "None of it makes any sense. I just know I need to get over there and fry some catfish while she gets this mess sorted out."

"Need me to go by the jail and lend a hand?"

"Are you serious?"

"Of course." Maddie nodded. "Consider it research."

"Research? Research for what?"

"For the speech it now appears I'm going to write."

The oven timer dinged.

Michael smiled at her.

"I'll take care of those. You go bust Raymond out of the joint."

Maddie felt like an old-timer at the county jail. After all, it hadn't been that many months since Charlie Davis drove her there to bail both Celine and Syd out after their altercation with Syd's former mother-in-law, Doris.

Actually, altercation was putting it mildly.

Celine had ended the argument with her former childhood antagonist by liberally dousing the angry socialite—an heiress to the Massengill fortune—with a dime-store douche.

Maddie didn't miss the irony that today's fracas had transpired at the Midway Café, too.

She began to wonder what Nadine was baking into the biscuits at that place.

If she'd ever stopped to think about it, she would've guessed that Tuesday nights at the county jail would probably be—*slow*. But tonight, the place was hopping. The small waiting room was jammed with people crowded onto benches or leaning against any available stretch of wall. They all appeared to be caught up in various states of anger or distress. Most of them she didn't know. But a few were patients she'd seen a time or two. They uniformly appeared mortified when they recognized her.

Byron Martin entered the room from a door that led to the processing area. He wasn't in uniform. Maddie thought he looked different in street clothes—oddly, more, rather than less imposing. It occurred to her to wonder what he'd been doing before showing up here on what, plainly, was a night off.

He noticed her right away and motioned for her to join him. He didn't seem surprised to see her.

"Nadine is in back with Raymond. She'll be out in a few minutes." He glanced back at the room full of people and grimaced. "Let's go to my office. You can wait in there."

"Good idea," she whispered to Byron. "I guess I should try harder to blend in so I don't attract so much attention."

He gave her an ironic look. "Yeah. You *do* that. Start by being shorter and maybe show a little more ink."

"Ink?" Maddie was confused.

"Ink. It means . . . never mind."

135

He led her down a short hallway and opened the door to his office.

"Have a seat." He gestured toward a battered chair with a faded seat cushion. "Judge Burris has set his bond at four thousand dollars," he explained. "Frankly, I think that's ridiculous. But they called him in off the golf course and even on a good day, he tends to get pissed when people slug it out in public places. Nadine said there was no way she could raise that much cash tonight, so it looks like Raymond is gonna be an overnight guest."

"You mean Azalea doesn't keep that much stashed in her ammo case?" Maddie asked.

Byron laughed. "I guess not."

Maddie shook her head. "What the hell happened? Michael said something about an argument over landscaping?"

Byron perched on the edge of his desk. "Apparently, the mayor had been after Raymond to remove some bushes at the entrance to the café parking lot. He alleged they were a nuisance because they blocked a clear view of the road heading east."

"So, Raymond slugged him?"

"Not exactly. Raymond and Nadine offered to prune the bushes so they'd be lower and less likely to block anyone's line of sight. Well. That wasn't good enough for our mayor. He showed up out there early this evening with a road crew and directed them to cut the things down. Mind you, all of this transpired while the café was open and gearing up for dinner. So, there were about fifty witnesses to what happened next."

"Which was?"

"When Watson's boys fired up the chainsaws, Raymond was out there like a shot. He tried to stop the crew from chopping up the shrubs. It turns out they were Rose of Sharon bushes that Nadine and Evelyn started from cuttings off their grandma's plant back in Georgia."

"Oh, no."

"Yeah. Raymond got into a shouting match with the crew—who said they were just following orders. Then he noticed that Watson was there, too, watching the show. Raymond didn't see him right off because he was driving Junior's loaner car." Byron shook his head. "Raymond said the asshole had it parked across three spaces, too."

That last part didn't make sense. Everybody knew that Junior only had one car he ever lent out. It was an old, hail-damaged Cutlass Ciera that had more pockmarks than paint, and was tricked out with a bright yellow winch bolted to the front bumper mount.

"Why was Watson using Junior's loaner car?"

Byron held up a hand. "Don't ask."

"So, that's when he slugged Watson?"

"No. That didn't happen until Nadine showed up—wielding a cast-iron skillet." Byron took a deep breath. "That woman is a force of nature."

Maddie smiled. "Remind you of anyone?"

Byron actually blushed.

Maddie took pity on him. "So, what happened when Nadine got there?"

"First, she threatened to decapitate anyone who touched the damn shrubs. Then she called Watson a . . . ," he picked up a sheet of paper from his desk and read the arresting officer's description, "'chinless bigot'—and told him he was trespassing on private property." Byron picked up a pen and jotted a note in the margin of the report. "I need to remember to ask her about that comment . . ."

"And *then* Raymond hit him?"

"No. Raymond didn't hit him until Watson made some provocative statements to Nadine."

"What kind of statements?"

"Let's see." Byron referenced the report again. "He called her, in order, a whining shrew, a loud-mouthed Aunt Jemima, and a fag hag." He lowered the paper. "For my money, I'm betting that Raymond punched his lights out to prevent Nadine from taking his head off with that skillet. If you ask me, the mayor should thank Raymond for saving his miserable life."

"Good god. Where's the mayor now?"

"Who the hell knows? Probably off figuring out whose bowl of Cheerios he's going to piss in next."

"You said that Nadine can't get the bond money together tonight?"

He nodded.

"Suppose I put it up for her? Quietly. Just between us."

"You have access to that much cash?"

"Well, not on me—but I've got it at home. We're replacing all the fencing in the south pasture and are paying the crew in cash."

"That would work. This is very generous. Are you sure about it?"

"Yeah. In fact, don't even tell Nadine I was here."

"How about I have Charlie meet you at the courthouse? She can bring the receipt back here after you post the bond. That'll save you a trip."

"Perfect." Maddie stood up. "Thanks, Byron. You're a good man."

"I don't know about that." He stood up, too. They shook hands.

"Maddie . . ." he began. "I'm . . . I want you to know . . ."

"That my mom is terrific?" she asked. "That you're behaving like a perfect gentleman?"

She could tell he was trying not to smile. He stood there like an embarrassed teenager.

"Something like that," he said.

"Stop worrying, Byron. I'm not freaking out."

"You aren't?"

She shook her head.

"That's a relief. Now if we can just get your mom not to, everything will be fine."

"Yeah." She grinned at him. "Good luck with *that* one, bucko. Now, get me the hell out of here before I run into Nadine—or any more of my patients."

It was a slow night at Aunt Bea's.

Bert and Sonny had taken to stopping in a couple nights a week after finishing up at Dr. Heller's because Sonny loved the fried chicken. Bert didn't much care for the chicken, but he did like the country steak. And Aunt Bea's had real mashed potatoes—even though he wished their corn wasn't that frozen kind that was always too yellow.

On Tuesday nights, the special was stew beef with cornbread and two sides. They both liked that. And Sonny picked up two desserts because it had been a mostly dry spring and the strawberries were extra sweet.

They sat in their usual booth—the one in the corner closest to the street. They liked this one because it was a holdover from way back, when the restaurant had been a Burger Chef. It was the only booth in the place that still had vinyl upholstery—in a wild, green and white design with silver sparkles. Sonny said it felt better on his back. Bert agreed. He liked the way the vinyl got warmer the longer you sat on it. And in the summertime, it pretty much worked in the opposite way.

Vinyl was an amazing invention. It didn't make sense that most restaurants now rejected it in favor of those hard, molded-plastic seats that were like sitting on the lid of a trash bin. Sonny said they did that intentionally so folks wouldn't tarry too long over their food. He said that was why most of these establishments played awful music, too.

"Nobody wants to hang around a place where they have to listen to old stuff that was bad even when it wadn't old."

The music didn't really bother Bert. He was more inclined just to tune out things he didn't want to hear. His ex-wife told him that was the main reason she wanted a divorce—because he never listened to her.

It didn't much help his case when he had to ask her to repeat what she'd just said.

But that was all water under the dam.

Wait . . . was that right? He always got that one wrong.

"Hey, Sonny?"

Sonny raised his eyes from his plate full of shredded beef and gravy.

"Is that expression water *under* the dam, or water *over* the dam?"

"It depends. Are you talkin' about somethin' good or somethin' bad?"

Bert had to think about that one. When his wife first talked about leaving and taking Buddy, it felt bad. But now that Buddy was back living with him, he had to admit that it worked out pretty good.

"I guess both," he said to Sonny.

"Then it's *over* the dam. Over the dam can be good or bad, depending on what kind of water it is."

That didn't help. Bert knew that introducing a new variable to the expression would make it even harder for him to remember it right.

"Why'd you ask?" Sonny followed up. "Are you still worried about using them wrong drawer pulls in Dr. Heller's kitchen? It only took us ten minutes to swap 'em out for the right ones."

"No. It's not that. I was just thinkin' about how I got Buddy back from Ruby."

"Well, you didn't have no way of knowin' she was gonna take up with that Bath Fitter guy and move to Canada."

"Yeah."

"Besides, Buddy was old enough to make his own decision about where he wanted to live."

Bert nodded.

"That boy's done a good job pickin' up extra work. And who knows what will happen with that helmet thing of his? He could end up owning this whole town."

It was true. Buddy'd taken to giving Henry Lawrence rides home from school on his scooter. And Buddy being Buddy, nothing would do but he'd make sure his little Bluebird had a helmet to wear. So, he just made one for him—out of Styrofoam and car tape.

It looked pretty good, too. Real authentic. Good enough that the high school football coach heard about it and asked Bert if he could look it over. Now the Chargers were all wearing headgear inserts based on Buddy's design. There was even talk about gettin' Azalea Freemantle to use her big-time video game contacts to set up a meeting with the NFL Players Association.

It was what they called a pipe dream. But sometimes, miracles happened.

"Things sure do seem to be hoppin' at the jail tonight."

Sonny wasn't kidding. Their booth had a good view of the Sheriff's Department. The parking lot was filled up and there were cars lining the street in front of the courthouse.

"Is this the lottery night or somethin'?"

People tended to act crazy when those jackpots got so big—and right now, the PowerBall was up over four hundred million.

"No," Sonny explained. "Them drawings is always on Saturday."

"Well, what do you think's goin' on, then?"

"Prob'ly somethin' to do with the full moon."

"Idn't that Junior's loaner car parked over there in front of Harold's place?"

Sonny's boy, Harold, ran the local beauty shop, Hairport '75.

"Looks like it," Sonny agreed.

"I hadn't seen that hunk a junk on the road since the tornado."

"Well, I was at the mayor's office yesterday mornin', and I heard that somebody spray-painted all kinds of mess on his car. I suspect it's out at Junior's gettin' cleaned up."

"Why were you at the mayor's office?"

"Stink bugs."

Sonny was the town exterminator—in addition to helping Bert out with renovation jobs.

"Ain't it a little early for stink bugs?"

"Not this year." Sonny used a hunk of cornbread to mop up some gravy. "Everything's comin' on too soon. Them stink bugs are like a warning shot. It's gonna be a long, hot summer."

"Good thing we got that AC working at Dr. Heller's."

"Well, don't tell nobody that it ain't been inspected, yet."

"What in thunder is the holdup on them inspections? It never took this long before."

"I asked about it yesterday. That Halsey girl that works there

141

looked embarrassed. She said the inspections department is all backed up."

"Backed up with what?" Bert asked. "It ain't like there's a new construction craze around here."

Sonny shook his head. "I think she knew it wadn't true. She wouldn't look me in the eye."

"I feel sorry for them people. It ain't right what that man gets away with."

"Harold says you just gotta play the game."

"He still messin' with Harold?"

Sonny nodded. "He's forcin' him to put in some kind of special holding tank and remediation setup for all them hair dyes and perm solutions. Harold says the expense might put him out of business." Sonny tsked. "It ain't like he was flushin' all that mess down the toilet. He was already savin' it all in a big drum and sending it off to a place in Blacksburg that takes care of all that."

"Sure sounds like a nuisance thing to me."

"Don't it?" Sonny pulled one of the small dessert bowls over and dug into the strawberry cobbler.

Bert took the other one. "For what it's worth, he gives Buddy a hard time, too."

"Mark my words. Someday, somebody's gonna hurt someone."

Bert laughed. "Ain't that an Eagles' song?"

"How would I know? I don't listen to that modern music."

"That ain't modern music, grandpa. It's older'n Buddy."

Sonny shrugged and took another bite of the cobbler.

"Hey, hey." Bert gestured toward the entrance. "Here comes Doc Stevenson."

The big glass door opened and Maddie Stevenson entered. All conversation in the restaurant stopped as the smattering of diners watched her approach the counter.

A few folks called out hearty greetings. She smiled and waved back at them all.

"That is one fine-lookin' woman," Sonny muttered.

Bert agreed. "She takes after her mama."

"But she's tall, like her daddy. And she's got his way with people, too."

"He was a good man. We're all lucky she came back here to live after he passed."

Maddie placed her order and stood back to wait while they pulled it together for her. That was when she noticed them sitting in their corner booth.

"Hey, guys," she said with a smile. She walked over to greet them. "How're things going out in Bridle Creek?"

"Just fine, Doc." Bert started to stand, but she stopped him.

"Don't get up. I can't stay. I'm just picking up something to take home."

"You workin' late?" he asked.

"Sort of." She smiled at him. "I'm on my own tonight, and I had an errand to run in town. I thought I'd stop in and pick up some contraband for dinner."

Bert could see the server filling a Styrofoam container with fried chicken.

"Sonny says they make the best wings," he agreed.

"True. But I'm getting the strips." She lowered her voice. "That way, I don't have to hide the bones from Syd."

"Why?" Sonny asked. "She don't like fried chicken?"

Maddie laughed. It was a rich sound that made everything in the place seem classier.

"It's not the chicken. It's what eating the chicken does to my cholesterol."

Bert couldn't speak to the doctor's cholesterol, but everything else about her seemed to be humming along just fine.

"You look pretty dang healthy to me," Sonny said.

Bert kicked him under the table.

"Hey!" Sonny grabbed his leg. "Why'd you do that?"

"I didn't do anything."

"You just kicked me." Sonny was rubbing his shin. "*Hard.*"

"You *guys* . . ." The doctor didn't seem offended. "How is Mom's place coming along?"

"Just fine," Bert replied. "She got that piano all tuned up today."

"Yeah," Sonny chimed in. "She was fixin' some special dinner tonight."

Bert tried to kick him again but Sonny yanked his leg out of harm's way.

"Why do you keep doin' that?" he complained.

"Why do you keep flappin' your jaws?" Bert replied.

Maddie held up a hand. "It's okay, guys. I know about Mom's social life."

"You do?" they asked in unison.

She nodded.

The server called out to tell her that her takeout order was ready.

"I need to scoot," she said. "Thank you for watching out for Mom. I know she's in good hands with you two." She smiled at them and walked off to retrieve her food.

They watched her leave the restaurant and cross the parking lot toward her Jeep.

Sonny was still rubbing his shin. "You had no call to kick me like that," he complained.

"Yes, I did. You're worse than a old woman."

Sonny looked back at him with a blank expression. "What's that supposed to mean?"

Bert rolled his eyes. "You don't need to be tellin' tales on Dr. Heller—especially to her daughter."

"I didn't tell her nothin' she didn't already know. You heard her."

Bert ignored him. Something more interesting was brewing outside.

"Here comes trouble," he said.

"What is it?"

"Look." He pointed out the window. "It's Junior's loaner car."

"Well, I swanny. Why'd the mayor stop behind Doc Stevenson's Jeep?"

"I dunno," Bert said. "But it looks like he's gettin' out."

"Hells bells," Sonny said. "He looks hoppin' mad."

"This ain't gonna be good."

Dr. Stevenson was now out of her Jeep and the two of them were standing between their vehicles having words. They made an odd pair. The tall doctor topped the mayor by at least six inches. It was almost comical to watch him stand there fussing and squawking up at her like an angry catbird. He kept pointing at the courthouse and shaking his finger at the doctor. She seemed a lot calmer than he was. But all that changed when he stepped closer and poked his long, skinny index finger into her collarbone.

"Uh, oh . . ." Bert knew this wasn't gonna end well.

Doc Stevenson slapped his hand away so fast her arm was a blur. Even from this distance, Bert could tell her blue eyes were blazing like fire.

He fumbled for his cell phone.

"What the heck are you doin'?" Sonny asked.

"What do ya think?" Bert was already dialing. "I'm callin' her mama."

Maddie counted to five before she put the Jeep in park and got out to see why the mayor had blocked her into her parking space.

She didn't have to wait very long.

It was clear that he was seething with anger—he wasn't trying very hard to conceal it. His face was beet red. As a clinician, she couldn't help but notice how the cast to his complexion accentuated the purple contusion on his jaw.

Apparently, Raymond had a good right cross.

"How dare you interfere with due process." He spat the words out at her.

She folded her arms.

"Mr. Mayor, I have *no* idea what you're talking about."

"Don't play coy with me, Doctor Stevenson." He thrust out an arm and pointed to the courthouse across the street. "I *know* what you did. This matter does *not* concern you."

"Mr. Watson?" Maddie sighed. "It's been a long day and I'm

tired. Will you kindly move your—*conveyance*—so I can go home and enjoy my food while it's still hot?"

"Oh, no. I'm not finished yet." He took a step closer to her. "Don't think I'm unaware of how much you enjoy inserting yourself into the middle of everyone else's business around here. You may choose to regard yourself as local gentry—but you're no better than the rest of those deviant freaks you choose to associate with."

Maddie took a deep breath. She hadn't slugged anyone since the seventh grade, but right now he was making it hard for her to resist the temptation to give it another try.

"I'm not certain which aberrant freaks you're referring to, Mr. Mayor. But I can assure you that any combination of them would be preferable to my present company." She glared at him. "Please move your car. *Now.* This conversation is over."

He ignored her request.

"You think you're better than everyone? That you have some exalted right to do and say whatever you want because you went to the best schools and had everything handed to you—while the rest of us are forced to work and fight for everything we have?" He shook his bony finger at her. "You're a perfect example of what's wrong with this country. And I, for one, am here to stop you and your kind from carrying out your godless mission to destroy the moral fabric of our town."

Maddie had a clear sense that if she didn't walk away from him—and soon—she'd end up occupying Raymond's spot in the jail cell. She was just about to turn away and head back inside the restaurant when Watson made a big mistake. He gave up on shaking his finger in her face and chose, instead, to drive his point home by jabbing it into her clavicle.

Maddie reflexively smacked his hand away with so much speed and force it caused him to lurch sideways and nearly lose his footing.

"Do not *ever* touch me again," she hissed.

He looked at her with surprise and more than a trace of wariness.

She glared back at him.

Their wordless faceoff continued until he cut his eyes away. "Um, Doctor Stevenson?"

The voice came from behind her.

She turned around.

It was Bert Townsend. He was holding out an open flip phone.

"I got your mama on the line," he said. "She wants to talk to you . . . *right now.*"

The drive to Bridle Creek took less than ten minutes, but it was long enough for Maddie to bring her blood pressure down from the stratosphere. Now that she had a few minutes and as many miles separating herself from the events in the parking lot, she could reflect on the creative way Bert and Sonny had brought the altercation to an end.

It was pretty inspired.

Nobody had called her mother to express concern about her behavior since . . . well. She really couldn't recall another time. This was a first—for her and for her mother.

To be fair, she wasn't prone to getting into trouble. At least not the kind of trouble that snowballed into an occasion for her to punch somebody's lights out.

Gerald Watson. *What an ass.*

No. That wasn't strong enough. The man was more than contemptible, brutish and provincial. He was dangerous. She knew that now. She'd seen it in his eyes when he confronted her. There was a raw, naked ugliness there that terrified her. She was certain that David's decision to challenge Watson in the upcoming election would escalate the mayor's rhetoric and energize his increasingly hostile attacks on all the "aberrant freaks" in the community.

Freaks like her . . .

It was a paradox. Returning to Jericho to live after her father's death had been a relatively easy decision to make—even though she harbored no illusions about the social and political

147

conservatism of the area. To be fair, she'd never felt directly affected by either—and she felt the sting of the mayor's words when he accused her of being "local gentry." It was true that she benefited from the luxury of an implied status that came with her position. For many years now, that status had allowed her to live an idealized life, tucked up inside her pastoral bubble on the periphery of the hardscrabble world that gave rise to dark prophets like Gerald Watson.

But those days were over.

It seemed ironic to her that David had been so quick to hone in on the ominous threads that linked Watson's recent string of administrative edicts. She'd been guilty of passing off his epic rants about the mayor as just the latest examples of his penchant for overreaction and excessive statement. It was true that Watson had always been a self-righteous jerk. But David had been the first to recognize that the mayor's simmering homophobia had finally reached its boiling point when the country's slow march toward marriage equality finally landed squarely in the middle of Jericho's town square.

That so-called abomination was the proverbial beam in the mayor's eye—and it was leading him into a myopic frenzy of lashing out at anyone he regarded as complicit.

Tonight's events changed everything. It wasn't that she no longer saw the goodness and simple beauty that defined this remarkable place called Jericho. She did. But she also understood that caring enough to preserve those qualities came with a price—a price that meant surrendering her comfortable seat on the sidelines.

Self-styled autocrats like Gerald Watson succeeded by preying on fear. They wrapped their accusations and empty promises in righteous indignation, then hawked their own twisted brand of miracle cures to the public like patent medicine.

The adage was true. Once the scales fell from your eyes, you could never see things the way you did before. And what she saw now was a once bright and vivid landscape dissolving into a palette of bleak and sinister hues.

◊ ◊ ◊

When Maddie pulled in behind the refurbished bungalow, she was surprised by how much progress Bert and Sonny had made on the exterior. All the shutters were in place now, and they'd nearly finished cladding the chimney with reclaimed river rock. That had been Celine's idea. She liked tying the house more directly to its setting—high on a bluff overlooking the river.

Maddie had thought her mother was crazy when she announced her decision to buy the old house that sat abandoned for decades, on the edge of an overgrown pasture in a remote part of the county. But Celine had been right about it—just like she'd been right about so many other things.

On their first walk through it, her mother observed that any structure determined enough to persevere and remain standing through nearly two centuries of catastrophic weather events and human neglect deserved their respect.

She said the house had good bones.

Even Bert and Sonny said the process of setting the place to rights would be as much about undoing the things that were wrong, as it would be about adding back refinements like insulation, centralized heat and indoor plumbing. Those things were just window dressing, they said. The house already had all the things it needed to be good and livable. They just had to uncover it, clean it up and stay out of its way.

Looking at the place now, Maddie realized how true that was. She had no doubt that her mother would thrive out here. Probably more than she had in any of the places she'd lived before. She believed this was true because her mother was finally giving herself permission to be happy—and that was a sea change in attitude and behavior that Maddie was determined to support.

She collected her bag of food and went to meet her mother, who waved at her from the unfinished patio. It was a balmy night. Maddie could see that Celine had a makeshift table set up for them. She was apparently confident that the storms firing up tonight would skirt around them as they had the last few nights. Faint flashes continued to light up the ridges off to the northeast. She hoped Syd and Roma Jean weren't piloting that battered book wagon home in a downpour.

Celine stood up to greet her.

"The prodigal daughter returns."

Maddie rolled her eyes. "Better thirty-seven years late than never, I suppose."

"I won't argue with that. Do you need to heat up your food?"

"No." Maddie set her bag down on the table and gave her mother a hug. "Right now, I could eat the bag."

There was a rumble of thunder, but it still seemed distant enough not to pose a threat.

They both sat down.

"I made us some hot tea. Chinese Gunpowder. It seemed appropriate given the circumstances. Or would you prefer something stronger?" Celine smiled at her. "I know from experience that brawling can make one thirsty."

"Yeah. Byron and I were reminiscing about that earlier when I went by the jail."

Celine seemed momentarily flustered by Maddie's mention of Byron. But she chose to follow up only on the second part of Maddie's observation.

"Why were you at the jail?"

"You didn't hear?"

"I guess not. But then, I don't tend to monitor police band radio."

"I just assumed you had your own conduit to goings-on in local law enforcement."

"Maddie?" Celine laid a hand on her arm. "We can discuss Byron later. Right now, I want to hear about how you ended up staging your own version of *High Noon* in the parking lot at Aunt Bea's. Okay?"

"Okay. Fair enough."

Celine withdrew her hand and reached for the teapot. It was a beauty—one Maddie had not seen before.

"Where'd you get that one?" she asked. Celine loved tea and had an impressive collection of pots from all over the world.

"You like it? I think it's my favorite." She held it up and rotated it so Maddie could appreciate it from all angles. "I got it last week in North Carolina—in Seagrove."

"It's beautiful. I like the color of the glaze."

"They call it bronze. It's vintage Jugtown—a very traditional design. One the potters there have been making for generations. Something about it seemed right for the house, you know? A perfect synthesis of old and new. I love everything about it. The weight. The balance. The old-signature domed lid. It pours perfectly, too."

Celine was right. The teapot's simple elegance derived from its restrained but masterful combination of form and function.

"I agree. It looks like a piece of art." She held up a mug so her mother could pour her some of the strong, fragrant tea. "Why were you in Seagrove?"

"Sonny told me about a blacksmith there. I wanted to find someone who could replicate the original, box-style rim locks on the interior doors." She refilled her own mug and set the pot back down on its trivet. "As you may know, such antiquities are woefully absent from the hardware bins at Home Depot."

"Any luck?"

"Oh, yes. The good news is that the blacksmith there can make the locks for me. The bad news is that it may take a year to get them. Apparently, he has quite a backlog of special orders."

"I knew I should've gone into a trade." Maddie unpacked her Styrofoam box of chicken. "What will you do in the meantime?"

"Fortunately, one of the advantages of living alone is that you rarely have to close doors." Celine regarded Maddie's food with a raised eyebrow. "Are you really going to eat all of that?"

Maddie's face fell.

"Not at the rate I'm going. Please don't tell me you're going to rat me out to Syd?"

"Of course not. I was simply going to ask if you'd consider sharing it with me."

"Oh." Maddie brightened up. "Sure. Want part of this biscuit, too?"

"Only the part that hasn't been soaking in that lake of mayo from the coleslaw."

"I know." Maddie picked up the biscuit and blotted its underside on a paper napkin. "I don't understand why they make it like this."

"Your Oma was fond of saying that all gentiles thought mayonnaise was a food group."

Maddie paused mid-blot. "Did she really say that?"

"Oh, yes. She was quite a bigot."

"You never mentioned that before."

Celine shrugged. "You were too tender to hear it before."

Maddie broke off the dry part of the biscuit and handed it to her mother. "So, why are you telling me now?"

"Because now you're an accomplished street-fighter who thumbs her nose at adversity."

"I wouldn't go that far."

"No? Then how about setting the record straight. Tell me what actually happened between you and the mayor tonight."

While they ate chicken strips and drank their tea, Maddie filled her mother in on the evening's chain of events. She ended her story at the point where Bert showed up, holding out his cell phone and meekly telling Maddie that he had her mama on the line.

"That was a pretty inspired intervention," she said. "The mayor was as flabbergasted by it as I was. I assume it was your idea?"

"Mine?" Celine pointed a finger at herself. "Oh, no. I was as surprised as you were. All Bert said when I answered the phone was that you were about to get into a fist fight with the mayor and I needed to talk you down—*immediately*. The next thing I knew, you were on the line—sounding, I might add, just like your father did every time *he* got caught in the middle of a colossal lapse in judgment."

"Hey. I did not *have* a lapse in judgment—colossal or otherwise. I was minding my own business, trying peacefully to exit the parking lot with my hard-earned victuals, when that sorry excuse for a public servant accosted me and called me an amoral affront to decent society."

"He actually said that?"

"Well," Maddie clarified. "I think his exact phrase was 'aberrant freak,' but it's the meaning that matters, not the vernacular."

"So, you decided to slug him?"

"No." Maddie rolled her eyes. "I did *not* decide to slug him. He made the mistake of jamming his eerily long index finger into my collarbone and I slapped his hand away. I won't deny that I *would've* slugged him if he tried to touch me again." She shivered. "There's something seriously creepy about that man, Mom. I think he's genuinely evil."

"What are you going to do?"

"Do?" Maddie was confused. "Do about what?"

"I think it's fairly obvious that you've catapulted to the myopic center of his crosshairs. I doubt he'll let up on you, now."

"Well, he can just bring it on. I'm not afraid of him."

"I'm sure you aren't. But what about Syd? And Henry?"

Maddie didn't immediately catch her meaning. "What about them?"

"He may use them to get back at you."

"He wouldn't dare."

"Don't be too sure of that. If he's as dangerous and unscrupulous as both you and David suggest, he'll be certain to use anything at his disposal to damage your reputation."

"Such as?"

"Take your pick. You're a lesbian. You live with another woman—out of wedlock—and the two of you are de facto foster parents to the innocent child of a disabled veteran. Your live-in lover is a divorcee who happens to be an outspoken, county-paid peddler of banned books. Your best friends are gay men who make a living performing same-sex marriages, and who knows what other manner of Bacchanalian rites, at their secluded B&B. Your aging mother amuses herself by translating German porn and is actively scandalizing the county by sleeping with the sheriff—who, by the way, is twelve years younger than she is." Celine paused in her recitation. "Any of that resonate for you?"

Maddie was stunned. "I see you've given this some thought."

"Not really. I'm just quick on my feet."

She took a moment to consider all her mother had said.

There was another rumble of thunder—closer this time. It appeared that tonight, the storms would not pass them by. The irony of that fact was becoming hard to mistake.

"This is a lot to take in."

"I know it is."

"Um. Mom?"

"Yes?"

"Is it possible that all of that was just an elaborate way for you to fess up that you're sleeping with Byron?"

"Maybe. Or it could have been a masterful exercise in hyperbole."

Maddie smiled at her. "I don't think so."

Celine sighed. "You're right. I needed to come clean. One of us needed to say it."

"I'm glad you told me. Although, you did bury the lede in your litany of horrors."

"Unfortunately, that's always been my style."

"True," Maddie agreed. "But now you've got an opportunity to change that."

"Meaning?"

"Meaning . . . Byron is a good man. It's obvious he cares for you. Why not give yourself another shot at happiness?"

"The difference in our ages . . ." Celine didn't finish her statement.

"What about it?" Maddie asked.

Celine didn't reply.

There was a flash of light followed by a rumble of thunder. A solitary drop of rain landed on the teapot and rolled down its domed lid.

"Mom?" Maddie leaned forward. "It does not matter. Not one bit. The only person who cares about it is you."

"I don't need this complication in my life right now."

"Well, hell." Maddie sat back. "Who *does* need the complication that relationships bring? It's a tradeoff—like the unwelcome side effect of a medicine that can save your life. And if you're lucky, you end up getting a hell of a lot more happiness than frustration out of the bargain."

Celine gazed back at her without replying. Maddie knew better than to try and press her point. Eventually, her mother shook her head and smiled.

"Who taught you how to argue?"

"*You* did."

"No wonder you make such a compelling case."

"Does that mean you agree with me?"

"Not entirely," Celine demurred. "But it does mean I'll take your suggestions under advisement."

"I can't ask for more than that."

"Good." Her mother pushed back her chair. "It's starting to rain. Let's get all of this inside before we get soaked."

"Okay." Maddie began collecting her food containers and silverware. "I wanted to come in and see the piano, anyway."

"Maddie?" Her mother laid a hand on her arm. "One other thing before we leave this topic?"

"What?"

"I wasn't kidding about the rest of what I said to you. I've known men like Gerald Watson. Don't underestimate him, and don't take him for granted."

"I won't."

"And whatever else happens, do not allow him to bait you again like he did tonight."

"I'll take it under advisement."

Celine gave her a wry smile and picked up her prized teapot.

"Then it appears I can't ask for more, either."

Chapter 6

The roads in this part of the county were barely drivable on a good day. They were mostly a latticework of ruts, connected by prehistoric slivers of pavement.

But today, getting from point A to point B was worse than usual. It was more like competing in a demolition derby. The ruts were all filled with water from last night's rain—and that made it impossible to tell which ones were deep enough to do real damage to the undercarriage of a car if you hit them.

David's Mini bottomed out again. For about the tenth time, the top of his head slammed into the frame of the car's cabriolet top.

"Damn it!" He compulsively tried to fluff the hair on the crown of his head.

It was a fool's errand. There was no amount of product that could get his hair to stand up to this magnitude of slammage. He looked at his reflection in the rearview mirror.

If this keeps up, I'm gonna have to borrow one of Michael's rugs . . .

Nobody knew that Michael was losing his hair. Well. At least *Michael* thought nobody knew. David thought it was obvious. He had tried numerous times to tell Michael that the various crown-toppers he was using were like cheap animal pelts.

Not that *expensive* animal pelts would be any more authentic . . .

Michael kept them all discreetly organized on a shelf at the back of their closet. David thought they looked like swarthy hamsters in a police lineup.

It was a touchy subject. One they couldn't talk about without arguing.

Just like this canvassing. Michael was growing impatient with how much time David was spending going door-to-door to make his case for why he was running for mayor. But he *had* to. As a write-in candidate, the only hope he had to stay on the ballot was to get name recognition by personally introducing himself to the voters. Assuming, of course, that he could interest anyone *to* vote in the upcoming primary. In an off-year election when there were no big statewide or national contests, the turnout in this area tended to be . . . low. That is, if you called *nine* percent participation "low."

He figured that all he had to do was pique the interest—or arouse the ire—of half that many people to clear the first hurdle. His approach was simple. If the average estimates were right, then one in ten people in this county were gay. And even if they weren't, most of them either knew someone or were related to someone who was. And if *that* inducement fell flat, he knew they all got hairdos, sent funeral arrangements, had kids who took music lessons from his mama, or used their Groupon discounts to eat food cooked at queer-owned eateries.

Besides, Watson was a "come here." He wasn't local and nobody knew his people. Whereas, David's ancestors had been showing up on the birth and baptismal rolls at the Methodist church for more than two centuries.

The simple truth was that, in these parts, blood was always thicker than umbrage.

So, he made his house calls, and he spent ninety-nine percent of each visit catching up on how his mama was doing now that she was retired—and whether or not he thought that new maximum security prison they were building out at Danby would bring all kinds of undesirables into the area like they said. Of course, David was never really sure who "they" were—but he did a fair amount of speculating anyway.

He only had one stop left to make today—at Celine's. He needed to drop off the next few chapters of the book they were working on. *More Tales of Rolf and Tobi: Two Hot Farm Boys at a Biergarten* promised to be an even bigger seller than their first foray in the burgeoning German slash fic genre. Michael thought he was crazy to keep working on the anthology, but David insisted the books were entirely too specific to show up on anybody's radar in Jericho.

He hit another mud-filled pothole, sending a wave of muck up the driver's side of his car. This damn mud factor was another thing. Already his car looked like it had a bad case of *scorbutus*. He'd learned all about the pernicious skin disease from a Nat Geo special on Civil War prisons . . .

Someone was walking along the roadside up ahead. He slowed his car to a crawl so he wouldn't risk splashing them with muck as he passed. When he drew closer, he recognized the young woman. He stopped and called out to her.

"Hey, Dorothy. Where're you headed?"

She seemed startled but not wary. She walked over toward his car. She was carrying a tied-up Food City bag.

"Hey, Mr. Jenkins. Today is bookmobile day." She held up the plastic bag. "I got off the school bus over here so I could wait for it."

"Where does it stop?"

"Up at the crossroads." She pointed ahead, in the direction she'd been walking.

"What time does it get there?"

She shrugged her narrow shoulders. "Some time around four."

He looked at his watch. "That's more than an hour from now."

"It's okay. I don't mind waiting."

David didn't like the idea of the girl being alone out here on a desolate road for that long. Another thought occurred to him.

"How will you get home from here?"

"Walk."

"Walk? Dorothy. That's gotta be more than five miles."

She shook her head. "It's not that far. I take a shortcut across the river."

"There's no bridge around here," he began. Then he realized

what she meant. "You mean you take a shortcut *through* the river?"

She nodded.

Dorothy intended to wade across the river? After more than two inches of rain?

There was no way he was letting that happen.

"Couldn't your father come and pick you up?"

Her eyes widened and she took a step back from the car. "*No.* I mean, no—he's too busy. He won't have time to come. Please don't tell him, Mr. Jenkins. I don't want to bother him at work."

"Hey." David held up a hand to ease her agitation. "Don't worry, Dorothy. I won't call him. But I tell you what—how about you ride along with me? I have to drop something off at Dr. Heller's house, then I can bring you back to the bookmobile."

She seemed reluctant to accept.

"Look," David continued. "I think Henry's gonna be there having a piano lesson. I bet he'd wanna go with you to get some new books. I can drop you both off."

He was careful not to mention that he'd also wait around afterward, and drive each of them home.

"A piano lesson?" she asked.

David smiled at her. "Yeah. His gramma just got her big piano moved back here from California. If I know Henry, he's not very happy about it." He reached across the front seat and opened the passenger door. "Come on. Hop in. I know she'd like to meet you."

She hesitated only a few seconds before acquiescing and joining him inside the car. She took care to secure her bag full of books on the floorboard between her feet before putting on her seatbelt.

David continued his careful progress along the rutted road.

"I thought school was already out?"

"We have three more days," she replied.

"Why's it so late this year?"

"We have to make up for snow days."

They rode along in silence for another quarter mile.

"You know," he observed. "I think we'd make better time if we just drove up through the ditch."

"I don't think so," Dorothy pointed out. "Not unless your car floats."

David looked over at her. Her expression gave nothing away.

"Did you just make a joke?" he teased. "I don't want to be hasty, but it sure sounded like a joke."

"Was it funny?" she asked him.

"It was, actually."

"It was a joke," she said.

"This from the woman who wades across the river and calls it a shortcut?"

"It *is* a shortcut."

"Do you float?"

"I can if I have to," she explained.

"Well. This hunk of metal does *not* float."

"Then it should stay out of the ditch."

David laughed.

"You know, Dorothy? I think this is the start of a beautiful friendship."

She didn't reply but he could tell by her posture that she was more relaxed. For one thing, she loosened the vice-like grip her feet had on her bag of books.

"What's that thing?"

He was surprised by her question. She was pointing at the storage well between their seats.

"You mean this?" David picked up the short, metal instrument and handed it to her. "It's a swanee whistle."

"A what?" Dorothy turned it over in her hands.

"An old-fashioned slide whistle. But this one's a pitch pipe."

"What's a pitch pipe?"

"Blow into it." David nodded at the whistle. "Give it a try."

Dorothy timidly blew into it. The sound it emitted was a thin, tinny hiss.

"No," David corrected. "*Really* blow into it."

She tried it again. This time, an earsplitting, perfect C rang out.

161

David jumped and hit his head on the convertible top. Again.

"See?" He looked in the mirror and fluffed his hair. "That gauge on the end changes the pitch when you blow into the whistle. That way you can use it to tune different musical instruments—or make sure you're singing in the right key. Which, by the way, the choir at First Methodist Church could *definitely* use."

"Is that why you carry it around—so you can fix bad singing?"

"No, but that's an interesting concept." He warmed to the idea. "I could be the next great superhero, and save the tone-deaf multitudes from having to sit through excruciatingly bad cantatas."

"Superheroes wear special outfits."

"Honey," David waved a hand, "that would be the *least* of my problems. Unlike most men, I happen to look fabulous in Spandex." He thought about it. "What I *would* need, though, is a great name. You know? An alter-ego."

"How about Calliope?"

"Calliope?" He looked at her. "You mean like those obnoxious steam organs?"

"No. Like the Greek goddess of poetry."

"*Goddess?*" David asked.

"Oh." Dorothy immediately seemed embarrassed. "Sorry . . ."

"No, no. I'm *good* with the whole goddess idea. I'm just not sure about the *name*. It's a tad too . . . *carnivalish*. Don't you think?"

"What about Orpheus? He was Calliope's son."

"What's with you and all the Greek mythology references?" he asked.

She shrugged. "I like it. I read some books about it."

"Is that what's in there?" David pointed at her grocery bag full of library books.

"No. I have books about it at home."

"I thought that topic seemed a tad dense for Roma Jean's bookmobile." He pondered Dorothy's suggestion. "So. Orpheus, you said?"

She nodded.

"I don't think so . . . it sounds too much like . . . *orifice*. I'd never live it down."

Dorothy smiled.

David thought it was remarkable how much a simple action like smiling could alter her appearance. She really was a pretty girl, with her shiny blond hair and green eyes. She looked almost like a younger version of Syd—except for the weariness and resignation that bound her up like an ill-fitting garment.

He knew from personal experience what that was like, and he tended to recognize it in other people right away. And he didn't have to wonder much about where it came from; his own father had been a lot like Dorothy's.

He also knew if he asked her any questions about it, she'd be as skittish as a long-tailed cat in a room full of rocking chairs. Just as he'd been at her age, whenever anyone asked him about *his* home life.

Honor among thieves. They all abided by the unspoken pact of silence.

He took the turnoff for Celine's. The lane leading up to her house was an immediate improvement over the county road. It was obvious that Bert and Sonny had been after it with the grader.

"You're gonna love this place," he said.

He parked the car and turned off the engine. "We need to bring that pitch pipe along with us. It's for Celine."

Dorothy handed it to him. "Does she use it to tune her piano?"

"No. I think she's giving it to Buddy."

"Buddy? Why?"

"Well." David retrieved a file folder from the back seat and opened the car door. "It turns out that Buddy likes music."

They walked together toward the house. David could hear a halting and jumbled sequence of notes forming a disjointed refrain from *The New World Symphony*. Apparently, Henry was grinding his way through volume one of *Alfred's Piano Book for Beginners*.

Celine was such a traditionalist . . .

The back door was open but David knocked loudly on it anyway.

163

"Anybody home?" he called out.

The music abruptly stopped and he could hear the pounding of small feet. Henry raced around the corner and made a beeline for them.

"Uncle David! Dorothy!" Henry hurled himself at David. "Gramma C. told me you were coming."

"Hi ya, Sport." David hugged him. "Dorothy is gonna go with you to the bookmobile. I thought I'd give you both a ride." He waved at Celine, who entered the kitchen at a more sedate pace. "That is, as soon as your piano lesson is over."

"It's over," Henry insisted. "Isn't it over, Gramma C.?"

Celine sighed and looked at David. "How many notes did you hear?"

"About eleven, give or take."

"I guess that counts." She smiled at Dorothy. "Hello, Dorothy. It's nice to see you again."

"Hi, Dr. Heller." Dorothy looked around the big kitchen. "Your house is really pretty."

"Show her the piano, Gramma C.," Henry insisted. "She wants to take lessons." He looked at Dorothy. "Don't you, Dorothy?"

"Well . . ." Dorothy seemed embarrassed by Henry's suggestion.

"You and Miss Freemantle are always talking about how ladies play the piano," he continued.

"That's just in books." Dorothy gave Celine an apologetic look. "Miss Freemantle was telling me about *Pride and Prejudice*."

"One of my favorite books." Celine nodded. "Although Elizabeth Bennet enjoyed playing the piano about as much as Henry does."

"See, Henry?" David nudged him. "You're in good company."

Henry looked confused. "Who is Liz Beth Bendit?"

"She's the heroine in one of those hallmarks of so-called *great* literature that nobody's ever read—right Celine?" David batted his eyes at her. "Unlike *this* little gem *we're* working on." He held up the file folder that was fat with pages of untranslated German erotica.

"Yes, David." Celine conceded. "That's *exactly* right. Now, why don't you and Henry fix us all something cold to drink?" She extended a hand to Dorothy, who hesitated before taking it. "I'm going to show Dorothy the piano."

'Sounds good to me." David put the file folder and the battered pitch pipe down next to a bright blue bowl full of peaches that sat atop a table by the window. "Any requests?"

"Chocolate milk!" Henry cried.

"Seriously, dude?" David walked toward Celine's fridge. "You need to aim your sights a little higher."

Dorothy had never seen anything like Dr. Heller's piano.

It sat off to one side of the large room she called her studio, away from a row of windows that overlooked the river. The room had a high ceiling and two walls covered with white bookcases. The shelves were all filled with what had to be hundreds of books. There wasn't much other furniture in the room—just two chairs, a footstool and a couple of small tables. The tables were covered with books. And music. There were big, loose pages of music everywhere.

There were paintings on the walls, too. A couple of them were very modern-looking—big squares of color on giant canvasses. But there was one that seemed different from the rest. It was a black chalk drawing of a young woman and a dark-haired child. She thought the woman in the picture looked an awful lot like Dr. Stevenson—but she was afraid to stare at it too long, and she was too shy to ask Dr. Heller about it.

But the piano was different. Even though she tried, she couldn't do anything but stare at it. That was mostly because it was the biggest thing in the room. Although Dorothy figured it would be the biggest thing in any size room—even one five times this big.

It was black and shiny and it sat there without making a sound—but even its silence seemed loud. She stood beside it with her eyes closed and imagined she could feel the vibration from the last notes it had played. They surged up from the plank

165

floor into her shoes, up her legs, and along her arms to reach her twitching fingertips. She thought about Mr. Jenkins and his swanee whistle. He said it could help a bad choir find the right key.

He was right.

In that one moment, she knew—the way she always knew when it mattered—that something finally had come along that could make right her own chorus of bad voices.

She raised her hand to touch it, but stopped herself in time. It didn't belong to her.

"Don't be afraid of it, Dorothy." Dr. Heller sat down on the padded bench in front of the keyboard and patted the space beside her. "Come and sit down with me. Come and see that there is nothing here to fear."

How did Dr. Heller know what she was thinking?

"I don't want to hurt it," she said.

"You won't hurt it." Dr. Heller smiled at her. "I promise. It's bigger and stronger than both of us."

Dorothy sat down beside her. She could see their faces reflected in the shiny panel behind the keys. They looked the same, but different—just like those strange shapes that stared back at you when you stood in front of fun house mirrors.

"Do you want to try it?" Dr. Heller asked.

She watched the head that was hers, and not hers, nod.

"But I don't know what to do," she said.

"That's okay." Dr. Heller reached over to take hold of her right hand. "Lucky for you, I do."

Dr. Heller positioned her thumb and two fingers over three keys.

"A chord is built by combining notes one, three, and five." She touched each of Dorothy's fingers as she counted. "One, three, and five. Notes C, E, and G. And keys one, three and five are played by fingers one, three and five. Okay?"

"Okay."

"Good." Dr. Heller withdrew her hand. "Now press down on all three keys at once."

Dorothy complied. The piano made a big, perfect sound.

"Congratulations, Dorothy." Dr. Heller leaned into her. "You just played a perfect C major chord."

"I did?"

"Yes, you did."

Dorothy was still holding her fingers in place over the keys. "Can I try it again?"

"Of course."

Dorothy repeated the chord. It sounded perfect. Just like the first time. *It was incredible.* She could have stayed there all day, just playing the same three notes over and over.

"Are there other chords?" she asked Dr. Heller.

"Oh, yes. Many other chords—both major and minor."

"Can I learn them, too?"

"Do you want to learn them?"

Dorothy nodded.

"Henry told me that you're going to be staying with him three days a week after school lets out. Is that correct?"

"Yes, ma'am. In Troutdale."

Dr. Heller smiled at her.

"I think we can work something out."

Roma Jean was having a slow day. Normally, that drove her crazy, but today it gave her a chance to think through everything she and Miss Murphy had talked about last night on the drive back from Roanoke.

It rained cats and dogs most of the way home—especially through Blacksburg. It got so bad that Miss Murphy suggested they pull off the highway and find a place to wait out some of the bigger bands of storms that were rolling through. That was okay with Roma Jean. She wasn't too nervous about driving the bookmobile these days, but super-bad weather like they'd had last night made it harder than usual to gauge things like safe stopping distances. Nobody believed her, but that was the real reason she ran into so much stuff. She always knew where she wanted the truck to stop, but sometimes it had its own idea about how much farther it wanted to go.

They got off the interstate at the exit for Claytor Lake and found a Dairy Queen that was still open. Miss Murphy only got a cup of coffee, but Roma Jean got a large Orange Julius and a Dilly Bar.

Charlie always made fun of what she called Roma Jean's "pre-teen palate." But ever since she'd been a little girl, Roma Jean had loved Dilly Bars. Probably that was because the only time she ever got one was when her family went on vacation to Virginia Beach. They always stopped off in Danville to eat because it was close to halfway, and her daddy would treat them all to an ice cream after dinner.

Roma Jean always associated Dilly Bars with happy times, and being on the front end of something good. But last night, the experience of eating one quickly turned into something different. That was because they ended up having what she now thought of as "The Talk."

They hadn't been sitting down very long when Miss Murphy cleared her throat and said there was something she'd been putting off discussing with her. It only took about two seconds for Roma Jean to blush up to the roots of her hair. She could feel the heat spreading up from her neck.

She didn't have to wonder what Miss Murphy wanted to talk about. They'd been together all day long and she hadn't brought up *anything* until now. Well, at least she hadn't brought up anything out of the ordinary. They did have their usual conversations about books and whether they were doing enough stops out in the western part of the county. But the way Miss Murphy introduced this topic left no doubt what it concerned.

"I'm *really* sorry." She said it before Miss Murphy could get her first sentence out. "I know I shouldn't have done it, but I *had* to. Once I knew about it, I couldn't stop myself."

Miss Murphy was tapping her index finger on the side of her coffee cup. She looked concerned but not angry. At least *that* was a good thing.

"Roma Jean," she said. "If you were that upset about it, why didn't you come and talk with me? Before you acted?"

"I'm sorry. I really screwed up, didn't I?"

"I wouldn't say that. It *is* your life and you get to make your own decisions about what you do and with whom. So, deciding to act on something that matters to you is not a bad thing." She smiled. "Not unless it involves something like robbing a gas station or getting 400 body piercings."

Roma Jean blinked. *People got 400 body piercings?* She couldn't even think of that many places on her body to hang things. Not unless you counted . . . *gross.*

She knew she was blushing again.

Miss Murphy was being all nice about it, but Roma Jean felt like a deer in the headlights.

"I tried really hard to be careful and not attract attention," she explained. "But it happened during a lunch break and I know a bunch of people up there saw us. I promise it didn't take very long and I got out of there as soon as we finished." She lowered her eyes to the table where the vanilla center of her Dilly Bar was beginning to seep out onto a pile of napkins. "Charlie said I'd probably regret it, too. But I figured that was just because she had more experience and was used to how you felt after you did something like this."

"How *do* you feel?"

Roma Jean raised her eyes to Miss Murphy's face. She didn't look mad. But then, Miss Murphy almost never got mad—at least not with her.

"I feel . . . okay."

"Are you really sorry about what happened? Or is that the way you think you're supposed to feel?"

"I don't know. Maybe a little of both."

"Roma Jean? Do you truly think what happened was a mistake? Because you need to know that no one has the right to pressure you into doing anything that you aren't ready for—and just because you were tempted to try something, it doesn't mean that anything about who you are has changed."

"Nobody pressured me. I wanted to do it."

Miss Murphy looked . . . relieved.

"I'm very glad Charlie didn't pressure you or push you into doing something you weren't ready for."

"No, ma'am." Roma Jean wanted to make sure Miss Murphy knew she acted on her own. "Charlie tried hard to talk me out of it."

"She did?"

Roma Jean nodded. "She tried to make me promise not to do it, but I knew I was going to the next time I went up there."

"Up there?" Miss Murphy looked perplexed. "Up where?"

"Whitetop."

"Whitetop?"

"Yes, ma'am. That's where I met him."

"Him?" Miss Murphy's green eyes grew as big as salad plates. "Roma Jean? Exactly who did you—engage with—up there?"

"Mr. Sanchez."

"Mister . . . *Carlos* Sanchez?"

Roma Jean nodded. "I thought you knew that?"

Miss Murphy flopped back against the booth. "I have no idea what to say . . ."

"Does this mean you're mad at me?"

"I don't know what I am, Roma Jean." She slowly shook her head. "Carlos has a wife and three children."

"I know. That's why I did it."

"That's . . ." Miss Murphy stared at her, then squinted her eyes. "Roma Jean? Exactly what *did* you do with Mr. Sanchez?"

"I warned him. About the mayor."

"Warned him? Warned him about what?"

"Charlie told me the mayor was going to start rounding up people who didn't have the right paperwork and send them back to Mexico. I couldn't let that happen to Mr. and Mrs. Sanchez. They're so nice. And Henry is best friends with Héctor and Gabriel."

"So, you went to tell Mr. Sanchez about what was going to happen?"

170

Roma Jean nodded. "Isn't that what you wanted to talk with me about? I figured one of the other people who saw us talking called the mayor to complain."

"No. No that wasn't what I . . ." Miss Murphy shook her head. "What did Carlos say when you talked with him?"

Roma Jean sighed. "Well, you know his English isn't really good, but I think he understood what I was trying to tell him. He pulled out his wallet and showed me his immigration card."

"Thank god for that."

Roma Jean picked up her Dilly Bar and did her best to prevent any more ice cream from leaking out, but it was hopeless. The frozen inside had mostly melted, and it was oozing out through every crack in the hard chocolate coating.

She looked out the big plate glass window that overlooked the parking lot. The rain had mostly slacked off. Water was standing all over the place in big puddles. Roma Jean noticed they all had that oily, rainbow thing forming around their edges.

She knew that Miss Murphy would want to get back on the road soon. But something about their conversation didn't make sense to her.

"Miss Murphy?"

Miss Murphy was collecting their napkins and empty cups. She paused and looked up at Roma Jean.

"I was just wondering," Roma Jean began. "If you didn't know anything about my visit with Mr. Sanchez, what was it you did want to talk with me about?"

Miss Murphy took a slow, deep breath. Then she smiled.

"Let's go and get you another Dilly Bar . . ."

The rest of their conversation had been *really* embarrassing. Although Miss Murphy tried hard to be sensitive and not ask about any details that were too personal.

But one thing she *did* make clear was that Roma Jean couldn't have any more meetings with Charlie on bookmobile stops— even though nothing really inappropriate had happened—yet.

It was the "yet" part that Miss Murphy took the most time to warn her about. And her warning was less about protecting the library than it was about protecting Roma Jean's right to take her time figuring out what she wanted.

"This isn't something you need to rush into, Roma Jean," she said. "And there isn't any right or wrong way to be. Take the time you need to figure out what your heart wants, and what your mind will allow the rest of you to embrace."

"Is that what you did with Dr. Stevenson?"

It was a pretty bold thing for her to say. Roma Jean had never made a direct reference to Miss Murphy's relationship with Dr. Stevenson before. As soon as she asked the question, she wished she could take it back.

But Miss Murphy didn't seem bothered by it at all. Her serious expression just melted into a big, goofy smile.

It was a whole lot like watching what happened to her first Dilly Bar.

"You know what, Roma Jean? I think it's high time you started calling me Syd."

Peggy Hawkes tapped on Maddie's office door at four-thirty and told her that an emergency case had just walked in.

Maddie quickly got up from her chair and reached for her jacket. "What is it?"

Peggy stepped inside and lowered her voice. "It's Curtis Freemantle. He cut his hand on a slicer, but it doesn't look that deep. I told him I could take care of it but he insisted that he wanted to see you—*alone*." She took a quick look over her shoulder. "I don't think he's here because of his hand, if you catch my drift." She gave Maddie an exaggerated wink.

"Okaaayyy." Maddie picked up her stethoscope and looped it over her neck. "Show him into room two."

Peggy nodded and left her office.

Maddie stood rooted in place and listened to the sound of Peggy's crepe-soled shoes creaking along the corridor toward the waiting room. It gave her a minute to stare at the ceiling and curse her bad luck.

There could be only one reason why Curtis Freemantle wanted to talk with her—privately—and it probably had everything to do with his daughter and a certain Sheriff's deputy.

Sensitive chats. My favorite.

She waited until she heard Peggy ushering Curtis into the examination room. Before she left her office to see him, she picked up the framed photo of Syd that sat on her desk.

I wonder if you'd come roaring over here if I sent you a 9-1-1 text? Fat chance.

Syd would see right through her. Maddie knew *exactly* how she'd reply: "Put on your big girl panties and deal with it."

She replaced the photo and went to meet Curtis—avoiding the temptation to hike up her drawers on her way out of the office.

She found him sitting on the edge of the examination table when she entered the room. Peggy had wrapped his hand in a couple of clean towels and had it resting on a rolling tray. Maddie could see a few spots of blood on the front of his shirt.

"Hey, Curtis," she said. "What have you managed to do to yourself?" She walked over to the sink and washed her hands.

"Hey, Doc," he replied. "I was slicing up some of that boiled ham for Natalie Chriscoe, and just got careless."

Maddie dried her hands before sitting down on a stool in front of him.

"Let me take a look at it."

He nodded.

She carefully unwrapped his hand. Peggy was right. The cut was clean and not very deep. She was confident that it wouldn't require stitches.

"Well the good news is that I think we can avoid needles," she said. "But I do want to soak it in some antiseptic solution before we close it up with some Steristrips."

"Okay," he said. "I felt kind of silly comin' over here, but Edna said I should get you to look at it. And then Natalie chimed in and told as how her cousin once cut himself on some of that hard salami and didn't do nothin' about it. She said it went all septic on him and he ended up losing two of his fingers." He shook his head. "Ain't no deli meat worth that."

Maddie filled a small basin with a Betadine solution and pulled on a pair of nitrile gloves.

"I don't think you need to worry about that, Curtis. I'd say you won this battle with marauding cold cuts." She smiled at him. "Let's soak your hand in this for a few minutes, just to be sure there isn't any kind of debris in the cut."

She helped Curtis submerge his hand in the pan of liquid.

"Does that sting at all?"

He shook his head.

"Good. I'm going to give you some antibiotic cream to take home, too. I want you to keep this dry and dab the cut with a bit of the cream every time you change the bandages. Okay?"

He nodded.

"You let me know right away if it feels worse or begins to look red and puffy."

"Okay, Doc."

Maddie was just beginning to wonder if maybe she'd been wrong about an ulterior motive behind Curtis's visit when he shattered her hopes.

"So, Doc? I was kinda hoping maybe we could talk for just a minute about Roma Jean?"

Shit . . .

"Roma Jean?" Maddie asked him. "Is she not feeling well?"

"Oh, no. It ain't nothin' like that." He took a moment to consider his statement. "Least, I don't think it's nothin' like that."

"No?"

"No, ma'am. I wanted to ask if you noticed anything—*different*—about her lately? You and Miss Murphy, that is."

"Different . . . how?"

She knew she was playing dumb, but it seemed important to have Curtis actually state what was on his mind. She wanted to be careful not to blunder into something that lay beyond what he was prepared to discuss.

"Well," he looked down at his hand, soaking in the antiseptic

174

rinse. Tiny bubbles covered the surface of the cut. "Folks have been talking about how much time she's spending with that Charlie Davis. At first, me and Edna didn't think nothin' about it, but now we wonder if maybe she's . . ." He shrugged, and didn't finish his sentence.

"Curtis?"

Curtis looked up at her. He had bright, hazel-colored eyes. Maddie had never really noticed them before. They were clear and very pretty. And right now, they looked scared to death.

"What is it you want to ask me?"

"I don't wanna give any offense."

"I don't think you will."

"Well. Edna and me was wondering if maybe you thought Roma Jean was . . . was maybe like you and Miss Murphy?"

Oh, man . . .

"Are you asking me for a medical opinion, Curtis?"

"No, ma'am." He shook his head. "I'm just asking you as a friend—and as somebody who cares about Roma Jean like we do."

Maddie relaxed a little bit.

"Curtis, you do know it wouldn't be right or fair for me to express any kind of opinion about Roma Jean—especially about something in her life that's so personal?"

"So, she hadn't said anything to you about it?"

Great. There was no way to answer this question without confirming his suspicions—or violating a previous confidence of Roma Jean's.

She decided to take a different approach.

"Curtis? Is there a reason why you and Edna don't feel comfortable just talking with Roma Jean about your concerns?"

"Oh, no." He seemed alarmed at the idea. "We couldn't do that. What if we're wrong?"

"What if you are? Roma Jean is an adult, and she has a good head on her shoulders. She'll know if you're asking from a place of concern versus one of judgment."

He didn't reply.

"Or is that the problem? You're afraid to ask because of how she might answer?"

He nodded. "It ain't that we have any real problem with it, Doc. We know that people these days can love whoever they want to love. Nobody much cares about that anymore. It's just that . . ." He waved his free hand in frustration. "Me and Edna just wanted Roma Jean to find some nice fella and settle down. Maybe have a bunch of grandbabies? It don't look like that's gonna happen now. And that makes it hard for us to ask her about it. We don't want her to think she let us down if it ends up being true. And right now, I don't think neither of us could hide how sad we'd be—and that ain't fair to her."

"Curtis? There's not a thing in the world I can say that could help you be a better parent to Roma Jean. You just proved that you're an expert on all the parts that matter."

He looked unconvinced.

Maddie patted him on the arm. "You're a good dad. Roma Jean knows that. She'll talk with you when or if she has something to share."

"I hope so."

"I *know* so. Now," Maddie lifted his hand from the antibacterial bath, "let's get you bandaged up and on your way." She smiled at him. "I don't want Natalie to miss out on her boiled ham."

"Oh, heck," he said. "She already took it on with her—that and about six pounds of roast beef and turkey. She said they was having some big to-do at Cougar's tonight. Something about getting a contract with Wheaton? I guess they're getting into that moving business big time."

Maddie wasn't sure that was good news—not if it meant James would be gone on more overnight hauls.

She finished applying the bandages to Curtis's hand.

"You try to keep this dry for at least the next twelve hours, okay? Then dab some of this cream on the cut before you put new bandages on it. I'll put a few extras in a bag for you."

"Okay. Thanks, Doc."

"It was my pleasure, Curtis. You be more careful with that slicer."

176

"Yes, ma'am." He got to his feet. "I want to thank you for not getting upset when I asked you about Roma Jean. I hope you know Edna and I think you and Miss Murphy have been real good role models for her."

"Thank you for saying that, Curtis. We're very fond of Roma Jean."

Curtis nodded and turned to leave, but paused before reaching the door. He turned back around to face her.

"That Charlie Davis?" he asked. "I heard she was good friends with the granddaughter of Nelda Ray Black, and all. But is she good people?"

This was one question Maddie had no problem answering.

"Yes, Curtis. She's very good people."

He gave her a short nod and exited the room.

Maddie dropped back onto her stool.

I so should've listened to my mother and gone into psychiatry . . .

Syd knew she was taking a chance by showing up uninvited. It wasn't a type of behavior she normally indulged in, and she wasn't sure what kind of reception to expect. To be fair, Lizzy had every right to refuse to see her at all.

She had forgotten how desolate it was out in this part of the county. Lizzy was still living in the riverfront bungalow that had once belonged to David's eccentric aunt, Iris. There had been a time, after Beau Pitzer's attack, when it seemed that Lizzy might part from her pioneer spirit and look for a house closer to town. No one would've had trouble understanding that. The memory of what could have happened to each of them the night Beau showed up at Lizzy's bungalow, half-crazy on meth and looking for money—and something else more sinister—was still terrifying. Syd hadn't been back out here since that night, and she felt the unwelcome reminder of that experience wake up inside her like a restless dog.

Which, she could see, were *also* plentiful out here.

She passed yet another house ringed by a yard full of furry

mastodons. The ungainly beasts wasted no time proving their fondness for snacking on wayfaring strangers. Her Volvo, which now ran on about three of its five cylinders, had a hard time outrunning the pack. One of the dogs managed to sprint alongside her car—snapping and salivating—for at least a tenth of a mile. Long enough for her to observe that it had a pronounced underbite and dark markings around its muzzle.

She thought it looked a lot like the mayor.

It was another unseasonably hot day, and she had all the windows down. The Volvo's air conditioning, which had worked poorly twenty-three years ago when the car was new, was now completely useless. She worried that one of the more enterprising dogs might actually contrive to leap inside the car. It was a relief when she finally turned off the county road and made the slow descent along the lane that led to the small bungalow.

She wondered if Lizzy now had a dog.

If she does, I'm not getting out of the car.

Syd was impressed by the changes Lizzy had made. For one thing, the monster-sized stacks of firewood that David's Aunt Iris had surrounding the place like a stockade had obviously been burned or sold off. That change alone made the setting look more inviting. The house itself now sported fresh paint, replacement windows and a new front porch.

Lizzy's Subaru was in the driveway. Syd had gambled on the likelihood that she would've come straight there after the clinic closed at five. It was now just past five-thirty. Since Syd hadn't said anything about her errand, she was hopeful she'd make it back to the farm before Maddie got there, which usually was about seven o'clock. Unless, of course, they had Henry. On those nights, Maddie arranged her schedule to be home in time for an early dinner.

Syd didn't have to worry about screwing up her courage to knock on the door. Lizzy apparently heard her car pull up and came out onto the porch to greet her. Syd thought she looked surprised but not wary. She took that as a good sign. Lizzy looked tired. Her fair complexion looked paler than normal, although her thicket of red hair seemed as wild and vibrant as ever.

She made a determined effort not to look at Lizzy's waistline.

She got out of the car and walked over to the steps.

"Hi, Lizzy. I guess my whole element of surprise just went out the window?"

"Oh, I wouldn't say that." Lizzy leaned against the porch railing. "But it's good to see you, regardless."

"Is it?" Syd was dubious.

"Of course, it is." Lizzy motioned for Syd to join her on the porch. "Wanna come up here and have a seat? It's too hot inside the house."

"Okay." Syd joined her and they walked over to where Lizzy had an enormous wicker settee and two matching armchairs. Overhead, a big Panama fan moved in slow circles, pushing warm air around. "Is your air conditioning on the blink?"

"No." Lizzy sat sideways on the settee and propped her feet up on a big striped pillow. "I just hate having to turn it on this early in the season. You know how it is—once you crank it up, it pretty much runs nonstop for six months."

Syd nodded. "I think this summer is going to be another one for the record books. Of course, we seem to be saying that now about every summer, don't we?"

"No kidding. I picked a supremely bad time of year to get knocked up."

Syd wasn't sure how to reply.

"It's okay." Lizzy filled the conversational vacuum. "The rabbit died and now the cat's out of the bag." She gave Syd a wry smile. "Are there any other animal euphemisms I missed?"

"Um. How about bacon in the drawer?"

"In foal?"

"Stung by a serpent?" Syd added.

"In pig!" Lizzy proclaimed.

In pig? Syd was perplexed. "I haven't heard that one before."

"I think it's a precursor to getting bacon in the drawer."

"Oh." Syd shook her head. "Who comes up with this stuff?"

"Men."

"Of course." Syd rolled her eyes. "Bless their hearts."

"Yeah," Lizzy agreed. "They're pretty much assholes."

"Especially my brother."

Lizzy seemed surprised. "I won't deny that he's missed a few opportunities to regale me with demonstrations of his caring and sensitivity. But I'm surprised to hear you share that assessment."

"Why? I'm horrified by his behavior." She hesitated. "And my own."

Lizzy didn't offer a response. Syd took that as implied permission to continue with her apology.

"I had no right to interfere in your private life the way I did, Lizzy. I was wrong to share my conjecture with my brother. I was wrong to discuss *anything* about your relationship with him. You also need to know that Maddie never broke your confidence. I drew my own conclusions based on what she didn't say, and guessed at what I thought might be true. For that—and for my interference—I am deeply sorry, and I apologize."

Lizzy listened without interruption. She took her time to respond when Syd finished.

"I don't blame you for wanting to help your brother, Syd. Even though he's acting like an ass, I know this is hard for him, too. And for you. I don't doubt that you had good intentions."

"I'm still mortified about what I did. Maddie was furious with me. *Is* furious with me," she corrected. "Rightfully so. I don't expect you to forgive me, but I hope you'll believe me when I tell you that I honestly thought he'd behave like a grown-up—finally." She slowly shook her head. "I was wrong."

Lizzy sighed. "I think we're both victims of the same malady."

"What's that?" Syd asked.

"We both love him."

"I guess that's—good?"

"Trust me. It doesn't feel like it right now."

"Lizzy, I completely understand if you choose not to answer—but do you know what you're going to do?"

Lizzy shifted her position on the settee. "I thought I did. I was sure that this wasn't something I was ready for—especially if I had to go it alone. It's always been one of those hypotheticals you live with, you know? In the background. At least, women do. We all know it's a possibility—whether it's something we want to do or not. I mean . . . I'm sure it was something you thought about, too. Before you were married. While you were married. Hell. Maybe even now?"

Syd smiled. "While Maddie does have unsung talents, I'm happy to share that *those* rumors are false."

"Please don't shatter my illusions. I need my fantasies right now."

Syd's surprised reaction to her comment must have shown on her face.

"Not *that* kind of fantasy," Lizzy clarified.

"Thank god."

"But, doesn't it piss you off that we live in a world where women still have to wrestle with everyone else's moral judgments when we make what should be personal choices about our own lives?"

"Yeah. It does."

"I don't mean to completely reject Tom's stated religious scruples about abortion. But, really? If his Catholic upbringing is so damn sacred to him, then how the hell could he be so cavalier about wagging his junk around out of wedlock? If you ask me, that whole wingnut brand of morning-after piety is nothing but a bunch of male chauvinist bullshit. How dare he suddenly get religion and insist that his faith and values need to drive any decision I choose to make about my *own* body?"

"He doesn't have that right, Lizzy. Nobody does. He should respect and understand that this is your decision to make."

"Wanna know something? If he hadn't acted like such a self-righteous asshole, I would've gladly asked him to help me sort through this. I honestly thought that maybe—just maybe—he'd surprise me and decide that he actually *was* ready to make a commitment to us. Well. Here was his big chance. But all I got from him was a big ole nothin' burger of recrimination for not telling him sooner—and a lecture about what all he was and wasn't 'comfortable' with."

Syd was very glad her mother wasn't hearing this.

Tom wouldn't be able to walk straight for a year . . .

"Lizzy, I don't have words to tell you how much I regret my brother's behavior. I wish I could change this outcome. You cannot imagine how much I wish I could change it—change *him.*"

"Yeah." Lizzy gave a bitter-sounding laugh. "I wish you could change him, too. As it is?" She laid a hand over her abdomen. "I just need to make my peace with going it alone."

"For what it's worth, you're not alone. You know that Maddie and I are here, and we'll help and support you in any way we can."

Lizzy met her eyes. "You say that now—but how will you react when I call you at three in the morning with a squalling infant?"

Syd knew she needed to tread carefully. She didn't want to overreact or put too great a value on anything Lizzy hinted at.

"Even then," she said.

"Oh, shit. I don't even know what I'm saying. I change my mind about every two seconds." Lizzy sat up. "Wanna come inside and have a glass of wine?"

Syd demurred.

"Don't worry," Lizzy added. "As tempting as it is, I haven't succumbed yet. I'll just have a tonic on the rocks, with a slice of lime, and pretend it's the world's biggest VT."

Syd stood up. "Why not make it two, and we'll pretend together?"

"Works for me."

Lizzy got up and led the way inside. She stopped halfway across the living room.

"Uh, oh. Do you mind making them?" She gestured toward her kitchen. "I feel a sudden need to hit the bathroom. I think that hot dog I had for lunch is about to make another appearance."

"Oh. Sure. No problem. Take your time."

Lizzy hurried off toward the back of the house.

Syd found the tonic and limes in Lizzy's ancient refrigerator and opened half a dozen cabinets before finally locating a couple of tall glasses. She was just beginning to coax the ice cubes out of a metal tray when Lizzy walked back into the room. She looked pale and distressed.

"What's wrong?" Syd set the ice tray in the sink.

Lizzy sank down onto a stool. She appeared so unsteady that Syd walked over and placed an arm around her shoulders. "Are you okay?"

She looked at Syd, but her brown eyes seemed unfocused. "I guess we don't have to worry about late fees on that *Name the Baby* book I checked out last week."

Syd noticed she was holding a tied-off plastic bag.

"Lizzy . . ."

She nodded. "I'm pretty sure I just had a miscarriage."

"Oh, honey . . ." Syd pulled her close.

"I called Maddie from the bathroom." Lizzy's voice was small. "She's waiting for us at the clinic."

The Bixby Bowladrome was having a "renaissance."

At least, that's what the owners had decreed a year ago when they made the bold decision to rebuild after the tornado tore off the roof and demolished two of the outside walls. The way they saw it, they couldn't shut it down.

The place had become world-famous.

That was because it was here, on this very spot, that Deb Carlson's flame-red Camaro finally came to a rest after being swept up in a maelstrom that blazed a path of destruction across three counties. The epic storm hurled Deb's beloved car around like an eight-cylinder wrecking ball. After its epic reign of terror ended, the car landed, light as a feather, across three lanes at the south end of the bowling alley. It remained there for nearly three weeks—until it was removed to a more distinguished final resting place.

It was as close to a holy relic as they could get in these parts.

The owners wanted to create a permanent memorial to the famous car when they rebuilt the Bowladrome. So, they painted a bright red outline of the Camaro across the lanes in the exact spot where the car landed. Of course, those lanes quickly became the most popular—especially on league night. People would call up weeks in advance to reserve them for special events. And it wasn't just because of the snazzy paint job and the status of getting to bowl on sacred ground. It was also because in the last year, bowlers had managed to rack up five perfect 300 scores—but only on those hallowed lanes.

Rita Chriscoe told James it was no accident. She pointed out that when the universe dealt you a perfect hand of cards, it was up to you to play them.

And that's what they were celebrating here tonight—a windfall alliance that would soon catapult their upstart trucking company into the big leagues. James wasn't too sure how "big league" a franchise contract with a commercial moving company was, but he did have to hand it to Jocelyn and Deb—the two of them had transformed their fledgling flag car business into a local powerhouse. Cougar's was on their way to becoming one of the biggest haulers of domestic freight in southwest Virginia.

The one thing he wasn't too sure about was how much the nature of the work would change now that they would be taking on more long-distance moves. The trip to Los Angeles to get Dr. Heller's piano was one thing. He pretty much viewed that contract as a one-off. But if these overnight trips became more common, that would mean he'd be away from Henry more.

It wasn't that Syd and Maddie minded taking care of Henry. In fact, James was pretty sure the opposite was the case. It was hard for him to admit that his son was better off staying out at their farm than he was when James tried to find someone to stay with him at their small apartment over Junior's garage. Henry never complained, but James could always see the excitement in his face whenever he knew he was going to be staying in his room at the farm—the big front bedroom with all the airplane pictures.

Airplanes. Dr. Stevenson had her own airplane . . .

How could he compete with that?

There was a roar from the crowd. Deb Carlson had just rolled another strike. It was her fourth in a row. Heads were nodding.

Money was changing hands. It looked as if Rita's sister-in-law, Natalie, was holding.

Anticipation that it might be happening again spread through the place like wildfire.

Cougar's Quality Logistics had lucked out tonight and got access to the premier spot because Natalie still had an "in" with the management. Their contingent was all spread out across a cluster of tables that sat just behind the trio of coveted lanes.

"Why don't you get on up there and give it a go?" Rita asked him. "That leg of yours won't make no difference. You won't bowl no worse than the rest of them jokers."

"No thanks." James refilled his glass with beer from the pitcher on their table. "Besides, I don't want anything to do with that word."

"What word?"

"Handicap."

Rita looked confused. "Who said anything about a handicap?"

James gestured toward the group bowling at lane twenty-three.

Rita rolled her eyes. "You mean that dickhead in the MAGA hat? Purvis Halsey?"

James nodded.

"The only ass *that* idiot could find with two hands is the one hangin' off Yolanda Painter's backside." She shook her head in disgust. "His *brain* is the only thing around here that needs a handicap."

"It's okay. I never did like bowling much—even before the army."

James rarely made any mention of his military background—much less his disability. He could see the surprise register on Rita's face.

"You do know folks around here call you a war hero?" she said. "They're grateful for your service."

"I'm no hero."

"Now why in thunder would you say that?" Rita gaped at him. "Didn't you get one of them purple hearts?"

"Give me a break. I was riding in a truck that hit a bomb. It didn't take any heroism to get my leg blown off."

He could tell that Rita wasn't sure what to say. She sat and fidgeted with her scorecard and stub of yellow pencil. James felt bad for making such a blunt comment when she was just trying to be nice.

"I'm sorry," he said. "I didn't mean to bite your head off. I just don't deserve to be called a hero. Especially now."

"How come I feel like you ain't talking about Afghanistan?"

He smiled at her. "You're a smart woman, Rita."

"Hell." She refilled her own glass with beer. "If I was so damn smart then why would I be investing in hemorrhoid cushions instead of real estate?" She took a healthy swig of beer. "I had a shot once at making something good out of my life. I blew it. Don't you be doing the same thing."

"You think I'm blowing it?" he asked.

"It don't matter what I think. It only matters what you think."

He didn't reply. He didn't think he needed to. That didn't appear to be a deterrent to Rita.

"It don't take no rocket scientist to see that you ain't happy with the way things is workin' out. So why not make a change before you get dug in any further?"

"It's not that simple. I have a kid. I can't just pick up and go."

"Who says you can't? It ain't like anything's keepin' you here. Not unless you're gonna tell me you just love them deluxe accommodations in that penthouse up over Junior's garage?"

He had to smile at that description. Rita sure knew how to turn a phrase.

"I don't have any ties here. Not really. But Henry does. He's made a lot of friends. I wouldn't feel right taking him away from that."

"Well, kids are pretty good judges of character. Kind of like dogs. Maybe he knows things you don't?"

"Yeah. Maybe."

"It ain't like you couldn't learn from him."

They were interrupted by a loud chorus of moans.

"Well, shoot." Rita slammed her pilsner glass down on the table. "*Bed posts.*"

James looked up at the scoreboard. Deb Carlson had just rolled a seven-ten split.

"Well, that's that." Rita drained what was left in her glass. "Guess there ain't gonna be no perfect game tonight."

"No," James agreed. *Not tonight, and not any other night, either.*

It was a busy night by the pond. By Maddie's count, Pete had taken at least half a dozen flying leaps off the porch to chase unwelcome critters off. Eventually, he decided enough was enough and his shift for the night was finished. Now when thirsty intruders approached the water, the big yellow dog would simply lift his head and emit a low, rolling growl.

"Yeah, big guy." Maddie reached down and scratched between his ears. "You give 'em hell."

Syd emerged from the house carrying two oversized tumblers of . . . something. She handed one to Maddie and reclaimed the seat beside her—after moving Rosebud.

Maddie sniffed the contents of the glass.

"Oh, boy. Is this the good stuff?"

"It is as far as I'm concerned."

Maddie took a cautious sip. *So luxurious.* How was it possible to make grapes taste like liquid amber? She swallowed. *And fire?*

She held the tumbler up to examine the miracle brew in the moonlight. "Is this the French stuff?"

"Yes, honey. This would be the French stuff." Syd nudged her arm. "Like all cognac."

"Oh, come on. You know what I meant."

"Yes, it's the D'ussé."

The VSOP was Maddie's current favorite. She slid lower into her chair. "You're spoiling me."

"I think you deserve it."

"I don't know about that." Maddie sighed. "I wish we could've sent some of this home with Lizzy."

"Me, too." Syd sipped from her own glass.

Maddie noticed a change in the music. They'd been listening

to Murray Perahia's new recording of the Bach *French Suites*—a gift from Celine. But now there were sensuous sounds of someone crooning over lost love. It was . . . perfect, actually. Soft and smooth. Warm and mellow.

Just like the French stuff.

I let a song go out of my heart . . .

"Who is this?" she asked Syd.

"Catherine Russell. I thought we both could use a change."

"You'll get no argument from me on that." Maddie listened to a bit more of the song. "This is beautiful, but kind of doleful."

Syd nodded. "I thought that seemed right for this evening."

"Yeah." Rosebud jumped up onto Maddie's lap and immediately started to knead. Maddie grimaced and returned her to the porch floor. "This cat is a freak."

"She's certainly persistent." Syd patted the side of her leg to distract the cat from her pursuit of Maddie. "Do you think Lizzy will be okay?"

"Eventually. I mean—physically, she's fine. Although this will be a shock to her system."

"And her emotions."

"Yeah. There's no dodging that roller coaster ride, I'm afraid. But Lizzy is a nurse, so she'll know what to expect."

"What do you think happened?"

Maddie shook her head. "It's impossible to say. This early in a pregnancy? It could have been anything. The human body is enormously self-righting. It's difficult to tell someone that a spontaneous abortion is often the body's best way to resolve a problem. But . . ." She didn't finish her statement.

"I fear that Lizzy will punish herself for her ambivalence."

"I wouldn't have said that before. But now, I think you're right. It did seem like she was making her peace with the idea."

"I thought so, too."

Rosebud tried to get on Maddie's lap again, but Maddie cut her off at the pass.

"I was surprised when Lizzy called and said you were there with her. When did you decide to talk with her?"

"Almost immediately after I realized what an idiot I'd been by talking with Tom." Syd made another futile attempt to draw Rosebud away from Maddie's chair. "Were you angry?"

Maddie looked at her with surprise. "Angry about what?"

"That I went to see Lizzy."

"No." Maddie reached over and laid a hand on her arm. "Of course not."

"I'm glad." Syd met her eyes. "I need you to know how much I regret what I did. I promise you that I'll never break your confidence again."

Maddie gave her arm a gentle squeeze. "I know that. But thank you for saying it, just the same."

"Do you think we were right to let her go home alone?"

Maddie nodded. "She's a big girl. She said she hadn't told her parents about her pregnancy yet. But she was going to call her mother."

"I'm glad."

"She also made sure I knew how much it meant to her that you came out to see her. I think she was very relieved that you were there with her."

"I hope that's true." Syd sighed. "I wonder if she'll tell Tom?"

"You mean tonight?"

Syd shook her head. "No. I mean *ever*."

"I can't imagine she wouldn't."

"I can."

Maddie was perplexed. "Why would you think that?"

"You mean, apart from the fact that he behaved like a complete knuckle-dragger and forfeited any right he might have to the information?"

"Well. There is that . . ."

Syd gave a bitter-sounding laugh. "The pathetic part of this is that he really does love her."

Rosebud made another ill-fated attempt to climb onto Maddie's lap, and was summarily evicted.

"If that's true," she asked Syd, "then why do you think he behaved the way he did?"

"You're asking *me* this question? Aren't you the one with all the advanced medical degrees?"

"Nooo," Maddie drawled. "That would be my mother." She batted her eyes at Syd. "I skipped all my psych classes, remember?"

"You are so full of shit."

"Hey, I never professed to understand anything about the male psyche."

"Well, that makes two of us."

Maddie drained the rest of her French stuff. "Thank god Henry is more transparent."

"At least he is for now. We should enjoy it while it lasts."

"I don't know about you, but I hope it lasts forever."

"That reminds me." Syd shifted in her chair to face Maddie. "You never really filled me in on how your conversation went with his unfortunately named teacher."

"You mean Mr. Hozbiest?"

Syd nodded. "The very one."

"Yeah. The little troll refused to speak with me."

"What?"

"He said, and I quote, 'You're not his parent.' I thought about throttling him, just on principle. But I couldn't force the conversation. We'll have to talk with James about it."

"That really infuriates me."

"It does me, too. But we have to accept that we have no real standing in Henry's life. At least, not legally," she added.

Syd stared out across the lawn. Maddie could sense her frustration. It really was an untenable situation for them— one with no real remedy.

"Did you see that?" Syd was pointing toward the pond.

"What?" Maddie tried to follow her gaze.

"I swear I just saw a lightning bug."

"No. You couldn't have. It's too early."

"There it is again. Look. Near the bracken fern."

Maddie squinted her eyes. Sure enough. She saw a faint flash. Then another.

"My god."

"The soothsayers are right. It's going to be an early summer."

"And a hot one," Maddie agreed.

"I wish we could slow it down."

"What?"

"This." Syd spread her hands. "All of it. *Everything*. I just want to drag my feet or tie an anchor to the moon—anything that will make it all last longer." She looked at Maddie with eyes full of sadness. "He's going to be gone from us. He'll grow up or go away and we won't have had enough time with him."

Syd was right. There was no argument Maddie could make that would change the outcome.

She took hold of Syd's hand. "I know."

Syd leaned her head against Maddie's shoulder. They watched the slow dance of the fireflies and listened to the dying strains of another jazz classic.

Chapter 7

Charlie was surprised when Roma Jean called her and asked if they could get together after church for a picnic. She was even more shocked when, instead of saying they'd meet up someplace neutral, Roma Jean said Charlie should pick her up at home.

That had never happened before.

It wasn't that Charlie had never met Roma Jean's parents. She had. But showing up at their house to retrieve their daughter for something that looked a whole lot like a date was something new. The prospect was exciting but also nerve-wracking. For one thing, she had no idea what to wear, and she ended up changing her clothes five or six times. They were going on a picnic, so that meant she needed to be casual. But to her, that implied wearing jeans or cargo shorts—which might make her look too butch. On the other hand, trying to look "feminine" would be a stretch for her on a good day.

Charlie never could pull off wearing girl clothes. It wasn't that she looked bad, or anything—it was more about how the garments made her feel. Clumsy. Awkward. Like she was a phony—pretending to be something she wasn't. And none of that had anything to do with being *female*. Charlie had no problem with her gender.

Especially lately . . .

No. It was the *uniform* women wore that caused her problems. She supposed that was part of what made getting a job in the sheriff's department appeal to her. It took that whole wardrobe issue right off the table.

She retrieved her service revolver from its safe in her bedroom. *Having access to you fixed a bunch of stuff, too.*

Going to work for Byron solved a lot of problems in her life. For one thing, it allowed her to break free from her father, who had threatened to kill her when he found out she was gay. He damn near made good on his promise, too—until Byron got wind of it from the guidance counselor at school and managed to get her away from him. Whatever he had said to Manfred Davis must've made an impression because her father packed up his Chevy one night and took off without looking back.

Charlie had no idea what had happened to him after he left Jericho. The last her grandma heard, he'd taken up with a woman from South Carolina and was working third shift at an airbag plant in Cheraw.

Airbags. Things that were made to explode on impact. They were perfect for him.

She didn't miss him. She didn't miss any part of her childhood. The only thing she regretted was not having the chance to learn how people in normal families related to each other. That's why she didn't blame Roma Jean's parents for being worried about her. That's what people who cared about you were supposed to do— worry about you and try to protect you from making mistakes.

Even though Charlie knew in her heart it wasn't a mistake for Roma Jean to be with her.

She was sure of it.

Roma Jean was unlike anyone Charlie had ever known. She was like that big milkshake blender at Dairy Queen—filled to the brim with every wonderful thing you could think of, and running flat out. Shy. Blunt. Clumsy. Confident. Funny. Sad. Smart. Clueless. Sassy. Scared. She was all those things—tumbled together inside the best Blizzard ever made.

Charlie once took some web design classes at Alleghany Community College when she first went to work for Byron, and part of her job was maintaining the department's website. One of the first things they talked about was how you needed to know the difference between subtractive and additive color. One system started with white and ended with black—and the other started with black and ended with white. The whole point was that black and white were the results you got when you either subtracted or added all colors together. Whether you were adding or subtracting, it took all colors to reach opposite ends of the spectrum.

It was a tough concept to grasp and she never really understood it.

Not until she met Roma Jean.

Roma Jean was a perfect mix of all colors. And her contradictions proved how opposites could coexist in perfect harmony. It made no sense, and it made all kinds of sense. And it didn't take Charlie very long to figure out that adding a hefty dose of Roma Jean to the darkness of her own life was resulting in a fantastic explosion of light.

That meant she could afford to be patient while Roma Jean figured things out.

She just wished *she* could figure out what to wear . . .

In the end, she decided to go with jeans and a lavender polo shirt. The jeans were comfortable, and the shirt was pretty enough to pass as *halfway* girlie.

She took a last, wistful glance at her revolver before locking it up in the gun safe between the front seats of her car. It was unlikely she'd be needing it on a picnic.

She smiled. *Not unless Roma Jean made more of those awful deviled eggs.*

The last time she made them, she experimented with beet juice and red wine vinegar and they ended up looking like appetizers from a party at Freddy Krueger's house.

Roma Jean had said they could take their picnic lunch up to the Highlands state park near Mouth of Wilson. There were wild ponies up there—and caverns with a spring-fed underground lake that was big enough to swim in. The destination was a popular one for campers, folks hiking the Appalachian Trail and ham radio operators. And there were plenty of picnic shelters, too—although

Charlie was hopeful she could tempt Roma Jean to consider a site in a less trafficked area.

They had things to discuss.

She parked her cruiser behind Roma Jean's Caprice and tried to avoid checking her hair in the rearview mirror before getting out. It looked like both of Roma Jean's parents were at home. Edna's Impala was pulled up beneath the carport next to Curtis's Silverado pickup.

The Freemantles only bought Chevys.

Charlie knew better than to go to the front door. Nobody in the county did that. If you did, it was clear that you were either up to no good or were selling something nobody wanted.

Roma Jean yanked the kitchen door open before Charlie was halfway through her first knock. She guessed that meant Roma Jean had been standing there watching her walk up. She looked fantastic. Her long red hair was loose today and she'd already changed out of her church clothes.

"Hey, Charlie." She stood back and held the door open so Charlie could join her inside. "Mama is just packing our food."

Edna was standing at the kitchen counter loading Ziploc bags and hard plastic containers into a soft-sided freezer bag with a giant "Food City" emblem on its side. She made what felt to Charlie like nervous eye contact before directing her attention back to the bag. She didn't say anything.

Charlie took the plunge.

"Hey, Ms. Freemantle. It's nice to see you."

Edna did look at her then. She even smiled. Well, she smiled a little bit.

"Hey, Charlie. I think you girls picked a good day for a picnic." She looked out the kitchen window. "It's already getting hot."

"Yes, ma'am." Charlie racked her brain trying to come up with other small talk. "I guess we just have to hope it doesn't pop a storm later on."

"It's not supposed to." The voice came from the doorway and it belonged to Roma Jean's father. "But you two oughta plan on being back early, just the same."

"Yes, sir." Charlie nodded at him. "We sure will."

Roma Jean rolled her eyes. "I already told you that I'm not going to evening church. You all can go on without me." She looked at Charlie. "They always have those nighttime services early in the summer. I don't get it. It's not a nighttime anything if it's still daytime."

"They just do that so folks can have more time off in the evenings," Edna clarified.

"More time off from God?" Roma Jean asked. "How do they think that makes sense?"

"It's just a kindness, Roma Jean." Curtis walked over to the counter and took a peek inside the cooler.

"Well it seems to me if they *really* wanted to be kind, they'd just quit having them period." Roma Jean faced Charlie. "People drive like lunatics getting outta there so they can make it home in time to watch *24.*"

"Now, Roma Jean, you know those services only run *that* late when they're in revival." Edna finished packing the bag.

"I don't know how they can call anything that happens there 'revival' when most of those people are on life support."

Charlie fought to stifle a laugh.

"It's true," Roma Jean insisted.

Charlie looked at Curtis. "I promise to have her home before it gets dark," she said.

"Well . . ." He didn't finish his statement.

Edna handed the cooler to Charlie. "You girls be careful driving."

"They're takin' that police cruiser, honey," Curtis said. He looked Charlie in the eye. "I expect they'll be safe enough."

Curtis's meaning was impossible to miss. Charlie gave him a meek nod and followed Roma Jean, who was already halfway out the door.

Once they were in the car and had backed out of the driveway, Roma Jean shifted on the seat to face Charlie.

"That went a lot better than I thought."

"It did?"

"Oh, yeah." Roma Jean nodded vigorously. "When I told mama this morning that we were going on a picnic, she didn't say *anything* for almost ten minutes. And believe me, that's like a lifetime of silence from her."

"What happened then?" Charlie was trying hard to remain calm. She was almost afraid to hear what Roma Jean would say next.

"She just started pulling things out of the refrigerator for us to eat. The market had a big sale on pasta salad this week—but it was that kind with the tricolor bowties, and most people around here don't trust anything but regular macaroni. So, we had *tons* of it left over. And she gave us the rest of that boiled ham that Daddy was slicing for Cougar's when he cut his hand. There wasn't any blood on it, or anything, but he figured nobody would want to buy it once the word got out."

"That was it?" Charlie was surprised. "She didn't ask you anything else?"

Roma Jean shook her head. "I figure that means either she doesn't want to know, or she *already* knows and doesn't want to talk about it."

"You didn't say anything else to her? I mean, about . . . well. About us?"

Roma Jean smiled at her. It made Charlie's insides go soft. She had to concentrate on keeping the car between the painted lines.

"I told her you were picking me up at home because it was time for them to meet you."

Charlie knew she was going to blush. And she knew the more she tried not to, the redder she would get. It was strange to feel so happy and so embarrassed about it all at the same time. But if Roma Jean had said that to her mother, it must mean that she believed it herself.

Yes. They had things to discuss.

She stole a glance at Roma Jean, who was still giving her that million-dollar smile.

"Did you really mean that?" she asked.

Roma Jean reached across the console and laid a hand on

Charlie's thigh. In all the time they'd spent alone together, she'd never done something so . . . forward. But Charlie saw her do it like it was the most natural thing in the world.

"Of course," Roma Jean replied. "What do you think I meant?"

Henry didn't usually have piano lessons on Sunday, but today was different. His daddy was on a trip to someplace in Kentucky, so he was spending the afternoon at Gramma C.'s until Syd came and picked him up at suppertime. He'd stay with them out at the farm until Tuesday, when his daddy got back. Henry didn't mind a bit. Now that it was staying light longer, he could be outside later after supper. Every night, Syd would let him walk down to the pond with Pete and feed the fish. And when she knew for sure he was coming to stay, she would save leftover pieces of melon rinds in a big bucket with other stuff like carrot tops and old lettuce. Henry's cow, Before, *loved* all of that—especially the pieces of melon. Maddie said that was because they were special treats and probably tasted like candy to her. When Before would see him coming across the yard swinging his red pail, she'd leave her clumps of grass and hurry over to the fence to wait for him. She'd cram herself up against the rails and moo like crazy until he got there and started shoving the big hunks of leftovers between the boards.

Syd told him to always be careful not to get his fingers too close to Before's mouth, but Henry knew she'd never bite him. Not unless it was an accident. They were friends, and friends never hurt each other on purpose.

At least that's what Buddy told him.

Henry missed his animals a lot. His daddy said they weren't allowed to keep any in their apartment—not even goldfish. It helped a little bit when he could stay up late and watch shows on Animal Planet with Buddy—even though Buddy didn't stay with any one program very long.

Not unless it was Shark Week.

Buddy seemed to like those programs a little bit more. Henry even asked Miss Freemantle if she could find some good story-books about sharks that he could check out. He would ask Buddy to read them to him. He thought that maybe Buddy would even read these books forwards first—even though stories about sharks probably wouldn't change very much if he did read them backwards.

He asked Dorothy if she thought that was true and she said it probably was. She supposed it was because sharks were the oldest things alive. She said anything that could survive that long probably swam ruts in the ocean that were so deep, there wasn't anything new left to learn about.

That wasn't true about *The Incredible Journey*. Something new happened on nearly every page of that story. Sometimes, Henry would stay awake late into the night worrying about how the animals were going to get out of trouble—or wondering if they ever would make their way back to their family. One time, he fell asleep holding the book and had a dream that he and Dorothy were the ones lost in a strange place. They were alone in a big field full of yellow flowers that covered everything. They were running. He didn't know why they were running or if somebody was chasing them. But it didn't matter. They both kept running as hard as they could. There was a noise behind them. The closer it got, the more it reminded him of something. He woke up before he could figure out what it was. That was when he heard Buddy's scooter running beneath his open bedroom window.

He hoped that maybe Dorothy could finish reading the book to him today. She was here at Gramma C.'s house, too. She stayed with him nearly every day now that school was out. When Gramma C. came over to pick him up, she asked Dorothy if she'd like to come along and get another piano lesson. Dorothy had to think about that for a while, but Gramma C. said she'd be sure to get her back to Troutdale in time to meet her daddy when he came to fetch her.

Dorothy was inside having her lesson now. Henry could hear her playing the same pieces of music that he was supposed to be learning. But even though this was only her second lesson, her playing already sounded better than his. He didn't mind. Not if it meant Gramma C. had somebody who liked practicing a whole lot more than he did.

He kept hearing a single note coming from someplace outside the house. It played over and over, but only when Dorothy made the same sound inside. It didn't sound like a piano and he was pretty sure it wasn't any kind of bird. He stood still and listened to it until he could figure out where it was coming from. Then he followed the sound around the house to the sunny side, where an old fence divided Gramma C.'s yard from a pasture that nobody used anymore.

It was Buddy. He was working in this part of the yard planting flowers. There were big flat crates of them stacked all over the place. He was digging, but he kept stopping and blowing into this strange little whistle whenever Dorothy played that same note.

"Hi, Buddy. What is that noise you keep making?"

"Three, five, seven," he said. Then he blew the whistle again. "Three, five, seven. C major."

"You're making a C major sound?" Henry asked. "Like the one on the piano?"

"Three, five, seven. C major," Buddy repeated.

"That's a funny whistle. Does it only play one note?"

"C major makes other notes right."

Buddy blew the whistle again. This time, the music stopped.

"Where'd you get it?" Henry asked. He pulled over an empty flower crate and sat down on it.

"Quiet lady gave me C major," Buddy explained. "It makes other notes right."

"Gramma C. gave it to you?"

Buddy nodded. "C major makes other notes right."

"Are you going to plant all of these flowers here?" Henry could see that Buddy had dug a whole bunch of holes in an unusual pattern. It reminded him of the fun shapes he and Maddie drew on sheets of paper with an old pen-toy of hers called a Spirograph. Henry thought the designs they made all looked like spider webs or honeycombs. But they used special tools to make the perfect shapes. Buddy was making this one in a big patch of dirt with only a blue pointed shovel.

There was something else, too. Buddy had all the flowers set up by colors in the same order. Each crate was the same. Two yellows, two greens, three blues, five purples, eight reds, twelve oranges. Henry counted them all again to be sure.

He pointed at the rows of flowers arranged in all the crates. "Why are the yellow ones first?"

"Goldenrod," Buddy said.

Henry was confused. Goldenrod was Buddy's name for Dorothy.

"What does she have to do with the flowers?" Henry asked.

"Goldenrod is magic for Bluebird. One, three, seven, five." He dug another hole. "Golden magic makes other things right."

Henry looked at the winding spiral of holes Buddy made in the dirt. It was hard to imagine how all the flowers would look when they got planted and grew bigger. He guessed they'd all blend together and make the pattern that held them together hard to see. But Buddy would always know it was there.

Now Henry knew it, too.

"What on God's green earth is that disgusting smell?"

Michael and Nadine were busy at the stove. Michael didn't need to turn around to know who'd just entered the kitchen at the café.

"Hello, David."

"Lord have mercy." David walked over and peered into the skillet. "What are you two killing over here?"

Nadine tried to slap David with a dishtowel, but he danced out of her way.

"Don't you come into this kitchen and talk smack about *my* food, boy."

"Seriously." David pinched his nose closed. "What *are* you two cooking? It smells like a Bulgarian ghetto back here."

"A Bulgarian ghetto?" Michael glared at him over the tops of his glasses. "And you'd know this because?"

David waved a hand. "It was on one of those Anthony Bourdain adventures."

"That man couldn't cook his way out of a Bojangles drive-through." Nadine rapped her spatula against the side of a big Dutch oven full of simmering collards and cabbage. "Taste that and see if it needs more red pepper flakes."

Michael complied. "Nope. I think it's perfect."

"Perfect?" David looked back and forth between them. "Perfect for what? Are you gonna spread it around the perimeter of this joint to keep the mayor and his goons away from your shrubs?" He inched closer to them and took another cautious sniff. "It might just work."

Michael and Nadine exchanged glances.

"I hate to say it, Nadine . . . but he might be on to something, there."

"Oh, really?" She waved her spatula in the general vicinity of the dining room. "And I suppose if one of those brain surgeons out front sat down in front of a typewriter for long enough, he'd hammer out *War and Peace*, too?"

"Yeah." David lowered his voice. "By the way—who *are* those guys? I thought it was a mortician's convention when I walked through there."

Nadine rolled her eyes. "They're the Elders from the Conference."

"Conference?" he asked. "There's a mortician's conference going on? How come Harold didn't know about it?"

"Harold?" She seemed confused.

"He means Harold Nicks." Michael added more salt to the collard and cabbage mixture. "He does all the hair for Buford's Mortuary."

"Yeah. And if you ask me, he's hasn't been doing his best work lately. There's been a noticeable dip in loft on the last few hair helmets he's created out there." David perched on the edge of the prep table. "I barely recognized Hazel Maldonado. That woman never left the house unless her hair was halfway to glory. Who knows? Maybe old Manuel just didn't want to spring for the extra-long casket it'd take to accommodate all that backcombing. They say those bigger ones go for about 500 bucks a foot. If you ask me, it's more that Harold's been forced to cut corners on product to save money. Gerald Watson has just about run them out of business with all that remediation stuff. Not that I'm against protecting the environment—but it's not like Harold was dumping activator down the storm drains."

Nadine glared at him. "Boy, do you ever pay attention to the mess that comes outta your mouth? I said they were Elders from the *Conference*—not undertakers."

"She means the Methodist Conference," Michael explained. "They're meeting out at Bone Gap."

"Bone Gap?" David was confused. "Why would they come all the way over here to eat?"

"Want me to give you the short answer?" Nadine picked up an iron skillet.

David held up both hands. "No, ma'am. I get it."

Nadine slammed the empty skillet back down on its shelf. "That's the smartest thing you ever said."

"What are you doing out here, David?" Michael asked. "I thought you were taking Astrid to the groomer's?"

"Desirée had a gallbladder attack, so they canceled." He shrugged. "I thought I'd take advantage of the free time and do a little canvassing out here."

"David has decided to run for mayor." Michael brought Nadine up to speed. "Since he's a write-in candidate, he's making the rounds to tell people they'll actually have a choice on the ballot this year."

David nodded energetically. "The average voter turnout around here is about five percent—unless there's a presidential election. Then it roars all the way up to about nine. It's pathetic. No wonder that homophobic kumquat keeps getting reelected. Nobody likes him, but he keeps running unopposed."

"Until now," Michael added.

"Wait a minute." Nadine wagged a finger at David. "*You're* running for mayor?"

He nodded.

"*Against* Gerald Watson?"

He nodded again.

She faced Michael. "And *you're* in favor of this?"

"Against my better judgment." Michael smiled at her. "Shocking, isn't it?"

Nadine scoffed. "That's one word for it."

"Oh, come on, Nadine. You can't tell me that you and Raymond would prefer to have that wingtip-wearing ferret calling the shots around here for another year." David caught a glimpse of his reflection inside one of the stainless-steel frying pans hanging from a pot rack on the wall near the stove. He raised a hand and smoothed back his dark hair. "I pledge right now to protect your shrubbery from malicious malcontents wielding chainsaws. And P.S.—I have better fashion sense."

"Well, fashion is about the only kind of sense you can lay claim to, boy." Nadine shook her head. "Don't you know that man is dangerous? I saw it in his face the day he came out here and threatened us." She elbowed Michael out of the way and gave the odiferous vegetable medley a vigorous stir. "It was like looking at a shark's eyes—dark, deep and dead. You mark my words—no good can come out of this for anyone. Least of all you."

"How can you say that, Nadine? While I'll admit that David's methods can be . . . *eccentric* . . . I think it's damn courageous for him to take Watson on. He doesn't have to do this."

"That's true," David agreed. "I could continue to sit back and bask in my newfound celebrity as the best-selling editor of a landmark story series."

"Landmark?" Nadine whirled around and pointed her spatula at him. "Don't you dare mention that smut in my kitchen."

"*Smut?*" David was horrified. "It's not smut, it's *literature.*"

"It's *pornography*, and your mama should snatch you up by the short hairs."

"It's not pornography—it's *erotica*." David threw up his hands. "Why does everyone have such a problem with that distinction?"

"Boy? The only 'distinction' that people around here are gonna have a problem with is the one you two get busy with when the lights go down. He'll make sure of that—I can guarantee it." She glared at Michael. "I thought you knew better than this? People who try to dance with that devil end up in jail—or *worse*."

"Worse?" David asked. "What do you mean by *worse?*"

Nadine raised a hand like she was testifying in church. "I'm not one to gossip."

"Well, honey, who is? You can't drop a bead like that and not explain it." David went in for the kill. "It's not *Christian*."

Nadine snatched her skillet off its shelf again.

Michael intervened. "I heard some of those rumors, too."

"What rumors?" David asked.

"You know. Speculation about what really happened to Watson's wife."

"What speculation? She OD'd on pain killers." David rolled his eyes. "Hard to blame her for *that*. There ain't enough opioid on the planet to get you through doing the nasty with him."

Nadine's eyes blazed. She brandished the skillet like a claymore.

Michael intervened again—this time by grabbing hold of her wrist.

"Don't do it, Nadine. I'll need that pan later to fry up all those leg quarters. If you kill him, they'll impound it as a murder weapon."

"Good thinkin', love chunks." David got to his feet. "I gotta scoot. I need to pick up a couple rolls of canvas and run 'em out to Celine's. Buddy is gonna make me some banners for the debate."

Nadine shot an alarmed look at Michael.

"He's debating Watson at the town Fourth of July picnic."

"Lord have mercy." She shook her head.

"That reminds me." David walked over to a storage closet and retrieved a battered-looking box that was stashed behind some sacks of yellow cornmeal. "Raymond told me I could borrow your spray paint, Nadine." He pulled out a can and examined it.

"Rust-Oleum Old Forge Blue. *Solid choice.* Junior said this is great stuff and he'll probably have to sandblast it off Watson's car."

Nadine made a lunge for him, but Michael held her back.

"Yeah. Better part of valor, and all that." David scurried toward the door. "TTFN, y'all."

Jocelyn Painter set a box bulging with hardcover discards and dog-eared paperbacks down on the circulation desk.

"I think I got some real beauties in here," she told Syd.

The library's annual book sale was in full swing. It only lasted a week, and today was the first day. It was also the only reason Syd had the branch open on a Sunday.

Jocelyn was always one of the first patrons to scour through the scores of donated items, collection duplicates or damaged books that Syd routinely culled from the shelves. In a normal year, she'd hold the sale in the deep of summer—when the area would be teeming with campers, hikers and whitewater junkies. It was a great way to boost traffic in the branch and generate a bit of revenue. But this wasn't shaping up to be a normal year—not in any way. Everything seemed to be coming on early. Temperatures were already climbing into the upper 80s—unheard of for June. And there'd been so much rain that the water in the river had surged to near record levels. That prospect made serious rafters flock to the area sooner in the season. Campers, too—although rising waters were beginning to threaten some of the more popular RV parks.

None of the locals seemed to shed many tears about that last part. They complained that the big RVs descended upon the area like a brood of locusts, and tended to leave the same level of carnage behind when they moved on. They didn't eat in the local restaurants or stay in any of the hotels. They just parked their giant, high-dollar rigs beside the water and ruined the best views.

But they also bought books. Especially cheap, disposable ones—or, as Syd lovingly called them, "fire starters."

That's why regular patrons like Jocelyn made it a point to show up on the first day. "I want to make sure I get to skim the cream off the top," she'd explain.

Syd realized that Jocelyn's definition of "cream" was specific. She could be counted on to snap up any books about engine repair—no matter how old the edition or the vehicle in question, cookbook compilations published by any of the area churches, books or magazines about NASCAR, field guides to birds from *any* part of North America, old mysteries with yellowed pages written by dead authors (they had to be dead), and, oddly, biographies of unknown (or lesser-known) people.

Jocelyn really liked those.

Syd pulled Jocelyn's haul from the box so she could tally up her purchase.

"Okay, let's see what all you found this time."

She stacked the books according to price. Hardbacks were two dollars. Paperbacks were seventy-five cents—unless they were written by "dead people," in which case they were fifty cents. Syd knew better than to charge the full discounted price for any book that had no shot at a sequel.

Jocelyn had amassed quite an impressive set of titles.

Two Raymond Chandler novels. One dollar.

One Chilton manual for a 1972 Ford Pinto. Two dollars.

Three Audubon guides to birds of the Upper Midwest. Two dollars and twenty-five cents.

One favorite casseroles cookbook compiled by First United Methodist Church. Seventy-five cents.

Biographies of Gene Rayburn, Sam Ervin, Linda Kaye Henning, Donny Osmond, and some hippie lounge singer named Bruno Williams. Three dollars and seventy-five cents.

Four Spencer detective novels by Robert B. Parker. Three dollars.

Syd was surprised. She held up one of the books. "Are you branching out?"

Jocelyn looked confused. "What do you mean? Ain't they mysteries?"

"Yes, they are. But Robert B. Parker isn't dead. At least, not yet."

"He's not?"

Syd shook her head.

"Well, dang." Jocelyn took the books back from Syd and set them aside. "Maybe if he's dead by next summer, these'll still be here."

"You never know," Syd agreed. She continued tallying up the books.

One history of NASCAR series racing at Watkins Glen. Seventy-five cents.

One creased and tattered copy of *Tipping the Velvet*. This one was in such bad shape that Buddy had repaired the torn cover with car tape. Syd raised an eyebrow.

Jocelyn was quick to clarify the selection. "That one's for Rita," she said.

Syd smiled. *Seventy-five cents.*

"Okay. Your grand total comes to," Syd did a quick calculation, "ten dollars and fifty cents."

Jocelyn handed her a twenty-dollar bill. "You keep the change and add it to that Friends of the Library fund. Cougar's Quality Logistics is proud to support literacy in this community."

"Thank you, Jocelyn. That's very generous."

"Can I get a receipt? That Natalie is all about them tax write-offs."

"Oh, are you getting these for the business?" Syd opened a drawer and pulled out a pad of receipts.

Jocelyn nodded. "Cougar's has moved into the big leagues since we signed on with Wheaton Van Lines. We're running so many long-distance hauls now we can barely keep up. Natalie says we're gonna have to take on more drivers." She shook her head, and Syd detected a faint trace of perm solution. "I don't see as how right now, though—not if them Fleetwood contracts dry up." She leaned over the counter and lowered her voice. "Natalie says their business is good right now, but they'll likely go belly-up if things in this economy don't turn around. It'll be just like Oakwood Homes all over again." She sighed. "I hope that day doesn't come.

It's a sad state of affairs when God-fearing taxpayers can't afford to have a new home delivered."

"I guess that's true," Syd agreed.

"That's why Natalie convinced us to diversify our business model. These here books?" She indicated the box Syd was repacking. "These'll be part of our corporate library—to give our drivers somethin' to do on the road besides drink beer and waste money on scratch-off cards."

"I have noticed that James is away on overnight trips a lot more," Syd observed.

"Well, that's true. But don't you be worrying that we're working him to death on purpose. He's always the first one in line to ask for them longer runs. Sometimes, we have to say no to him, just so other drivers can get a shot at the higher-paying trips."

Syd's interest was piqued. "James is asking you for more overnight work?"

Jocelyn nodded. "The only reason me and Deb don't really mind is because we know you and Doc Stevenson like having more time with his boy. We ain't in the business of busting up anybody's family life."

Syd smiled. "I know that, Jocelyn. And, yes—James knows we're always happy to have Henry stay with us."

"Well, between you'n me," she said in a confidential tone. "I suspect maybe James is thinkin' about leavin' the area and doin' somethin' different."

"Leaving?" Syd was alarmed. "Has he said anything to you?"

"Nope. Not yet. But Rita says he's real unhappy and doesn't feel like things is workin' out for him here."

Syd's heart sank.

Leaving? That would mean he'd take Henry away, too . . .

Jocelyn noticed her distress. She reached across the circulation desk and patted Syd's hand. "Don't you go worryin' about this. I shouldn't even of brought it up. My big mouth causes all kinds of trouble. You forget I even said anything."

Forget?

That wasn't very likely.

Syd knew it would now be impossible for her to think about anything else.

She felt dazed.

"Where would he go?" she asked Jocelyn.

"Honey," Jocelyn squeezed the top of her hand. "He may not go anyplace. Rita just said he was *thinkin'* about making a change—about maybe going back in the army."

"The army?"

Jocelyn nodded.

Syd's shoulders slumped.

Oh, god . . .

"Thinkin' and doin' are two different things. You know that." Jocelyn gave her hand a last warm squeeze. "I am truly sorry I upset you with my loose talk. I oughta be horse-whipped." She picked up her box of books. "Are you gonna be okay, honey?"

Syd had no idea how to reply. She handed Jocelyn her receipt and tried to smile.

"I'll do my best."

She watched Jocelyn leave, then sat down on a stool.

Fear and sadness swirled around her like invading armies, amassing along every border.

Armies . . .

James was thinking about leaving—and that would mean Henry would be leaving, too.

How would she survive it? How would Maddie survive it?

Their lives would never be the same.

She stood up and headed for the phone in her office. She needed to call Maddie. *Now.* In her haste, she knocked a book off the end of her reshelving truck—and when she bent down to pick it up, she realized what it was. Richard Brautigan. *So the Wind Won't Blow It All Away.*

She stared at it briefly before flinging it across the room.

"Legato. Staccato. These are perhaps the most important things to understand and to master."

Dorothy sat on the bench beside Celine with a straight back. Her left hand rested on her lap. Her right wrist was up. Her right hand was arched over the keyboard. Her fingers were fixed in Position One. This was only their third lesson, but already, Dorothy was showing incredible promise. A lot of that came from her intensity and ability to focus. Celine had never come across that in anyone so young—apart from her own daughter.

But Maddie had never had the patience or the inclination to learn the piano. Celine always suspected that was a kind of protest position that was as much a referendum on problems in their relationship as it was an expression of her distaste for the discipline.

Thank god, those days were in the past. Although Maddie still refused to play the piano and would always find an excuse to disappear when it was time for one of Henry's lessons. Celine figured it was her way to avoid guilt by association.

"Don't worry if the actions feel unnatural at first," Celine explained to Dorothy. "It can seem difficult to do because we're not used to making our fingers work independently."

"Say those two words again?" Dorothy did not look up from the keyboard.

"Legato. Staccato. *Legato* is an Italian word which means 'tied together.' In music, this means the notes should be played fluidly and evenly, with no space between them. *Staccato* is another Italian word. It means 'detached.' This means staccato notes should be shorter and more distinct—with defined spaces between them. In music, these differences in the way notes are played is called *articulation*—and it's very like the way we use words in speaking. Seamless when we're animated or agitated. Cropped and punctuated when we're conveying more precise thoughts or emotions. Does that make sense?"

Dorothy nodded and looked over at her—but she still held her hand rigidly in Position One.

"So, the way the notes sound has to do with the feelings behind them?"

Celine smiled at her. "To me it does. What we're paying attention to with legato and staccato is the function and importance of silence between the notes. What does or does not happen between the notes—how much silence there is or isn't—informs the message and meaning of the music. That's articulation."

"How do you know how much silence is right?"

Celine thought about Buddy. He would be better positioned to answer this one. After all, Dorothy was asking a question that was as much about life as music.

"The truth is that sometimes we don't know. But the composers who write the music give us notation and direction to guide us. We will learn to follow those as we go along."

Dorothy looked down at her left hand. "I don't know how to start."

"I can help you with that. You begin slowly, until you are comfortable. Each finger plays one note, followed by another. Then another. Until you can play them all in order without thinking."

"What happens after that?"

"After that, you learn to do the same thing backwards."

Dorothy looked at her with a panicked expression.

"It's all right," Celine reassured her. "Do you remember when you first learned how to walk?"

Dorothy shook her head.

"But now you walk without thinking about it. Right?"

Dorothy nodded.

"Can you walk backwards?" Celine asked.

"Mostly. But sometimes I bump into things."

Celine thought about her own clumsy attempts to reverse direction. She bumped into things, too. But most of her obstacles were internal. She had the sense that maybe Dorothy's were, too.

"We all do," she explained. "But we keep practicing until we get it right."

Dorothy hunched her narrow shoulders. "I don't want to make mistakes."

"None of us does. But making mistakes isn't fatal. It's the thing that makes us human."

Dorothy removed her hand from the keyboard.

"What's the matter?" Celine asked.

Dorothy shrugged. "I guess I don't want to be human if it means making mistakes."

"Oh, honey." Celine moved to place an arm around her shoulders, but was stunned when Dorothy lurched away from her. It took Celine a moment to collect herself.

"I'm . . . I'm so sorry, Dorothy," she said.

Dorothy had swiveled away from her on the bench and sat slightly bent forward with a hand pressed against her right upper arm. "It's okay," she muttered. "I'm not upset or anything."

Celine understood in an instant that whatever this was about, it wasn't about music—and it certainly *wasn't* okay. She also intuited that Dorothy probably had legitimate reasons to avoid being touched. And she noticed for the first time that the girl was wearing a long-sleeved sweater on a day when the temperature had already hit eighty degrees, and was still climbing.

"Dorothy?" She knew she needed to proceed carefully. "Will you turn around, please?"

Dorothy took her time complying, and when she did, it was very slowly. She would not make eye contact with Celine.

"I'm okay. I just . . . I hurt my arm and it's sore. That's all." She continued to hold on to it.

Celine also noticed the girl's upper body was making a faint rocking motion. It was so subtle it would've been easy to miss if they'd been sitting further apart.

But they weren't sitting further apart.

They were only inches away from each other. Right now, however, that distance seemed like a thousand miles.

"How did you hurt your arm?" Celine asked the question as gently as she could.

Dorothy still wouldn't look at her. "I fell and hit it."

"You fell? When did you fall?"

"Last week at church."

"Does your father know?"

"*No.*" Now Dorothy did look at her—with eyes full of fear.

"*Please* don't tell him. It's just a little sore. I don't want him to know about it."

"All right. All right." Celine did her best to keep her voice soft and calm, despite all the alarm bells going off inside her head. "Will you let me look at your arm, Dorothy? Just to be sure it's really okay? You don't have to worry—I won't say a word about it to anyone. It'll be just between us." She made what she hoped was a reassuring smile. "I promise."

Dorothy hesitated.

"I *am* a doctor you know—just like my daughter. Only I prefer to torture my patients with a piano instead of a stethoscope."

That got a small smile out of her.

"Okay," she said.

Celine had to stop herself from reaching out to help when she saw Dorothy wince as she shrugged her way out of the lightweight sweater she was wearing.

Her right bicep and upper arm were covered with dark, ugly bruises. There was some slight swelling along the outer edge of her arm. Celine thought the bruising there had a distinctive pattern—like finger marks.

Someone had grabbed her. Hard enough to leave bruises.

She noted some of the same discoloration on Dorothy's left upper arm—but not as pronounced.

"Could you rotate your arm for me, Dorothy? Just out in front, back behind you, straight up and to the side? And tell me if it hurts to move it in any one way more than the others?"

Dorothy carefully moved her arm in slow arcs in each direction.

Celine watched her face. "How does all of that feel?" she asked.

"It's just sore," she replied. "I hit it hard when I fell."

"Did you fall inside or outside?" Celine asked. "I don't see any cuts or scrapes."

"Inside. I slipped on the floor at Sunday school."

"Does that happen to you a lot?" Celine noticed some slight bruising along the base of her collarbone. "I only ask because I know how slick some floors can be after they've been polished."

"It happens sometimes."

"Dorothy? May I look at your back? Just to be sure there isn't anything seriously wrong with your shoulder blade?"

Dorothy hesitated.

"I promise it will only take a few seconds," Celine assured her.

Dorothy nodded and slowly turned around.

"I'm going to raise your shirt, now," Celine said. "Don't be afraid, okay? I'll be very careful."

Dorothy didn't reply, but she didn't flinch or pull away when Celine took hold of the hem of her T-shirt and carefully lifted it up.

What she saw didn't cause her more alarm, but it didn't exactly lessen her concern, either. Dorothy's smooth, young skin was clear, but crisscrossed with a couple of faint, red lines. Old scars, perhaps? Shadow reminders of—what? Pattern injuries? Deep scratches?

It was hard to tell.

And harder to be sure about what it all meant. One thing was for certain, though—the bruising on her arm and collarbone did *not* come from a fall. Dorothy was lying about that. Why? Who was she protecting? And what was she afraid of?

Right now, Celine simply had more questions than answers. She knew she needed to do something. But what? Approach Dorothy's father about it? But she couldn't do that without divulging that Dorothy was coming to her house for piano lessons—something Henry said Dorothy wanted to keep secret from him.

Maybe she should share her concerns with Byron first? After all, Dorothy's father was hardly approachable.

Celine lowered her shirt. "All done. Your shoulder seems fine. But I want you to try to be more careful."

Dorothy turned back around and allowed Celine to help her put her sweater back on. She seemed a bit more relaxed.

"Are we going to finish my lesson now?" she asked.

"No. I think we've practiced enough for today, don't you? And I want you to take it easy on that arm—no more acrobatics of any kind until it's healed. And that includes the keyboard." She stood up. "Why don't we go outside and see what kind of progress Buddy and Henry are making with my garden?"

"Okay."

Dorothy followed her into the kitchen, where the big double doors that led to the patio were standing open. A warm breeze was blowing in from the south. It smelled sweet and clean—like it had rained someplace miles away.

"You know, Dorothy," she said. "I'd be interested in your opinion about the pattern Buddy's creating with the plants. It's very . . . unusual."

"Is it because of the numbers?"

Celine was surprised by her question. Her face must have shown it, because Dorothy followed up before she could respond.

"Buddy always does numbers. It's like he sees them in everything."

Numbers.

Dorothy was right. It *was* about the numbers. She couldn't believe that hadn't occurred to her when she stole a peek at the flowerbed earlier. The strange spiral configuration he was creating with the repeated color sequence of the plants made sense now.

At least, it made sense in a Buddy kind of way.

He was planting her flowers in a Fibonacci sequence.

Celine led the way outside, into a small slice of world defined by warmth and perfect order.

"Let's talk about numbers," she said. "Let's talk about the *language* of numbers, and the spaces that exist between them."

"Like the music notes?" Dorothy asked.

Celine smiled at her.

"Exactly like that."

Charlie was halfway home when she got the call. Sundays were generally slow nights, but the weather had gotten so much warmer that people were spending a lot more time outdoors, engaged in recreational activities.

"Recreational" in the law-and-order context meant drinking, cheating, fighting and wrecking cars—usually in exactly that order.

Daylight Savings Time was to blame, too. That crazy extra hour that got tacked on to the end of every day caused more problems than it solved. Byron was fond of saying it turned "the gloaming" into "the groaning." Charlie agreed with him. She didn't understand why they kept mucking around with the clock like that. Why not just let day be day, and night be night? It was no accident that most of the bad or stupid things people got up to in the summer happened during that extra hour of so-called "daylight."

It didn't really "save" anything. And it wasn't really like daylight, either. It was more like some kind of weird half-light that wasn't exactly day and wasn't exactly night. It was in between—an eerie sixty minutes of hollow light that made everything look flat—like it was part of a movie set. Probably that was part of what led people to think they could act out in any ways they wanted—no matter how wrong or "uncharacteristic" the behavior was. And when it was over, night would drop down like a curtain at the end of a bad play—fast and hard. No easing into it, and no time to get ready for it. People would pretty much be stuck in the middle of whatever mess they'd started—and most of the real damage would happen while they fumbled around in the dark, trying to find a way to get out of it.

But this time, she was actually happy to have the extra hour between day and night. She used it to race back to the Freemantles' house so she could keep her promise to get Roma Jean home before dark. They barely made it, too. When they pulled into the driveway, Roma Jean's father was outside puttering around in the carport, pretending to work on their riding lawn mower. At least, Roma Jean said he was pretending.

"He can't even change a lightbulb," she told Charlie before they got out of the car. "And that mower hasn't run since 1997, when I was born."

"Why does he keep it, then?" Charlie asked her.

"Who knows?" She unclipped her seatbelt. "A better question is, why does he keep it in the carport? The good mower just sits out back underneath a tarp. He leaves it out there in all kinds of weather. Mama says the Freemantle men don't respect machines. Except for Chevys. They always treat those with respect."

"Like their women?"

"Hush." Roma Jean swatted her on the arm. "Don't you start that here. Daddy has ears like a barn owl."

"Sorry," Charlie apologized. She ducked her head and spoke more softly. "I had a great time today."

Roma Jean blushed. But that wasn't unusual. Especially lately.

"I did, too," she whispered, before they got out of the car to greet her father.

When Charlie had set out to pick Roma Jean up that morning, she had no idea their relationship would take such a turn. It wasn't something she'd planned on. To be honest, she didn't plan on it because she thought it would never happen—even though she hoped with all her heart it might. But she vowed she would never push Roma Jean into anything she wasn't ready for.

As it turned out, Roma Jean ended up being a lot more ready than Charlie could have imagined.

It all happened so naturally, too. Without any hoopla or big buildup—just like the best things in life always did.

They ate their picnic lunch atop one of the many balds—large outcroppings of rock and low grasses. The Appalachian Trail crossed that part of the park, and right now it was ablaze with rhododendron—brilliant white and fuchsia blossoms that huddled in great clusters and shimmied in the warm breezes blowing across the high meadows. They didn't talk much. They didn't have to. It was clear to each of them that something had changed. They drank a bottle of iced tea and ate pasta salad and bites of ham from the same containers—sharing a fork, just like an old married couple. Some wild ponies grazed nearby. They didn't seem bothered at all by the two humans invading their space. It was so warm, fragrant and relaxing that Charlie wanted nothing more than to stretch out on the soft grass and nap in the sun. But Roma Jean suggested they hike, instead, and try to walk off the meal.

So, they did—choosing to venture along the Cabin Creek Trail because it ended at a spectacular waterfall. The hike down was long, and they were tired and sweaty by the time they reached the falls. It was getting later in the day and the area was deserted, probably because of the two-mile trek back to the parking area near the cutoff for Massie Gap. Charlie really wasn't looking forward to that part. But the breathtaking view of the falls was worth the torture it would be getting back to the car.

So was the way Roma Jean looked.

Her short-sleeved cotton blouse was sticking to her skin in all the right places. And she'd tied her mane of red hair up in a loose and rakish knot, exposing a long slope of neck that was usually hidden from sight. Charlie's view of that smooth-looking swath of pale skin felt strangely illicit. The innocence and intimacy of the experience surprised her. It was hard not to stare at it as they sat together on the edge of a moss-covered rock and cooled their bare feet in the clear dark pool of water collecting at the base of the waterfall. It was even harder to keep from touching it—so hard that she finally sat on her hands to still them.

The roar of the water cascading down from more than thirty feet above them was deafening. It was so loud that communicating with words was impossible without shouting. And neither of them wanted to shout. So, they sat without speaking and moved their feet around in lazy circles, watching how the sunlight shining though the red spruce and big-toothed aspen trees made the falling spray glitter like diamonds. Roma Jean was leaning back on her elbows with her head tipped up toward the narrow opening at the top of their private world. A dozen shifting rays of light made brilliant patterns across her long body. Charlie thought she looked just like the women in those old religious paintings—the ones who were having visions or being blessed by God. She could not remember another moment like this one—a split-second when every good thing, real and imagined, came together in a quiet storm of feeling. The immediacy of it overwhelmed her. It stole her breath and swept her heart up into an avalanche of emotion that dwarfed the power of the crashing water. Her emotions were so palpable, she was afraid Roma Jean would notice—and reject her for behaving like a love-crazed lunatic.

But if Roma Jean did notice Charlie's distress, she didn't seem bothered by it. Not at all.

She lowered her head and looked over at Charlie. Her expression was calm and beautiful. She smiled and leaned forward to kiss Charlie gently on the mouth. Charlie didn't move. She was afraid to. But Roma Jean kept right on kissing her—with more intent and greater urgency. Charlie closed her eyes and listened as the beating of her heart drowned out the noise of the water raining down around them. When Roma Jean's mouth opened beneath hers, Charlie thought she might pass out.

Just as abruptly, the sweet contact ended and Roma Jean backed away.

Charlie opened her eyes, afraid they'd gone too far. Afraid to see the doubt and uncertainty that she knew would be staring back at her from Roma Jean's luminous eyes.

But Roma Jean wasn't looking at her. She was sitting erect, and calmly unbuttoning her blouse.

Charlie watched with disbelief and elated panic as Roma Jean removed the rest of her clothing and revealed herself—naked and unashamed. She gave Charlie a small, special smile that contained her signature mix of coyness and shyness before sliding off their rock into the cold water. Charlie watched the expression on her face change from confidence to shock as her body reacted to the abrupt change in temperature. She hovered above the surface for only a moment before submerging herself in the flood. Charlie could see her beautiful form moving and flashing like bits of gold beneath the clear water. When she rose back up like a wave and stood with water streaming across her shoulders and breasts, Charlie was too stunned to move.

Roma Jean said something, but the noise of the waterfall combining with the noise raging inside Charlie's head made it impossible for her to hear.

"Are you coming in?" Roma Jean shouted her question this time.

Charlie remained frozen in place—still sitting on her hands to keep them from shaking.

Roma Jean waded over to where she sat. Charlie had to fight not to gape at her beautiful body and the things the cold water had done to it.

Roma Jean placed her wet hands on Charlie's thighs. The sensation was thrilling—like being frozen and burned at the same time.

"I want you to come in with me," she whispered. "Now."

Charlie could barely make out her words, but she didn't need to. She knew in her viscera what Roma Jean was asking—what she was offering. Freely.

Charlie slid off the rock into Roma Jean's arms. She was still wearing her clothes, but she didn't care. The cold water surrounded them, but she didn't care about that, either. Roma Jean wrapped her arms around Charlie's neck and pulled her head down.

"I love you," she murmured against Charlie's mouth. "I know it and I'm not afraid."

Charlie let go of her own fear. She knew with certainty that once they embraced this prospect, their lives would never be the same. Like the wise men of old, they would go back another way.

Wound together like vines on the towering trees that had stood watch over this sacred spot for generations, they drifted as one toward the cascade of falling water.

The rest of that experience would be something Charlie would relive again and again. Probably forever. The thought of it all made returning to everyday life impossible. That meant she didn't want to be the first responder to somebody else's Sunday night misfortune. If she couldn't be with Roma Jean right now, then she wanted to be left alone with the warm memory of their day together.

The radio in her cruiser erupted again.

"Car four, this is dispatch. Do you copy?"

There was no ignoring it now. If the dispatcher was trying this hard to reach her, it had to be important. She picked up the handset.

"Dispatch, this is Davis." She let out a deep breath. "Whattaya got?"

"Hey, Charlie." It was Selma Dees, the chain-smoking central dispatch operator who'd ridden shotgun on the seamier side of life in this county for nearly thirty years. "Sorry to roll you out on Sunday night, but things is heatin' up and we're short-staffed. We got a report of a 10-37 out on Highway 58, just west of Baywood."

"I copy." A 10-37 was a suspicious vehicle. "What kind of car?" Charlie asked.

"White Ford Ranger. It's got Virginia tags and an army bumper sticker."

"Ten-four. Any passengers?"

"Affirmative. One occupant. Could be 10-55. Proceed with caution."

"Roger that. I should be at the scene in about six minutes."

"Copy that. Advise if you need backup."

"Ten-four. Davis out."

Charlie took a shortcut on Redd Road and turned onto Highway 58 near the river bridge. She didn't have to travel very far east before she saw the small pickup, pulled off and parked near the entrance to a public boat landing on the west-bound side of the highway. There was a man seated inside, behind the wheel. She saw no other passengers or pedestrians. She made a quick U-turn and flipped on her blue lights before pulling to a stop behind the truck. She retrieved her service revolver from its safe between the front seats and got out of the car.

The driver rolled down his window as she approached. It only took Charlie a moment to recognize him. It was James Lawrence.

"Hey, James," she said. "Is everything all right? You having some car trouble?"

"I'm okay," he replied. "Nothing's wrong with the truck. I just wanted to stop here and think through some things. I guess I could've picked a better spot to do it."

Nothing about his demeanor suggested to Charlie that James had been drinking. And she saw no evidence of any open containers inside the vehicle. He did have some manila folders and envelopes on the passenger seat, alongside a bag from Popeyes Chicken.

The nearest Popeyes was in Wytheville. She knew that because Roma Jean loved their spicy tenders and told Charlie how she always stopped there on her way home from college at Radford.

"You heading home from Wytheville?" Charlie pointed at the bag.

"Yeah. I picked up some chicken and biscuits for Henry. He loves this stuff."

"He's not alone in that." Charlie thought James seemed vague and slightly out of it. Not intoxicated. Just—distracted. "Tell you what, James. How about you move your truck down there by the boat ramp and get off the roadside here? It would be a shame if somebody didn't see you parked here and hit you from behind. That is, unless you're ready to head on?"

"No," he said. "If it's okay, I think I'd like to hang out here a little longer. Is that a problem?"

"Not for me," Charlie said. She had an instinct that leaving him alone right now was not a good idea. Byron had taught her that when she had these inklings about people, she needed to pay attention to them. "In fact, if you don't mind, I think I'd like to join you. I've got a few things to think over, too."

James looked from her to the things piled on his passenger seat. Then he started his truck.

"Sure. Okay. That's fine. We can maybe find a place to sit."

"I think there's a picnic table down there." Charlie tapped the roof of the pickup with the flat of her hand. "See you in a minute."

Back in her car, Charlie took a moment to give Selma Dees an all-clear before turning off her blue lights and stowing her service revolver. She followed James down the gravel access road to the boat landing.

The trash bin was overflowing with food containers and empty beer cans. Charlie shook her head.

Sundays...

James was already out of his vehicle and walking toward a battered picnic table that sat at a precarious angle a few feet from the water's edge. Track marks in the dirt made it apparent that it had been dragged to this location to keep it out of the water. All the rain they'd been getting recently had pushed the river level up quite a bit. It was especially obvious through here, where the river took a wide turn beyond the bridge and continued its slow trek north to join forces with the Gauley River in West Virginia.

Charlie helped James seat the table on more level ground. Then they both sat facing the water, on top of the table with their feet resting on the bench. Charlie felt awkward for intruding on James's solitude, but something nagged at her about his mood.

Morose. That was the word for it.

She'd read about that just last night in *The Stranger You Seek.* Profiler Keye Street was looking for a serial killer in Atlanta, and managed to become a target herself. *Morose* described her mood while she sat alone and tried to think things over.

Of course, all those Krispy Kreme doughnuts helped Keye through *her* rough patches.

Charlie had no idea what to do to help James. It was clear he was fighting his way through something.

"I come here a lot," she said, just to break the silence.

James looked over at her. "You do?"

She nodded. "Especially at night, when it's quieter."

"Don't you worry about being down here alone?"

Charlie raised an eyebrow.

"Oh." James rolled his eyes. "I guess you don't." He seemed to notice for the first time that she wasn't carrying her service revolver. "You didn't bring your gun?"

"I felt like I'd be pretty safe with you, James." She smiled at him. "Don't go proving me wrong, okay? I'd never live it down at work."

"I promise you don't have to worry. Not about that, anyway."

"That's a relief." She picked her next words carefully. "So, are there other things we might need to be worried about?"

He looked at her again. Charlie couldn't tell by his expression whether her question interested or irritated him.

"There's nothing," he finally said. "Not anymore."

Charlie wasn't sure how to follow up on a statement like that, so she watched the water instead.

"The water is pretty deep through here," James observed.

At least he was trying to make conversation. "It's all the rain we've had," she said.

Of course, talking about the water reminded Charlie of her afternoon. She was grateful for the darkness that mostly hid her face. She knew she was blushing.

"I don't like water much," James added. "Never have."

"Really? Why not?"

He shrugged. "I don't like things that aren't solid." He gestured toward his prosthetic leg. "Especially now. I need to know where the bottom is, so I can be prepared for it."

"I guess that makes sense. But I've always been the opposite. I like the feeling I get when I'm floating—and I let the water carry me along to places I might never go, otherwise."

"Don't you worry about getting back?"

"I never let it take me far enough that getting back is a problem."

He nodded. "That's a kind of control thing, too."

"I guess it is."

"I wake up at night sometimes and think my leg is still there. It feels so real—like I could get up and stand on it. I even think I can move my toes." James pulled a loose splinter of wood off the tabletop and tossed it toward the moving water. He looked at Charlie. "You can't make it in a place where what's real and what isn't get mixed up like that."

"So, you have to stay where you can see the bottom?"

"Pretty much. At least, that's what I think I've figured out."

Charlie really had no idea what they were talking about, but she knew it didn't really matter if she understood what James was explaining. It only mattered that *he* understood it. And right now, it seemed to her that he did. He wasn't a danger—not to himself or to anyone else. She knew that.

And he had a bag of chicken and biscuits in the car for his son.

"It's good when you figure things out," she said. "Everybody is better off when that happens."

James didn't reply right away. He sat and stared at the water. Then he got to his feet.

"That's what I think, too," he said.

They didn't talk on the short walk back to their cars.

Charlie followed James's truck back up the access road and waited while he pulled out onto Highway 58. He waved a hand at her before disappearing around the bend that led to the river bridge.

Chapter 8

Henry's hands were covered with Old Forge blue paint. So was most of the makeshift drop cloth they'd assembled with old tarps borrowed from Junior.

They were making banners for David to use at his Fourth of July debate.

In fact, Buddy was making the banners and Henry was "helping." And Dorothy was there to keep an eye on Henry while his father was at work.

Keeping an eye on Henry right now meant trying to prevent him from looking like a Smurf.

Buddy didn't seem bothered at all by Henry's attempts at helpfulness. Instead, he created things for Henry to do so he'd feel useful. Buddy used long strips of car tape to mask off wide, alternating stripes of blue and white. Henry was then allowed to spray the exposed areas with Nadine's cans of Rust-Oleum. While Henry did that, Buddy was cutting out stencils for the lettering.

"NO PLACE FOR H8"— the signs would read. Followed by David's first name and phone number.

David had said he didn't need to include his last name, and could use his phone number instead of a website because everybody in town already knew him, and they could just call him up with questions. He said most people would do that anyway, so why bother with the Internet?

It seemed like a good idea.

Buddy didn't really approve of the abbreviation, *H* and the number 8, for "hate." He said it wasn't right. But David told him that *nothing* about hate was right, and this was just a kind of shorthand to get people's attention. That explanation didn't stop Buddy from muttering pretty much nonstop about all the ways H8 wasn't right.

Dorothy thought she might be able to distract him by reading aloud while he painted and cut stencils. They only had two chapters left to go in Henry's library book, *The Incredible Journey*. So, while Henry and Buddy crawled around on the big sheets of canvas that were laid out flat on the ground behind Junior's garage, she sat in the shade on top of an old oil drum and read the exciting final scenes of the book.

It wasn't long before Henry became so engrossed with the story he stopped "helping" Buddy and wandered over to claim a spot on the ground at her feet. He sat staring up at her intently while she read the exciting conclusion of the story of Tao, the Siamese cat, and his two canine companions, Luath and Bodger. The courageous and determined animals traveled more than 300 miles across the Canadian wilderness to be reunited with their family. Along the way, they had endured more hardships and misfortunes than Dorothy could count—many so sad and traumatic that she worried about the ultimate outcome of their adventure almost as much as Henry did. But now, at last, a happy ending appeared to be in sight. The weary trio were about to be reunited with their beloved humans.

"They stood at the road's end, waiting to welcome a weary traveler who had journeyed so far, with such faith, along it," Dorothy read.

"It's them," Henry cried. "They hear them barking! They know they're home!"

"Together journey their end might they that," Buddy quoted.

"What?" Dorothy was surprised. She didn't think Buddy had even been listening to her. She looked down at the last page of the book, then back and forth between the two of them. "Did you guys already read the ending?"

"Buddy always reads books backwards," Henry explained.

"Oh." It was true. Buddy had just recited the last line of the story—backwards. "I guess I don't need to read it, then."

"No! Please read it, Dorothy," Henry pleaded. "I want to hear it read front-wards."

Dorothy read the last line to please him.

Henry fell back against the grass, happy and satisfied, clapping his blue-stained palms together. "They made it home. They made it home." He repeated the simple phrase over and over.

"It's not finished."

Dorothy looked at Buddy, who was busy painting letters on the banners.

"What do you mean, Buddy? I read the whole thing." She held up the book so he could see it, but he didn't look at it. He didn't take his eyes off the banner.

"It's not finished," he said again. "Goldenrod has more story to go. More story for Bluebird."

"I don't understand?" Dorothy turned the book over and looked at its back cover. "Is there another book about these same animals?"

"More story," Buddy said. "No place for hate. Hate needs to leave so the story can be finished."

"Do you know what he means?" Dorothy asked Henry.

"No." Henry shook his head. "But it's okay because Buddy knows. Buddy knows everything."

"More story to go," Buddy repeated. "No happy ending until hate goes away."

Dorothy gave up trying to decipher Buddy's cryptic comments. "Who wants lunch?" She hopped down off the barrel.

"I do!" Henry climbed to his feet. "I want Popeyes!"

Henry still had chicken and half a biscuit left from the dinner his father had brought home the night before. Dorothy packed her own food at home and brought it along with her every day to Troutdale—and she usually brought extra for Henry, too—just in case there wasn't something handy to eat in the small apartment. Buddy always traveled with his own beat-up lunchbox and thermos strapped to the back of his scooter. He was very scrupulous about eating his own food.

"Are you ready for lunch, Buddy?" she asked.

"No place for hate," he said. "The space between sounds is smaller. When it's done, the story will be finished."

Dorothy wasn't sure what that meant, or what it had to do with lunch.

"That means no," Henry clarified. "Come on, Dorothy." Henry grabbed her hand and pulled her toward the back of the garage and the steps that led to their apartment. "Let's go get some chicken."

"Okay." She allowed Henry to lead the way.

They tiptoed carefully around the banners. The areas that Henry had painted looked like a big mess, but she knew that once Buddy pulled the car tape off, the edges of the stripes would all be sharp and straight. She was anxious to see how they'd look once they were finished and hanging up. It felt strange to be involved in making these, even though she wasn't actually *doing* any of the work. But it meant a lot to her that Mr. Jenkins— *David*, as he kept telling her to call him—wanted her to help out with this project. It made her happy that he wanted her to be part of something—something that mattered. She liked that—even though she knew she'd never be able to talk about it at home.

Just like her piano lessons. She could never talk about those, either.

They had reached the narrow flight of wooden steps that led to the second floor of the garage. Henry raced on ahead of her. She watched the comical flash of his blue hands as he flew up the steps. But Dorothy paused and took a last look over her shoulder at Buddy, who was still bent over the wide sheets of canvas, painting tall letters with a small brush. He must have sensed her staring at him because he suddenly lifted his head and looked back at her. It only lasted a few seconds, but it was long enough to make her feel strange. Even from a distance, she could tell how clear his eyes were. They were such a pale blue they looked almost white. She didn't think Buddy had ever looked right at her before.

She didn't think Buddy ever looked right at *anybody*—except his father, and maybe Henry. But he stared right back at her now like he was seeing her for the first time.

Then he spoke.

"Goldenrod," he said. "No place for hate."

Just as abruptly, he lowered his gaze and resumed painting.

Dorothy slowly followed Henry up the stairs, aware of something churning inside her. It wasn't that she felt afraid—but she did feel . . . exposed. Even though she wasn't sure why, or about what.

The space between the sounds is smaller, he said.

Was he talking about music? Like Dr. Heller?

Or did he mean something else?

And why did he always talk in riddles?

His eyes were so clear—just like the water she crossed in the shallowest part of the river.

He looked right at me, she thought. But it was more than that. *He saw me*, she thought.

And for the first time, I saw him, too.

Maddie had a plan.

And having a plan was unusual for her because she didn't normally have plans.

She had strategies.

But this time, it was a *plan*. A good ole, bona-fide, dyed-in-the-wool, true-to-life, homespun plan.

It *was* noteworthy that she didn't always have the best track record when it came to putting her understandably infrequent plans into action. Memories of that nightmare incident with Michael's revered stand mixer, "Gloria," rose to mind. All she'd wanted to do was cook a special dinner for Syd—by herself. Michael had been gracious enough to tutor her on the barest essentials of French cooking—and had allowed her to use his kitchen at the Riverside Inn. Needless to say, things progressed from bad to worse and from worse to apocalyptic at light speed.

Her elaborate four-course meal ended up being a portable family feast from KFC, and Michael's kitchen got a free spring cleaning courtesy of her new best friends at SERVPRO.

She didn't even want to *think* about what had happened to Gloria . . .

But that was then. This time, things were going to be different. For one thing, she was going to introduce as few variables as possible. That meant making use of a familiar setting, ensuring there would be a minimum amount of prep work—and that, only of a kind already in her wheelhouse—and timing it all to avoid intrusions . . . altogether.

She also vowed that no Kitchen Aid appliances of *any* kind would be allowed within a hundred miles of the happy event.

So far, things were working out just fine.

Celine had been ecstatic when Maddie made a late afternoon visit to her bungalow and told her what she was planning.

"It's about damn time," her mother said.

"You know—I *could* say, 'Et tu, Brute?'"

"I don't think so."

"Oh, come on, Mom. It's not like you aren't still a candidate for this." Maddie made a playful smirk. "We could make it a double-truck, and save big on the cheese straws."

"Cheese straws?"

"Yeah. You know." Maddie made little curlicue gestures with her index finger. "Those great little baked cheese cracker things that are ubiquitous at these events? They're usually on a silver platter next to the bowl of mints."

Celine gave her a withering look. "I *know* what cheese straws are. Although I constantly marvel at how you fell heir to such an eerily unsophisticated palate when your father was a near-gourmet cook."

"Who knows?" Maddie shrugged. "I think my aptitude for appreciating the culinary arts was stunted by the boiling of one too many cream sauces."

"You don't *boil* cream sauces."

"I rest my case."

Celine rolled her eyes.

"So, Mom?" Maddie got down to the point of her visit. "I was wondering about something. And it's perfectly okay for you to say no."

"You want to give Syd Oma's ring?"

Maddie blinked. "How did you know I was going to ask about that?"

"You mean apart from the fact that you've been fiddling with your ring finger ever since you got here?"

Maddie looked down at her left hand. "Shit."

Celine reached across the table and patted the top of her daughter's hand. "It's okay, honey. Mothers know things."

"You sound like Syd talking about Henry. It's like she has this x-ray vision that allows her to see into his psyche."

"That's a pretty accurate description of how it works. Although I'd venture to guess that Henry is far less transparent."

"*Less* transparent?" Maddie squinted her eyes. "Are you suggesting that I'm more transparent than a child?"

"Let me think about it . . . yes."

"Jeez, Mom. Take all the time you need."

Celine laughed at her.

Maddie sulked.

"Don't sulk, Maddie. It's bad for your posture and it leads to premature sagging."

"Sagging?"

"Oh, yes." Celine nodded. "Fortunately, there is now a whole range of over-the-counter enhancements that can remediate the gravitational effects of aging."

"And you know about this because?"

"Bert and Sonny tend to listen to a lot of talk radio. At first, it annoyed me. But after a while I became fascinated by the socio-cultural insights the amusement offered." She took a sip of her tea. "One should never shy away from a learning experience."

"As I am discovering this very moment . . ."

"But to answer your unasked question—yes, I'd be thrilled for you to offer Syd Oma's ring."

"Really?"

Celine smiled at her. "Yes. Really."

Maddie struggled to conceal her excitement before realizing that she didn't need to conceal it at all.

"I'm happy," she said. It was a simple statement, but it perfectly summarized her feelings.

"I know you are. And I couldn't love Syd more if she were my own daughter. And seeing you this happy makes me happy."

"That matters to me, you know. I want you to be happy, Mom. In every way."

"Well. I'm a work in progress." She waved a hand at their surroundings. "Just like this old house."

Maddie looked around the newly up-fitted kitchen, where they were seated. "I'd say you're both holding up pretty nicely."

In typical fashion, Celine ignored the compliment. "There is one thing I wanted to ask you about," she said. "Why now? Not that any time wouldn't be right because you two are so perfect together—but why now—so long after the Supreme Court ruling removed all legal barriers?"

"I don't know. It's not like we haven't talked about it—of course we have. I guess neither of us thought it would change anything about how we defined ourselves as a couple—as a *unit*, so to speak. I mean, previously, Syd was necessarily a bit gun-shy from being so recently divorced—even though she understood that the circumstances for that were entirely different. Still. It's a big thing for any two people—regardless of the social or political implications."

"All of that is still true," Celine agreed. "What changed your mind?"

Maddie laughed. "You wanna know the truth? I think it was Gerald Watson."

"The *mayor?*"

"Yeah. How about it?" Maddie shook her head. "Something inside me clicked that day in the parking lot at Aunt Bea's. For the first time in my life here, I had to confront how dearly bought everything I'd always taken for granted was. Our sweet, sleepy town has changed—just like our world has changed. None of the rules we used to play by are being followed anymore. And people like Watson? They're popping up in positions of power all over the place. It's like living in a monster-sized game of whack-a-mole. You knock one down—and ten more spring up. Each of them more frightening than the last. So why not cleave together with the ones you love and make what may well be your last, best stand against the gathering storm?" She absently stroked her bare ring finger. "I love Syd—more than I ever thought possible. And not only do I want to show it—I feel an obligation to honor the depth of my commitment to her in every way possible. Now. Publicly. While I still have the means and the right to do so."

"That's quite an answer."

Maddie smiled at her. "I've had some time to think about it."

"I'm happy about this, Maddie. For both of you."

"Aren't you making a wild assumption that she'll say yes?"

Celine narrowed her eyes. "I don't think so."

"I hope you're right."

"I feel certain that I am. When do you plan to do this?"

"If Syd's in agreement, I was thinking of having the ceremony before the end of the summer—maybe even invite everyone in town—make it a kind of public event? See if we can't help goose business at the inn a bit. Watson has really eaten into their profits this year with all his efforts to short-circuit the gay wedding industry. And, by the way," she winked at her mother. "You're welcome to bring a plus one."

"Nice try."

Maddie laughed. "Think I can ask Henry to be my best man?"

"Of course. But what about David? Won't his feelings be hurt if you don't ask him to stand up with you?"

"I was thinking about asking him to be my maid of honor."

"Ah. Good plan." Celine smiled. "Henry will look adorable in a tuxedo."

"Oh, no," Maddie held up a hand. "No tuxes. No gowns or leisure suits. No powder-blue ensembles or wrist corsages for the mothers-of-the-brides. Strictly casual."

"You're making a lot of suppositions, here. What if Syd wants something different?"

"She won't."

"You sound awfully sure about that."

"Mom," Maddie smiled at her. "I'll be lucky if she lets me wear *pants*—much less anything else."

"Well, you do have great legs."

"That isn't what I meant."

"I *know* what you meant. I was trying to ignore the picture in my mind's eye."

"Of course you were." Maddie got to her feet. "So. I have to head back to the clinic. Wanna give me the ring?"

"I will as soon as I find it."

Maddie looked crestfallen. "You don't know where it is?"

"I know generally where it is—but it'll take me a while to unpack it."

"But, I wanted to ask her this weekend."

"Don't pout, dear." Celine stood up, too. "I'll be sure to find it and bring it to you on taco night."

"Oh." Maddie brightened up. "That'll work. Give me a heads-up when you're on your way and I'll meet you at the car. I can hide it in my workbench in the barn."

"Good plan." Celine hugged her.

Her mother was right. It *was* a good plan. And when you had a good plan, you didn't need to strategize.

Now, she just needed two things: She needed Syd to say yes—and she needed the three capricious Fates who seemed to make a career out of thwarting her best-laid plans, to take an extended holiday and cut her some richly deserved slack.

She was fairly certain about the first part.

It was that *second* part that always came with a floating decimal point.

Syd agreed to meet her brother in a public place because she knew meeting him in private would make it impossible for her to resist the temptation to kill him.

They agreed to connect at Freemantle's Market for an early

238

lunch. They weren't alone in that idea, either. The place was jammed. Curtis and Edna had their hands full running the register and handling all the deli orders—although she did notice the dearth of boiled ham. Curtis gave her an energetic wave with his bandaged hand when she entered, and pointed toward the back of the market where an uneven line of small tables snaked around stacked towers of Cheerwine and Pabst Blue Ribbon. Tom was already there, watching the entrance and drumming his fingers on the tabletop. Syd was surprised to see Byron Martin and Charlie Davis seated back there, too—huddled over their table in deep conversation about something.

Two minutes after Tom and Syd returned to their table with their hot dogs and drinks, it became clear that Tom wasn't much in the mood for eating—or for polite conversation.

"She dumped me," he said without preamble.

Syd barely managed to bite back her immediate response—which was to smile and say "good."

It wasn't that she didn't feel sorry for her brother. She did—*kind of.* In the same way you'd feel sorry for someone who stupidly lost their car because they kept leaving it parked with the keys in the ignition.

Feeling genuine empathy for Tom was difficult because he had acted like such an unrepentant jerk—and it was hard to keep from reminding him that he had only himself to blame for his present distress. Whenever she did feel tempted to take it easier on him, she simply channeled their mother. Where selfishness was concerned, Janet Murphy took no prisoners. If she'd known anything about her son's recent behavior, the heat and force of her indignation would've singed the hair off his head—and he'd probably still be walking with a limp.

The long and the short of Tom's dilemma was that Lizzy had cut him loose with little ceremony and less discussion—presumably because of his "epiphany" after her miscarriage. Tom explained that he had gone to see her and shared that he'd undergone a revolution in his thinking about their future. Suddenly, he was ready to make a lasting commitment to her—starting, of course, with an immediate offer to rekindle their physical relationship.

Profoundly. Bad. Timing.

It was no surprise to Syd that his professions of attachment were met with more outrage than skepticism. Tom said that Lizzy had actually slammed her front door in his face and told him to keep his hands—and all of his other parts—the hell away from her property.

"Why would she say something like that to me?" he fumed. "I'm not some low-life intruder."

Syd understood Lizzy's double entendre right away, and took pains to clarify it for her brother.

"Sex, Tom. She's talking about *sex*. The kind you won't be having with her."

He looked baffled.

"Work with me, okay? Her 'property' in this context, means her 'body.' In simple terms—she's saying you ain't gonna be hittin' it anymore."

He blinked. "I don't get it. Why not?"

"Really? Do you seriously not understand that?"

He threw up his hands. "I guess not."

Syd sighed and looked around the market for inspiration.

Byron and Charlie were still in earnest conversation about something. Byron caught her eye and gave her a wink.

Natalie and Rita Chriscoe were there, too. They were seated at the table just beyond Charlie and Byron—beside the giant vending machine that dispensed scratch-off lottery cards. As usual, Natalie was sporting a flashy-looking nail job—but this one looked elaborate, even for her. Her fingertips were alive with an explosion of starbursts and brightly colored stripes. Syd recalled Jocelyn telling her that Buddy had shown the manicurists at Hairport '75 a technique for making intricate designs using car tape. This had to be some of their handiwork.

It was pretty impressive.

Cheetos were on sale. Fifty one-ounce bags for $16.99.

Maddie probably had already laid in stores for the winter . . .

Edna was restocking cigarettes. She wondered if David was still sneaking out to buy stealth packs of Camels.

"Hello?" Tom snapped his fingers. "Anybody home?"

Syd looked back at him. "I'm sorry. Was I ignoring you?"

"Um, *yeah*."

"Tom? The only advice I can give you right now is to step back and give Lizzy some space. She's just been through a very traumatic experience—emotionally as well as physically. You need to respect that—*and* you need to respect her."

"I *do* respect her."

"I'm sure you think you do—but showing up at her door and offering to hop back into the sack is not the best way to demonstrate the depth of your attachment."

Tom's face colored. "It wasn't like that. I said lots of other stuff, too."

"Yeah? Well maybe the other 'stuff' needs to be expressed without any caveats."

"What the hell does that even mean?" Tom flopped back against his plastic chair. "You might as well be speaking a foreign language."

Syd ran a hand through her hair. This was getting them no place. It was time for a different approach.

"Tom? Let me ask you something. Can you imagine a future with Lizzy in your life?"

"Yes," he said without hesitation. "Of course, I can."

"Okay. Now answer another question. Can you imagine a future without her?"

This time, he didn't have a ready response. He dropped his eyes and stared at their uneaten lunch.

"Give her some space, Tom. And give yourself some time to think about the things that really *do* matter—things that have nothing to do with your next booty call. Maybe then, she'll know that you're approaching her for the right reasons, not simply biological ones."

He still didn't reply. He sat there plucking at the cardboard boat that held his hot dog.

"Tom?"

He looked up at her. Syd could tell he was trying not to cry.

"Do you love her?" she asked.

He nodded.

"For right now, that's enough. Just sit with that for a while. You don't need to do anything else."

"Could you—" he began, before Syd cut him off.

"Absolutely *not*. I made the mistake of interfering once before. It was unconscionable on my part. A complete violation of professional ethics *and* of Maddie's trust in me. I won't do it again. Ever."

He sighed. "Okay. I guess I understand that."

She reached across the table and squeezed the top of his hand. "The one thing we haven't discussed is how *you* feel about Lizzy's miscarriage."

They both jumped at the loud noise made by a stack of boxes toppling to the floor.

Byron Martin leapt to his feet to avoid being clobbered by a cascade of Red Velvet Oreos—also on sale this week. But that wasn't the only threat. The cookie display had been knocked over because Gerald Watson had exploded into the market, and surged over to Byron's table like an angry tide. His narrow face looked pinched—and, even from a distance, Syd could see thick, purplish veins sticking out on his forehead.

It was clear to everyone in the place that he was mad as hell—and he wasn't trying to conceal it.

"Don't think for one minute I don't know what you and your little minion here have been up to at Whitetop," he bellowed at Byron, while shaking a bony finger at Charlie.

Byron held up a restraining hand. "Mr. Mayor, I suggest you calm down. If you need to speak with me about something, we can step outside."

"I don't think so, Sheriff. The citizens of this town deserve to know what you've been doing to thwart justice and interfere with due process."

Byron folded his arms. "I have no idea what you're talking about, Mr. Watson."

"Oh, don't you?" Watson whirled to face a stunned-looking Charlie Davis. "How about we ask Barney Fife, here? Maybe she can fill us in on how her little *girlfriend* knew we were planning an INS raid at the tree farm this morning? And when we got there, they were mysteriously short-staffed. A well-timed outbreak of the Spanish Flu."

Charlie's eyes grew wide. She looked at Byron and quickly shook her head.

"What's the matter, Barney?" Watson spat out the words. "Cat got your tongue? Or maybe it's just tired from all the extracurricular workouts it's been getting during your romantic trysts on the county bookmobile?" He shot a contemptuous look at Syd. "Not that we could expect our local librarian to care. After all, the apple doesn't fall far from the tree, does it?"

Syd was stunned. Watson was plainly unhinged. Everyone in the market was riveted to his tirade—including Roma Jean's parents.

"Okay." Byron dropped his arms. "That's *enough*. Either you zip it—or we can continue this conversation downtown."

"Don't you *dare* threaten me, Sheriff. I don't need any lectures in proper behavior from someone who spends his nights tom-catting around with an over-the-hill pornographer."

Byron's eyes blazed. Charlie quickly stepped between the two of them. Syd saw her grab hold of Byron's arm—probably to prevent him from clocking the mayor, who still sported a hint of bruising along his jawline from Raymond's right cross.

At this rate, people in town will be lining up to take shots at Watson.

Curtis Freemantle approached the scene. He was wielding a big block of something that looked like . . . olive loaf.

"Lissen, fellers," he said. "This ain't good for business—or the merchandise." He gestured toward the litter of Oreos that were strewn across the floor. "Me and Edna would appreciate it if you all would take this thing outside."

Watson looked at Curtis like he was something the cat dragged in.

"Oh, *I'm* bad for business?" he sneered. "That's rich coming from the father of a *pervert*. But I suppose having a lesbian for

243

a daughter quit hurting your bottom line once she stopped handling the food."

Curtis turned white, but he stood his ground.

"Our daughter is a good girl," he said in a quiet voice. He looked at Charlie, then back at Watson. "She hadn't done nothin' to be ashamed of, and we're proud of her. Now you need to leave this store. Right now."

Watson's nostrils flared, but he didn't say anything else. He squared his shoulders and straightened his striped tie.

"You haven't heard the last of this," he said to Byron. "I intend to file a complaint with the state."

He glared at Syd before turning on his heel to head back toward the exit. He'd only taken two or three steps when he tripped over something and went sprawling, face-first, into another tower of boxes—the Cheetos this time.

Syd heard someone chuckling.

"Have a nice trip, asshole."

It was Rita Chriscoe.

Watson quickly got back on his feet.

"Who fucking tripped me?" he sputtered.

Rita raised her hand and fluttered her fingers at him.

"*You* . . ."

If they all thought he was mad before, there was no known technology sufficient to measure the mayor's rage now. He flung a bag of the cheesy snacks at Rita. She caught it with one hand and calmly got to her feet. She walked over to stand just inches away from him.

"Go ahead," she cooed. "Let's *do* this. Right here." She waved a hand. "*Now.* In front of all these wonderful witnesses."

Syd could see Watson taking rapid breaths. But, amazingly, he held his tongue.

"Whatsa matter, *Gerry?*" Rita leaned even closer to him, so their faces were just centimeters apart. "Ain't you got somethin' to say to me?" She waited a few seconds before shaking her head. "No? Well if that ain't a damn shame after all these years. I'd dearly *love* to have a public conversation with you about . . . *things.*"

Watson stood clenching and unclenching his fists—but he never spoke. Their standoff continued until Rita gave a bitter laugh and reclaimed her seat. She casually tore open the bag of Cheetos he'd thrown at her and ate one. The crunch reverberated through the market like a gunshot.

"Hey, Curtis?" Rita called out to Roma Jean's father. "Add this here bag of snacks to the mayor's tab. He's in a *generous* mood today."

She crunched and cackled as Watson made a beeline for the door.

Maddie was waiting in the driveway when Gramma C. and Henry drove up. Pete was there, too. His ears were perked up and his tail was swinging around in big loopy circles.

Henry was pretty sure Pete knew when it was taco night. That was because Pete liked tacos almost as much as he did. Syd even pretended not to notice when he'd accidentally drop bits of shells for Pete, who always stood guard beneath Henry's chair.

He wasn't allowed to give him any more beans, though.

They had to have one of Maddie's "conversations" about that after one night when Pete had really messy poopies and Maddie had to wash the fur on his hind end *three* times. She wasn't very happy about that—and Pete looked really embarrassed, too. He pretty much sat around the rest of that night with his wet end backed into a corner.

Henry unhooked his seatbelt and opened the car door. He rushed over to Maddie and gave her a big hug. She lifted him off the ground and swung him around.

"Hi ya, Sport," she said.

"Hi, Maddie. Gramma C. isn't staying for tacos. She's eating supper with the Sheriff."

"Oh, really?" Maddie set him down and kissed the top of his head. He proceeded to tackle Pete and give him belly rubs and back scratches. Maddie looked at Gramma C. "Do tell?"

"Thank you, Henry." Gramma C. was out of the car, too. She

handed Maddie Henry's Batman backpack. He was staying over since James had an overnight run to Paducah. "I appreciate the help."

Maddie laughed at her. "Does this breaking news alert imply that this is a public outing . . . no pun intended?"

"No. It only implies dinner. At Byron's house."

"Well, that's a change that is not without significance."

Gramma C. nodded. "I suppose so. I thought I'd take a bit of your advice."

"It's about damn time." Before Gramma C. could correct her for swearing, Maddie added, "What goes around, comes around."

Gramma C. just shook her head.

"I have something else for you," she said.

"Oh." Maddie sounded happy. She looked over at the house before walking around to Gramma C.'s side of the car. "You found it?"

"Of course I did. It was exactly where I thought it would be—in the very last of the forty-two boxes I checked."

Gramma C. handed Maddie a tiny package. She stuck it into the front pocket of her pants.

"Thanks, Mom. This means the world to me."

"It does to me, too." Gramma C. smiled at her. "Now. Where is Syd? I want to say hello to her before I scoot to meet Byron."

"She's in the kitchen—lining up implements of torture."

"Oh? Are you grating the cheese again?"

"Not until I retrieve my brass knuckles."

"Your what?" Gramma C. asked.

Maddie nodded. "I ordered a set at Amazon Prime. Did you know they're listed under kitchen implements—right along with garlic rollers and herb snips? I figured they must be part of the Tony Soprano collection."

Gramma C. shook her head. "I worry about you sometimes."

"Well, don't." Maddie winked at her. "I'm about to do the smartest thing in recorded history. Who knows? Maybe I'll get an honorary Mensa membership out of it."

Gramma C. patted her on the cheek. "Hold fast to your dreams, dear."

Maddie hugged Gramma C. "You have fun tonight."

"I'll do my best," she said.

"C'mon, Sport," Maddie said. "Let's go see what treasures Rosebud has left behind in the barn."

"Okay, Maddie." Henry scrambled to his feet. "Bye, Gramma C.," he called out. "See you for lessons tomorrow."

"Bye, sweet boy. I'll come get you and Dorothy in time for lunch."

"Can we have some more of that yellow soup?" He looked up at Maddie. "Gramma C. makes yellow soup out of *squash*. It's really good."

Maddie looked horrified. "What have you done to this child?" She put an arm around Henry's shoulders. "Come with me. I have *Cheetos* in the barn."

Henry could hear Gramma C. laughing as he went with Maddie.

Sure enough, Rosebud was asleep on top of Maddie's workbench.

"Shoo!" Maddie waved an arm at the cat. Rosebud just yawned and stretched out even more. Her fluffy black and white head was resting on a pair of work gloves. Maddie sighed. "This tuxedo cat is a pain in my . . . tuchus."

Henry rushed over to pet Rosebud, who began purring at decibels rivaling a coffee grinder.

"What's a *tuchus*, Maddie?"

Maddie slapped her own butt. "It's this part, right here."

"That's a funny word."

"I know it is." She joined Henry and the cat. "My Oma used to say it."

"What's an *Oma*?"

"It's another word for Gramma."

"Why are there so many different words for the same things?" he asked. Rosebud was on her feet now, rubbing her head against Henry's hand. "It makes learning stuff harder."

"You can look at it that way. Or you can see that learning about how different people use language is exciting—and teaches you things about their lives and their family histories." Maddie set Henry's backpack down on a stool. "For example—we call you by many names. *Sport. Short Stack. Short Stop. Sweet Boy.* And Buddy calls you *Bluebird.*"

"Those are nicknames."

"Right. Just like *Oma* or *Gramma* are nicknames for Grandmother."

"And *Asshole* is a nickname for Rosebud?"

Maddie's mouth fell open. "Um. Well . . ."

"You call her that a lot. What does that teach me about our family?"

"Okay. Uh . . ." It took Maddie a while to answer. "So, Sport? It's time for you to learn about *another* interesting language concept. It's called, *entre nous.*"

"On-tray-new?" Henry asked. "What does that mean?"

"It's French. And it means 'between us.' Like a secret. Just between you and me."

"On-tray-new." Henry repeated the words. "Do we have a secret?"

Maddie nodded. "We do now."

"Can we tell Syd about it?"

"Nope. Nope." Maddie shook her head. "That's why it's *entre nous.* Just between you and me."

"Okay, Maddie." Henry stroked the cat. "Your special nickname is on-tray-new, Rosebud," he told her.

"Good job, Sport." Maddie patted Henry on the back. "I knew you'd get it."

Maddie stashed the tiny box from Gramma C. behind some old vacuum cleaner parts. Then she clapped her hands together.

"Whattaya say we go eat some tacos?"

"Yay!" Henry cheered. "Can Ass . . . *Rosebud* . . . come, too?"

Henry thought Maddie was going to say no, but she didn't.

"Why not?" she said. "She'll just follow us, anyway."

Henry picked up the chubby cat and raced off toward the house, where Syd was making their dinner.

◊ ◊ ◊

Henry was racing along the fence line, pulling up handfuls of wild onion and garlic and stuffing them into a battered tin bucket—treats for his beloved heifer, Before.

Maddie and Syd were following along at a more sedate pace. It was just after the solstice—the longest day of the year. It was impossible to believe that now the hours of daylight would begin their slow decline.

"Why does Henry keep saying everything is 'entre nous'?" Syd asked.

Maddie feigned ignorance. "I have no idea. Probably something he picked up at Mom's."

"That seems odd."

"Not really." Maddie shrugged. "Maybe it's some piano term."

"Piano term? I don't think so."

Maddie decided to change the subject. "Are you ever going to tell me about the drama today at Freemantle's? Peggy said it was a near-riot, and they had to call the sheriff's department to break it up."

"What?" Syd looked up at Maddie. "How did Peggy hear about it?"

"You're kidding, right? That woman has better sources than *BuzzFeed*. She practically gave me a transcript."

"Well, trust me," Syd clarified. "Her sources are a bit off on one point of fact. It *was* all pretty damn dramatic, but nobody called the sheriff. He was already there—at the center of the action."

"Really? What caused it all?"

Syd shook her head. "Watson came storming in there, looking for Byron. He was loaded for bear, too. Ranting about a raid up at Whitetop. I gather he was trying to round up 'illegal' workers at the Christmas tree farm—but nobody showed up for work. He blamed Byron—then Charlie and Roma Jean—for tipping them off." Syd squeezed Maddie's arm. "It was horrible, Maddie. The terrible things he said . . . the accusations he made about Roma Jean and Charlie . . . all in front of her *parents*—not to mention everyone else in the place."

"What on earth did he say?"

"Can't you guess? And he left little to the imagination. He even suggested that Roma Jean's 'perversion' was because of her association with me."

Maddie stiffened and stopped walking. She turned to face Syd.

"He said *what?*"

"Calm down, honey." Syd tugged at her arm. "That wasn't the worst of it. Not by a long shot."

"It got worse than *that?*"

Syd nodded.

"Do I want to know how?"

"Probably not. Suffice it to say he made some rather colorful allegations about Byron—and your mother."

"That rat bastard. I'm gonna kill him . . ."

"Yeah? Well you might have to get in line. I thought Byron was going to take his head off. Charlie had to step between them. And you'd be proud of Curtis—he stood up and defended his daughter's honor. It was a pretty remarkable moment." Syd pulled Maddie's arm closer to her side and resumed walking. "There was one rather intriguing exchange between Watson and Rita Chriscoe."

"Rita? She was there?"

Syd nodded. "She and Natalie were having lunch. When Watson started to leave, Rita stuck her leg out and tripped him. Watson went sprawling. We all expected him to get completely unhinged. But when he saw it was Rita, he just clammed up and stood there in front of her—not saying anything—while she taunted him and dared him to take her on. I'm telling you, Maddie—she's *got* something on him. He's terrified of her. It was obvious."

"Well. You did say she had an affair with his wife. Maybe his ego can't take the reminder?"

"Maybe," Syd agreed. "Or maybe it's something more than that. When I got back to the library, I did a bit of research on Eva Watson. Do you know anything about the circumstances of her death?"

Maddie shook her head. "It happened before I came back here to practice. But I understood it was a suicide."

"Correct." Syd nodded. "A drug overdose. Sleeping pills. It was ruled intentional, but many people who knew her well questioned that finding—including Rita. Apparently, Eva had a deep-seated mistrust of *any* kind of medicine. She wouldn't even take aspirin for a headache. And her body was discovered in a motel room in Galax—along with several suitcases containing most of her belongings. Not very typical behavior for someone intending to take their own life."

"No. But maybe she didn't want to be at home to leave a legacy like that for her family?"

"Maybe. But I don't think so."

"What do you think happened, then?"

Syd shook her head. "I honestly have no idea. But I feel sure that Rita does—and I think that's why Watson is afraid of her."

"He's a dangerous man, Syd. We all need to stay away from him. And we need to find a way to keep Roma Jean out of his crosshairs."

"I know. I've already talked with her about that."

"Good."

Henry had finished filling his bucket and was heading back toward them at an uneven lope.

"Take it easy, Sport," Maddie called out to him. "Before isn't going anyplace."

It was true. The big heifer was ambling along the fence beside them, munching at stray clumps of grass. She wasn't in any kind of a hurry. And she seemed to have an uncanny sense that Henry was headed her way with a super-sized serving of redolent comestibles.

"Her diet is out of control," Syd murmured.

Maddie laughed at her.

"What?" Syd nudged her with an elbow. "Look at her. I swear she's gained a hundred pounds this month."

"Honey. She's a *cow*. This is what they do—graze and gain weight." She smiled. "Nice work if you can get it."

"Oh, don't even go there. I found your stash of Cheetos in the barn."

"You did? And, by the way, they aren't 'stashed.' I just haven't brought them into the house yet."

"Right."

"They were on sale," Maddie explained.

"Of course they were."

"It was a great deal."

"I'm certain it was."

"You like them, too."

"I don't deny that."

Maddie sulked. Then she got an idea.

She gave Syd a playful nudge.

"We could maybe share a bag later, after Henry goes to bed?"

Syd considered her suggestion. "I'm listening."

Maddie lowered her voice. "I'd lick the orange dust off your fingers."

Syd looked her up and down. "Please continue."

Maddie bent closer and whispered something in her ear. By the time she finished, Syd's eyes were glazed over.

"Really?" she asked, in a small voice.

Maddie nodded enthusiastically.

Syd cleared her throat and cast about for Henry, who was busy shoving garlic bulbs through the fence.

"Shake a leg, Sport," she commanded. "It's getting late."

Henry looked up at the sky. "It's not even dark yet," he complained.

"It will be by the time you have your bath and story." Syd clapped her hands together. "Come on. Come on. Time is money."

Henry gave Before his final few handfuls of greens, then wandered over to join them.

"I'll go on ahead and get your bath started, Henry." Syd took off for the house. She wasn't exactly running, but it was clear she was in a hurry.

Maddie and Henry watched her go.

"Why's she going so fast, Maddie?"

Maddie put her hand on Henry's shoulder. "It's . . . well." She chose her words carefully. "I can't really tell you," she said.

Henry looked confused. "Why not?"

"Because," Maddie bent down to whisper. "It's *entre nous*."

When Byron announced that he was cooking dinner for them, Celine just assumed it meant he would grill something—probably from an animal he'd shot and killed himself.

She prided herself in believing there was no judgment in this assumption. After all, hunting was something the men in this county just did—like watching NASCAR on Sunday afternoons and voting Republican.

But then, Byron hated stock car racing, and he was the first registered Democrat ever elected sheriff in this part of the state.

Still, she knew he probably enjoyed hunting and likely had a big chest freezer stuffed to the gills with venison, humming away in some remote corner of his back porch.

Wrong again.

Byron was a vegetarian. Correction. Byron was a *pescatarian*. He'd eaten fish at Celine's several times now. It never occurred to her that they'd never had meat—so there wasn't a reason for him to share this dietary detail with her.

He didn't have a chest freezer, either.

Or a back porch.

He was proving to be a man of many contradictions.

None of that made navigating her predicament any easier. She knew she was clumsily blundering from encounter to encounter with him, trying to keep her bearings and maintain a steady heading. But every time she thought she had a handle on the contours of the landscape and had plotted a safe way through it, something would change. Dramatically.

Like right now.

Byron had told her to take the Fairwood Road turnoff, just after she passed through "downtown" Troutdale. The apartment over Junior's garage was dark. The rest of the town looked deserted, too—probably because everyone was at the Methodist Church playing bingo. The church parking lot was overflowing with cars, and a dozen or so more lined the roadway out front. She was certain she recognized Bert and Sonny's pickup trucks parked nearest the entrance—which meant they'd arrived early enough to command the premier spaces. She wondered if Buddy played Bingo, too . . .

Doubtful.

This part of the county didn't have many residents, but the people who did choose to live out here on the fringes seemed to be overflowing with gratitude. No matter how humble the dwelling, every scrap of yard sported a sign proclaiming, "Thank you Jesus!"

She didn't have any trouble finding Byron's lane—it was set off by a large mailbox that looked like it had been used for target practice. It sagged from its mounting post and the reflective letters that spelled out MARTIN were neatly ringed with bullet holes.

Byron's small house sat atop a narrow ridge that afforded an unobstructed view of Mount Rogers, the highest peak in Virginia. His acre of land was nestled along one of the many switchbacks that once had been part of the old Marion and Rye Valley Railroad. Back when the area's large stands of virgin timber seemed limitless, Shay-powered steam locomotives hauled logs that had been cleared from thousands of acres across this remote part of the Virginia mountains to sawmills in Marion and Fairwood. The trains had stopped running more than eighty-five years ago, and all that remained of the legendary railway were a few abandoned grades, and the occasional rusty spike that somehow managed to push its way back out of the earth. The old-timers who remembered the railroad were mostly gone now. But Byron said that sometimes, late at night, if you listened through the wind, you could still hear echoes of the big trains rumbling over Iron Mountain.

Celine parked her car and Byron met her on his front porch,

which connected to a catwalk that ran the length of the house. A floppy-eared yellow dog danced around their feet. This was Django, a stray Labrador and—*something*—mix that had managed to survive a fire that consumed the abandoned house he'd been living in. His front left paw had been badly singed and he'd lost two toes. No one wanted to claim the castoff pup, and the local veterinarian said it didn't make much sense to try and save the dog's foot if he was destined for euthanizing by animal control. Byron supposed that was true, so he wrapped the wounded creature in his jacket and placed him on the front seat of his cruiser for the short ride to the county shelter. At some point along the way, though, the dog had managed to drag itself across the big bench seat and rest its chin on Byron's thigh.

Django didn't go to the shelter that night. And veterinary surgeons at Virginia Tech had managed to save most of his left foot. If you hadn't known about his rocky start, you'd never have guessed at what all he endured to be where he was today.

Byron had explained to Celine that he named his furry companion after his favorite jazz guitarist, Django Reinhardt—who'd suffered a similar physical loss after barely escaping a Gypsy caravan fire.

"They have a lot in common," he explained. "Reinhardt learned how to compensate—with a vengeance. And this little guy," he patted the dog's head, "can tree a squirrel faster than I can swat a fly."

Celine had never spent much time around dogs, until she got to know Maddie and Syd's dog, Pete. It had been a surprise to her to learn how profoundly *human* dogs were—along with sensitive, intuitive and forgiving. In fact, they were more human than most humans. She regretted that she'd lived so much of her life without making time or space for pets. It was something she intended to change as soon as the renovations on her house were complete.

In the meantime, she supposed keeping company with Pete and Django would have to tide her over.

The view from Byron's catwalk took her breath away. The sun

was setting over the Blue Ridge and everything was alive with color. Endless ranges of mountains were painted in broad swaths of indigo, purple and pale lavender. She tried to count them all but gave up. They were too numerous—and they were on a collision course with the advancing night, which now was gaining steam on an evening sky exploding in last gasps of pink and orange.

She didn't realize that Byron had gone into the house until he reappeared, carrying two glasses of dark red wine. Whatever he was cooking smelled divine. The scent of it followed him back to where she stood, watching the light drain from the landscape.

"I could look at this view forever," she said.

"So could I," he replied.

Byron was standing with his back against the wood and cable wire railing, and he wasn't watching the sunset. He was watching her watch the sunset.

"Don't say things like that," she demurred.

"Why not?" He handed her one of the glasses. "It's true."

She decided to change the subject. "What are you cooking? It smells wonderful."

"It's a tagine. Please tell me you like Moroccan food?"

She nodded.

"Thank god. This one is eggplant and chickpea. I got some fresh mint and cilantro at the farmer's market this morning." He rolled his eyes. "I had to serve some papers on one of the vendors and he was being a bit—elusive. So, I had to track him down at the actual farm. I took advantage of being out that way and got some eggplant, too. It looked pretty nice—even though it's a bit early in the season. I guess it's all this warm weather we've been having."

"How did you learn to cook Moroccan food?"

"Oh, that's easy. I spent four years in North Africa while I was in the army."

Celine was surprised by his answer. And even more surprised to realize how little she actually knew about his history.

"I didn't know you were in the army," she said.

"Oh, yeah. A lifer. Twenty-two years."

"Really? I thought this area was home to you."

"It is. I just ran away from it for a while—kind of like you did."

Celine had to smile at his comparison. "I guess I did run away. Funny. I never really thought about it like that."

"See? We're just a couple of renegades. No wonder we fit together so well."

Celine tried the wine. It was wonderfully complex. Big and rich with a soft smooth finish.

Just like Byron.

The thought flustered her. Thank god it was nearly dark. She hoped that would help conceal her discomfort.

"What is this wine? It's lovely."

"You like it?" He held up his glass and tried to examine the wine in the fading light. "I do, too. It's a Super Tuscan. They're a real bargain these days. You get a lot of bang for the buck."

"It's very like a Chianti."

"Good nose." He smiled at her. "Would you like to come inside? I need to tend to the food a bit."

"I'd love to."

She and Django both followed him through the big atrium doors that led inside.

Byron's house was small—just four rooms and a bump-out space that contained his home office. But the kitchen and main living area were open, spacious, and very comfortable-looking. A large stone fireplace took up most of one wall. He also had a lot of books. She didn't want to be too nosey, but she was extremely interested in finding out what he liked to read. That he liked to read at all was a delightful enough surprise—and she was certain that his tastes were likely to be more varied than her own. She couldn't remember the last time she'd read something that wasn't a dissertation abstract or some unremittingly dull article in the *JAMA*.

There was no television—at least not in this room. She found that refreshing.

The whole place was modest, efficient and tidy. It was also

uncluttered, although he did have some interesting pieces of rustic-looking pottery and faded kilim rugs scattered about—probably all artifacts from his years in the service. She wanted to ask more questions about that.

Stacked beside the door that led to his small office was an impressive tower of boxes. They were all the same size—except for one—and they were all emblazoned with the Amazon.com logo. Celine was intrigued.

"Doing some early Christmas shopping?" She gestured toward the tower.

Byron chuckled. "Nope. They're mailboxes."

"*Mailboxes?*"

"Yeah. I'm sure you noticed the condition of mine when you drove in."

"Well. Yes."

"Being the county sheriff earns me a lot of the kind of attention I'd rather avoid. Fortunately, most of my detractors are satisfied to take their dislike out on my mailbox." He laughed again. "I have to replace it five or six times a year." He waved a hand toward the pile of cartons. "God bless Amazon Prime."

Celine was incredulous. "You buy them in bulk? Why not just get a box in town, at the post office?"

"Nah. That'd take all the fun out of it."

"Fun?"

"Sure. I get to laugh at what lousy shots they all are."

Celine shook her head. There was still a lot about life in this county that she did not understand.

"What's in the smaller box?"

Byron smiled at her. "Car tape."

"Car tape?" Recognition dawned. "Let me guess . . . Buddy?"

"Yep. He makes all the reflective letters for me."

"Of *course* he does. He also used it to rewrap all the handles on my gardening tools."

"He's a genius with that stuff."

Byron walked into the kitchen and began fussing over the tagine.

She noticed that he had a small table set with two places. And there was music playing. Jazz. Brubeck, maybe? She wasn't sure. She'd have to brush up on the genre. Maddie's father had loved jazz. She recalled how Davis and his best friend, Arthur Leavitt, would drag her with them to a succession of ratty, smoke-filled clubs down on Bleecker Street. She was pursuing her medical degree at Columbia then, and Davis would come up to New York from Penn on the weekends. He and Art were both in med school there—and they were inseparable.

That all seemed like a lifetime ago. It *was* a lifetime ago.

Let the dead remain buried. Didn't that idiom also apply to dwelling in the past?

Django wandered over to a plush-looking corduroy dog bed and flopped down on it with a grunt.

Yes. It was very comfortable here. Not in the least like the man-cave she had feared.

"You're pretty quiet." Byron's voice startled her. "Rethinking your decision to come out here?"

Celine watched him ladle two generous servings of the fragrant vegetable stew over bowls of couscous. Then he topped them with rough-chopped cilantro and slivered almonds.

No. She wasn't rethinking her decision to come here tonight.

She was rethinking the forty years it took to get her here . . .

Chapter 9

So far, Maddie's plan was coming together without a hitch. She had everything in place for tomorrow.

Michael and Nadine were going to take care of the food—there was no way she was risking a repeat of that Valentine's Day fiasco. She was picking up flowers in town today—dozens of tulips in every color. Syd's favorite flowers were tricky to come by this late in the season—but Gladys Pitzer told the new shop owner, Ryan, where to get them.

"I want to make sure he gets *real* ones," she confided to Maddie. "Not them hothouse kind that never seen the outside of a Walmart." She cut her beady eyes at Ryan, who was busy fluffing an arrangement of dyed carnations and fat, glittered marshmallows skewered on long reeds. "These gay boys get up to some strange approaches when you ain't watching them."

Yep. Everything was in place. Now she just needed tomorrow to come.

And she needed Syd to say "yes," too. The good news was that she was less worried about that part.

Rosebud jumped up onto her workbench. *Again.*

Her target was undoubtedly Maddie's open bag of Cheetos. Maddie had been "working" in the barn since breakfast, trying to make some headway on her passion for repairing broken appliances. The Cheetos? Well. They were just part of another kind of passion—one that involved her unrequited love for junk food and sometimes paid *other* kinds of dividends.

She put the protesting cat back on the floor, then reached behind some boxes of screws to retrieve Oma's ring so she could examine it for about the four-hundredth time. She'd polished it to within an inch of its life. But even with all of that, the unique patina of the tiny gold ring carried inside it reminders of the life her Oma had lived. The Hebrew inscription inside the band was faint, but still readable. *Ahava.* I give love. She smiled.

That part was right, too.

Her grandparents had met as children in their native Salzburg. When Hitler annexed Austria in 1938, the Heller and Weisz families had wealth and connection sufficient to secure safe passage to England for their children, as part of a Kinder-transport convoy that allowed children under age seventeen to enter Great Britain on temporary travel visas. Josef Heller and Madeleine Weisz, each permitted to carry one suitcase of belongings and their beloved violins, said their somber farewells under cover of darkness outside the Vien Westbahnhof railway station, because their parents were not permitted to accompany them to the platform. "Be good children," Papa Weisz said, as he blessed them. "Study hard and be obedient. We will write to you, and we will come to be with you soon." Surrounded by Nazi soldiers, Josef and Madeleine boarded the night train with other dazed and terrified-looking children. The doors were sealed shut for the long journey to a port in Belgium, where they boarded a ship bound for Harwich, England and a "temporary" home with distant relations.

They never saw their families again.

Josef and Madeleine were never separated from each other until the day death claimed him at age seventy-six. They both entered music conservatory at London's Guildhall before emigrating to the United States in 1952, where they raised their daughter, Celine, and enjoyed distinguished performance and teaching careers in New York City.

Maddie recognized the telltale sound of crunching before she realized that Rosebud had climbed back onto her workbench.

"Seriously?"

When she reached over to grab the cat, her sleeve caught on the edge of a tray containing half a dozen tiny set screws she'd removed from the outer housing of an old GE chrome and Bakelite toaster. The tray went flying and so did Rosebud, who quickly managed to nab another Cheeto before jumping down on her own.

"*Great.*" Maddie glowered in disgust as she watched the tuxedo cat's ample backside disappear beneath her Jeep. "Thanks, a lot, ass . . . *cat.*"

She'd never remember to quit calling Rosebud by her nickname.

She set the ring down on the workbench next to the bag of Cheetos and got to her knees to search for the screws. She found the first four right away, but the remaining two took forever to find because they'd somehow managed to fall into Henry's tin bucket, which still held a few garlic bulbs.

When she stood up she was amazed to discover that the wily Rosebud had contrived to slink past her and was enjoying unobstructed access to a world of cheesy delights.

"Good god," she muttered. "What *is* it with you and these things?"

Rosebud seemed completely at ease. She just blinked up at Maddie and continued crunching away on her treasures.

A fine ring of orange dust ornamented the cat's muzzle.

Maddie reclaimed her seat and dropped the handful of screws onto the tray.

"I should just give you your own damn bag," she said.

Then she realized the ring was no longer where she'd left it.

With an increasing sense of dread, she searched the entire surface of the workbench—and the floor beneath it.

No ring.

Nothing but the scattered parts of a toaster, and a surly, overfed tuxedo cat, now calmly licking cheese powder off her paws.

Oh, dear god . . . do not even tell me this just happened . . .

Instinct took over before it could be replaced by panic.

She raced to the door and shut it so Rosebud couldn't escape.

Okay. Okay. I need to call somebody. But who? It's Saturday.

"Tom!" she cried. "Of course."

Syd's brother was in vet school. *Perfect.* He could tell her what to do.

She fumbled for her cell phone and found his number. He answered on the third ring.

"Hello?"

"Tom?" she said. "It's Maddie."

"Hey, Maddie. I'm glad you called. I've been wanting to talk with you."

"Oh. Um. Yeah." Maddie felt like a schmuck. She hadn't talked with Syd's brother since Lizzy's miscarriage. "How've you been doing?"

"Not too good, to tell the truth. I was hoping you could help me out."

"Um. Help you out?" Maddie was doing her best to keep an eye on Rosebud.

"Yeah. Has Lizzy said anything to you about me?"

Only that she hopes you burn in hell, she thought.

"No. Not a word, Tom," she said. "But then, it's all pretty personal, and I haven't wanted to intrude."

Maybe I should open another bag of Cheetos? Just to keep her occupied until I can figure out what to do . . .

"I'm pretty miserable about it all," Tom continued. "Syd told me just to sit in it and give it time."

"That sounds like her," Maddie agreed.

"Do you think she's right? Do you think Lizzy will talk to me in time?"

Maybe after hell freezes over . . .

"Sure. Of course she will." Rosebud's bath was proceeding. She was playing the cello, now. "Just keep the faith."

Keep the faith? Did she really just say that to another human being?

"Okay. I'll try." Tom sighed. "So. How're things with you?"

Finally . . .

"To tell the truth, Tom—I've got a bit of a situation here. I need some veterinary advice."

"Sure. What's up?"

"Well." She took a deep breath. "What can you tell me about cat digestive processes?"

"I really love it here." Roma Jean was staring out at the big bend in the river.

They were at the boat landing just outside town—the same place where Charlie had sat with James Lawrence last week. Charlie had brought Roma Jean here after their lunch date, just so they could spend a bit of time together before she had to go on duty at three o'clock.

"I do, too. It's my second favorite place in the county."

Roma Jean looked at her. "*Second* favorite? What's your first?"

Charlie nudged her. "You know . . ."

"Oh." Roma Jean blushed. She gave Charlie a shy smile. "Mine, too."

"I wish we were back there right now."

"Maybe it's good we aren't," Roma Jean said.

"Why?"

"For one thing, it's broad daylight and there'd be people all over the place."

"That's true," Charlie agreed. "We might need to find some-place more private."

"You mean like your house?"

Charlie looked at her in surprise. Roma Jean was wearing a yellow sundress and the skin on her bare arms was as smooth as ivory. Charlie remembered how soft and warm they felt against her hands and had to fight an impulse to touch them.

"Haven't you thought about it?" Roma Jean asked her. "About us going there?"

"Um." Charlie wasn't sure how to answer. "Have *you* thought about it?"

"Of course, I have. A lot."

"Really?"

Roma Jean rolled her eyes. "Yes. Really." She discreetly slid her hand across the bench they were seated on and laced her fingers with Charlie's. "I want us to be together again. Don't you?"

Charlie could barely speak. She looked at Roma Jean and nodded.

They were distracted by a bunch of whooping and hollering. A flotilla of canoes was making its way downriver—likely part of an excursion group traveling from Sparta to the outfitter's post in Fries. Roma Jean quickly withdrew her hand and they both waved at the happy paddlers.

"It'd be a great day to be on the water," Charlie said.

"It'd be an even better day to be *in* the water," Roma Jean replied.

Her meaning was impossible to miss. Charlie couldn't get over the change in Roma Jean's demeanor—and it was every bit as thrilling as it was surprising.

"I'm not sure I know you," she teased.

"Oh, you know me all right," Roma Jean replied. "Warts and all."

"I don't recall seeing any warts."

Roma Jean swatted her. "You know what I meant." Her hand crept across the bench again. "I'm not sorry about what we did," she whispered—although only Charlie was close enough to hear her.

Charlie squeezed Roma Jean's warm hand. She could feel their pulses pounding away together.

"I'm not sorry, either. It's the best thing that's ever happened to me."

"My parents told me what the mayor said about us." Roma Jean looked up at her. Her hazel eyes were bright with determination. "They asked me if it was true."

Charlie's heart sank. "What did you say?"

"I told them he was wrong. I'm *not* a pervert," she tightened her hold on Charlie's hand, "but I *am* in love with another girl. If that makes me a lesbian, then so be it." She smiled. "Aunt Evelyn always did tell me I had a good head on my shoulders. I just decided it was about time to start using it."

Charlie was speechless.

Roma Jean tugged at her hand. "Don't you have anything to say?"

"I . . . you really told them that?"

"Of course, silly."

"What did they say?" Charlie was afraid to ask this question, but she needed to know the answer. Roma Jean's father and mother hadn't made eye contact with her after the run-in with the mayor at their market. And Charlie was too shy and embarrassed to try and speak with them about the awful thing the mayor had said about her and Roma Jean.

But Roma Jean didn't seem that bothered by it all.

She just shrugged. "They didn't say much. But that's pretty typical for them. They never do say much—unless it's about Chevys." She rolled her eyes. "Or Jesus. Daddy kind of grunted and said that was about what he thought. Then he kissed me on the forehead and went outside to change the oil on the Impala. And Mama asked if you liked chowchow. I guess they got a big shipment of it in because they're stocking up on picnic stuff for the fourth of July celebration next weekend. I took that as a good sign. If she cares about what you put on your hot dogs, it must mean she's gonna ask you if you want to go with us to watch the fireworks. That's about as close as they'll ever get to saying it's okay for us to be together."

Charlie listened to her story with amazement. How was a simple coming-out process like that even possible? Not that Roma Jean's parents wouldn't still spend time struggling with their own fears and disappointments about their only child's decision—even though the only *real* decision any of them had to make had nothing to do with the truth of who they were—it was all about whether they could accept it, and tell the truth about it to the people they loved. She remembered when her own father found out about her first sexual foray with another girl at church camp. He had beat her so badly she ended up in the hospital. That was when Byron intervened and changed the course of the rest of her life. Her father decamped for parts unknown, and

Charlie went into foster care until she was old enough to enter the police academy in Bristol. She never looked back—and Byron never gave her a reason to. He was the closest thing to a real parent she'd ever had.

Roma Jean tugged at her hand. She gave Charlie a shy smile. "So?"

"So?" Charlie repeated.

"So, doofus." Roma Jean shook her head. "Do you wanna go with us to eat chowchow and watch the fireworks? *Officially?*" She smiled. "As my girlfriend—just like the mayor said you were?"

Charlie did smile now—so big and wide she didn't care how goofy it made her look.

"Just try and stop me," she said.

Maddie made the text message short and sweet.

It was an old signal. One they'd used since childhood—back in the dark ages when they had to communicate via pagers and walkie-talkies, instead of cell phones.

S.O.S. Clinic. NOW.

Tom had told her what she needed to know. If Rosebud *had* ingested the ring, she likely would pass it without complication—so long as it didn't get twisted up inside her intestines on its way out. He was optimistic that wouldn't happen because the ring was small and didn't have any gemstones. But the best way to be certain of that—*and* to determine where the ring was on its journey back out?

X-ray her.

Fortunately, Maddie had everything she needed to accomplish this task at her clinic. What she didn't have was someone to help her wrangle the cat—who seemed more than usually irritated and determined not to cooperate. Obviously, she couldn't ask Syd. And calling Lizzy seemed inappropriate with everything going on in her life right now. That left her other nurse, Peggy.

Absolutely. Not. In. A. Million. Years.

Peggy was biologically incapable of keeping a secret for more than two point five seconds—and that figure was rounded up out of charity.

Enter David. It was a risk, of course—but mostly because he'd derive a lifetime of pleasure out of tormenting her for yet another epic example of her penchant for misfortune.

Getting Rosebud into the car and to the clinic was more of a cage fight than a game of strategy. Fortunately for Maddie, Syd was working at the library all afternoon so she didn't have to worry about trying to sneak out with the cat. Rosebud seemed determined to make the trip as difficult as possible. Tom had told her not to agitate the cat any more than necessary, so Maddie followed more than chased Rosebud around the barn before finally cornering her behind a big bin of fish food. She was smart enough to already have the car door open on the Jeep—but not smart enough to remember to use the cat carrier Syd purchased after they decided to keep the stray. Thankfully, she had the presence of mind to put on a thick pair of work gloves before picking Rosebud up. Good thing, too, because the cat wasn't any too happy about being put into the car against her will. However, once Maddie deposited her inside the Jeep, Rosebud seemed to relax and go with the flow. She curled up and looked placidly around the interior—probably making an assessment about how long it would take her glamour-length nails to tear the leather interior to shreds.

Maddie also expected the cat to amplify her resentment by peeing all over the back seat.

As soon as she arrived at the clinic and had carried Rosebud inside, she took Tom's advice and gave her twelve milligrams of diphenhydramine to help her relax. She enticed the cat to take the medicine by administering it in solution form—and mixing it with the liquid from a can of tuna from the stash of lunch items Peggy kept in the clinic's small kitchen. She kept the cat corralled with her while she waited for David to arrive. He hadn't texted back, but that didn't worry her.

It was a moral absolute. The S.O.S. summons was always heeded. *Always.*

She didn't have to wait long.

She heard gravel flying as a car roared into the parking lot. Its door slammed—then the clinic door was thrown open.

"Cinderella?" David bellowed. "Where are you? What's going on? Who's dead?"

She heard him running down the hallway from the back door.

"In here," she called out. "The kitchen."

David was running at full tilt, but managed to put on the brakes before he passed the small canteen. Maddie watched him skid past the door sideways before managing to stop and reverse course.

What the hell is he wearing?

In the flash of him she'd seen sliding by, he looked exactly like a hieroglyphic of a dead Pharaoh—headdress and all.

He came into the kitchen like the wind.

"What are you doing in here? Are they already dead? Do I smell fish? How can you eat at a time like this? Who is it? Syd? Celine? Henry? My god . . . *what took you so long to text me?*"

Maddie got to her feet and held up her hands. "David. Calm down. Nobody's dead."

"What do you *mean* nobody's dead?" He cast about the kitchen, plainly looking for hidden corpses. "You never use the code unless it's an *emergency.*" He noticed Rosebud on the counter, cleaning out the rest of the tuna from the open can. "What is that cat doing in here?"

"I repeat. *Calm down.* I need your help to x-ray the cat. I think she swallowed a piece of jewelry."

"Jewelry?" He looked at the fat cat, then back at Maddie. "The cat found *jewelry* at your place? I doubt it. That'd be like finding King Tut's tomb."

"David? King Tut's tomb was discovered in *1922*. And apropos of ancient Egypt, what is up with this outfit?"

David was wearing most of what looked like a fussy peignoir set. This one was a gauzy lime-green creation with a billowing hem and blousy, three-quarter-inch sleeves. He had fuzzy rainbow-colored slippers on his feet and his head was wrapped in a Canyon Rose spa turban. He also had random lengths of wide, shiny tape stuck all over the arms of his ... lingerie.

He was wearing a facial mask. It smelled vaguely like cucumber.

"*Hello?*" He waved a hand across his ensemble. "S.O.S. means 'emergency.' *Remember?* I didn't take time to change into evening attire—I rushed over here as fast as I could." He was still fuming. "I can't *believe* you played the S.O.S. card and nobody's dead ..."

"I'm *sorry* to disappoint you, okay? I'm not kidding. This *is* an emergency. I think Rosebud swallowed Oma's wedding ring."

"What were you doing with Oma's wedding ring?" His eyes grew wide. "*No way?*" He collapsed onto a chair and fanned himself. A few of his nails looked impressive. He'd obviously been halfway through a French manicure, too. "I need a moment ..."

"David. Will you *please* relax. I was going to tell you. I want us to have the ceremony at your place."

"Our place?" He looked at her through his spread fingers. "How *big* of an event are we talking?"

"That depends." Maddie pulled out a chair and sat down, too. "How big does it have to be to get me out of the doghouse for not telling you sooner?"

"Well, let me think." He tapped an index finger on his chin. "Remember the Rolling Stones concert in Rio?"

Maddie sighed. "Yes."

"Yeah. Bigger than *that.*"

"We'll see what we can do. But first I have to get the ring back from ass ... *Rosebud.*"

"What made you change your mind?"

"About?"

David rolled his eyes. "Marriage."

"I didn't change my mind. I just realized that there were no longer any good reasons to wait. And it seems to me that right now is a good time to make a public declaration about my complete and unabashed commitment to the woman I love."

271

"Well, you'll get no argument from me about that." He smiled at her. "I'm happy for you, Cinderella. This has been a long time coming. And you were smart enough to know the right one when she came along."

"I had a little help from my friends." She patted his bare knee. "My best friend, most of all."

"Yeah. It's still going to cost you plenty."

Rosebud grew tired of toying with the now empty tuna can. She swatted it and it clattered to the floor.

Maddie sighed. "Showtime."

When David tried to stand up, one of his stray pieces of tape caught on the edge of the table.

"Damn it!" He yanked it free.

"Why do you have all those pieces of duct tape hanging from your sleeves?"

He gave her a withering look. "It's *not* duct tape. It's *car* tape. Buddy told me it was great for hair removal."

"Hair removal?"

"Yeeeeesssss." David made the word sound like it had five syllables. "If you must know—when you texted, I was man-scaping the Furry Prince."

"The furry . . ." Maddie held up her palm. "You're right. I don't want to know."

"Not *that* furry prince, Tori Spelling—the *other* one. Michael." He shook his head. "That man's mother must've been an orangutan. He's got more rug than New York Carpet World. And, trust me. You *don't* want to see it right now—his chest looks like a bad imitation of that stars-n-bars pattern they always mow on the courthouse lawn on Lee-Jackson Day."

"Yeah. TMI." Maddie walked over to retrieve the yawning cat. "By the way, did you get a chance to look over the speech I wrote you for the debate?"

"Yeah. Nice job, Cinderella. I have to say, though, I was hoping for a few more fireworks—no pun intended."

"In your case, I thought less was more."

"Probably. Though I wouldn't say nay to some Gettysburg

Address flourishes, you know? Maybe ramp up the crowd a bit?"

Maddie carried the cat over to where David stood. "Since Lincoln was consecrating a cemetery on the site of a blood-soaked battlefield, I think we should look elsewhere for dramatic inspiration. Something that fits you more stylistically."

"Really?" David stroked the cat's head. "Like what?"

"I dunno? *Hello Dolly?*"

"*Hello Dolly?* Are you kidding?" He took a second to consider it. "On the other hand, the Divine Miss M. *is* doing that limited-run Broadway revival . . ."

"My thoughts exactly. Now. Let's get this done, shall we? I want to strike while the iron is comatose."

David followed her across the hall to the room containing her x-ray equipment.

Maddie set Rosebud down on one of the smaller tables.

"Grab us two of those lead-lined aprons over there." She pointed to a small closet.

"Wait a minute. We're staying in the room with her?"

Maddie was stroking and massaging the cat to get her to relax and stretch out. It seemed to be working. Rosebud was actually purring. *What a hedonist . . .*

"Yes," she said to David. "We're staying in the room with her. We have to keep her lying still to get a good image. I need to see where the ring is in her digestive tract and be sure it's not going to cause any tears or blockages."

David handed her one of the heavy aprons.

"Oh, no, Miss Thing. There is *no way* I am staying in this room and letting you zap my 'nads with microwaves. What if they drop off?"

"I think I can promise you that if they drop off, it won't be from radiation—it'll probably be from the over-application of car tape. Now, unless you can convince me that you're pregnant, you need to put on your apron and start massaging this cat. I have to get the machine set up properly."

David sighed and complied. "She seems pretty calm. What was in that can of tuna? Xanax?"

Maddie chuckled. "Close. Twelve milligrams of diphenhy-dramine."

"Hmmm. I wonder if it would work on Michael?"

"In a larger dose, it probably would. Do you want to take some home?"

"Do I *know* you?" David was scratching along the cat's back-bone. Rosebud's purring reverberated off the walls of the small room. "Dispensing drugs without a license?"

"I *have* a license." Maddie measured Rosebud's abdomen and set the correct exposure time. "That's what those letters M.D. after my name stand for—remember?"

"Yeah, yeah. I remember. You were a colossal drag for about *eight* years acquiring them. Now let's get this party started. I have a date with a cranky, partially epilated stud muffin."

"Whatever. Let's get her on her side and stretched out as far as possible. I want a good lateral view of her abdomen. When she seems good and relaxed, just move your hands away from that area and hold her head still. I'll keep her back legs stretched out. It will only take a second to get the image."

"*You'll* hold her feet? Don't you have to leave the room to take the photo?"

"No. I have a foot pedal. Okay. On the count of three. One. Two. Move your hands and hold. *Three*." Maddie pushed the pedal and the machine whirred. "All done. Perfect."

"That's it?"

"Yep." Maddie removed the digital plate and placed it into a scanner. The radiograph of the cat's interior popped up on a track-mounted computer screen about five seconds later. Maddie tapped a small white circle that glowed inside the cat's abdomen. "Bingo. Thar she blows."

David peered at the screen. "That's the ring? Boy. They aren't kidding when they say gold goes with anything."

"It looks fine. See how it's moved into her intestine? With luck, she'll evacuate this with her next bowel movement."

"How long will that take?"

"Hard to say. It looks like there's some stool in there right now. With luck, I'll have it before tomorrow."

"Is that when you're popping the question? *Duh.*" David smacked his forehead. "No wonder you asked Michael and Nadine to cook for you. I should've put two and two together."

"I really am sorry I didn't tell you sooner, David. It all came up kind of quickly."

"No worries, Cinderella." He smiled at her. "You know how happy this makes me, right?"

Maddie nodded. "Be my maid of honor?"

"Words I never thought I'd hear *you* say." He pointed at the x-ray. "But at least I won't have to carry *that.*"

"True. Though I do plan to clean and disinfect it first."

"Yeah. *Whatever.* Although, I *have* been looking for the right occasion to wear that tulle veil I got last month at LulaKate." He grinned at her. "Okay, I'll do it."

"Thanks, pal. There's no one else I'd rather have at my side. Although . . ." Maddie hesitated.

David smelled a rat. "What is it?"

"I will ask *one* small thing of you."

"And that is?

"Veil notwithstanding, you cannot wear this outfit."

Celine was surprised when James Lawrence called and asked if she could keep Henry a bit longer. He said he had a special errand to run and would be home later than planned. She told him to take his time. She enjoyed spending time with her two star pupils—even though she was scrupulous about making certain Dorothy was dropped off in time to meet her father for the ride home.

Dorothy was very determined to avoid being late.

Celine fetched both Henry and Dorothy in Troutdale on her

way back home from Byron's. Since Byron had the day off, he had persuaded her to stay on for breakfast, which naturally turned into lunch.

Naturally.

It hadn't really taken much persuasion on his part.

She should have been horrified by her behavior, but she wasn't. If asked to explain it, she wouldn't say that she'd experienced a revolution in her feelings. It was more like a quiet insurrection—as if all her battle-ready arguments laid down their arms and fled to the safe cover of the hills, where they planned to hide out until the conflict ended and their services were no longer required.

The feeling was new to her, and new things were generally suspect. She preferred to live her life in the safe haven of "The Known." Life was easier and less complicated when her emotions were kept under house arrest. It wasn't the strange sensation that came along with giving in to a passion she could no longer manage or compartmentalize that bothered her—it was the shocking admission that she'd made a conscious choice to stop *trying*.

Byron's tagine was the culprit. The catalyst. The cause. It was all of those, and a heavenly host of other *c* words—like crazy, compulsive and confounding. That intoxicating, unlikely stew of his had pushed her headfirst off the plank of reason into an abyss of pure sensation that was as mysterious as it was fathomless. And its success had everything to do with combinations—another damn *c* word. Exotic tastes and flavors that had no known reason to work together combined to create an explosion of "Just Right." Eggplant. Chickpeas. Dates. Almonds. Cilantro.

Not things that normally would beckon, "blend us all together and see what happens."

Well, she saw all right. And for her, the metaphors were too numerous to ignore.

As abstract relationship ingredients, she and Byron made *no* sense. There was absolutely no good reason why they should work together. And yet?

They did work. Easily. Seamlessly. Abundantly. At one point in the evening, when she tried to give voice to her concerns, Byron laughed at her.

"Do you wanna know why this works—*really* works—despite all the energy you keep putting into finding reasons why it shouldn't?"

"Of course I do."

"It's because inside this rough-and-tumble exterior, I have a secret." He leaned toward her. "I'm really a lesbian."

Celine tapped a finger against the stem of her wine glass. "I wonder how you'd look wearing this eggplant?"

"I'm an autumn." He batted his eyes at her. "So probably pretty good."

She tried not to laugh, but it was a losing battle.

He reached across the table and took hold of her hand. "Surrender, Dorothy. Life in the Emerald City is rumored to be great. Why not give it a whirl?"

He was right. And she'd run out of arguments. Resistance was futile. And it was time for her to emerge from the shadows and embrace what was left of the light. Wasn't it Somerset Maugham who wrote that surrendering to happiness was a defeat better than many victories? If so, it was past time for her own human bondage to end.

With that admission, there was only one course of action available to her.

She tugged at his hand.

"Be my date for the Fourth of July?"

All the contours of her life changed in an instant, when he smiled and said yes. They were going to make a public appearance. As a couple. In front of her daughter. *In front of the entire town.*

It was still too much to take in.

Celine could hear Henry's sweet voice drifting in through an open window. He was chattering away nonstop while Buddy stained the trim on her front porch railings. As was his habit with any project, Buddy was following a complex pattern that she was certain related to an obscure mathematical formula. Henry was watching him work and asking endless questions about topics that ranged from what Buddy thought the weather would be like next weekend for the fireworks, to if Buddy thought that dog barks worked the same way as human language. Buddy was rarely prolix with his responses to any questions, but Celine marveled at how Henry could manage to engage the young man in conversation so effortlessly—better, even, than Buddy's father, Bert.

Celine had earlier decreed that today should be a day without lessons. In her world, music was a discipline. And discipline was the precursor to art. Life was a discipline, too—and before today, she'd always believed that the hard work, study and practice that were required to transform music into art were the same tools required to craft a successful life. But today she had gained new information that challenged her long-held thesis.

Life was an *art*—not a discipline. And sometimes it was better to play, than to practice playing.

She got no disagreement about that from Henry, who did little to conceal his excitement at the reprieve. But Dorothy appeared disappointed. So, Celine suggested a compromise.

"Instead of practicing, how about we listen to some music *about* practicing?"

"Can it be piano music?" Dorothy asked.

"Absolutely. In fact, I know just the thing."

She selected her prized 1981 recording of Glenn Gould playing Bach's *Goldberg Variations*. One aria with thirty variations—all sharing the same bass line. It was a stunning tour de force—an enduring textbook about what was possible to achieve at the keyboard in terms of performance, precision, technical finesse and compositional genius. She had no doubt that Dorothy would find the music as mesmerizing and as pleasing as she did.

She had another thought, too.

Byron had given her a jar of homemade jam—made from Clingstone peaches trucked up from Georgia. He said they were sweet and delicious and smelled like the promise of summer.

"Why don't we make some tea and share this wonderful jam with the boys?"

"What are we gonna eat it on?" Dorothy looked around Celine's kitchen, which was still far from fully stocked.

"Good point. What do we have?" She walked to her pantry and opened its narrow door. The shelves were mostly empty. "Well, it looks like our choices are red rice and quinoa crackers or Health Warrior Chia Bars."

Dorothy looked distressed. "What are chia bars?"

Celine closed the pantry door. "Something we'd never get Henry to eat."

"We could make biscuits." Dorothy suggested.

Biscuits? Celine had never baked biscuits in her life.

"I'm afraid I don't know the first thing about how to do that," she apologized.

"I could make them."

"You know how to bake?"

"Some things." Dorothy shrugged. "I know how to make biscuits pretty good."

"You do?" Celine smiled at the girl. "Would you like to teach me?"

"Okay."

"What ingredients do we need?"

"Just a couple things. Butter. Self-rising flour. Buttermilk."

"I don't have buttermilk," Celine noted. "But I have whole milk and we could sour it with some white vinegar."

Dorothy looked confused. "Is that the same thing?"

"It will be in just a few minutes. See? That's the beauty of science."

"I guess so. I'm not very good at science."

"Well, I'm not very good at cooking—so maybe we've arrived at a good division of labor. How much buttermilk do you need?"

"I guess about two cups. Maybe a little more."

Celine assembled the ingredients. "Do you need measuring cups or a scale?"

"No, ma'am. I just kind of eyeball it. They usually turn out okay."

"Is it all right if the butter is cold?"

279

Dorothy nodded. "It's supposed to be."

Celine got Dorothy a large mixing bowl and a couple of rubber spatulas. "What else do you need?"

"Maybe a fork? A knife to cut the butter. And a rolling pin."

"A rolling pin?"

"You don't have one?"

Celine shook her head.

"We can use a liquor bottle."

Celine raised an eyebrow.

"I saw it on TV on one of those cooking shows," Dorothy explained.

"Does it need to be a certain kind of liquor, or will any type do?"

Dorothy seemed unsure about how to answer.

"I'm joking." Celine went to her freezer and pulled out a bottle of Grey Goose. "Is it okay if it's cold?"

Dorothy nodded. "We need to make the oven hot."

"Okay, chef." Celine walked over to her bright red Viking range. "What temperature?"

"Hot."

"Could you be a little more specific?"

Dorothy shook her head. "Our oven at home doesn't tell the temperature anymore. I just turn it way up and watch them while they're baking."

"A quandary." Celine looked at the oven dial. "How about we compromise? Let's use 435. It's a lot hotter than 350, but not as hot as 500."

"That should be okay." Dorothy was scooping flour out of the bag. "I like this music. Each part is the same, but different."

"That's correct. It's why they're called *variations*."

"Who was Goldberg?" Dorothy was cutting the stick of butter into smaller chunks and adding it to the bowl of flour.

Celine set about souring the milk.

"There is some discussion about that. Goldberg was believed to have been a student of Bach's—a very talented harpsichordist. Some believe the Variations were composed for him."

"But this is a piano."

"Yes. The composition has been transcribed for many instruments, including piano. This recording is very famous—performed by Glenn Gould, one of the greatest pianists of all time."

Dorothy was now cutting the butter into the flour with a fork. "How many variations are there?"

"Thirty."

"Thirty?" Dorothy seemed shocked. "Have you ever played them?"

Celine nodded. "A long time ago. When I was in school studying music—before I decided to become a doctor."

"You studied music?"

"Yes, I did."

"Where?"

"At Juilliard in New York—where my father was a teacher." She sniffed at the milk to check its progress. "Both of my parents were musicians."

"What was your name then?"

Celine was confused by her question. "I'm not sure what you mean."

"Wasn't your name different then? Before you got married?"

"Oh. No." Celine smiled at her. "I kept my full name—even when I got married."

"What's your middle name?"

Celine smiled at Dorothy's sudden inquisition. It was unlike her to be so forward.

"It's Weisz. My mother's family name. What's your middle name, Dorothy?"

"It's Gale."

Dorothy Gale? "Like Dorothy in *The Wizard of Oz?*" she asked.

Dorothy nodded. "My mama loved that story."

"I can see why." She thought about Byron's remark to her just that morning. *Life in the Emerald City is rumored to be great.* "It has a lot to teach us about hope and the things that matter."

"Was your daddy mad at you for changing your mind about school?"

Celine thought about how to answer her question. "Mad" didn't come close to describing all the things her father had been when she told him her decision. His sadness and disappointment had been harder to bear than his anger.

And her mother's reaction had been even worse. Hers had persisted for decades and tainted the rest of their relationship. Celine wore the stigma of her mother's disapproval like a shroud, and it colored everything she did—even when she became a mother herself.

"Yes," she told Dorothy. "He was very upset with me."

"Did he hit you?"

Celine was stunned by her question—but she tried fiercely not to show it.

"No," she said in a voice as casual as she could muster. "He didn't." She tried to make her next statement as innocuous as possible. "I guess I was fortunate."

"Yeah. My father wouldn't have been that nice."

"Does he hit you?"

Dorothy shrugged. Celine listened to the sound of her fork clacking against the side of the stoneware bowl. "I need the buttermilk, now."

Celine picked up the measuring cup and carried it over to the table where Dorothy was working.

"It's been sitting long enough to be good and spoiled." The irony of her own words was enough to make her want to scream.

In the next room, Glenn Gould was moaning and humming his way through another Variation. They were coming fast and furious now. Celine wondered how many variations of the same question she would need to try before finding the right one to reach Dorothy.

The door to the garden flew open and Henry came rushing inside. Buddy followed him more slowly.

"We finished the porch, Gramma C." He noticed what Dorothy was doing. "Are you cooking something?"

"Dorothy is making biscuits for us. I have homemade jam from Sheriff Martin."

"I love biscuits!" Henry looked at Buddy. "Don't you love biscuits, Buddy?"

"Five is imperfect," Buddy said. "Half of ten is not right. Ten is the number for God."

"What does that mean?" Henry looked at Dorothy. "Are you making five biscuits?"

Dorothy shook her head. "I think he means the music."

"Are you talking about the music, Buddy?" Celine asked. "Could you hear it outside?"

Henry nodded. "He heard you talking about it. He counted all the notes."

"Ninety-five bars," Buddy said. "Nine plus five equals fourteen. Four plus one equals five. Five is half of ten. *BACH* is inside the center number. B plus A plus C plus H means two plus one plus three plus eight. Fourteen. One plus four equals five. Bach is five. Bach is the center number. The center number is not perfect. Bach is half of ten. Half of perfect. Ten is God. God makes the center right."

No one said anything. Mostly because there wasn't any response to make.

Dorothy picked up the Grey Goose bottle and began rolling out the biscuit dough.

Variation eighteen began. Celine was curious to see if Buddy would notice the canon. She didn't have to wait long to find out.

"Row the boat. Row the boat," he said. "All good things are three."

"Are we going to row a boat?" Henry asked.

"No, sweetheart." Celine ran a hand over Henry's mop of hair. "Buddy means that some parts of the music have repeats in them—like the song 'Row, Row, Row Your Boat.' Isn't that right, Buddy?"

Buddy looked at her with his clear eyes. "Bach signed the music," he said.

She smiled at him. "Yes, he did. I'm glad you like it."

Buddy turned around and headed back for the door. Before he went outside, he stopped in the doorway. "Five biscuits are not right."

Celine laughed. "Dorothy? Can you get ten biscuits out of that dough?"

"I can if you have a small glass," she said.

"Yay!" Henry ran to the counter. "You can use my Spiderman glass. It's little."

Celine stood in the center of her new kitchen and closed her eyes as the mystery, form and substance of Bach's perfect universe swirled around her.

Divine grace came in many forms. And lately it had been raining down around her like manna from heaven.

God bless the families we make.

Maddie's most recent starring role in Theater of the Absurd was thankfully nearing an end.

She'd just bundled Rosebud into the Jeep and left the clinic for home when she got a text message from Syd.

Flat tire. Hwy 21 near Little Wilson. Come and rescue me for old time's sake?

Maddie didn't miss the irony of Syd's appeal for help. Another flat tire along the same stretch of road where they first met so many years ago? What were the odds of that happening?

She thought about running home first and dropping the cat off—but she didn't want Syd to wait alone on the side of the highway any longer than necessary. And she didn't want to risk having Rosebud evacuate in a place where she'd be unable to find the ring.

One thing she had *no* doubt about was the cat's ingenuity when it came to ways to torment her.

She watched Rosebud in the rearview mirror. The fat tuxedo cat was striding back and forth across the seat behind her, sniffing at the air coming in from one window before shifting to the other.

Asshole.

David had made her swear to call him the instant Oma's ring

reappeared. Maddie offered a hundredth mental apology to her late grandmother. Oma's legacy included avoiding capture and imprisonment in a Nazi death camp and surviving to lead a stunning, decades-long career as assistant concertmaster in the Metropolitan Opera orchestra.

Enter Rosebud . . .

Orson Welles has nothin' on me . . .

She tried to come up with a reasonable explanation for why she was showing up with the cat in tow. Syd had an uncanny ability to smell a rat at a thousand yards. No good reason occurred to her. Maybe she could just tell Syd that Rosebud swallowed—*something*—and she had to x-ray her to be sure she was okay.

That might work. But what could she swallow that wouldn't kill her or pose a medical emergency?

A screw? A washer? A brad tack? She glanced at the cat again. *A couple rounds of ammo?*

How about an entire bag of Cheetos—including the bag?

Bingo.

That idea worked on a couple of levels. It was believable. And it would immediately distract Syd by tempting her to indulge in her favorite pastime—chewing Maddie's ass about her diet.

Yep. It was a winner. All the way around.

The road ran along close to the river through here. It was late in the day and she could see flashes of sunlight on the water through the trees. She rounded a bend near the intersection of Little Wilson Creek and saw Syd's decrepit Volvo on the side of the road.

Syd was sitting on a grassy bank above the car. Reading. Maddie smiled.

She's so damn gorgeous . . .

Syd never went anywhere without a book. Considering her irrational attachment to her ancient and unpredictable mode of transportation, it was a good strategy.

Maddie flashed her lights to get Syd's attention, and waved when Syd looked up and spotted her approaching. Syd waved back and got to her feet while Maddie parked.

"Fancy meeting you here," Maddie said.

"I know." Syd walked over to greet her. Maddie gave her a quick hug and kiss. "It's like déjà vu all over again." She smiled at Maddie. "I know I could've done this by myself, but I'm sentimental. This is nearly the same the spot where I had my last flat tire."

"I know. I remember it well." Maddie patted the hood of Syd's old Volvo. "I owe you one."

"We *both* owe her one. As I recall, depending upon the kindness of strangers worked out pretty well for me last time."

Maddie raised an eyebrow. "Think lightning might strike the same spot twice?"

"I'm counting on it."

"Well, where this hunk of metal is concerned, I'd say the odds are in your favor."

"Hey." Syd popped Maddie on the arm. "Any car can have a flat tire—even a brand-new one."

"Sweetie. This thing is older than Inger Stevens." Maddie considered her comment. "In fact, this thing probably belonged to Inger Stevens before you acquired it."

"Very funny. If you ever get tired of lancing boils you should consider becoming a stand-up comic."

"From your mouth to God's ear. Which tire is it this time?"

Syd sighed and waved a hand at her car. "Front right."

"Honey . . ."

Syd held up a hand. "I know what you're going to say. I'm thinking about it. Okay?"

They'd had so many protracted discussions about Syd's refusal to get another car that they now could have the entire conversation without saying anything. Maddie just shook her head and headed for the back of the car to retrieve the spare and the jack. "What were you doing out here, anyway? I thought you were just working at the branch today."

"I was. Then I got a call from Edna Freemantle. She wanted to talk with me about . . ." She stopped abruptly and squinted at Maddie's Jeep. "Am I seeing things—or is that Rosebud in your car?"

"No." Maddie bounced the spare to the ground and rolled it to the front of the car. "That's her, all right."

"Is there . . . *some reason* . . . you're driving around with the cat?"

"Yeeees," she dragged the word out. "I was working in the barn. She ate my bag of Cheetos."

"So, you decided to take her for a ride? What for? A chaser?"

"Very funny. She ate the *bag*, too. I called your brother to see if she'd be okay. He said I should x-ray her to be sure there weren't any complications—so I took her to the clinic. You'll be glad to know she's fine."

Syd laughed. "I bet that process was a barrel of fun."

"I called David to help me out."

"David? Okay, this one is sure to make national news."

"Yeah. Remind me to fill you in on his latest fashion don'ts. Will you hand me that tire iron?"

Syd complied. "Remember to jack it up *before* you remove the lug nuts."

Maddie gave her a withering look. "You're never going to let me forget that, are you?"

"Probably not." Syd gave her one of her best Sandra Dee smiles.

"Well, as long as you took your time and gave the idea real consideration . . ." Maddie began to loosen the lug nuts. "What did Edna want to talk with you about?"

Syd sighed. "She didn't tell me on the phone and, as you can see, I never made it out there. If I had to guess, I'd say it's probably about Roma Jean and Charlie."

"That's ironic. Curtis came to see me last week for the same reason." Maddie grunted as she fought to work the last lug nut free. "*Damn.* This thing is rusted in place. It won't budge."

"Use your foot."

"My what?"

Syd tapped her on the shoulder. "Back up and watch a professional show you how this is done."

"Okaaayyy." Maddie obeyed and moved out of her way.

Syd rested a hand on Maddie's shoulder for balance, positioned her foot on the edge of the tire iron, and stomped down on it with all her weight. There was a resounding crack as the arm of the tire iron snapped in half. Syd's momentum carried her right after it, and she would've ended up face down on the pavement if Maddie hadn't reached out and yanked her back.

She ended up sprawled across Maddie's lap in a most unladylike posture.

"Now I see why *this* technique is so effective," Maddie drawled.

Syd was flustered. "That wasn't supposed to happen."

"I dunno. I'd say it worked out just fine."

Syd slapped her wandering hand. "You're a pervert."

"True."

"What about my tire?"

Maddie pulled her closer. "What about it?"

"It's a goner."

Maddie kissed her neck. "Why should it be the only one?"

"What are *you doing?*"

"I think it's called taking advantage of the situation."

"I *get* that part." Syd shifted around so she could look at Maddie's face. "You do realize we're sitting in the middle of a state highway, right?"

"Um hm." Maddie kissed her. "You talk too much."

Syd relented. *Briefly.* After a few blissful moments, she pulled away.

"It isn't that I'm—not—enjoying—this," she said, a tad unevenly. "But we do have a—bit of a—situation here."

"That would be true," Maddie agreed.

"Well. What do you think we should do?"

"You think we need to do something?"

Syd looked at her with wonder. "Do I *know* you?"

"In fact, you do—better than anyone."

"So?"

"So?" Maddie repeated.

Syd rolled her eyes. "Do you have any ideas?"

Maddie looked at her. In that one ridiculous but perfect and unscripted moment, she *did* have an idea. The best one she'd ever had. And it required nothing. No planning. No strategizing. No flowers. No catering. Not anything but the two of them, here together, stranded along the same damn stretch of road where they had first met so many years ago.

She took Syd's face between her grimy hands.

"I love you," she said.

Syd looked confused, but she went along with it, anyway. "I . . . love you . . . too?"

"I want to be with you," Maddie said. "Always. So we can face whatever else life throws at us—together. I want to fall asleep beside you every night, and have your face be the first thing I see every morning. And when it's my time to leave this world forever, I want the memory of you and the life we spent together to carry me across the heavens into eternity." She cleared her throat. "So. Here's my humble but heartfelt idea. Will you marry me?"

Syd's face was a confluence of a hundred shifting emotions.

"Do you mean it?" she asked. Her voice sounded small—like it was coming from a hundred miles away.

Maddie nodded. "I mean it." She tugged her closer and gave her a shy smile. "So, whattaya think?"

Syd still seemed dazed. "I don't know what to say."

Maddie chased off a tiny surge of panic. "Well, 'yes,' would be a helluva start."

"Oh, my god . . ." Syd laughed and hurled herself at Maddie. The force of it knocked them both over. "*Yes.* Oh, my god, yes. *A thousand times, yes.*"

They rolled around on the ground beside the battle-weary car, embracing and laughing like fools. Finally, Maddie came to her senses and remembered something—the most important something.

Rosebud.

"Honey," she said. Syd was on top of her, kissing her collarbone. "Honey?" She pushed Syd up with her forearms. "Wait a minute. I forgot something."

"Oh, I don't think so." Syd moved in again, but Maddie stopped her.

"No. *Really*. Lemme go and get it. It's important."

Syd sat up with a grunt. "It better be."

"It is. I promise." Maddie kissed her on the forehead and climbed to her feet. "I'll be right back."

"Back? Where the hell are you going?"

"I just need to get something out of the car. Don't go away."

"Fat chance. My legs are like jelly. I doubt I can even stand up, much less go anyplace."

Maddie opened the car door and scooped out the protesting cat. Rosebud had been napping, and she wasn't very happy about being so rudely awakened. Maddie walked back to Syd and knelt in front of her. She held the cat up between them.

"I forgot the most important part," she said.

"The cat?" Syd asked with a raised eyebrow.

"Well. Sort of." Rosebud continued to squirm. Her fat body swayed between Maddie's hands like a furry pendulum. "I wasn't lying when I told you that Rosebud swallowed something. But it wasn't just a few Cheetos."

Syd's jaw dropped.

"Yeah. She ate Oma's ring, too."

Syd blinked. Her eyes filled with tears. "You're giving me your grandmother's ring?"

"I will be," she handed the cat to Syd, "in another four to six hours . . ."

In the end, they decided to leave the Volvo parked where it was and call Junior to have it towed out to his place in Troutdale. They'd decide what to do about it later. Right now, all Maddie wanted was to get home with Syd, and spend a quiet evening looking at the stars and planning the rest of their lives.

This time, they opted to leave the scene of a flat tire together. Maddie thought it was about damn time—and Syd's response to her proposal suggested that she thought so, too.

They didn't talk much on the ride home. But they held hands like schoolgirls and gave each other shy smiles whenever their eyes met. The perfect symmetry of it all overwhelmed them both. After so many years, ending up precisely where they started— only to begin a new chapter in their lives together—was sweetly sentimental and demonstrably perfect. Maddie would be forever grateful that, for once, she was sharp enough to know the right moment when it presented itself.

She was amazed by how simple it had been. Like all the most important things in life, asking Syd to marry her hadn't turned out to be supremely complicated or impossible to orchestrate. And contrary to every expectation she'd ever had, it didn't call for a thousand moving parts.

It only needed two.

Maddie confessed to Syd all she had planned for the "big event." Syd laughed and said she hoped they still could enjoy the catering. Maddie hoped so, too—mostly because she'd asked Nadine to make a big batch of Grandma Harriet's fried chicken.

Rosebud resumed pacing as soon as the car started moving. Maddie was quick to tell Syd that they needed to keep the cat with them until the ring materialized.

It was nearly dark when they turned onto their lane. Maddie was surprised that Pete didn't greet them, running alongside the car and barking like he usually did. When they drew closer to the house, she saw why.

James Lawrence was there—sitting on one of the lower steps that led down from the porch. She could see the tip of his cigarette glowing in the fading light. Pete sat on the ground at his feet, seemingly glad for the company. She cast about for Henry, but didn't see any sign of him—not along the pasture fence where Before was nosing around looking for stray tufts of grass. And not by the pond.

"Is that James?" Syd asked. "Do you see Henry, too?"

Maddie shook her head. "No. I think he must've come alone."

"I hope everything is all right."

Maddie heard the underlying hint of anxiety in her voice. She squeezed her hand.

"Try not to worry. I'm sure it's nothing."

They parked the car.

"I'll go and get the cat carrier out of the barn," Syd said. "You go meet James."

"Okay. Come join us on the porch?"

Syd nodded. "I'll be there in two minutes."

When Maddie approached, James stood up and ground out his cigarette on the toe of his boot. He stashed the butt in his pocket.

Pete rushed over to greet her as she approached. She stopped and scrubbed his head before walking over to greet James.

"Hey, James. This is a nice surprise." Maddie extended her hand. When James offered his, she shook it warmly.

"I'm sorry for just showing up like this," he apologized. "It was kind of last-minute."

"No. Not at all. Syd had a flat tire out near Little Wilson. That's why we're getting home so late."

James looked concerned. "Did you have to leave her car out there? Want me to go take a look at it?"

"One of the lug nuts was so rusted I couldn't get the wheel off. We called Junior and he said he'd go and fetch it. I'm glad you didn't get the call." She smiled. "Syd broke the tire iron trying to force it with her foot."

"I think that must be something they teach women to do in Driver's Ed." He seemed to think better of his observation. "No offense, ma'am."

"None taken." Maddie smiled at him. "That car is so damn old, I'm amazed the axle didn't break before the tire iron."

"I'll check it out tomorrow."

"Thanks. But between you and me," Maddie lowered her head and spoke more softly, "as the county coroner, I happily give you leave to pronounce it DOA and consign it to a pauper's grave."

James smiled. "She sure does love that car. Henry says the engine sounds like the popcorn machine at Twin County Cinemas."

"Yeah. Except it doesn't smell as nice." She decided to take the bull by the horns. "How is Henry?"

"He's fine. He's over at your mother's. I asked if she would watch him a while longer tonight so I could come over and talk with you and Syd."

A free-floating wave of panic crashed up against her best-laid plans for the second time that night. This time, it had all the earmarks of a harbinger. Something bigger was right behind it, and it was heading right for them.

Syd made her way toward them, carrying Rosebud's crate with both hands. The container was listing dramatically to stern, suggesting the extent of the cat's unhappiness with her new accommodations. Pete was jogging along beside her.

James watched her approach with a look of befuddlement.

"We have to keep an eye on the cat," Maddie explained. "She swallowed something she shouldn't have so we're watching her until she passes it."

"Oh. I wondered."

"Hi, James." Syd smiled at him. "It's always good to see you."

Maddie relieved Syd of her burden. "I was just telling James about Rosebud's . . . condition. How about we all go have a seat on the porch?"

"I second that idea." Syd linked arms with James and led him toward the steps. "Anybody want something to drink?"

"I'm fine," James said. "I got a big tea at Aunt Bea's on my way out here."

"In that case," she added, "anybody need to use the bathroom?"

James smiled. "I took care of that, too."

They reached the porch and James helped Maddie haul a third Adirondack chair over so they could sit together. She carefully positioned Rosebud's crate between her chair and Syd's. Pete reclaimed his usual spot at the top of the steps and proceeded to keep a watchful eye on everything transpiring between the house and the pond.

It appeared to be a quiet night.

At least, so far.

Maddie filled Syd in on the reason for James's visit.

"James said Mom agreed to watch Henry tonight so he could come and talk with us." Maddie noticed the immediate hitch in

Syd's breathing. She tried to give her a smile of encouragement.

"Is everything okay, James?" Syd was never one to mince words—especially when every needle on every dial seemed to be pointing straight toward something portentous, if not downright catastrophic.

"I hope so." James dropped his eyes to the porch floor. "At least, I think it will be—with your help."

"You know we'll always do anything we can to help you and Henry," Maddie said.

"I do know that." James looked at her. "Sometimes, it's been hard for me to accept it. I felt like I took advantage when I had to ask people for so much support. I think I was too stubborn about that and it ended up hurting Henry more than helping him. I'm sorry about that now." He looked at Syd. "I want to try and fix it—and that means I need to change some things. So that's why I came out here tonight—to tell you both what I've decided to do."

Maddie reached over and took hold of Syd's hand—as much to stop her own from shaking as to offer support for what she felt certain would follow.

"You're leaving, aren't you?" Syd asked. The bluntness of her question hung in the air between them like a dense fog.

After a moment or two, James nodded.

"I have to. I just can't make it here. I've known it for some time, but I just kept hoping things would get better." He shook his head. "They haven't."

Syd was squeezing Maddie's hand like a vice. Maddie was afraid to look at her—afraid to see the hurt and sadness in her eyes. "I'm very sorry to hear that, James." It took an effort for her to keep her voice steady—but nowhere near the effort it took to keep from standing up and throwing her chair through a window. "Sorrier than I can say. I wish we could do more to change things. You and Henry are family to us, and we care very much—about both of you."

"I know that," he said. "I think that's the only thing that made it possible for me to make this decision." He looked down at

Rosebud, who was batting in frustration at the door of her cat carrier. "Lately, I've been a lot like that." He pointed at the cat. "Trapped. Not able to move forward. Not able to move any way at all." He shook his head. "And this?" He extended his prosthetic leg. "Out here, it's a crutch. A handicap. I'm like half a man. And you know what?" He looked back at them. "Buddy is right. Half is not finished."

Even though her heart was splintering, Maddie couldn't summon the energy to argue with what James was saying.

He was right.

"What have you decided to do?" Syd's voice was soft and low.

"I know now that I need to be in a place where I fit—where who I am makes sense and I know what I'm supposed to be doing." He used a hand to pull his leg back from its extended position. "I've only ever had that one other time. Just one. So, last week, I drove over to Wytheville to see an army recruiter. I reenlisted."

Syd gasped.

"James," Maddie said. "Are you sure about this?"

"Yes, ma'am." He nodded. "That night when I got back home, I sat at the kitchen table watching Henry eat his box of Popeyes chicken, and I knew I'd done the right thing. Living out there in Troutdale over that crummy garage? That's not what he needs. *Nothing* about that life is what he needs."

"Where will you go?" Maddie asked. "Have they told you yet?"

"Oh, yeah. I made sure of that. I'm going to be part of the transportation corps—a coordinator. I already passed the physical. I was lucky that there were MOS positions in that area. All the long-distance work I've been doing for Cougar's was a big help. I'll be doing the same kind of thing—just for the army. They're sending me back to Fort Hood. It's not my favorite place to be stationed, but I don't think I'll be there very long. With this kind of assignment, they keep you moving around."

"When do you leave?" Syd asked. Maddie could sense her unasked question: *When will you take Henry away?*

"Three weeks," James said.

"Three weeks?" Syd repeated. She looked at Maddie with desperation.

"Well," he added. "That's if I meet one condition."

"What's that?" Maddie asked.

"I can't take Henry. I can't reenlist as a single parent—and I wouldn't want to, even if the army allowed it."

Maddie and Syd exchanged glances.

"What does that mean, James?" Syd leaned forward on her chair. "Are you asking us to take care of him for you?"

"No. I'm asking you to do what I haven't been able to do—what I can't do." He looked back and forth between them. "I'm asking you to be his parents. Permanently."

Permanently? Maddie was sure she hadn't heard him correctly.

"Do you know what you're asking?"

"Yeah," he nodded. "I do. I'm not sure about very many things, but I'm sure about one thing." He paused. "Well. I'm sure about *two* things, really. I'm sure about how much you love Henry—and I'm damn sure about how much he loves the two of you. You make him happy—happier than I could ever make him. You give him a safe and beautiful place to live—a place that's full of love and happiness. This dog? His cow? The fish? His bedroom with the airplane pictures? *Everything* he loves—is here. *With you.*" James wiped at his eyes with impatience. "I love my son—and I always will. But with you, he'd have a life that's full of possibilities—and the chance to do things I can't even imagine, much less know how to make happen for him." He leaned toward them. "If you agree to make him yours, I know I'll never have to worry about him again. And I'll know I finally got it right."

Syd had tears running down her face, and Maddie knew she wasn't far from it herself.

But she owed it to all of them to be sure James understood what he was asking.

She extended a hand toward him. He took it without hesitation.

"James. We need to be very clear about something. If Syd and I agree to do this—to adopt your son and raise him as our own—

it must be done legally. No halfway measures. No trial basis. No going back if you change your mind. We couldn't put Henry through that—and we couldn't put ourselves through it, either." She looked at him with great intent. "We wouldn't survive it."

"I understand that. Believe me, I won't change my mind." He looked at Syd. "This is right. He belongs with you."

Syd reached out and took James's other hand. He stopped trying to fight his tears.

"I'd just ask one more thing, if I can," he said.

"Of course." Maddie squeezed his hand. "Anything."

"I want to stay a part of his life. If that's okay with you? Just so he grows up knowing I didn't abandon him."

"Oh, James." Syd got up and hugged him. "Henry would never think that. You'll always be his father. And you'll always have a place here with us. Always."

"Thanks." His voice was muffled. Syd just wrapped him up tighter.

Maddie saw his shoulders shake as he fought to control his sobs. That did it. She gave up trying to corral her own emotions. She stood up, wrapped her long arms around two of the best people she'd ever been blessed to know—and commenced crying like a baby.

If she'd thought about it, she'd have realized how ridiculous they all looked—sobbing into each other like crazed extras from the last act of *Hamlet*.

But she didn't think about it—and she didn't care.

Just for tonight—*just for a few perfect moments*—God was in his heaven, and all was right with the world.

Chapter 10

No Place for H8.

David's campaign slogan, resplendent in twenty-four-inch-high Rust-Oleum Old Forge Blue letters, proclaimed to anyone interested in dessert that there would be a mayoral debate right after the picnic ended, but plenty of time before the start of the fireworks.

That was because his banners were well-positioned behind the food tables.

He knew people.

This year, Nadine and Michael were doing all the catering for the annual Independence Day celebration.

When Nadine saw the big, blue and white banners, she clucked her tongue and told David they looked like signs hawking a Greek Festival. He responded by making a flamboyantly rude gesture and chastising her for the limited color palette.

"Listen, Paloma Picasso—don't blame *me*. Next time you decide to make one of your midnight graffiti runs, stop by the tire store first and spring for a broader assortment of colors."

He managed to dodge the cheese biscuit she hurled at him. It landed on the ground near Django's feet. He sniffed at it before taking a cautious bite. Astrid looked on with indifference. She only ate imported cheeses . . .

Dogs were welcome at the annual celebration, too.

It looked like a record turnout this year. This was only Syd's third time attending the town gala, but it was already one of her favorite things about life in the small mountain community. Everyone came out. On this one day a year, all differences were set aside. That was because, in Southwest Virginia, patriotism and a good piece of fried chicken trumped any kind of disagreement.

Any kind.

Although, Syd did notice that Azalea Freemantle kept off to herself to avoid any accidental encounters with Yankees. But she did look especially festive today, decked out in a rakish black cap with "RockStar" emblazoned across the front, and wearing a pair of blinding white Nike Cortez sneakers.

"Hey, Blondie?" David dropped a quick kiss on Syd's cheek as he danced by on his way to . . . something. "Nice bling."

Syd held out her left hand and smiled. Rosebud had finally delivered the ring a little before midnight—about six hours after swallowing it. What a night that had turned out to be. Her head was still reeling from Maddie's proposal—and the bombshell James Lawrence had dropped on them.

They were going to adopt Henry . . .

James had said he wanted them to tell Henry about the change together—as a family. So, they did—the very next day—seated around the big kitchen table at the center of their home, surrounded by dozens of late-season tulips in every imaginable color.

Henry was sad to learn that his daddy was going back in the army—but he brightened up considerably when James promised his son that he'd never go back to "Afistan"—and that he'd always be a part of his life. Maddie had explained to Henry that the big upstairs bedroom next to his would now be known as James's room—and that whenever his daddy could come back to visit, he would stay there with them.

Syd looked beyond the crush of people lined up at the beverage station to where Henry, James and Maddie were playing catch with a battered old Frisbee of Pete's. Each time one of them threw it, reflected sunlight would flash off the strips of shiny silver tape Buddy had used to repair several splits along its rim.

The three of them made a happy tableau, laughing and tossing the worn-out toy back and forth. Pete raced around between them, not quite understanding why they were so obsessed with such an annoying game of keep-away.

Syd smiled as she watched them. She wished she could stop time—freeze everything just where it was. *Right at that very second.* She closed her eyes tight and savored the image, committing it forever to a place among the most hallowed moments of her life.

"*Dorothy Gale?*" Byron didn't believe it. "That's not possible. *Nobody* is really named Dorothy Gale."

"It's true," the girl insisted. She looked up at Celine for help. "Tell him."

"You're on your own with this one." Celine shook her head. "You can't change his mind about anything once he has it made up." She looked over at Byron. "I learned that one the hard way."

He laughed.

They were just finishing their dinners, and Dorothy was sitting on the ground, petting Django. "Can I give Django another cookie?"

"Sure." Byron handed her a Ziploc bag containing an odd assortment of dog biscuits. "But not too many. He's already been stuffing his face with hot dogs and anything else that lands on the ground."

Dorothy took an oblong, peanut-shaped biscuit out of the bag. Django brightened up at once. He flopped over on his side and sat back up in one spastic motion, then sat staring at her with an expectant look in his big brown eyes.

Dorothy giggled. "What was *that* supposed to be?"

"That's his uptown version of rolling over." Byron nudged Celine. "He agrees with me, and believes it's the thought that counts."

Celine rolled her eyes. "I'm not certain I endorse the wisdom of rewarding an inferior performance."

"Oh, really?" Byron asked. "How many inferior performances have you had to endure lately?"

"None yet." Celine plucked a cherry tomato off her plate and plopped it into Byron's mouth. "I'll be sure to let you know if it becomes a problem."

Dorothy was holding the dog biscuit up to her nose. "This smells like bananas."

"That's right," Byron explained. "They're peanut butter and banana. Django's favorite."

Dorothy gave the nearly apoplectic dog his treat.

"Do you have a dog at home, Dorothy Gale?" Byron asked.

She shook her head.

"Not even a *little* one?" He held up a thumb and forefinger. "Dorothy Gale doesn't have a Toto?"

"No. Papa doesn't like dogs."

Byron exchanged glances with Celine. "We're definitely not in Kansas anymore," he said.

"Maybe Django can spend some time at my house," Celine suggested. "and you can play with him there?"

"Really?" Dorothy looked up at her with excitement. "Would that be okay with you, Sheriff Martin?"

He smiled at her. "I think we might be able to work something out."

His words made her feel warm inside—and special. Just like when Dr. Heller said the same thing to her about learning to play the piano.

Django had finished his biscuit, and now had his head resting on her leg.

Yes. She'd like to have a dog.

That was because dogs were nicer than most people.

She looked back up at Sheriff Martin and Dr. Heller, who were arguing about who would get the last deviled egg on the plate of food they were sharing.

She patted Django's head.

But, sometimes, people were just as nice as dogs . . .

◊ ◊ ◊

"Girl, you keep blowing through them Camels at this rate, and we're gonna have to go open another carton." Jocelyn waved a hand back and forth to try and clear away the fog of smoke that hung in the air between them.

"I can't help it." Rita took a deep drag and blew out another chest full of sweetly scented smoke. "Ever since I got started up again, I can't seem to get tapered off."

"It's always like that," Natalie chimed in. "Like the Good Book says, 'The dog returns to its vomit.' You can't never control an obsession once you give back into it. It pretty much takes over your life."

"Ain't that the truth." Jocelyn tilted her tightly coiffed head toward a nearby table where the mayor was making nice with the crew from Buford's Mortuary. "Look at that slimy rat bastard over there drummin' up votes."

"Hell." Natalie waved a hand that was ablaze with her brand-new, stars-n-stripes manicure. "That man don't have a lick of sense. And if them dumb coffin-wranglers don't know better'n to listen to his line of empty promises, then they've got about as much goin' on as their customers—the ones that arrive at their establishment as *freight*, if you know what I'm talkin' about."

Rita did not disagree. She couldn't seem to take her eyes off Watson. She'd been all het-up about him ever since their encounter at Freemantle's Market last week.

Prick . . .

Truth be told, he was the reason she'd started smoking again.

She had more than one reason to be "obsessed," as Natalie called it.

It didn't help her ability to resist temptation when James Lawrence told her about his plans to reenlist in the army. They'd really become friends, and she was gonna miss his company on those long overnight hauls. His announcement pretty much blew a Freightliner-sized hole in the expansion plans for Cougar's

Quality Logistics, too. They'd be SOL until Jocelyn and Deb could hire another driver who could fill in on the cross-country runs.

She'd miss James for more personal reasons, too. He was really the first person in years who'd given her the time of day—in any way that went beyond the normal "Hey, howdy" kind of way that was typical of most of her relationships in Jericho. It wasn't that he ever said all that much. But there was something different about the *way* he was quiet. They could be driving along for three to four hours at a stretch and not say anything—but Rita still had a sense that James was understanding everything—even the things that were left unsaid.

He was a rare man in her experience. And that meant a lot because Rita didn't much care for men. But after getting to know James, she had wondered more than once how her life might've been different if she'd had a friend like him a hundred years ago, when things had gone so far off the rails for her.

It was pointless to make herself crazy by wondering about all the ways the past could've been different. It wasn't different and it couldn't ever be changed. That's why it was called the past. The best thing she could do was try to shake the dust of it off her feet and go on without looking back.

She watched Watson leave the table full of undertakers and move on to another group—the crew from the tire store this time. He must've sensed her staring at him because he cut his beady eyes over and looked right at her. She reflexively raised her fingers to her mouth, and rapidly wagged her tongue back and forth between them. Judging by how quickly his face turned red, she knew he understood the gesture.

He abruptly changed direction and walked away without so much as a backwards glance.

"Just what in the hell are you doin'?" Natalie slapped her hand down. "There's *children* around here."

"Don't waste no more energy tryin' to poke that badger," Jocelyn added. "There ain't nothin' to be gained by it."

"Just *look* at him," Natalie. pointed out. "He's over there commiseratin' with that other Grade A piece of shit—Hozbiest."

"Them two sure are cut from the same bolt of cloth." Jocelyn gave a disgusted laugh. "Well, maybe that makes sense. They do say that birds of a feather flock together."

"Yeah," Natalie agreed. "Especially when they're both *turkey buzzards*."

Rita took a last, long drag on her cigarette. They were right. Why was she wasting any more of her time worrying about that pencil dick?

She ground out her cigarette and got up.

"Gimme your car keys, Natalie."

Natalie looked up at her. "What for?"

"Because we got about another hour until them fireworks get started. If we're gonna stay, I gotta go get more smokes."

Natalie fished the big ring of keys out of her oversized pocketbook.

"Here." She slapped them against Rita's outstretched hand. "Don't say none of us didn't try to save you from yourself and all them bad instincts."

"Come on."

Roma Jean grabbed Charlie's hand and started leading her away from the shady spot where they'd been hanging out beneath a couple of aspen trees.

"Where are we going?" Charlie complained. "Roma Jean? I don't wanna go out in the sun. *It's hot.*"

"There's somebody I want you to meet."

Charlie gave up on trying to slow her down. She had no idea where they were headed, but Roma Jean seemed determined to drag her past just about every damn resident of the town to get to their destination. More than one person raised an eyebrow as they passed. Others waved. A few whispered behind their hands. Some even gave them wide smiles. An oblivious Roma Jean just trudged right on, still dragging Charlie along by the hand.

They were nearly at the river when Charlie saw a small group of people sitting in a semi-circle on aluminum lawn chairs. They had a portable picnic table set up and it was loaded with plates, cups, a giant vat of iced tea, and leftover plates of chicken and slaw.

The Freemantle clan had staked out their traditional Fourth of July spot near the water. This was one of the best places to get an unobstructed view of the fireworks—and they were quick to claim it every year. Sometimes, Cletus actually drove down here the night before and set up their tables and chairs, just to be sure nobody else would have a shot at moving in on their prized domain.

Charlie felt a jolt of misgiving when she realized where Roma Jean was taking her. It wasn't that she wanted Roma Jean to keep their relationship a secret. She didn't. But she wasn't sure that parading their newfound attachment around in full view of her extended family during the town's most popular holiday celebration was the best idea she'd ever had.

They were all here, too. Roma Jean's parents. Her aunt Evelyn and Uncle Cletus. Her crazy grandma, Azalea. Aunt Evelyn's nieces, Nicorette and Maybelline, were there, too. So was Nadine's husband, Raymond Odell. There were even a couple of distant cousins from out near Bone Gap.

Roma Jean practically skidded to a halt in front of her Aunt Evelyn's chair.

She was still holding on to Charlie's hand.

"Aunt Evelyn?" she said. "I wanted to be sure you got to meet Charlie Davis." Roma Jean looked up at Charlie and gave her an electric smile. "We talked about her." She shifted her gaze back to her aunt. "Remember?"

Evelyn didn't say anything. In fact, no one seated in the family compound said anything—except Roma Jean's Gramma Azalea, who dropped her chicken leg and asked if Charlie's people were related to Jeff Davis, the former president of the Confederacy.

Charlie opened her mouth to say "No, ma'am," but Roma Jean cut her off.

"Yes, she is," Roma Jean declared. "Her people moved here

from Kentucky right after 'The War of Northern Aggression.'"

While it was true that Charlie's ancestors actually *did* relocate to Virginia from Kentucky, it was a boldfaced lie to suggest they had any relationship to the family of the famed former president.

Roma Jean's eccentric grandma pushed her half-finished plate of chicken and broccoli slaw off the chair beside her and patted the seat with a bony hand. Charlie noticed her bright white shoes. She hadn't seen Nike Cortez sneakers on anyone since Eazy-E got buried in a pair.

"She wants you to come over and sit down beside her," Roma Jean whispered. When Charlie didn't budge right away, Roma Jean gave her a shove. "Go on. *Get over there.*"

Charlie looked at Aunt Evelyn, who was clearly sizing her up. After a moment, Aunt Evelyn slowly shook her head and fluttered a hand toward Azalea.

"You'd best get moving, young lady," she said. "If you're gonna be part of this family, you'll make out a lot better once you stop asking questions and just learn to do as you're told." She elbowed her husband, who lounged in the chair beside her, watching the show with a half-smile on his face. "Ain't that right, Cletus?"

Cletus cleared his throat.

"Yes, dear," he said. He winked at Charlie. "It surely is."

Charlie gave Aunt Evelyn a shy smile before dutifully walking over to sit down next to Gramma Azalea.

"Well, Roma Jean," Charlie heard Aunt Evelyn say. "I see you went with happy. Now, that's *smart.*"

Charlie didn't hear Roma Jean's response because Gramma Azalea was already beginning an energetic narrative about how Jefferson Davis contracted malaria in the Mexican-American War, and never had a shot at a successful presidency because everyone knew that Alexander Stephens was a conniver who undercut Davis, and was really a Yankee sympathizer . . .

"How much longer you think we need to wait before we can start telling folks we're fixin' to get things fired up?"

Sonny and Bert were hauling munitions from their trucks down to an ideal launch pad along a rocky bank beside the river. Buddy was helping them get organized for the big finale of the evening. His job was to set up the launch apparatus and make sure it was good and secure.

Buddy had brought along a couple extra rolls of car tape just to be sure they didn't have any mishaps like last year, when that one stand fell over and shot a bottle rocket up the bank and right into the dessert table. They were lucky nobody got hurt—but it did take out about five of Peggy Hawkes's untouched lemon chess pies.

More than one person had taken Bert aside earlier today and told him they'd slip him a couple of sawbucks if he could do the town the same favor this year . . .

Bert looked up at the sky. The sun was already below treetop level, but they still probably had another good hour or so before it would start getting dark enough to commence.

"I'd say another hour and fifteen to twenty minutes," he told Sonny. "'Sides, we can't start nothin' until they get that debate over with."

"Shucks. I forgot about that."

"No place for hate," Buddy said. "Ten canons before hate goes away."

"Ten cannons?" Sonny looked at Bert. "What does he mean by ten cannons? There ain't no cannons this year, is there? I thought they outlawed that after that guy got killed shootin' one off in that accident down in Shelby."

"They did," Bert agreed. "Buddy? There ain't no cannons this year. Just the fireworks that me and Sonny set off, like usual."

"Ten canons," Buddy repeated. "Row, row, row the boat. Three times ten. Bach is in the middle."

"Now he's talkin' about some music he heard out at Dr. Heller's," Bert explained. "But I don't know where he came up with that cannon idea."

"'God has made them a kingdom and they shall reign on earth,'" Buddy said. He wound a length of silver tape around a tripod to secure it to a stake in the ground. "Revelation happens at five and ten. Five is not finished. Ten is God."

Buddy had set up ten tripods in two rows of five. Each tripod was separated from the next one by five feet—plenty of space for Bert and Sonny to safely reload the fireworks after each volley was discharged. They probably had enough munitions for a twenty-minute show—about half as long as last year. That was because the mayor's office had cracked down on this part of the celebration. He said the noise it created was disruptive to people in the area who didn't attend the festivities.

Bert had no idea who that could be. Pretty much everybody who lived within a thirty-mile radius came out for the Jericho Fourth of July fireworks. Anybody who didn't attend either lived way off in another county or were so deaf they wouldn't be able to hear the explosions even if they were sitting a couple hundred yards up-river with all them Freemantles.

"Hate stops when the canons are through," Buddy said. "God redeems the imperfect. Ten replaces five."

Sonny looked over their setup, then back at Bert. "Do you think he means that having ten tripods is too many?"

"Hey, Buddy?" Bert asked his son. "Do we have too many tripods set up?"

Buddy shook his head and tore off another long strip of silver tape.

"Ten is perfect," he said. "*Ten is God.*"

Bert looked at Sonny. "Looks like we're all good." He took another gander at the sky. "Not much else to do here until show time. Why don't you two go watch that debate—maybe get another bite of dessert? I'll stay here and watch the gear."

"Works for me." Sonny put down his tools and headed back toward the crowd. "I could go for another slice of Nadine's rhubarb pie."

"You go on, too, Buddy." Bert added. "Bring me back some of that pie."

Buddy put down his roll of tape and followed Sonny along the narrow path that led away from the water. Just before they reached the wooden steps that led up to the picnic area, he stopped and looked back at the river.

"No place for hate," he said.

Maddie knew she'd probably regret what she was about to do, but she resolved to do it, anyway.

After a lot of cajoling, coaxing and pleading by more than half a dozen of her closest friends, Lizzy Mayes had finally relented and agreed to attend the holiday celebration. Syd and Maddie were thrilled to see her there and immediately asked her to join them. Lizzy begged off, insisting that she'd already promised to eat with some nurses from the hospital in Wytheville—but she did say that she'd reconnect before the fireworks started and spend the rest of the evening with them.

Maddie was worried about her.

She didn't seem to be rebounding after her miscarriage. She'd lost weight and her normally vivacious temperament was more than a little bit subdued. She didn't think Lizzy was suffering any medically induced side effects from the experience—at least not physical ones. No. It seemed more to Maddie like she was ... sad. It was a tough needle for Maddie to thread. She didn't want to presume too much, and she didn't want to invade Lizzy's privacy any more than they already had—even though Lizzy had been quick to tell her how much Syd's visit meant on the day she lost the baby.

That ended up being the real tragedy for Lizzy. Even though her relationship with Tom fell apart, she had made her decision to go forward with the pregnancy—on her own.

But it wasn't to be.

Maddie could tell that Lizzy was now rethinking everything in her life—even whether she wanted to stay on in this area. The grant that funded her position was up for renewal in another few months. Prior to recent events, there had been no question about her desire to continue working with Maddie and keep living in her little bungalow on the river. But now?

Losing Lizzy would deal a huge blow to Maddie's practice. She was a top-notch nurse practitioner who coupled keen diagnostic ability with a warm and engaging demeanor—a rare combination in medicine. She was also blessed with a professional disposition that inspired immediate confidence. And that was a huge asset in a backcountry area where people had a nearly inbred mistrust of modern medicine. Maddie would be sorry to lose her as a partner and trusted colleague.

She'd also be sorry to lose her as a valued friend.

It was that latter motivation that drove her to undertake such an uncharacteristic course of action today.

She'd seen Syd's brother, Tom, arrive about an hour ago.

He looked just about as morose and dejected as Lizzy did . . . *It was ridiculous.*

And it was about time for something to change.

She kept a watchful eye on Lizzy and saw her opportunity when Lizzy excused herself from her group and headed for the bank of rented port-a-potties that had been hauled in for the occasion. Miraculously, there were no lines just then, so she knew Lizzy wouldn't be gone for long.

This was her chance.

Tom was standing with them, listening intently while Syd filled him in on the sordid story of how Rosebud swallowed Oma's ring, and the hilarity that ensued when Maddie enlisted David to help her x-ray the beleaguered cat.

"Excuse me, sweetheart," she said to Syd. "I'm sorry to interrupt you, but I really need to speak with Tom. *Now.*"

Syd raised an eyebrow at her tone, but she didn't object to her request.

"Of course," she said. "Go right on ahead."

"Thanks." Maddie took Tom by the arm and led him in the direction Lizzy had just gone.

"What's up?" Tom asked. "And where are we going?"

Maddie stopped just short of the path that led to the portable restrooms. She knew that she only had a minute or two before Lizzy reappeared.

She had to work fast.

"Tom," she said. "I'm going to make this short and sweet. Sometimes in life, you have to take the bull by the horns."

He looked confused. "I'm not sure what that's supposed to mean."

"It means that when life hands you lemons, you make lemonade."

"Okay." Tom laid a hand on Maddie's shoulder. "Has someone been dipping a bit too freely into the hard cider?"

Maddie shook his hand off.

"Listen, dude. I'm preparing to do something I *never* do—and your total want of sense is *not* gonna mess it up. So." She took hold of his shoulders. "Whatever the hell happens here—just follow my damn lead. *Capisce?*"

Tom looked more than a little wary, but he wisely complied.

Lizzy appeared seconds later. Maddie saw her eyes widen when she noticed them standing there. She stopped and cast about for an escape route—but Maddie was too fast.

"Hold up there, Cherry Ames," she called out. "You're not going anyplace just yet."

Maddie hauled Tom over to where Lizzy stood.

She noticed that neither of them would make eye contact with the other.

"Okay." Maddie folded her arms and adopted her most authoritative stance. "Here's the deal. I'm going to make this as profoundly simple as possible. You two can love each other or hate each other—but indifference is not an option. You can forgive, do your level best to forget, start over, and get busy planning a future together that will, in my humble and informed estimation, result in prodigiously energetic and geometrically successful attempts at procreation—*or*—you can walk away from each other forever and go down in history as two of the stupidest and most moribund losers *ever* to squander a shot at real happiness." She took a long, slow breath. "Now, do us all a favor and take a few minutes to talk it over."

They were now sneaking sidelong looks at each other. At least that was a good sign.

"That's pretty much it. Thanks for your attention."

Maddie laid a hand on each of their shoulders, and turned them to face each other.

She nodded at them, then turned on her heel to walk away. She didn't look back—not even after she rejoined Syd, who watched her approach with an open mouth.

"What on earth did you *say* to them?" Syd asked with amazement.

"Why?" Maddie replied, nonchalantly. "What are they doing?"

"Well. Let's just say if they don't stop soon, someone's going to turn a fire hose on them."

Maddie smiled at her.

"I love it when a plan comes together . . ."

"Will you please calm down." Michael pointed beneath the table that was loaded with desserts. "You're upsetting the dogs."

"*The dogs?* Who cares about the dogs? I'm having a nervous breakdown and you're worried about the *dogs?*"

"David. It's just a fifteen-minute debate." Michael tried to placate him. "You've been practicing nonstop for days. All you need do is stand up there and read the speech Maddie wrote for you. But . . ." he hesitated. "There is one *little* bitty, teeny, insignificant thing you might want to reconsider . . ."

"What?" David was bent over the table, using a stainless-steel iced tea pitcher as a mirror. He'd been fussing with his bow tie for the last half hour. Something about it was still not right.

"Well," Michael continued. "I've been giving some thought to that new finale you improvised."

David glared up at him. "And?"

"I'm not sure ending with that *Evita* medley is the best idea."

"*What do you mean it's not a good idea?* Are you *kidding* me with this?" David was apoplectic. "You wait until *now*, when it's," he checked his watch, "*ten minutes away* to tell me this?" He picked up a stack of napkins and began to fan himself. "I'm going to pass out. I know it. I never should've eaten that three-bean salad . . . you know what legumes do to me. Oh, my god, *oh, my god . . .*"

Michael was stunned when Nadine appeared out of nowhere. She grabbed David by the shoulders, spun him around, and slapped him soundly across the face.

"What the hell is the matter with you, boy?" she demanded. "Nobody in this crowd wants to listen to you standing up there making a damn fool of yourself."

David was dazed, but at least he'd stopped his tirade.

Nadine stood in front of him, wagging an index finger in front of his face. David's eyes locked on her finger and watched it sway from side to side like a hypnotist's medallion.

"I'm only going to say this to you *once*—so don't expect me to repeat it." Nadine leaned in closer. "Nobody—I mean *nobody*—sings 'Don't Cry for Me, Argentina' but Patti LuPone. *Get it?* Not Joan Baez. Not that Welsh lounge lizard Tom Jones. Not Andrea *damn* Bocelli. Not Karen Carpenter. Not Shirley Bassey—and sure as *hell* not Olivia Newton-John. And before you open that blaspheming mouth of yours, boy—not your precious Madonna, either."

David blinked. "Nadine? Is that you?" He looked around. "Where am I?"

"You're in a place where you stand up, read your speech, then sit down and shut up. You leave the damn show tunes on Broadway, where they belong." She reached out and straightened his bow tie. "Now get outta here and let me straighten up this mess before the fireworks."

"Okay, Nadine." David started to walk away, but stopped and turned back to face her. "You really think Patti LuPone was better than Madonna?"

Nadine glowered at him and picked up an iron skillet.

Nadine never seemed to go anyplace without one . . .

"Okay, okay . . ." David held up his hands in a pantomime of surrender and skittered behind Michael. "I just thought I'd ask."

"I wish I had the guts to change my fate."

Rita was firing up another cigarette. It was her fifth one since she'd come over to sit down next to him. James hadn't started out intending to count them, but she was burning through them so fast it was hard not to notice.

"Do you maybe want to ease off those a little bit?" he asked.

"Why?" she huffed. "It don't matter how fast you smoke 'em. They'll kill you just the same if you take your time."

"Maybe," he said. "But what if you change your mind and try to quit again?"

"That ain't likely."

"Why do you say that, Rita?"

She looked at him. "Remember what you said to me about when you knew that going back in the army was the right thing for you to do?"

"I'm not really sure," he admitted.

"Well, I remember. You said it happened late one night while we were drivin' back together after droppin' off one of them doublewides in Wheeling. You said you looked out ahead at all those miles of empty road and thought you were seeing a nightmare vision of your future—long, dark and empty." She took a drag off her cigarette. "That's what you told me. That's when you said you knew you needed to make a change."

"I guess that was true," he said. "I didn't mean for it to imply anything about your life, though. I hope you know that."

She laughed. "Of course, I know that. I don't know how you made it overseas. You'd be likelier to turn the dang gun around and shoot yourself before you'd hurt anybody else—even one of them terrorists."

James was embarrassed by her observation—probably because he knew she was right.

"Well, it turned out I didn't have to shoot anybody. Maybe I got lucky."

"You think losin' a leg is lucky?"

He shrugged.

Rita finished her cigarette in silence.

Henry ran over to ask if they wanted to go with him to get more dessert before the fireworks started.

"Uncle David is gonna give his speech—and then we get to go to the river with Maddie and Syd to watch the big explosions," he said. "Buddy told me they have *ten* cannons. Come on, Daddy," Henry grabbed his hand. "Come on Miss Rita. Let's go get a good spot."

James got to his feet.

"Come on, Miss Rita." He held his free hand out to her. "Let's go watch the show. Who knows? Maybe we can pretend we're blowing up all the things in our pasts we'd like to forget?"

Rita took her time to think it over, but finally grabbed hold of his hand and stood up. She ground out her cigarette and dropped the butt into the empty Pepsi can she'd been using as an ashtray.

"Way ahead of you, soldier," she said.

"I'm telling you. If you don't try some of this bread pudding, you're missing out on one of the two best things in life."

Dorothy looked up at David.

"What's the other one?"

He bent down and lowered his voice. "I'll tell you later, when Michael isn't around."

Dorothy sighed. She really couldn't make up her mind. There were so many kinds of desserts on the table to choose from— more kinds than she'd ever seen in one place before.

"I don't know which one to pick," she said.

"Well, that's not hard to solve." David grabbed a plastic tray. "Take one of each."

"One of each?" She looked at him with wonder. "I could never carry all of that."

"Here's a news flash," he said. "I'll help you."

Dorothy was dubious.

"No. Really," David said. "I'm going to be famished when this debate is over. I always eat when I'm anxious. Don't you?"

"No." Dorothy shook her head. "I pretty much don't eat anything when I'm worried about stuff."

"David," Michael hissed at him from behind the table. He furiously waved his hand at him, like he was trying to warn him about something.

"Yes, my furry prince?" David asked. He didn't get to ask anything else because someone grabbed him from behind and yanked him backwards. "Not again," David began . . .

"You stay away from her," a voice bellowed.

Dorothy felt her insides cramp. She was afraid she was going to be sick all over the desserts.

"Hey, get your hands off him," Michael yelled. "You're messing up his suit."

"You go to *hell*," her father roared. "And *you*," he shoved David backwards. "You keep your filthy hands off my daughter."

Dorothy reached out to try and stop her father from hurting David.

"Papa, *please*. Don't do this. He was just helping me pick out a dessert."

Her father roughly shoved her away. The force of it made her stagger back against the table.

"Hey!" Michael cried. "Stop that—*right now!*"

Dorothy held her hands up in front of her face, expecting her father to strike her.

"What's the matter with you?" David stepped forward and grabbed her father by the arm. "You don't treat a child like that."

Her father smacked his hand away. "Don't you *dare* lay your filthy, perverted hands on me."

Her father was smaller than David, but a lot angrier. He lunged at him and knocked him off his feet. David staggered back against the table and the whole thing collapsed under his weight.

"Papa," Dorothy was crying now. "*Please stop*. Please don't hurt him. He didn't do anything."

Michael was trying to help David to his feet. People were rushing over to see what the fracas was about.

Her father wasn't backing down—not from any of them. She'd seen it in his eyes. She knew this time, there'd be no calming him down. And no getting away from his wrath.

This time, he was going to keep going until he was finished.

The best she could do was try to get him away from everyone else, and pray that it would be over soon.

More and more people were crowding around. Everyone was talking at once and asking questions about what happened. She saw people she recognized from town. Buddy was there. So was James Lawrence. He stood there at the edge of the crowd with Henry and that woman he worked with at Cougar's. Even Junior was there. And Mr. Hozbiest.

They kept on coming.

Her father was becoming aware of the crowd now, too. She saw him make an effort to compose himself and straighten his suit.

Michael was helping David back to his feet. He was covered with gooey fruit and icing. He looked different to her—and it was more than how shocked he was from being pushed down by her father. He looked . . . *younger*. And he looked afraid.

Her father turned around and began to address the crowd.

"This man," he pointed a long finger at David, "laid hands on my daughter. This man tried to infect her with his twisted ideas and profane instincts. *This man*," he raised his voice, "wants to corrupt the lives of *all* our children. He seeks to lead them astray and lure them onto the same twisted path of sin and aberration that he follows." He pointed into the crowd of people who were standing there. Most of them were staring at the ground or nervously shifting their weight from foot to foot. It was clear they had no idea what to think or do—and that was what gave her father his edge. "Who among you doesn't know it? Who among you hasn't turned a blind eye while this man and his unholy coven have brought filth and dishonor to this once sacred place? Who among you hasn't made excuses for him because of his connections and his old family name? Who among you now has the courage to stand with me and reject this contemptible lifestyle that is an abomination to God and the laws of man?" He turned to face David, who sagged against his partner. He looked close to tears. "I tell you this much here tonight, *Mister* Jenkins. I will not sully my oath of office by standing up before the good citizens of this community and debating such a one as you. You are not even fit to be a candidate for the position of trust I now hold."

He grabbed Dorothy by the arm and roughly yanked her along behind him as he pushed his way through the crowd of people. As he dragged her away, all she could make out was a jumbled mix of shouted orders.

"Somebody go find the Sheriff!"

"Get those children away from here!"

"Go tell Sonny to start up them damn fireworks!"

Then she wasn't aware of anything—except how hard she was having to run to keep from stumbling. He kept on going, faster and faster, until they were far away from the people and the noise—and all that lay before them was a darkening sky and the distant sound of rushing water.

Gerald Watson hurled his daughter down on the bank of rocks and sand that ran along this stretch of river.

They were both out of breath from the wild, frenzied retreat from the pandemonium above.

But one thing was clear. *Watson was still mad as hell.*

He was striding around like a crazy man, kicking at stones and tearing at loose bits of scraggly, crooked tree limbs that projected from an enormous hunk of driftwood. The thing was so gray and decomposed that it probably had been deposited here decades ago, when the last great flood that consumed the area pushed the water level high enough through here to leave all manner of debris behind when it finally receded.

Dorothy cowered on the ground and watched him in that

deathly quiet way of hers—that way that no child should ever know.

Finally, he stopped his mad pacing. With eerie and terrifying calm, he took off his jacket and folded it before laying it over a dry pile of rocks.

"You made me do that," he said to her. "You made me lose my temper, and look what happened."

He walked closer to where she lay, now curled into a fetal position.

"Goddamn you. *Look* at me when I talk to you." He kicked at her feet. "I am still your father."

She looked up at him with eyes like a frightened doe.

"I'm sorry, Papa."

"You're sorry? *You're sorry?*" He scoffed at her. "Well I am sure *glad* to know you're sorry."

He unfastened his belt and pulled it free from the loops of his trousers.

"How about you count the ways for me? How about you give me one 'sorry' for every lash?" He wrapped the end of the belt around his hand and raised his arm.

Dorothy raised her arms to cover her face.

An earsplitting sound rang out. It was shrill and deafening—like the screech of a deranged fox.

Watson was startled by the sound—long enough for Dorothy to scramble to her feet and try to get away from him. She made a frantic dash for the water, but he chased her into the shallows and caught hold of her by the hair. He slapped her and half-dragged, half-carried her back to the sandy bank.

The earsplitting whistle sounded again—closer this time. The girl seemed to recognized it.

Dorothy saw him first.

"Buddy, no!" She cried out. "Buddy, go back. Don't do this—*you can't help me.*"

Watson saw him now, too.

He sneered at the gentle intruder, who stood, uncertainly but calmly on the rocks, clutching his metal whistle.

"What are you doing here, you fucking moron?" he seethed.

"No place for hate," Buddy said. "Goldenrod won't be free until hate goes away."

"Oh, is *that* right?" Watson shook Dorothy off and surged toward Buddy, who raised his whistle to his mouth and blew it again.

"Papa, no!" Dorothy screamed. She scrambled to her feet. "Don't hurt him. Don't hurt him."

Watson raised his leg and kicked Buddy hard on the shin. Buddy cried out and fell to the ground, clutching his leg. His swanee whistle lay discarded on the ground beside him. He was rocking and chanting, "No place for hate. No place for hate. The canons are finished. Goldenrod will be redeemed."

"I'll show you redeemed, you worthless piece of shit."

Watson lifted his foot to kick Buddy again, but this time something stopped him. His body pitched forward and he crumpled to the ground, writhing and clutching his head.

Dorothy stood behind him holding a jagged hunk of driftwood.

"Get up," she shouted at Buddy. "Get up—*now.*"

Buddy slowly rolled into a sitting position beside Watson, who was lying on his back muttering and holding a hand against the side of his head. There was blood seeping out between his fingers.

"Buddy," Dorothy demanded. "Get over here, now. We have to get out of here—*we have to run before he gets back up.*"

Watson made a feeble effort to sit up, but failed and fell back against the dry ground.

Dorothy dropped the piece of driftwood beside her father's prone figure and extended a hand to Buddy. "Come on. We have to go. *We have to go, now.*"

Buddy looked up at her with his clear eyes—just like he had that day at Junior's, when he was painting the banners. Then he reached for her hand and let her help him up to a standing position.

"Goldenrod is redeemed," he said.

"Come on," she said. "Come on. We have to get help."

He leaned on her as they slowly backed away from where her father lay.

Watson had stopped moaning. His eyes were still open, but he wasn't trying to sit up. The fingers on his right hand twitched against the dirt.

Dorothy and Buddy retreated from the river as quickly as Buddy's leg would allow them to travel.

Just as they began their climb up the steep trail that led back to the safety of the picnic grounds, the first explosive volley of fireworks lit up the cloudless night sky, and threw everything along the river into bold relief. Watson lay on his back several feet from the water's edge. His unmoving figure cast a distorted shadow along the rocks as the sky overhead erupted.

The earsplitting booms and accompanying flashes of brilliant light went on and on—raining down along the persistent and slow-moving river that had taken thousands of years to push its patient way through these ancient and all-knowing hills.

"I found him."

Maddie was kneeling in the water near the river's edge.

The staccato booms and flashes from the fireworks finale were making it hard to hear, and even harder to see. Everything had a dizzying, surreal quality—like being trapped inside a strobe light. They'd been looking around down here for a while now. She only saw him because of the way the blue light reflected off his white shirt.

It was Watson.

And she could only be sure of two things.

He was face down in the shallow water. And he was dead.

Byron waded over to where she knelt beside Watson's body. "Is it him?" he asked.

"Yeah." Maddie stood up. "He's got a pretty nasty gash on the side of his head. He can't have been here long."

"No." Byron sighed. "Not likely."

He looked over the area where they stood. They were only a couple of feet from dry land.

The lights from the fireworks continued to flash and illuminate everything around them. He squinted at something. "Do you see that?"

"What?"

Byron directed the beam of his flashlight to an area just beyond the water's edge.

"There. On the bank. The dirt is all scuffed up—like something got dragged over it."

They looked at each other with sickening understanding.

Byron noticed something else. "I'll wager that's the piece of wood Dorothy said she hit him with." He cursed and cast about for Charlie, who was combing the area by the trail. "Davis!" he called out.

"Yes, sir?" Charlie responded.

"We need to secure this area and get some backup. It looks like we might have a 10-70."

Charlie hesitated only an instant before waving an acknowledgment at Byron and taking off at a run.

Byron slowly exhaled. "Helluva way to end a perfect day."

Maddie closed her eyes, not wanting to see any more of the spastic flashing lights that were making the bile rise in her throat—and not wanting to bear witness to the wrongful death that lay stretched out beneath her.

The deafening booms continued. They were closer together now, rolling faster and stronger in a frenetic race to the finish.

Byron was right. *It was a helluva way to end a perfect day.*

And it was a worse way to end a life.

She knelt next to the body of the man in the water, and set about doing her job.

Watson's eyes were open, but he wasn't seeing anything—not anymore.

His reign of terror had finally ended.

Its repercussions were just beginning.

About the Author

ANN McMAN is the author of seven novels and two short story collections. She is a recipient of both the Alice B. Lavender Certificate for Outstanding Debut Novel (*Jericho*) and the 2017 Alice B. Medal for Outstanding Body of Work. Her novel *Hoosier Daddy* was a Lambda Literary Award finalist. Her books *Sidecar* and *Three* won Golden Crown Literary Society Awards for Best Short Story Collection, and *Backcast* was awarded the Silver Medal for Fiction in the Independent Publisher Awards (IPPYs) for the Northeast Region. *Backcast* also received the Rainbow Award for Best Lesbian Book of 2016. A career graphic designer, Ann is a two-time recipient of the Tee Corinne Award for Outstanding Cover Design.

Ann and her wife, Bywater Books Publisher Salem West, live in Winston-Salem, North Carolina, with two dogs, two cats, and an exhaustive supply of vacuum cleaner bags.

Acknowledgments

Many people have asked why it took so long for me to return to Jericho. The answer is complicated. I could cite the literal reasons for the delay: a protracted process to secure ownership of rights to the series, the glittery allure of other projects, and the intrusion of real-life events that landed me squarely in the middle of a twenty-four-month season in hell. I could cite all those things, and they'd all be true. But there's another reason. The prospect of mucking around in the lives of all these wonderfully sleeping dogs frightened me more than a little bit. To be honest, I had no idea what kind of trouble I'd be starting if I woke them all up. Where would they take me? What kind of journey would it be? And if it didn't work out, would I have enough cab fare to get myself out of there?

For the most part, they treated me kindly. I enjoyed spending time with all of them again. They reminded me of old, endearing things I was sad to have forgotten—and introduced me to a slew of new things I'll be happy to forget.

No one writes in a vacuum—not unless they work for Oreck. None of this book would have been possible without the keen insight, collaboration, participation, determination and steadfast encouragement (often delivered in the form of a Nike-clad foot up the wiz wang) of my beloved Buddha. You make everything I do better, and I never want to learn what it would be like to write a book—or live a life—without you.

Ferret voices, notwithstanding . . .

To my Bywater family—Slumdog, Hot Lips, SKP, Marlo and Radar—I don't ever want to leave home without you. In fact, I pretty much don't want to leave home *period*—unless it's to go to Vermont. And even then, I want you all along for the ride. Thank you all for keeping our little joint by the Great Lake the best book mill on the planet.

Nancy Squires—you improve everything you touch, and I thank you for your superb job editing this book. [Do I need to add another pronoun here?]

Thanks to my beloved Nurse, Short Stack, Anna (Peg Leg), KG, Christine and Lou Lou for reading early drafts of the book. Since none of you gouged out your eyes, I took that as encouragement to keep writing. Thanks, too, to my sainted and truth-telling mother, Dee Dee—who told me it didn't suck, and noted that the cover worked very well on her coffee table.

Vermont owns the best part of my soul, and I'd be nothing without the people who make it so special— and who give me such a perfect space to write. Domina and HB. Susan and Cathy. Lee and John. My *entire* Shore Acres family. You are all very dear to me. And Danny? Thanks for saving my life. *Really.* (Now that I've buttered you up—can I have a burger?)

Father Frank, Flora and Biz—you make us feel loved and valued every single day. Every. Single. Day. Thanks for sharing The Big Journey with us.

Lee Lynch and Dorothy Allison—you inform and inspire everything I write. I shall always be indebted to you both. Thank you for your great contributions to our literature—and to my life.

Love and thanks are due to Christine "Bruno" Williams—the voice that launched a thousand Subarus. Bruno? People would line up to listen to you read the phone book. You always manage to make my words sound better than they are. Please continue this activity . . .

Skippy, Butch and Bucko—you know how much I love you.

Thanks are also due to Casey Otis and Kirk Sanders. Without you two, this book would not have been possible. Kirk? Thank god Gracie kept you on speed dial . . .

Lastly, I would be remiss and abrogate a sincere promise made to my dear friend, Sandra Moran Famous Author™ if I failed to make mention of the untold agonies endured by her mother, Cherie Moran, during her staggering 46-years of labor pains. Cherie gave up her meteoric rise to international prominence as the Skip of a Lithuanian curling team to bring SMFA into the world. I know I speak for all of us when I say we shall forever be grateful.

Fact.

SAPPHO'S
BAR AND GRILL

"Holy Hildegarde of Bingen! Bonnie Morris brings women's history to vivid, hilarious life in this whip-smart time travel tour de force." —ALISON BECHDEL, author of *Dykes to Watch Out For* and *Fun Home*

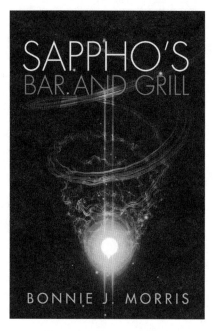

Sappho's Bar and Grill
Paperback 978-1-61294-097-7
eBook 978-1-61294-098-4

www.bywaterbooks.com

The Ada Decades

"Eminently readable, historically insightful, realistically romantic—Cam and Ada will stay in your hearts. We need them now more them ever, and we need this writer, Paula Martinac." —JOAN NESTLE, Lambda Award winning writer and editor

The Ada Decades

Print 978-1-61294-085-4
Ebook 978-1-61294-086-1

www.bywaterbooks.com

At Bywater Books we love good books about lesbians just like you do, and we're committed to bringing the best of contemporary lesbian writing to our avid readers. Our editorial team is dedicated to finding and developing outstanding writers who create books you won't want to put down.

We sponsor the Bywater Prize for Fiction to help with this quest. Each prizewinner receives $1,000 and publication of their novel. We have already discovered amazing writers like Jill Malone, Sally Bellerose, and Hilary Sloin through the Bywater Prize. Which exciting new writer will we find next?

For more information about Bywater Books and the annual Bywater Prize for Fiction, please visit our website.

www.bywaterbooks.com